Praise for *The Stockwell Lett*

"In 1854, Boston's most prominent men fought to make positive change, but it was the women standing quietly behind them who came together across lines of race and class to achieve the goals their husbands could not. In this powerful story of hope, dedication, and perseverance, Jackie Friedland takes an unflinching look at the devastating era of American history prior to the Civil War. This is a novel that you won't want to miss."
—KATHLEEN GRISSOM, *New York Times* best-selling author of *The Kitchen House* and *Glory Over Everything*

"Jacqueline Friedland is a gifted writer with an incredible ability to tell a gripping, page-turning story in any genre . . . Friedland's impeccable research and compelling characters immersed me in the period . . . Even if you don't usually gravitate towards historical fiction, this one will have you hooked from the outset. It's just that good!"
—SAMANTHA GREENE WOODRUFF, best-selling author of *The Lobotomist's Wife*

"Evocative period detail abounds in Friedland's work; characters are pulled directly from history."
—KIRKUS REVIEWS

"A riveting portrait of the women who risked everything to help usher slaves to freedom, Jacqueline Friedland's latest is told with a tender heart. Thanks to a cast of captivating characters, colorful period details and an ending that will have you cheering, the book will stay with you long after you finish. *The Stockwell Letters* is book club fiction at its best."
—BROOKE FOSTER, award-winning journalist and author of *On Gin Lane*

"*The Stockwell Letters* is an immersive work of fiction that plunges readers into one of the most fraught and urgent decades of American history. With assiduous research and a cast of complex and finely rendered characters, Friedland delivers a powerful literary punch. Showing both the best and the worst of human nature, Friedland's writing prompts every reader to ask: How can I stand up for what is right?"

—ALLISON PATAKI, author of
The Magnificent Lives of Marjorie Post

"Impressively researched, seamlessly written and deeply felt, *The Stockwell Letters* brings the abolitionist movement fully and completely to life. Friedland is an expert at showing us the motivations behind the actions; this is historical fiction at its very best."

—KITTY ZELDIS, author of
The Dressmakers of Prospect Heights

For *He Gets That From Me*

* 2022 *USA Today* Best Seller
* A 2021 *Kirkus Reviews'* Best Indie Book of the Year
* 2021 Reader's Favorite: Gold Medal, Fiction
* SheReads 2021 Book Awards: Best Book Club Pick

"It is hard to imagine a better novel for a book club discussion...A thoughtful and gripping family tale that will haunt readers long after finishing it."

—*KIRKUS REVIEWS*, STARRED

". . . a touching and provocative novel about the collisions of the emotional and legal meanings of family."

—*FOREWORD REVIEWS*

"Friedland spins a web of intrigue, questioning the truest expression of parenthood. Fans of Nicola Marsh, Tana French, and Hannah Mary McKinnon will race through this thrilling exploration of nature versus nurture and the sacrifices needed to keep loved ones together."

—BOOKLIST

"A heartfelt exploration of what it means to be a family, *He Gets That From Me* is a fascinating story of strength, humanity, love, and perseverance. This is one you won't stop thinking about."

—ALLISON WINN SCOTCH, best-selling author
of *Cleo McDougal Regrets Nothing*

"Jacqueline Friedland creates a host of complex characters in this nuanced, compelling exploration of what it really means to be a family, and why we should maybe think twice before heading to ancestry.com.

—LAURA HANKIN, *New York Times* best-selling author
of *The DayDreams, Happy & You Know It*
and *A Special Place for Women*

"A piercing, mesmerizing look into the fragility and resiliency of the human experience . . . a bold page-turner that will leave you breathless with anticipation. With *He Gets That From Me*, Friedland invites you to ask yourself the questions you didn't even know you needed to answer—about family, forgiveness, sacrifice, and love. An absolute home run."

—AMY IMPELLIZZERI, award-winning author of
Lemongrass Hope and *I Know How This Ends*

"Compulsively readable and ferociously insightful . . . *He Gets That From Me* cuts to the core of what it means to be family. An unforgettable book of our times."

—JAMIE BRENNER, author of
The Forever Summer and *Blush*

"*He Gets That from Me* is a potent reminder that we can't always choose what life hands us—but we can decide whether to rise to the occasion when faced with seemingly impossible choices. With expert plotting and unwavering empathy toward her characters, Jacqueline Friedland has written a novel as unexpected as it is riveting. I read it in a single sitting."

—CAMILLE PAGÁN, best-selling author of
This Won't End Well

"*He Gets That from Me* takes on timeless questions about parenthood and our presumptions about birth, biology, and family. Describing a modern-day arrangement between two dads and a surrogate, the story opens our eyes to the many ways a family can be created while also telling a suspenseful narrative full of unexpected thrills that keep the reader wanting more. A moving story throughout, it ends with a twist that will leave you thinking about the book long after you've finished reading it."

—MELISSA BRISMAN, ESQ., reproductive attorney

"Friedland has written characters who are so compelling and so lovable, and then she put them in the middle of such a suspenseful, entirely believable story of what can happen when modern-day technology complicates the most basic relationships between parents and a child. My heart was pounding as I read, far into the night. It's a must-read."

—MADDIE DAWSON, best-selling author of
Matchmaking for Beginners

For *That's Not a Thing*

✸ 2020 Readers' Favorite Book Awards: Gold Medal
  in Fiction—New Adult
✸ 2020 Readers' Favorite Book Awards: Wind Dancer
  Films Winner
✸ 2020 Next Generation Indie Book Awards Winner in
  Romance (Fiction)

"Exploring the messy concept of closure, this is a charmingly witty novel that fans of Emily Belden's *Hot Mess* (2019) and J. Ryan Stradal's *The Lager Queen of Minnesota* (2019) will eat up."
—BOOKLIST

"In *That's Not a Thing*, Friedland has created a delightful and generous novel about the type of love that never leaves us and the people we hope to become in the aftermath."
—LAURA DAVE, *New York Times* and international best-selling author of *The Last Thing He Told Me*, *Eight Hundred Grapes* and more

"An open-hearted lawyer is forced to choose between her fiance and her dying ex in Friedland's novel about love and forgiveness . . . A complex and compelling romance . . ."
—KIRKUS REVIEWS

"This tender, introspective romance from Friedland hangs on the difficult choice between new and old lovers . . . Fans of sensitively handled love triangles should snap this one up."
—PUBLISHERS WEEKLY

"Fun, flirty and fabulous . . . I devoured this read!"
—STEPHANIE EVANOVICH, *New York Times* best-selling author of *Big Girl Panties* and *The Sweet Spot*

"In life's journey, there are many types of love we encounter along the way—first love, rebound love, the one-who-got-away love, 'B'sherit' (soulmate) love, and conflict love (the one in your bed, the one in your head) . . . Friedland, with her fabulous descriptions and compelling characters, presents a little bit of everything in this emotionally-gripping tale that examines love, loss, loyalty, what ifs, what is, and ultimately, forgiveness. Protagonist Meredith Altman is my kinda girl—complicated, inspiring, and richly-drawn. *That's Not a Thing* has the unputdownable Jojo Moyes 'It Factor' that keeps those pages turning and burning bright . . . long after lights-out."

—LISA BARR, award-winning author of
The Unbreakables

"Friedland's *That's Not a Thing* is an unputdownable tale of old love meets new. Heartrending and evocative, this beautifully woven story captures the deep-seated emotions we carry—those of guilt, forgiveness, and what it means to be there for those we love. Friedland's sharp writing and emotional depth will leave you turning the pages, ending with a satisfying, albeit bittersweet conclusion."

—ROCHELLE WEINSTEIN, *USA Today* best-selling
author of *This Is Not How It Ends*

"Jacqueline Friedland is at the top of her game with this wholly engrossing page-turner about the complexities of love, loss, and loyalty. With richly drawn characters and a gripping plot, *That's Not a Thing* is undoubtedly THE thing to pack in your beach bag or pick for your book club. Friedland has done it again—another must-read!"

—AMY BLUMENFELD, award-winning
author of *The Cast*

"Fans of Jojo Moyes and Karma Brown will simply love Jacqueline Friedland's romantic, poignant novel, *That's Not A Thing*. In this dramatic and insightful story, Friedland explores tragedy, true love, and life's many 'what ifs'."

—AMY POEPPEL, author of
Limelight and *Small Admissions*

THE
STOCKWELL
LETTERS

THE
STOCKWELL
LETTERS

A NOVEL

JACQUELINE FRIEDLAND

SPARKPRESS

Published by SparkPress, a BookSparks imprint,
A division of SparkPoint Studio, LLC
Phoenix, Arizona, USA, 85007
www.gosparkpress.com

Published 2023
Printed in the United States of America
Print ISBN: 978-1-68463-214-5
E-ISBN: 978-1-68463-215-2
Library of Congress Control Number: 2023909022

Interior Design by Tabitha Lahr

For Abe, Asher, Shep, and Nava

ANN

Boston, 1836

———————

Six months after I met Wendell, I began to feel ill. At first there were only small signs. My appetite was less robust, and my limbs sometimes ached. I hardly paid mind to the symptoms, as I suffered no cough, no fever, no signs suggestive of a virus. But as the weeks wore on, the ailments progressed, refusing to be ignored.

There were days that spring when I couldn't leave my bed, the headaches throbbing so ferociously that even a sliver of sunshine caused pain behind my eyes. I felt myself a fool, knowing I exhibited no outward signs of illness. Yet, I was so overwhelmingly fatigued that I was forced to cancel many dates with Wendell, as well as several engagements with the Boston Female Anti-Slavery Society.

One Tuesday morning, Aunt Maria came to my chamber. As I opened my eyes and beheld the tray full of breakfast items in her hand, my vision began to blur. Maria's blonde hair seemed suddenly foggy, impossible to separate from the fair skin of her face. I was hit with a wave of nausea so acute that my eyes began to tear.

"I cannot," I managed to utter, as a force inside my forehead continued pushing outward, causing indescribable pain.

My aunt placed the tray on the bedside table, and then her soft hand was upon my forehead to take my measure. "Still cool to the touch. Perhaps a compress anyway," she said and then scurried from the room.

I must have fallen asleep then because when I awoke next, I found our family physician, the balding Doctor Henwick, speaking to Aunt Maria at my bedside.

"If she's not improved in two days' time," he was saying, "we will try leeching."

The mention of leeches caused my stomach to turn again, but I could hardly find the energy to say so.

"Try and get her to take some broth," he directed, and I managed to emit a moan in protest.

"Oh, darling," Maria said, rushing to my side. She took my hand in her own, but the contact was not a comfort. Her skin, which I knew to be smooth, felt like sand rubbing a wound. I prayed the doctor might find a way to help me, but I couldn't summon the words to tell him as much.

Shortly after Dr. Henwick left, I drifted off again and next awoke to the sound of Uncle Henry's voice floating up from the entryway.

"She's not been out from her bed in days, so a visitor would surely be unwise. The doctor has advised that she must rest as much as possible."

The voice that answered sent a small jolt through me.

"You'll let her know I called?"

It was Wendell, back from his travels. I longed to call out to him, but I could not so much as lift my head.

They exchanged additional words, too quiet for me to make out. I hoped I might feel well enough later to at least send him a note. I began to consider what I might say, but my thoughts were too muddy, the heat inside my head too thick.

OVER THE NEXT SEVERAL DAYS, there were moments when I awoke and felt perhaps I had improved only to discover, a short while later, that there were new ways to feel wretched. I could hear Aunt Maria and Uncle Henry arguing with increasing frequency outside my bedchamber, debating various aspects of my treatment, which doctor to call, whether I should try eating peaches again, or only grains.

"She cannot continue like this," Aunt Maria said late one evening after I had been abed nearly two months. "I'm beginning to fear the worst."

"You mustn't give up hope," Uncle Henry answered. "Think of Mary and Benjamin," he said, mentioning my deceased parents. "We cannot fail them. We cannot fail Ann."

I wanted to tell my uncle not to fret, that I knew the efforts to which they had already gone. Aunt Maria spoke the words that were in my thoughts.

"We've tried everything already, and nothing is having an ameliorative effect."

I heard a sob escape her then, and I was sorry to have caused my aunt such sadness. Perhaps it would be best if I sought to hasten my exit from this world instead, to join my parents wherever their souls had gone years earlier. Sadly, I had not the energy even for that.

And so the days passed, until I opened my eyes one afternoon to find Wendell beside me. He had clearly been sitting in the wooden chair for some time, as his head was in his hands, and he was thoroughly absorbed in sobbing.

I tried to push his name from my lips, but I could force out only an unintelligible sound. "Gra," was what I said instead.

"Ann!" Wendell looked up, his blue eyes pink and swollen.

Though it was wildly inappropriate for him to behold me in my dressing gown, I had neither the stamina nor the desire to protest, as I was delighted to lay eyes on him for the first time in so many weeks. I would have liked to smooth a hand over my hair, the brown tresses surely a tangled mess, but I reminded myself that with my dismal prognosis, it was beyond relevance in any case.

"My dear sweet Ann," he said in a near whisper as he reached for my hand.

Even in his sadness, he seemed to be brimming with energy and life. With his broad shoulders and vibrant complexion, he hardly belonged in my dark and musty sick room. As if he, too, understood that his usual vigor was unsuited for this visit, he seemed to make efforts to contain himself.

Inhaling a deep breath, he looked down at our joined hands, running one finger gently across the spot where our fingers met.

The tender gesture caused me a new pain, a shattering of my anguished heart. I'd come so close to having my own family again—and what a life I could have had with this man. To have lost it before it even began, it was almost too much to bear.

"Marry me, Ann," he said. He leaned closer, his light eyes focused on my own darker ones as he gently squeezed my fingers.

To my surprise, I found the strength to answer in cogent words, and I refused. "I'm dying."

"No!" Wendell argued, outraged. "You must get better. You will! And you will marry me!"

Oh, Wendell, I thought then. Such an idealist. The sign of a true aristocrat, ever an optimist and so sure that any problem could be solved if only one found the will. When I didn't answer, he persisted.

"Just say yes, and I will take care of the rest."

Even as my head pounded and my chest ached, I was utterly besotted by the golden-haired man beside me. I thought of all the reasons I should send him away and all the ways in which I did not deserve him.

"I will not yield," he whispered, as though he had heard my thoughts. "Please, just 'yes.'"

What could I do but nod?

I managed to keep awake for the remainder of Wendell's visit, though my eyelids grew heavier by the minute. After he departed, Aunt Maria's older sister, Caroline, appeared at my bedroom door. She entered and took a cloth from a stack on my bedside table, moving with it toward the basin.

"He nearly forced his way in," she told me as I closed my eyes. "Your uncle Henry turned him away so many times, but he'd not be deterred any longer. His love for you seems to grow only stronger."

She placed the cloth on my forehead, and I tried not to weep for what I would not have, sure as I was that death was coming to rob me of the life I dreamed.

ANTHONY

Richmond, February 1854

The lamplighter had long since fired up the streetlights by the time Anthony made his way back along 13th Street toward Millspaugh's Apothecary. It was well after the close of business, so he had to rap solid against the glass with his knuckles to be let in. His skin was cut and rubbed from the day hauling coal and guano down at the docks, but he was upbeat anyhow, fixing to show Master Millspaugh the $25 he had in his pocket. The wages he'd collected over the past fortnight were sure to be more than the man was expecting. It was money enough to prove that the arrangement they'd settled on was for the best. The apothecary had made a mistake leasing Anthony from Master Charles for the year when he didn't have near enough customers to keep an extra worker busy. But now the druggist's error had Anthony getting two weeks at a time to be in charge of his own time.

Master Millspaugh took his fair time getting to the door while Anthony waited out there in the cold. He was rubbing his hands up and down his arms and jiggling himself about when the door finally swung open.

"You didn't hurry back," the old man grumbled as he turned round and walked deeper into the store, expecting Anthony to follow behind him toward the back room. The shop had been closed near two hours, but the room was still rich with smells of lavender, coriander, camphor, and the other items Master Millspaugh would have been measuring out during the day. Anthony still hadn't worked out why the man hired him when he was so intent on doing everything round there himself. Anthony supposed Master Millspaugh wondered the very same and that was why he'd begun to let Anthony find other work on his own, so long as he brought back the wages he earned outside.

And there was work enough for a strong man like Anthony down at the docks. Not every day mind, but plenty of ships came and went needing their cargo cleared out. He liked to think that it was his preaching experience that made him a favorite hire among those sailors, that he had a way of making folks feel peaceful in his company. Going on and off all those ships in the harbor allowed him plenty of opportunity to talk with Northern sailors. So many of those men had a mind to tell him what was what up North.

"The wages," Anthony said, as he fished deep in his pocket to remove the bills he'd collected over the past fourteen days.

Master Millspaugh let out a low whistle as he reached for the money and started counting. Anthony kept his gaze on the lozenges topping the dispensary bench, giving the druggist something akin to privacy while he tallied the bills. Millspaugh counted it once and then started over again. When he finished the second time, he pocketed the money in the apron he was still wearing from the day.

"Twenty-five dollars," he said, and then the wrinkles on his forehead folded deeper. "I don't know about this, Anthony," he said. "Twenty-five dollars is an awful big sum for a Negro to be carrying around on his own."

"Yes, sir. Just like we agreed," Anthony answered, feeling proud that he'd managed to do what his employer maybe thought he couldn't. Weeks back, Master Millspaugh had noticed Anthony dividing tablets into equal groups to tally and realized the enslaved man he rented had a knack for numbers. After that, the druggist changed the rules between them. It used to be that Millspaugh wanted an accounting every night, even on days when no ships came in needing stevedores and there were no wages for Anthony to surrender. With Anthony's ability to figure, Master Millspaugh decided on a new plan. Anthony would get two weeks to collect wages however he saw fit, provided he handed over all money earned by the fourteenth day. Anthony had promised Master Millspaugh wages of $125 in total before the year was out. Anything above that, they agreed, would be Anthony's to keep.

"Someone might try to steal that kind of money off you," Master Millspaugh said, as though Anthony might be fool enough to let on about what was hidden in his own pockets. Anthony knew perfectly well that what they'd arranged wasn't legal. The druggist had rented Anthony for one full year from Master Charles Suttle, the man to whom Anthony belonged as property. Outside of Master Millspaugh's settlement with Master Charles, Anthony wasn't supposed to be finding his own jobs. He would surely do his part to keep secret his arrangement with the apothecary. Especially since an agreement allowing him to disappear for up to two weeks at a time could come to mean an awful lot.

Master Millspaugh kept looking from the paper bills back to Anthony, pursing his pale lips like he was sucking a rancid peanut. "Or someone might question how you came upon it. Twenty-five dollars," he said again, shaking his head as though he couldn't believe the size of it. "Best we switch back to daily pay-ups," Millspaugh said. "And I'll be expecting that $125 as fast as possible. Five, six months."

"But Master Millspaugh, sir," Anthony said, "I did everything you asked." Except now he understood his mistake in showing up with the large sum.

"Well now I'm asking something different, aren't I?" the apothecary said, as his cheeks started to redden. Anthony had worked with men like Master Millspaugh before, men who were more greedy than mean.

"But sir, you know there's days I collect nothing. I mightn't make twenty-five again anyway."

"I'll expect you tomorrow night for another accounting," he said, ending the discussion. "Goodnight, Anthony."

Anthony shook his head as he walked toward the narrow staircase at the back of the storeroom. He heard the front door open and close again as Millspaugh left for his own quarters, next door to the shop.

The fumes of Anthony's anger had him thinking cluttered thoughts. He'd been sure that their arrangement would allow him time to figure out his escape. At long last, he'd been well on his way, collecting money and the right kind of friends. He stepped into the small room he shared with Jeremiah, Master Millspaugh's houseboy. Jeremiah wasn't back from his day's work, and Anthony took advantage of the quiet to sit himself down on his pallet and think.

He knew why he was still in Richmond, why he hadn't left already. It had been about six years now since he got his hand hurt at the mill in Culpepper. All this time later, and he still had a piece of bone as big as a chicken foot jutting out from the wound at his wrist. Except now, that bone was dried up yellow and decayed. The day the accident happened at the Foote mill, that was when Anthony knew for sure that, someday, he would run. He was grown enough to understand, even then, that he couldn't spend his whole life captive to people like Master Foote, a man who would set a boy's hand in a sawmill just to teach him a lesson.

After he finished out his year with the Foote family and went back to Master Charles, he was finally allowed to get baptized, like he'd long been asking, maybe because Master Charles felt sorry about what'd happened to his hand. After that time, when Anthony had begun preaching to Black folk over there at Union Church in Falmouth, he began to worry that running North and stealing himself from Master Charles might be a sin. But once he came to Richmond and got to know Miss Colette, she lent him her copy of the Good Book. Even with some of its words being difficult, he knew what he was reading. There wasn't anything in those pages saying that Negroes were meant to be in bondage. He saw that of all the nations on Earth, God made them of one blood. Master Charles couldn't claim him as chattel under God's law any more than Anthony could claim Master Charles as his own property.

No, it wasn't fair to say it was religion tethering Anthony to Richmond anymore. But much as he wanted more time in Richmond near Miss Colette, they both knew when a thing was impossible. He had never so much as touched her hand, lest they both be damned. He knew better than to imagine a white woman for his own. Much as he pined for Miss Colette, he pined for freedom more. It was time now to take the opportunities for flight that might not come again to a man like him.

With Master Millspaugh demanding to see him nightly again, he'd now lost the advantage of being able to remain asunder fourteen days at a time. But he reckoned he could use the night's argument in his favor. If he failed to show up for an accounting during the first two-week period since their dispute, the druggist would figure he was still smarting about the changed terms and probably wouldn't start searching for him straight away. After that, all opportunity would be lost. He had no time to waste.

ON THE SECOND DAY AFTER THE QUARREL with Master Millspaugh, Anthony rose an hour before daylight and pulled from beneath himself a small bundle. The evening before, he had dressed in four layers of clothing and stowed what belongings he reckoned he could carry in his sack. He didn't have much. Just the hawk his father carved, a couple of potatoes, some coins, and an ointment the druggist gave him for when his wrist got to aching. He'd done all this preparing before Jeremiah returned from the Millspaugh kitchen. Jeremiah was a sly boy, and Anthony was in danger of betrayal if the child caught on.

He climbed quickly from his pallet, moving as quiet as his limbs could do. It wasn't just Jeremiah's ears he had to heed then, but Master Millspaugh's too. The druggist's home was accessed through an entrance beside the apothecary, and the man's sleeping quarters were near directly below the room Jeremiah and Anthony shared. Anthony was choosy with his steps as he crept down the narrow stairwell, feeling along the wall for guidance in the dark, taking care to prevent creaking. All the while, he worried about being caught.

When he finally reached bottom, he made his way to the window he'd unlatched the day before. He planned to climb from an open pane rather than risk the bell jingling at the door. He pushed at the glass, begging it to move silently, and then poked his head out just a crack, making certain nobody was about. The sky outside was still so dark, it felt a stretch to call it morning yet. Gas lamps burned all along the street, lighting shops across the way, and the air felt icy crisp, the way Miss Colette's maid, Adelia, liked to call cold-smoky. His eyes didn't find a single soul outside, save for a tabby crossing the cobblestones toward Grace Street. After offering up a swift prayer inside his own head, begging for Jesus to keep him safe, he hopped out and took off running.

He shotgunned himself to the east, keeping close to the shadows and the alleyways. The only sounds he heard were his feet pounding against stone and the huffing of his own breath. He had but one mile to travel before he would reach back to the same wharf he'd left the evening before—only one mile to cross until he'd be a full rung closer to freedom. Pushing himself through the February wind, his eyes teared up and stung with cold, but he kept putting the one foot in front of the other, following the route he knew, trying to keep himself away from the lamplight that littered every street. He just kept moving, as fast as his legs could carry him, stopping for nothing in his rush to reach the ship.

He was making good haste, but then, just as he rounded the corner toward 12th Street, he caught movement down the other end. He froze and backed himself against a wall. A figure, not more than a shadow, seemed to move toward him. He was scarcely breathing as he waited, trying to disappear into the bricks that were scraping up against him. As he watched, the figure became a man, a large white fellow in a dark coat and hat. The man fiddled with the door of a storefront, turning a key this way and that, struggling with the lock. Anthony noticed a barrel beside himself and crouched behind it. The fellow finally opened the door, but then he stopped and turned, like he could sense someone down the way. Anthony's breath caught in his chest as he made himself a statue. He couldn't be found. Not when he was so close. He called back on Jesus as he watched the man step out into the street.

The man passed in front of a light, and Anthony recognized him as the German baker. The fellow would surely know Anthony as Millspaugh's boy. Anthony wondered what he would do when the baker reached him, whether to fight or run, or simply accept that all hope was lost. But then the man bent low and retrieved a small package from the street, maybe something he'd dropped on his way. He turned back to the shop, leaving Anthony alone with just his thumping heart and the profoundest relief.

Once the door closed behind the baker, Anthony was back on his way, not sparing a second. He had only to hustle a couple more blocks, until, finally, he was at the dock, his neck slick with sweat. He found his sailor friend, Hayti, standing in the shadows and tapping his foot just where he'd promised, at the mouth of a clipper called the *Mary Will*. Before Anthony could speak even a word, the young man was shuffling him aboard. There were so many different sounds along the dock then, the lapping of the water against the jetties, the groaning and rasping of heavy ships anchored down, but as Anthony looked over his shoulder again and again, all he could hear was the clatter of his own fear.

He followed Hayti across the ship's foredeck, the two of them weaving around crates that were almost too hard to see beneath the moonless sky. Finally, they reached a stairwell toward the stern of the vessel, leading down to the cargo area where a space had been readied. Hayti shepherded Anthony deep into the hull, stopping only when they reached an open container. Anthony could smell salt, sweat, and something else pungent too, like fertilizer.

"Here," Hayti whispered, motioning to where Anthony should climb inside. It was a wooden carton, hardly large enough to contain a bushel of hay, much less a man standing six feet tall, but it was just as Anthony had already been told. He clambered inside, turning on his side to find a better fit, and placing his small sack atop his bent legs as he waited for Hayti to close him in. Feeling the tightness of the space, Anthony consoled himself with the knowledge that it would only be ten days' time, maybe fourteen if the journey ran long, before he'd be on free soil. As Hayti pulled the top across the crate, there was a sudden loud cry from above, almost a wail, and Anthony startled—

"Only the sails coming about," Hayti whispered. "Hush."

Anthony lowered himself down again, wondering how it was that his heart hadn't beaten itself clean out of his chest by then. He knew full well what happened to men like him if they tried escape and failed. Hayti made quick work of sealing the crate, and then he was gone. He'd promised to return with bread and water when he could. Anthony breathed in the cold musty air, questioning his choices, praying to God, and knowing that in that moment, he was as alone as he'd ever been.

COLETTE

Richmond, July 1852

The house in Richmond surrounded me like a perfect prison. With its gleaming white facade fronting South Fifth Street, and a grand entrance flanked by two Ionic columns, only a fool would have dismissed the power of a home such as the Randolph residence.

Inside the front hall, visitors would find a curved staircase and the long lingering scent of tobacco, pungent and unapologetic. A walk to the back of the house would reveal a dramatic portico, and not far beyond it, an entirely separate two-story structure that managed to hold both the kitchen and carriage house without obscuring views of the James River.

My esteemed husband told people he had the structure built as a wedding gift for me. As I was but fifteen years old when Elton, aged fifty then, chose me for a bride and negotiated with my father, there was ample time for design and construction before I reached truly marriageable age. The home, which continued to delight my husband, was conspicuous even in a residential area as lavish as ours.

Without children, my days as Mrs. Randolph dragged along. I found myself staring with increasing frequency toward the windows and the streets outside, where other Richmonders might have been engaged in endeavors more useful than my own.

"Mistress, the pink now."

Adelia thrust a spool of thread toward me, alerting me that I had almost blighted the floral edging on the handkerchief I was embroidering. It was meant as a gift for my sister, Fay, on her seventeenth birthday. I had been working too long with the green, forgetting the order of the pattern in my reverie.

"Thank you, Delly. You've saved the day now, haven't you?" I took the spool and tried to offer a true smile. Adelia, with her long slender arms and freckled nose, had been with me since I was a child, as a playmate before she progressed to lady's maid. My father had gifted her to me upon my marriage, and she was the only part of home I had with me still.

"Come now, Mistress," she told me in a tone that was at once supportive and remonstrative. "It's not but three days more until your visit with Miss Fay. And you'll be bringing her what will surely become her favorite new 'kerchief."

Despite the smile Adelia forced onto her own face, showcasing the large gap between her middle teeth, I could not find the strength to emulate her. *Bonne chance*, I was saved from disappointing her with my continued melancholy by the entrance of Tandey, the houseboy.

"If you'll be excusing me, please, Mistress," he said while glancing over his shoulder toward the front of the house. "There's a gentleman here to see you. And he brought a lady."

Adelia and I shared a look, as daytime callers were unexpected.

"Well, thank you, Tandey," I said as I rose and smoothed the tiered flounces of my silk skirt, which had grown rumpled after the full morning of sitting with my needlework. "What did they say their names were?"

"A Mister John Black and Mary . . ." He trailed off and

looked skyward, attempting to recall the woman's surname before looking back at me with trepidation.

I didn't try to hide my annoyance, sighing loudly even as I told him, "It's fine, Tandey. Just show them in." Never mind what I tried, that boy seemed just not to train. My husband was generally preoccupied when he returned from the factory in Shockoe Bottom, enough so that he hadn't yet noticed the deficiencies, but sooner or later, there would be repercussions for the child's lackluster performance of his duties.

When we reached the entryway, I saw an older gentleman, dressed in the way of clergy, and a slender woman about ten years my senior, attired in a neat but simple day dress. They were both lightly flushed in the cheeks, as one would expect on such a hot day.

"Good day, Mrs. Randolph," the man began as he bowed his head slightly. "I am Reverend John Black. Do forgive the sudden intrusion, but Miss Branson and I have found ourselves in a rather trying spate over at the Female Institute."

"The Female Institute?" I asked as though it was a place with which I was unfamiliar, but truth be told, I had followed the school's progress with great interest. The building, which had been constructed to resemble something of an Italian villa, housed a new school, one meant only for females. From what I understood, there was a great deal of learning happening inside its walls, despite many townsfolk objecting to the higher education of girls and young women. Before I allowed him to answer, I remembered my manners. "But forgive me, please come in and sit. Let me offer y'all some refreshment." I motioned back toward the parlor.

This time the woman answered. "I'm afraid we haven't time, Mrs. Randolph." Her voice was kind but strong. "Our teacher for the youngest girls was meant to arrive from the countryside two days ago. We got word this morning that she's fallen ill with the fever."

I hadn't any personal experience with scarlet fever, but I understood enough to know that the new teacher would not be arriving and that the school had been left in a lurch.

The reverend took hold of the conversation from there.

"As you probably know, Miss Lydia Melton has been given charge of the curriculum at the school since departing your parents' employ." He kept his hands clasped below his waist as if to steady himself as he spoke.

Bien sûr. I nodded. I had always been fond of Miss Melton, the woman who tutored both Fay and me, as well as seven of our female cousins before us.

"She has recommended you, expounding on your keen wit and deep patience. 'The most discerning young woman I've ever had the pleasure to edify' is what she said. She thought perhaps you would consider taking up the position." He glanced at his companion before adding, "At least until Miss Hart can convalesce and resume her post without endangering the welfare of the pupils."

Miss Melton's endorsement was both compliment and curse. I felt my chest puff up at the praise from my former teacher, but her suggestion was also an acknowledgment of my apparent barrenness. Married now nearly a year plus half, I knew perfectly well that I was being whispered about. Even my devoted husband, Elton, who was allegedly so besotted by my blonde curls and fair skin when he first met me at my parents' summer picnic, was beginning to complain about my failure to conceive. How many more nights I should have to suffer that portly man climbing atop me before he surrendered to defeat, I was not yet privileged to know.

My cousin Missy had been married three full years before she birthed her first child, and everyone was sure that her husband, Jules, had chosen poorly, that he would be deprived of heirs for his profitable iron mill. Yet now, Missy had five strapping children hanging off her at every family affair. Eighteen months wasn't yet a declaration. Perhaps if I emphasized the temporary nature of the teaching appointment to Elton, with promises to withdraw my service from the school the moment I conceived, he might allow it.

"It would be general studies then? Math and letters and the like?" I could hear the excitement building in my voice as I imagined it.

Miss Branson shook her head. "The girls are thirteen and fourteen years old, and all quite competent to be accepted at the Seminary. There would be higher level mathematics, literature, Latin, French."

I smiled at her mention of French, as my own mother had arrived in Virginia from Paris at the age of twelve. French was spoken more frequently in my childhood home than English. "I would certainly relish the opportunity," I told them, and Reverend Black's face lit up with relief. The appropriateness of a girl's seminary in Richmond was still a topic of debate, so I could understand why each defect might carry such heavy concern for those running it. "I can't hardly commit though until I've received my husband's permission, you understand."

"Of course." The reverend nodded vigorously as he shared a small smile with Miss Branson, both of them seemingly tickled already.

"I'll come visit y'all at the Seminary in the morning to confirm," I told them, hoping I would bring the answer we all desired.

ELTON WAS LATE RETURNING THAT EVENING, but Louisa kept our supper warming in the kitchen until his arrival. After we settled into our chairs at the chestnut dining table, Elton sliced into his roast pork, and I kept silent, knowing better than to interrupt his first bites.

He placed a forkful of the tender meat against his tongue and closed his eyes and mouth in tandem. I observed him as he considered the flavors. With his ruddy complexion and ever-tapering hairline, he was no longer a handsome man, but at least he was neat and well-attired, and his manners were impeccable, despite his excessive size. My husband certainly enjoyed his earthly pleasures, whether the tobacco he curated as his profession, the brandy he collected for sport, or the physical form of a wife more than thirty years his junior. I'd known for years prior to our marriage that Elton, and the elevated status my own family would gain from the union, would be my destiny. Even before his enormous successes in the tobacco industry, he had possessed great family wealth. With minimal initial investment, he also became the man behind one of Richmond's most successful tobacco factories, responsible for the production of Main's Tale tobacco. I'd known better than to protest when my daddy told me I'd be marrying such a prominent man.

When the meat was nearly finished from Elton's plate, he moved on to the creamed sprouts, and I ventured to break the silence.

"Did you have a lovely day?" I asked, forcing cheer into my voice.

Elton set down his fork and regarded me as though he'd only just remembered I was in the room. Lifting his napkin from his wide legs, he ran it once across his chin.

"As a matter of fact, I did," he told me with a proud smile, evaluating my appearance for the first time since arriving home. His eyes roved over my new silk gown and my neatly coiffed hair, parted down the middle and looped abundantly on either side of my face, and he seemed pleased. "We're increasing production again, renting additional slaves to work the leaves. Doing so much volume that we might strike a deal at only two cents per hogshead from one of the suppliers."

Elton did not expect me to engage on these topics, but he seemed to enjoy talking at me, as though to parse the moments of his day or perhaps simply boast to himself. I had, in my time as Mrs. Randolph, overheard enough talk from my husband and his associates to know that between his two brick factory buildings—the one on 14th and Cary, the other on 23rd and Main—he was producing over four hundred thousand pounds of usable tobacco each year. I knew he had upwards of one hundred slaves working the factories, sixty of his own and another forty that he hired from other owners. I understood that paying only two cents per hogshead was nearly unheard of and would be a victory that allowed for even greater profit, that this could be reason to celebrate. But Elton did not care for my opinions on these topics. He preferred when I nodded and smiled brightly without letting on that I understood anything other than the fact of my husband's greatness.

"Well, you must be just floating on air," I offered, and he agreed, going on to tell me about the several associates he'd spoken with and how they fawned over him and his accomplishments. I listened and nodded throughout his lengthy self-congratulatory statements. When he'd finally talked himself out, I found the time right to broach my own interests.

"We had visitors today," I started, as he listened with mild attentiveness. His eyes were focused on the low-cut bodice of my new frock. I explained about the open position at the Female Institute and finished by saying, "I feel it might be a way to fulfill my Christian duty until my days are occupied raising up your babies. And perhaps," I sighed dramatically, "the Lord might look so kindly on me for assisting these people that he'd help me and bless us with a child of our own." I gazed back at him, opening my eyes extra wide and arranging my features into an expression both innocent and youthful, as he seemed to like. I hoped he couldn't hear the pounding of my own heart, desperately bleating out its own pleas for a daily escape. If he knew how important this was to me, it would awaken his jealousy and turn his heart to brick.

His head cocked to the side, as if he was disappointed by having to endure such a request. "Sweetheart," he started, "it's not seemly. Educating females at that age. And to have my wife earning money. You'll have to tell them no."

"But I would only be with the youngest girls, the ones who are thirteen, fourteen." The words tumbled out in a rush as I raced to turn his mind. "And I'll tell them not to pay me. It will be strictly charity, and only short-term. Please, darling. The energy of the young girls, perhaps it will calm my nerves and help me toward carrying a child of our own."

Just then, Tandey appeared with the steaming cobbler, and for once, his timing was perfect. The scent of sweet peaches was sufficiently strong that Elton's attention was lulled toward the sizzling dish, away from his rejection of my appeal.

"Fine," he said, leaving me unclear whether he was granting Tandey leave to begin serving the cobbler or acquiescing to my request. I kept quiet as he waited for Tandey to place the cobbler before him. I prayed with all my heart that the child would not drop the cobbler in his master's lap and sour Elton's good mood, robbing me of this moment, this opportunity. To my relief, Tandey deposited our dessert without error.

As Elton carried his first spoonful toward his lips, he looked back at me pointedly. Then he offered one last edict.

"You'd best not make me regret it."

ANN

Boston, 1836–1837

To the surprise of everyone in the household, after Wendell's proposal, my health began to improve. Suddenly my wakeful periods were lasting longer, and I was able to take more food, even rice and biscuits. My aunts, Maria and Caroline, determined that Wendell's visit had been more beneficial to me than any other treatment, so they insisted that Uncle Henry admit him any time he came to call. Ours had never been a household to adhere strictly to the rules of propriety, and it seemed the decision to allow Wendell to repeatedly visit my bedchamber was no exception.

One Thursday afternoon, Aunt Maria was urging me to try a bite of chicken when I heard a visitor down below. Moments later, Wendell appeared at my doorway.

"I've brought you something," he said without preamble, and Maria took the bowl of stew from the room. He approached my bedside and reached into his jacket pocket, retrieving a small velvet box. "I bought it at an abolitionist bazaar and paid entirely too much for it." He smiled as he opened the box. Inside was a small blue cameo ring. "As an engagement ring," he said, as he lifted my left hand and placed the ring on my finger.

The ring sat too loosely on my limp hand, but I thought that perhaps, if I had more weeks of solid food behind me, my finger would plump back up and support the modest ring just fine.

"It's perfect," I told him, and I meant it—not only for its lack of ostentatiousness, but also for the fact that he had purchased it at an abolitionist fundraiser. He already seemed to understand every facet of my heart. Had he brought me something grand and flashy, I would have refused to wear it.

"And let it be a symbol that I will be your Gra for the rest of your days."

"Gra?" I asked, confused.

"It's what you called me," he reached for my hand again, "the day I proposed."

"I believe I had been attempting to speak your name. I thought that was rather obvious."

"Well, I think perhaps I prefer 'Gra,' at least some of the time," he said as he winked at me.

IT WAS SIX MONTHS LATER THAT WE WED. I wore a white dress set off by a pink sash on a fine October day. Though I still had aches and pains, my health was such that I was able to resume my usual routine most days. Only occasionally did I need to return to bed, and even then, the relapses lasted but a day or two at a time. Wendell and I honeymooned in Framingham and returned to Boston to continue our anti-slavery endeavors shortly thereafter. I was feeling so contented in our new life together that not even the prolonged refusal by Wendell's mother to accept me could put a damper on my general sense of joy.

My own parents had bequeathed me such a hefty sum of money at their death that I might have been the wealthiest woman in all of Boston at the time of my marriage. Unfortunately, when Sally Phillips regarded me, she saw only the daughter of former Boston Brahmins who'd been cast out of their place in high society when they began advocating for abolition of the enslaved. After their deaths, it was up to me to continue their mission. Despite my mother-in-law's disappointment at our nuptials and at Wendell's ever-increasing involvement in the anti-slavery cause, he and I were happy. And his mother was not wrong in her assessment that our joy was its most robust when we were advocating for the rights of others.

Just two months after we wed, we decided to attend a rally together at Faneuil Hall, one of the city's public meeting houses. Four weeks earlier, a journalist named Elijah Lovejoy had been murdered in Alton, Illinois, by a pro-slavery mob. The murderers had been reacting to Lovejoy's dissemination of anti-slavery information in the *St. Louis Observer* and had seen fit to shoot him dead. Although the upcoming meeting at Faneuil Hall was publicized as a gathering to support freedom of the press rather than abolition, many members of the Boston anti-slavery community were attending as well. As usual, the anticipated presence of several abolitionists inspired the attendance of some vocal anti-abolition Bostonians too. As we moved toward the entrance of the hall on that blustery morning, I saw that there were also many known free discussionists filing into the building. And then of course, there were the mobocrats, those who arrived simply for the opportunity to make trouble.

It was a relief to escape the frigid December wind as Wendell and I entered the hall. We found our seats about a third of the way from the front, where my aunts were already seated beside our friend William Lloyd Garrison, who we called Lloyd, and his wife, Helen. The walls of the building could only do so much to ward off the day's chill, and I sidled closer to my husband for warmth.

As the meeting opened, a Unitarian reverend from Boston's Federal Street Church took to the podium. The reverend opened with remarks deploring Mr. Lovejoy's murder and defending the right to free speech. Next to stand was local attorney Benjamin Hallett, a diminutive man whose job was to read out the resolutions that had been drafted by the reverend. The resolutions insisted that any infringement of the right to free speech must be resisted and that mobs must not act as the law. Mr. Lovejoy had violated no law in publishing anti-slavery sentiments, the resolutions further asserted. Equally important for our group's purposes, the resolutions declared that encroachment on the right to free speech must be resisted, whether with regard to abolition or any other political idea.

There was clapping all around, and I wondered if Wendell might rise from his seat to offer any additional words. Over the preceding year, he'd begun delivering anti-slavery speeches to small groups, and he'd displayed something of a knack for arousing a crowd. Back in January, he addressed the Adelphic Colored Union, and in March, he spoke to the Massachusetts Anti-Slavery Society in Lynn. Though he was a fine speaker, he had never addressed a group so large as the one assembled this day at Faneuil Hall. The meeting appeared to be reaching its conclusion, however, and there hardly seemed reason for him to add any sentiments to those which had already been shared. I could feel him pulling his cape more tightly around his shoulders, readying to confront the winter wind outside again.

Suddenly there was a commotion toward the back of the room. I craned my neck and caught sight of James Austin, the attorney general of Massachusetts, making his way up the aisle. Mr. Austin was a much loved and respected figure in our fair city, and he was also a vocal critic of abolition.

He marched toward the front of the room, and it quickly became apparent that he was planning to deliver a speech not listed on the program. The audience seemed rather delighted by the excitement of it, all eyes turning back toward the podium.

"My friends!" Mr. Austin began as he took the stage, "I

cannot agree with the abolitionist resolutions that have been read out today."

Someone let out a cheer at that, and Mr. Austin smiled into the crowd.

"Mr. Lovejoy, I'm afraid, was a scoundrel. The words he published attacked the rights of the good people of Missouri in their human property. I daresay that the members of the 'mob,' as it has been called by those here today, were doing their duty as patriots."

I couldn't help but gasp at his words. I turned to Wendell and saw that his face was reddening in reaction to the attorney general's assertions. All throughout our row of seats, my anti-slavery friends looked fit to burst. Lloyd sat with fists clenched, and Maria and Caroline appeared pale as bedsheets.

"They bring to mind another so-called mob," Mr. Austin continued, the creases in his forehead deepening along with the intensity of his words. "A group that operated in this very city only sixty-some-odd years ago as they captured the British tea and threw it to the harbor to make a point to those who threatened our own rights. I daresay those in the city of Alton were similarly orderly and similarly correct in their actions."

There were more cheers. I could scarcely believe Mr. Austin's words, or that he should so quickly arouse agreement from so many around us. Wendell quaked with fury beside me, and I felt my anger mingle with his, the two of us about to combust. Yet cheers and enthusiasm from the audience grew louder with each passing declaration from the attorney general.

"It was correct that the good citizens of Illinois and Missouri treated the offending journalist thusly," he called out into the crowd. "The mob did its duty in preventing a man from printing additional incendiary material. Mr. Lovejoy died nothing other than a fool's death. Let us do nothing further to support a traitor such as he!"

What a fickle crowd it was in which we sat. The man had fully turned them. Audience members stood and cheered. People shouted their approval while my friends and I looked on in horror. But suddenly, I remembered myself and who exactly was sitting beside me.

"Answer him," I said to Wendell.

Wendell looked back at me with a question on his face.

"You must answer him!" I repeated, feeling urgent and pushing against Wendell's arm, willing him to rise. "Otherwise, they will vote down the resolutions!" If the resolutions were rejected, our own rights to continue publicly advocating for abolition could be next to fall into question, or worse.

I watched as my words began to reach my dear husband. He looked up at Mr. Austin who stood at the front of the room, basking in the approval of the raucous crowd.

"Now," I pushed at Wendell again. "You must!"

Wendell's gaze shifted from the podium back to me, and then, thank heavens, he rose from his seat. As if finally remembering himself, he began moving toward the front of the room with purpose. I knew the oratory power of which he was capable, and I was hopeful that he was realizing his own strength in that moment too. Though Wendell was only half the age of the politician he was about to challenge, he walked like a man with no fear.

Other members of the crowd noticed Wendell approaching the front of the room, and a hush descended. Many in attendance already found my husband something of a curiosity. With his patrician heritage and exceedingly handsome face, he had shocked many among Boston's elite when he decided to reject his formerly lavish lifestyle in favor of joining the anti-slavery mission and taking a sickly bluestocking wife. I supposed they were anxious to see what outlandish behavior he might exhibit next.

As Wendell stepped to the podium, he gave the impression that he had planned all along to speak that day. He looked entirely at ease, as though there were no place more suited to his psyche than atop a stage with a crowd awaiting his words. He stood for a moment, with a calm dignity, looking out at the spectators. And then finally, he opened his mouth.

"Mr. Chairman," he began, his voice resonant and bold. "I hope I shall be permitted to express my surprise at the sentiments of the last speaker—surprise not only at such opinions from such a man, but at the applause they received within these walls. A comparison has been drawn between the events of the American Revolution and the recent murder in Alton. We have heard it asserted here, in Faneuil Hall, that the mob at Alton, the drunken murderers of Lovejoy, are worthy of comparison to those patriot fathers of ours who threw the tea overboard in 1773. Fellow citizens, is this Faneuil Hall doctrine?"

Shouts rang out from our sympathizers in the crowd then. "No! No!" some called, and I hoped that Wendell's eloquence, his noble bearing and calm logic, were reaching those who had been turned by Mr. Austin.

"The mob at Alton met to deprive a citizen of his lawful rights. They met to reject the First Amendment, a law that we ourselves created. We have been told that our fathers did the same when they threw crates of tea into Boston Harbor. Should it be that all mobs may now enjoy the glorious title of 'revolutionaries'? No! Lovejoy was well within his rights to free speech, and he should have been protected by our Constitution. He was not only defending the freedom of the press when the mob came to attack him, but he was under his own roof, in arms, with the sanction of the civil authority and the First Amendment. The men who assailed him went against and over the laws. To draw the conduct of our tea-spilling ancestors into a precedent granting mobs the right to resist laws we ourselves have enacted is an insult to their memory!"

Applause thundered out from the crowd. I dragged my eyes from my husband's face, and a quick survey of the room showed me an audience with wide eyes and rapt attention.

"Sir," Wendell continued, as though still addressing the chairman, when in fact he spoke to the room in whole, "when I heard the attorney general lay down principles which place the murderers of Lovejoy side by side with heroes of the American Revolution, like Otis and Hancock, like Quincy and Adams, I thought those pictured lips"—he paused and pointed to the portraits of those very men hanging in the hall before continuing—"would have broken into voice, speaking from their very graves, to rebuke such a disloyal American—the slanderer of the dead!"

Beside me, Helen grabbed my hand and squeezed in excitement. Wendell was a sight to behold. With his broad shoulders, the fine cut of his clothes, and his beautiful articulation, observing him was a sensory delight. The energy in the room had shifted entirely. I could feel him winning over the audience and destroying all that the attorney general had espoused. Had Wendell stopped his speech then, we probably would have left as victors already, but my husband was not finished.

"The gentleman," he said, referring again to Mr. Austin, "said he should sink into insignificance if he so much as acknowledged the principles of the resolutions we seek to pass. Shame on us, he asserts, for condemning the murder of a man who was acting within his rights under the First Amendment. On the contrary, for the sentiments *he* has uttered, on soil consecrated by the prayers of Puritans and the blood of our country's most devoted patriots, the Earth should have yawned and swallowed him up!"

"Yes!" I cried out before I could stop myself, but then I thrust my hand across my lips, loath to prevent even a single ear in the room from hearing every sound Wendell might utter.

"I am glad, sir," Wendell persisted, his shoulders straightening as he looked out over the crowded hall, a knowing smile playing at his lips, "to see this full house. It is good for us to be here. When liberty is in danger, Faneuil Hall has the right, it is her duty, to strike the keynote for these United States. The passage of these resolutions, declaring free speech a natural and inalienable right, in spite of opposition led by the attorney general of the commonwealth, will show more clearly, more decisively, the deep indignation with which Boston regards this outrage!"

Applause exploded around me then, like a hurricane, the force of which could not be denied. Cheers and shouts floated through the air, an excitement, a new momentum. Lloyd, Helen, and I were out of our seats jumping and clapping like everyone else. Even Aunt Maria and Aunt Caroline began hooting and carrying on.

When the chairman eventually quieted the crowd and put the resolutions to a vote, it felt as though every hand in the room was raised in favor. All of the resolutions were passed by overwhelming majority.

Wendell had done it! Reaffirming the right to free speech as a Constitutional privilege marked a crucial victory for the anti-slavery cause. I couldn't take my eyes off him at the front of the room, where he had clearly belonged all along. His own eyes found me in the crowd, and we beamed at each other across the many bodies and the clamor that separated us. Despite the physical distance between us at that moment, I had never felt closer to him.

ANTHONY

At Sea, February 1854

Anthony huddled in that dark box waiting and waiting for the boat to set sail. He couldn't say for sure whether he'd dozed or how long had passed before he finally saw a sliver of light creeping through one corner of the box. It was a relief seeing that pinprick of dawn pressing through the wood, knowing he'd at least be able to tell day from night throughout the journey. From somewhere up above, there soon came sounds of the day beginning, boots banging against the deck and men shouting back and forth to one another. As he waited for the telltale signs of sailing, he occupied his mind by silently reciting words of the gospel. Some hours passed, and eventually he fell asleep. What he knew for certain was that when he awoke, it was once again nighttime, and the ship was still not moving.

He began to worry that he'd been tricked, that Hayti was not his friend. He puzzled out every possibility while he waited. Maybe this ship was not setting to depart at all. *How long could a person manage inside that box*, he wondered. He tried to force himself into a steady place, but his mind wanted very much to run far away from him. Time became difficult to measure. At some point, he again heard shouts and calls of men above him. Finally, there was a new listing of the ship this way and that. And what joy, to realize that at last they were truly setting off!

That elation did not last long. They traveled what Anthony guessed was near fifteen miles down the river before he became certain he was going to die inside that box. He would never have expected there could be such rough water on a river. He couldn't imagine making it out to sea and being tossed about even more. The ship swung fiercely from side to side while Anthony stayed folded over himself in that crate. The bile was high in his throat, and he felt more wretchedness than he'd ever known. To spend ten days in this state, surely, it would be impossible.

He drifted in and out of sleep in between trifling attempts by his gut to vomit. At least he had so little inside his stomach that he was only heaving air again and again. At some point, he awoke to steps down in the hold. He hardly even had the energy to be frightened anymore. He sought only release from the box and the sickness. He felt sure there could be nothing worse than the fate he had been suffering. The footsteps came closer, and then someone was unfastening the cover from the crate.

"My friend," Hayti whispered. "Food."

"No, no, no," Anthony argued, pushing away the offering. "You must let me out. I can't abide the roiling. Please. Take me back." He started to move himself out of his sideways position, all his muscles tight with cramps.

"No," Hayti shoved against his arm. "You must stay. Take the bread."

Anthony felt a bundle drop onto his lap, and then already, Hayti was beginning to close him back in.

"No, please!" It was all he could do not to holler. "Put me ashore. Anywhere. I will surrender to the catchers, but at least to be on land." He was desperate, but he lacked the strength to fight as Hayti pushed him down again and directed him to hush.

And so the days passed, the seas growing rougher as they headed north against winds that caused the voyage to extend to nearly three weeks, rather than the ten days Anthony had expected. Each time Hayti appeared with bread, he refused Anthony's pleas, and gradually, too gradually, Anthony grew accustomed to the rocking.

TOWARD THE END OF THE JOURNEY, Anthony felt a new sharpness in the air, and he knew that they must be getting close. His toes grew numb inside his boots, and he waited with anticipation, gladder now that Hayti had not allowed him to jettison himself from the vessel. He tried to imagine what the city of Boston would look like and what he might do there as a free man.

Finally, he felt the vessel still, and he begged the good Lord yet again to please let him step off the ship without being discovered. The worry that they might be intercepted by slave hunters continued to plague him, even this close to the end of the journey. As the light coming through the crate changed to the brightness of morning, he heard familiar sounds above deck, shouts and shifting cargo, the commotion of men unloading at port, and he began to feel hope once again. He expected he would wait until dark before Hayti could release him, but dark arrived, and still, he was alone. As time continued to pass with no sign of Hayti, only hour after hour of quiet, Anthony wondered if he should try to bang his way out of that crate on his own. But he forced himself to remain patient. He was so very close now.

At last, as the gray of early morning light began creeping through that corner of the crate yet again, there were footsteps in the hull. Within moments, his cage was opening. Hayti was there, the sound of a smile in his voice as he whispered, "Come my friend; come see how it feels to be free."

Hayti helped him out of the crate. Anthony's legs were so stiff he could barely stand. After steadying him, Hayti watched a moment as Anthony stretched and groaned. Then he handed Anthony fresh clothing.

"You are a Northern seaman now, coming ashore as crew," he said.

Despite his aching joints, Anthony changed as quickly as he could, eager as he was to escape his own filth. Hayti bundled the soiled clothes into a sack and then they hurried toward the stairs. Anthony hardly had time to appreciate the icy fresh air above deck before they were hustling across the loading dock. The wharf where they'd landed looked similar to Richmond, just covered with more winter slush than he was used to. A few early morning workers were milling about, but nobody paid them any mind as they at last reached solid ground.

Anthony felt a jolt shoot through his veins as he recognized that he'd just taken his first steps as a free man. He thought of his mama, and her mama who she'd never known, and all the mamas and sisters and brothers and cousins and children who'd lived through days anything like his. He put the one foot in front of the other, moving toward his new life, and it was as if he were walking forward for all of them, each and every one.

COLETTE

Richmond, February 1853

E lton and I were in the dining room, just finishing our midday meal.

"Do you have something to tell me?" he asked as he pushed back his plate, where only the bone from a turkey leg remained amongst the drippings.

There was an edge to his drawl just then, and I wondered what he was getting at. There was only one secret that mattered, and I was certain I had done everything necessary to keep it safe.

"Why, I haven't the slightest idea, I'm sure." I blinked back at him.

"About your pet slave woman," he prodded. "Something you ought to share?" His jealousy about my affection for Adelia was chronic, yet I felt a rush of satisfaction at his words. I did not allow my face to betray my delight that the plan she and I hatched together was proving successful.

"You mean that she's been courting with a hired Negro?" I asked, as if it were utterly inconsequential. "He seems docile enough. I hardly expected you'd pay a mind to it."

"You're suggesting he's not on his own, not a freed darkie, then?"

"Heavens, no!" I gasped, as if I was scandalized by the very notion. There was a common conception amongst our set that close fraternization with free Blacks could lead to unrest among one's own crop of slaves. Folks grumbled on about it being bad enough that Negroes worshipped at the same churches together, the free and the owned crowing out hymns shoulder to shoulder. Allowing a romantic relationship between such a pair would rise to a different level of recklessness entirely. By comparison, my house girl dating a rented slave was relatively harmless.

"The Negro belongs to some fellow out of Alexandria. He's been hired out to one of the flouring mills; Gallego, I believe. Adelia tells me that the boy changes assignments every year. Last year he was with a tavern keeper out in Fredericksburg or Culpepper, so this will surely be only a brief dalliance."

It had been only two months since the day Adelia first noticed Anthony. He'd been walking just a short distance behind us as we made our way from the Female Institute back toward the house. As we turned onto Cary Street, I realized I'd inadvertently left certain textbooks behind and I asked Adelia to turn round and fetch them. At my mention of Collier's *English Literature*, Anthony emitted a startled noise, something akin to astonishment at seeing an old friend.

Adelia, of course, took umbrage at Anthony's listening in on us.

"If there's a reason you're studying us, boy, you best be stating your business right off," she said. We'd both turned around to face him, but she stepped in front of me, as if to block me from whatever threat he posed.

"Pardoning me to you both, Miss," Anthony responded, keeping his eyes on Adelia only, as decorum required. "I meant no disrespect. Just new to town, see, and taking it all in before my work starts."

"Mmpphh," was all Adelia responded.

Some impulse that I could not name struck me then. "Delly, take it easy on the poor fellow," I chided.

That was when Anthony's gaze finally strayed in my direction. I blush still, when I remember the moment his eyes found my face. It seemed as though he was trying to turn his eyes back to Adelia, but as he regarded me, it was as if he was powerless to look away. I felt my cheeks turn pink beneath his gaze. Finally, he seemed to remember himself and the fact that there could be consequences if he continued staring.

"It's no bother ma'am," he answered quietly, turning his gaze to the pebbles at his feet.

"Mistress," Adelia complained, "I'm not leaving you to walk by your lonesome while this man is stalking behind you. Coming up from Shockoe Bottom to cause trouble."

I believe we were all surprised by what Anthony said next.

"No, no trouble. I could fetch you the books, Mistress, if you'll just let me know where and also the place to be delivering them."

"That would be lovely," I told him, as I wondered why this Negro was so keen to get his hands on my books. Even so, I began telling him the address of the Institute, which was just up the road.

All the while, Adelia was hissing under her breath, admonishing me, but Anthony seemed to be rumbling with excitement to fetch what had been asked.

My suspicions were confirmed just a short while later. As I sat by the window of my bedchamber reading, I caught sight of Anthony arriving below with the books in his hand. He was rounding the side of the house and heading toward the kitchen, as I had directed. But before he reached the outbuilding behind the house, he stopped and crept close to a juniper bush. He looked to his left and right, clearly checking that no one else was about, and then opened one of the texts. After a moment studying the page, he began running his fingers across it. The set of his shoulders changed as he examined it, and his whole being seemed suffused with yearning and intent. Something in his posture told me that this was a Negro who knew how to read—or one who desperately wanted to learn. I felt myself connect with his longing in that moment, as I knew what it was to dream, to wish for something different. I must have moved suddenly in my realization, as the motion caught Anthony's attention and he glanced up my way. He closed the book in haste and began making straight away for the kitchen, where he would surrender his treasure.

IT WASN'T BUT SIX DAYS LATER WHEN I next laid eyes on him. All that time, I had been wondering if there was a way I could help him. As part of his job at the mill, he'd apparently been tasked with carrying letters and packages to the post office in town. Adelia and I were making our way to the dressmaker's when Anthony emerged from dropping the day's parcels. He was busy wiping at his shirt, swatting away flour dust from the mill. When he looked up, he almost collided with Adelia.

She met his eye and made that same sound of hers. "Hmmmph," she said, as she moved around him.

"Delly," I said in an upbeat tone, perhaps too indicative of my delight at this chance encounter, but I could hardly help myself. "It's our new friend. You must have started your work?" I asked as I tried to figure out how to suggest what I had been considering. Anthony seemed to jump a step away from me, and I imagined he was worried I might admonish him for his obvious interest in the textbooks.

"Yes, ma'am," he answered, keeping his eyes on my shoes.

"I've been teaching just down the street at the Female Institute," I told him. "Perhaps I will see you around town from time to time."

"Yes ma'am," he repeated, and I could hear hesitation in his tone, perhaps thinking I was issuing a warning, when in fact, I was aiming for the opposite. But then I had another idea.

"Adelia is friendlier than she seems," I told him.

"Ma'am?" he asked.

"You come round the house on a Sunday when you have time off. Maybe Adelia could show you a thing or two."

He looked up from the dusty road beneath his feet to where Adelia was standing just behind me. Adelia made some sort of grunt in his direction, like she could hardly be bothered to know him, but at the same time she squinted her eyes, examining him. I already told her the first part of what I'd been thinking, about finding a way to include Anthony in the lessons I provided secretly to Adelia. The second part of my scheme, that they should pretend to be courting as a way to conceal our subterfuge, had only just occurred to me. Much as Adelia had warned me off what I was suggesting, telling me again and again about how I was putting us both at risk, it seemed then that maybe she was reconsidering. I think we were both wondering what sort of man he might be, what type of character might be hiding underneath the flour and grist that had settled into his clothing.

"Yes, ma'am," Anthony said again. "After church be all right?" he asked.

"Of course," I answered. "I always tell my students it's best to start your learning with a clear head and open heart. Certainly your morning service should help with that." As I turned to Adelia, I sowed the first seeds of our subterfuge. Raising my voice slightly so that other passersby would be sure to hear, I made as if to chide her.

"No more dallying with your fellow, now, Adelia." And off I walked at a fast clip, heading toward the dry goods, with a smile on my lips and Adelia hurrying behind me.

With just a few well-placed comments since that day, I had successfully created the impression that Adelia and Anthony had found romance with each other. The ruse provided cover as to why people might notice them together from time to time. Meanwhile, I'd had several productive sessions educating them. I still couldn't say why I was so intent on including Anthony in our lessons except to confess that when he was near, I felt somehow less hollow inside myself.

I was drawn back to the present moment as Elton began fidgeting across from me, as if he was suffering some discomfort.

"Argh," he grunted as he pulled at his necktie, loosening it. The door at the far end of the room opened, and Elton's eyes shifted to watch Louisa enter. Netty, one of the older kitchen maids, followed behind her with a platter of pastries balanced in her hands. She and Louisa wore nearly identical black work dresses, with long, slim skirts and buttoned cuffs at the wrists. The white bonnets on their heads were freshly bleached and free of wrinkles, just as I had been taught to require.

"So long as they know they are permitted to proceed only under your supervision," Elton said as he looked back at me. "And at your pleasure." With that, he pushed back his chair and rose from the table. "I have an important matter to attend to," he told me as he tossed his soiled napkin atop his plate.

"But we've not had dessert," I protested, surprised to see Elton leave a meal before sampling every last offering.

"No," he answered as his eyes traveled regretfully to the pastel confectionaries filling the dish in Netty's arms and then back to the standing clock behind her. He ran his hand over his chest, as if he was suffering an ailment within, but I'd already learned not to ask after the condition. It seemed only to anger him each time I inquired. "It'll keep," he said.

As I watched his wide legs carry him from the room, I was glad about whatever obligation had taken him away.

"Come, Netty," I said, finding myself drawn to the pastries in my husband's stead. "I'll just help myself to one of the *petit fours glacée*."

She extended the silver platter, and I reached for the frosted square. As I sampled a small bite, savoring the sweet velvety texture against my tongue, Netty made as if to place the entire platter before me.

"No, that's fine, Netty. I mustn't overindulge, and better if we keep a hearty supply ready for Master Elton's return," I added as we smiled at each other. Elton's penchant for indulgence was well known in our home.

"Yes, Mistress." Netty nodded. "Hoping nothing's troubling him, then."

I shook my head as I let out a breath. "I can't very well say," I answered as we both looked back toward the door. Netty had been with Elton since long before I became mistress of the house, and she seemed to have some know-how in managing his moods. "For now, I best attend to my lesson plans for the week."

"Yes, Mistress," Netty said as she turned toward the back door and the kitchen beyond.

ANN

Boston, April 1851

W endell and I had long accepted that we would never have children of our own. Though our coupling was more frequent than one might have expected from a frail woman like myself, it failed to yield results, and so we felt doubly blessed that young Phebe had woven herself so seamlessly into our family.

"You'll sit by me with your lessons tonight?" Though I phrased it as a question, I knew the girl would not refuse. I had mustered the energy to vacate my sick room that afternoon, an accomplishment that had become exceedingly rare in recent weeks, and I thought both Phebe and I would like to make the most of it. In the few years since the girl had come to live with us, she and I had grown quite close, as if we were truly mother and daughter. Perhaps because I'd lost my own parents when I was near her age, I understood the strain of it all and could provide her with unique comfort. Just recently, and to my immeasurable delight, she had even begun referring to Wendell and me as "Father" and "Mother."

I took in Phebe's robust form, her figure looking more like that of a grown woman with each passing day. At fourteen years old, she already had a long, slender neck and shapely hips that refused to be hidden even under her modest day dresses. With her shining chestnut curls and bright eyes, she would never suffer for suitors.

The scent of the onions she was frying passed beneath my nose, and I struggled to conceal my revulsion. Even if my nurse, Betty, had been in the house baking her best biscuits, the ones with the luscious flakes and swirls of dough, I would not have found my appetite for them just then.

As I opened my mouth to suggest we wait for Wendell to return before eating, the door to our small home on Essex Street flung open with force, banging against the wall. Wendell burst inside, his friend Theodore Parker rushing in behind him.

"They've got a fugitive over at the courthouse! A runaway!" Wendell shouted as he ran past me and straight up the stairs toward the bedrooms.

Theodore stalled for a moment at the base of the stairs. A Unitarian minister and committed abolitionist, he had broken away from his church after they declared his anti-slavery views unchristian. Just one year older than Wendell, he already suffered a deeply receding hairline, but he still appeared young and hardy in the face. He offered me an apologetic smile for the intrusion as Wendell shouted down to him.

"Teddy, don't dally! Help me with the mattress!"

Phebe and I looked at each other.

"Mattress?" she asked me, still holding her spatula forgotten in mid-air.

"I cannot begin to imagine," I answered, using both my hands to push myself out of the soft chair where Phebe had settled me. I attempted to ignore the splintering pain that spread in my lower back as I began walking toward the stairs.

"Mother," Phebe admonished me, "you only just came

down. I'm sure they'll return any moment. Such haste as they've already displayed."

I let out a long sigh, knowing her advice to be prudent, but frustrated anew by my own inefficacies. I couldn't help the petty thought that it was I, so many years ago, who enlightened my husband to the burning import of anti-slavery, yet here I stood, relegated again to the home.

I maneuvered toward the front entry and peered out the small oval window beside the door, where I saw a covered cart waiting and three mattresses already peeking out beneath a tarp. Wendell was now walking backwards down the steps with one end of a mattress in his hands. Theodore, still obscured at the top landing, was presumably steadying the other end.

"They've got the man imprisoned on the third floor," he said, and suddenly I understood. They were planning to have the prisoner jump from the window. My dear husband and his associates on the Boston Vigilance Committee (BVC) were not going to wait for a physical altercation in the courtroom this time. The last time Boston authorities apprehended a runaway, back in February, members of the BVC had stormed the courtroom, using brute force to rescue the prisoner from certain doom. That particular fugitive, Shadrach Minkins, was now safely ensconced beyond the Canadian border, but the operation had been a great risk to the many involved. Perhaps more importantly, now that a group of angry abolitionists had stormed the courthouse once in the past, the guards would be ready for an attack this time, thus hindering the chance of another success. As harebrained as this mattress idea seemed, perhaps it was the wiser course indeed.

Wendell and Theodore maneuvered out toward the street, leaving the front door ajar while they positioned the mattress on the cart above the others. Wendell sprinted back into the house and planted a firm kiss against my lips. After a moment, he pulled back from me. With Phebe standing right there, he said,

"A better kiss, please. I'd like to feel enough of your form against my own to last me until I can be beside you in our bed again."

Speaking those bawdy words in front of others was certainly out of character for him. I recognized this flouting of convention as a sign of the growing ferocity in my husband, and I applauded it. With the exception of the forceful Minkins rescue, Wendell's primary weapon against slavery had always been his superior oratory skills. There was good reason that my husband had become known as the golden trumpet of the abolitionists. But it seemed that tonight he would again be prepared to use physical strength and cunning in the battle for one man's freedom.

As usual, I wondered how this champion of a man, this lion, could be fulfilled with a near invalid for a wife. What could I do but order him around from the safety of our own quiet home?

I looked toward Phebe as I smiled and told him, "I do believe with her mattress on the cart, you will find your usual spot occupied by our daughter tonight. Now off with you. A man's freedom is on the line!" I swatted his arm and sent him on his way, wishing I could be riding beside him, his partner in this crusade, like we had planned. But that was nearly a lifetime ago, before I took sick, before all the doctors, before the health retreats and water cures, before his constant edicts that I must stay away from too much commotion.

"Come, Phebe," I said as the door closed behind the men and we made our way back to our prior posts in the warm kitchen.

Phebe lifted the spatula again and moved a few of the wait-ing pancakes onto a dish for me. As I glanced down at the sad discs, so colorless and dense, I stifled a sigh and took up my fork. Another knock sounded then at the door.

Phebe peeped out the narrow window, whereupon she smiled. "It's just Helen." She grinned as she opened the door.

"My dears!" Helen was nearly panting, and I pictured her having run all the way to our door from her home on Dix

Place. Even winded as she was, her large bright eyes and shining brown hair presented the picture of good health. "You've heard?" she asked, looking at me. "They're heading back to the courthouse to save the man. Thomas Sims is his name. Lloyd's on his way to meet them at *The Liberator*," she added, referencing the abolitionist newspaper of which her husband, William Lloyd Garrison, was editor. "I'm not certain how long into the night they plan to wait."

"Well, you'll come and eat with us," I told her. Helen was so much a social being, always anxious for friendly companionship. I didn't even think to ask if anyone was looking after their children.

"Yes," she said absently as she made her way toward one of the chairs at our kitchen table. "Oh!" She held up a crinkled paper. "I hardly even realized I carried this with me."

It was one of the handbills that had been distributed the day before. I read the words from where I stood beside her.

> *Citizens of Boston! A free citizen of Massachusetts—free by Massachusetts law until his liberty is declared to be forfeited—is now imprisoned in a Massachusetts TEMPLE OF JUSTICE. THE KIDNAPPERS ARE HERE! Men of Boston! Sons of Otis, and Hancock, and Adams! See to it that Massachusetts laws are not outraged with your consent! See to it that no free citizen of Massachusetts is dragged into slavery without TRIAL BY JURY!*

I shook my head as if to clear it of the confusion. I'd read what men like Daniel Webster said about the importance of political compromise, and I'd seen scores of articles about the need to maintain social order and to continue the necessary evil of slavery. Yet, I still could not understand how liberty could possibly be an issue for debate among educated people.

Pursing my lips to prevent myself from reiterating all the same words Phebe and Helen had already heard me utter on the topic so many times before, I took my seat beside my friend.

As I rearranged the wool of my skirts to better hide the frailty of my thin legs, Phebe asked us, "What if the rescue fails? What will happen to him?"

Helen and I shared a glance, but I answered truthfully, "I suppose the poor soul will be sent back."

"I believe it was Savannah from where he escaped," Helen said. "I read that the man claiming ownership uses the prisoner for laying bricks around his plantation. Here." She dug into her bag for a folded newspaper and then handed it to Phebe.

We were all quiet for a moment as Phebe read the article.

"How awful," Phebe opined as she handed the paper back to Helen. "It says he escaped a first arrest before stowing away aboard a departing ship, only to be arrested a second time after settling into his new life as a free man. Not even three years older than I." She said the last wistfully, as if she was struggling to imagine being in Sims's position.

"Lewis Hayden and Thomas Wentworth Higginson are there at the courthouse," Helen said. Those men were known to be particularly bold about using physical force to support the Cause. I shuddered thinking of the violence that would likely occur that evening, but knowing in my heart that the consequences would be justified.

We were all silent another moment, simply absorbing the shamefulness of it all. But then something seemed to occur to Helen and she perked up.

"Elizabeth Bates heard that Sims stabbed one of the policemen in the thigh when he was arrested. At least the fellow had that one moment of vindication." Her pink lips tipped into a mischievous smile before she added, "They say it was Asa Butman."

I was lucky not to be personally acquainted with Mr. Butman

myself, as I'd heard only the worst of him. He was known to have been the lead deputy responsible for kidnapping Shadrach Minkins, and now it seemed he'd done the same to Sims. He probably deserved that stabbing and plenty more. Butman surely relished the new version of that frightful Fugitive Slave Act.

The new law required Northern states to apprehend any escaped slaves found within their borders and send them back to the state from whence they came. It put all Black citizens of Boston at risk of being kidnapped regardless of when, or even whether, they had escaped from enslavement. Even Blacks who'd been born free and lived in the North all their lives were now in jeopardy. Anyone could be labeled a fugitive slave, and there was little recourse for them to refute it.

If my husband and his compatriots were not successful tonight, Sims would be brought before a commissioner, not even a true judge, who would decide the man's lifelong fate. Under the law's parameters, Sims would be prevented from testifying on his own behalf, and he would be subject to a decision based only on the word of the Southerner claiming to own him. The law also included the particularly outrageous stipulation that any commissioner ruling in favor of the purported slave owner would earn $10, but those commissioners who ruled against the alleged owner would earn only $5 for conducting the hearing. There was no question that if Sims showed up in court in the morning, he would be sent back in the chains of bondage. As I lifted my knife to cut into my pancakes, I prayed that my Wendell would save the man from certain disaster.

THAT NIGHT AS I RESTED IN BED, I studied Phebe, who lay beside me in an easy slumber. What a blessing her presence had been. She was equal parts nurse, companion, and the daughter that Wendell and I would never have on our own. Her mother, Eliza, had been my nurse before she became one of the many in our city to be struck down by the cholera. Wendell and I did not hesitate to bring Phebe into our little home, just as the Chapmans had done for me after I lost my parents at that age. Phebe did not have the outsized inheritance awaiting her attainment of adulthood, nor a house to inherit like I did. Wendell and I were fortunate that we both came from means, and we would see to Phebe's care for as long as she needed. Even as she slept, the child brought me such comfort. Measuring the gentle rhythm of her inhalations as I awaited the return of my husband was the only way to soothe my frayed nerves.

Finally, with about two hours remaining before first light, I heard the quiet groan of our front door. I crept out from the bed without lighting a candle, hoping that when I met Wendell downstairs, he would have only triumphant news to report.

But what I found in our dim entryway told me otherwise. He had already lowered his body to the floor of our entryway, with his back against the closed door, head in hands, and his shoulders convulsing with silent sobs.

"Oh, dear Wendell," I whispered as I approached him. If I were a more agile woman, I would have dropped down beside him on the wooden floorboards, but I knew if I ventured groundward like that, it would be many days before my bones would forgive me.

As my husband lifted his head, his handsome face was marred only by the redness of his eyes.

"They knew we were coming," he told me, his deep voice suffused with sorrow. "There were nearly two hundred guards, and they put a new chain around the courthouse. They put metal bars across Sims's window. It wouldn't have mattered if we'd had triple the mattresses and as many men. There was no way for him to get past those irons to jump to the chaise below. All hope has been lost."

"Oh, that poor boy." My heart ached just thinking about

the prisoner's fate. "What next? There is no other endeavor to pursue before he goes to court?" I pushed.

"They've already ruled against him," he said, and I realized my prior assumptions that he had only just been caught must have been wrong. "They will march him down to the wharf quickly now, before crowds have time to assemble, cowards that they are. The young man will go back to Georgia. I suggested we find out the captain of the ship, offer him a bribe, but none backed me."

"I suppose the possibility of imprisonment has left many too frightened to assist."

"Higginson and Grimes said the same," Wendell said as he looked at me pleadingly. "But come, you must sit." He rose to his feet and ushered me toward the kitchen. "Will you eat some strawberries?" he asked, reaching toward the basket he brought home from the market the day before.

We heard creaking on the floorboards above and then Phebe's footsteps on the stairs.

"Is he saved?" she asked, rubbing a fist tiredly against her eye.

"Come, daughter," Wendell said as he reached out a hand in her direction and then repeated for her all that he had told me.

A faint knock at the door sounded, and I looked at Wendell in alarm. Much as I was proud of his courage, I was not keen on the idea of losing my husband to prison, should Mayor Bigelow think to make an example of him. I understood the mayor was still nursing his own embarrassment over the Shadrach affair, and perhaps now he would come after the movement's most visible leaders, like Wendell.

But Wendell only shook his head. "It's just Lloyd and Theodore with the mattress," he said as he rose to open the door. I was still clad in only my dressing gown, but there was hardly room for propriety on a night such as this.

Lloyd was the first inside. Abolition had been his whole life's work, and I could see from the set of his slender shoulders and the gray pallor of his face that he was shaken by the evening's events.

"Ann," he said, in greeting, as if he could only emit a single word or he would risk breaking down altogether. I thought of the strife Lloyd had already endured in pursuit of liberty for others, even being attacked by a mob outside of an anti-slavery meeting some years ago. The fact that he'd been rattled so thoroughly by the present case was telling.

Behind Lloyd followed Theodore. His necktie sat askew, and his eyes were wide beneath his spectacles as though he was struggling greatly to contain the rage boiling within him. He offered me barely a nod.

As the men carried the mattress back to Phebe's bedroom, I turned to my daughter. "Come, you must bear witness. Break your fast now so that you can all go and stand with Sims as he is marched back to the wharf."

"Yes!" Phebe declared, heartened, I thought, at least to have a task. She reached into the breadbox, taking out yesterday's sourdough. "But you cannot join?" she asked, knowing full well that I wouldn't have the strength to walk to the courthouse, nor would Wendell be pleased if I put my health in further jeopardy.

"No, I cannot," I agreed, feeling the ache of my disappointment at Sims's fate compounded by despair over my own limitations. I heard the clomping of Wendell's boots descending the stairs as I added, ". . . which is why you must go with your father and report back."

"Return to the courthouse?" Wendell asked as he reached bottom.

Phebe nodded as she handed the remaining bread to him and then hurried to go up and dress.

"Yes," I said, looking to all three men, "You must be there for the young man and bear witness to Boston's shame." How I longed to go with them and do my part for the Cause. "I will send all my prayers from here."

"Nonsense," Theodore nearly barked as he finished descending the stairwell to stand with us. "You'll join us. We have the cart just outside."

"But the other mattresses?" I protested, reluctant for them to risk discovery and repercussions.

"What better reason to travel with cushioning than transporting a woman who is generally confined to her bed?" Theodore asked. "You'd be helping us with camouflage I dare say."

"She is my wife to worry about, not yours," Wendell grunted at his friend. This was a common refrain from Wendell, and the sharp words hardly worried his companions.

Theodore's encouragement was enough to convince me and to quell Wendell's misgivings. I hastily followed behind Phebe to go and dress myself as well.

As I climbed the stairs, I heard Lloyd beg off to attend to an editorial he was working on for *The Liberator*. I suppose he thought his efforts would be better spent spreading the word via his periodical than being one more witness at the wharf. Or maybe he simply couldn't bring himself to watch Boston's disgrace as our city returned a fellow man to human bondage.

WHEN OUR CART APPROACHED THE courthouse, it was just after four in the morning. The early April air was frigid, and Wendell continued to fuss over me, badgering me to close my coat more tightly, to pull my hat over my ears, and so on. Though the sky was still dark, light was shining from lanterns and torches throughout the square, creating a spectral glow. I was shocked to find so many spectators surrounding the courthouse. Even in the low light, I could see there were nearly two hundred people. Police officers were also assembled in staggering quantities, with at least as many uniformed representatives of law enforcement present as there were members of the crowd to condemn them. Our path was obstructed by the many onlookers, and we were forced to leave the cart quite far from the center of the square.

"I fear you will suffer," Wendell said to me as he and Theodore hopped off the cart, "if you continue with us on foot." Phebe stepped gingerly from the side and nodded her agreement.

I looked toward the damp cobblestones behind him, where puddles lingered from the recent storm, and beyond that, to the growing crowd. Their agitation was palpable, and I knew he was correct.

"Here," he said, unbuttoning the cape from his overcoat and passing it toward me.

From experience, I knew better than to argue that he too might catch cold in the damp air. Instead, I spread it across my legs and reminded him to take great care with Phebe. Then I watched from my seat as they disappeared into the pulsating crowd.

As more torches were lit, a group of officers assembled in a hollow square formation. They marched to the east side of the courthouse, where Sims emerged, still shackled. I was too far to see his face, but I learned later that the man's cheeks were streaked by tears. They said he asked for a knife with which to stab himself, rather than return to slavery, but the knife was withheld. As Sims was guided to the center of the officers' formation, I could hear the outrage from the spectators at the travesty that was unfolding, yet there was nothing any of us could do.

The armed guards marched him down State Street toward the pier. Onlookers shouted helplessly into the air, "Shame! Shame!" and "Infamy!"

The procession of police and marshals armed with swords and pistols moved down State Street with Sims at its center, church bells tolling to signify the horror of what we were witnessing.

Before long, they were out of my sight. I learned later that a brig called the *Acorn* awaited Sims in Boston Harbor. By five o'clock, as Sims was led onto the deck, a voice was heard shouting from the crowd, "Sims! Preach liberty to the slaves!" The papers said Sims simply shook his bowed head before being led belowdecks and back toward the atrocities awaiting him.

WENDELL HAD SENT HELEN'S SON, YOUNG William Lloyd, Jr., to collect me from where I waited near the courthouse. After the boy deposited me at home, he set off with the cart to deliver the last borrowed mattress. My bones were aching from the outing, just as Wendell had suspected they would. Even so, I made my way to the writing desk in his study and began drafting the next speech my husband would deliver publicly.

Wendell's second-floor study sat above the milliner shop that was located next to our home. I could hear activity in the store below me as the merchant prepared to begin business for the day. As much as I wanted to surrender to distractions and wallow in my anguish over what I had seen at Courthouse Square, I tried to focus on the paper before me.

But instead, I had a sudden memory of my mother, dressed primly in a dark dress with a fresh bonnet on her head. In my recollection, she was preparing to deliver bedclothes to a woman named Jennie who needed the linens because she'd only recently arrived from South Carolina. I must have been about five years old at the time, and I hadn't understood then that the woman had recently fled slavery. Yet as I stared at the paper before me, I was hit by a fresh understanding that all people who'd traveled north to freedom, even those like Jennie, who'd come decades earlier, were at risk under the Fugitive Slave Law.

I imagined my graceful husband standing before a room packed full of Bostonians, preaching to them about these very risks, and finally, the words began to flow. As I drafted remarks intended to appeal to supposedly genteel members of society, the fervor of my feelings filled my head and drowned out the noises beneath me. I wrote about how the Union should not be used to sustain slavery, that nations are molded either by their great men or their masses. We had been brought to our current situation by our masses. Neither the North nor the South was showing proper statesmanship, and it was time to change. I lost sense of time as I wrote declaration after declaration about the importance of liberty, self-determination, and public opinion.

I was startled out of my concentration only when I heard the front door.

"It's just us, Birdie!" Wendell called, using one of his many pet names for me.

When he appeared at the study door, his chiseled features were haggard from lack of sleep and the disappointment of it all.

"I'm fine, Wendell. Go get some rest," I told him.

As if I hadn't spoken, he came and stood beside the cushioned chair where I sat, and I could smell the saltiness of the wharf on him. With a hand rubbing his eyes, he shook his head.

"One thing is certain," he said as he let out a slow breath. "Courts obliged to sit guarded by firearms will not sit long in Massachusetts. The commissioner who grants certificates shielded by armed men will not have many certificates to grant."

We regarded each other in silence for a moment as we absorbed the enormity of his words.

Wendell finally broke the spell. "Tea?" he asked.

I shook my head, having ceased to enjoy tea ever since I gave up cane sugar. Following the example of my Aunt Maria, I'd begun refusing to sweeten my comestibles off the broken backs of my fellow man. Wendell leaned over me and read some of the words I had written. I felt the warmth of his body as I watched him nodding in agreement at many of the sentiments. I knew he would be effective, resplendent as he always was, when he found the place to deliver this speech. As I gazed up at his stubbled jaw, his long nose, and deep-set eyes, I wondered again what he was doing with a weakling like me. While I seemed to get sicker with each passing year, my Wendell grew only lovelier.

"Have I some food on my face?" Wendell asked, catching me staring.

"Don't embarrass a lady. It's not seemly."

We smiled at each other a moment before Wendell moved to the room's petite sofa. As he sat, his face turned serious again.

"I cannot fathom what our next step should be," he said. "I am astounded that our own city of Boston has openly fettered a man and sent him to bondage. Have they forgotten that Massachusetts is a free state?" His voice rose, and a vein in his neck bulged along with his anger. "Yet now, any man can simply claim ownership of another, anywhere in the country. And regardless of the laws in the state where we stand, people everywhere are now bound by the rules of the South?"

We both knew the answer. Nearly three thousand Negroes had crossed the border to Canada after President Fillmore signed the Fugitive Slave Act because they knew it too.

Before I could respond, Phebe pushed her head through the door.

"I'm making scalloped oyster cakes. Will you have some?" she asked, attempting to buoy our spirits.

"None for me, thank you." Taking a morning meal rarely agreed with my digestion. Poor Wendell would have to suffer Phebe's experiments for the both of us.

One would not know from looking at our little home that we had sufficient funds to hire any staff we desired to cook our meals. Even so, it was common knowledge that we lived well below our means by our own choice. Besides, it brought such joy to Phebe to do the cooking that neither of us wanted to stand in her way. Luckily, Wendell seemed able to stomach anything she concocted.

"Sounds delightful," Wendell winked at me as he rose.

I felt a rush of joy looking at my little family, which was followed almost immediately by the guilt of relishing anything at all while Thomas Sims still sailed southward.

I knew already that this was not the last we would see of the Fugitive Slave Act, but I could not have known then the enormity of the havoc yet to come.

COLETTE

Richmond, February 1853

Three quarters of an hour after Elton had absented himself from our midday meal, I stood in a vacant classroom at the Female Institute. Throughout the previous half year, I had come to develop genuine affection for the girls under my instruction, both day students and those who stayed at the school as boarders. The teacher for whom I'd stepped in as substitute never recovered from that fever. Reverend Black told me they'd find a replacement in time, but he hardly seemed to be in any hurry. I liked to visit my empty room on Sundays, when the hallways were quiet and many of the girls had gone home visiting. I used the time to plan the coming week's lessons. This routine also lent itself nicely to my other endeavors.

I was just closing my mathematics text when I heard the light rapping of a twig against the window. I hurried into the dim hallway and opened the back door, just as I'd done on several Sundays preceding this one. As I pushed out the heavy door, I found Adelia waiting in the sunlight with a petite bouquet of winter jasmine in her hand. Anthony was idling just behind her.

"Let's make haste now, y'all," I said as I held the door ajar for them to enter.

The hallway was still empty as we hurried over the polished wooden floorboards back to my classroom. After I latched the door, I pulled a rough wooden box from the storage closet and placed it in the center of the room.

It was illegal to be educating slaves, and we all knew it. If we were found out, a lady such as myself might be assessed a hefty fine. And Elton would have my hide for the public embarrassment. The true risk, however, was to Adelia and Anthony. They could each be subject to fifty lashes, or worse. If we were observed here today, the box I was pushing would support my assertions that Anthony was building a contraption to hold the oversized dictionary I planned to display in the center of the room. The dictionary, Goodrich's new and revised edition, had arrived just days before, and now it sat waiting in a crate. I hoped its deliberate placement might help protect us in the event of our discovery.

"Here." I reached for my copy of Thackeray's *Vanity Fair* and placed it on the desk at which Adelia had seated herself. "You're first today."

She repositioned an empty inkwell so she could better center the book on the desk and then began flipping the pages. She landed finally at the start of the second chapter, where we had left off the week before. Then she began.

"In which Miss Sharp and Miss Sedley prepare to open the cam . . ." She paused there and her eyes darted up from the page to look at me, but I was not in the business of providing answers that would only hinder the learning.

"Go ahead," I prodded. "Just remember to work out the sound of each letter, one after the other."

She looked back at the words and began to make little hissing sounds as she whispered out each letter, first slowly, and then with gradually increasing speed. While we waited, my gaze strayed toward Anthony. He was unusually handsome, nearly six feet in height, and skin so smooth it made a person think of silks and satins. Save for the ragged scar on his one cheek, I found his face to be nearabout perfect.

Just then, Anthony glanced up and caught me staring. I felt my cheeks redden, and I pulled my eyes away as quick as a hand burned at the kettle. I was saved from further fumbling when Adelia burst out with the answer to the tricky word.

"Campaign!" She declared. "Prepare to open the campaign," she repeated the phrase and then kept on.

To be sure, Thackeray hardly made for easy reading, but I'd been working with Adelia on her letters since we were children. I still couldn't hardly say what encouraged me to take on the added risk of instructing Anthony, except that something struck me when I watched him thumbing through the pages of Collier's *English Literature*. Was it any wonder that I gravitated toward others who knew what it was to yearn for a different path? Joining the faculty at the Institute had been gratifying, but I knew my time at the school was limited. Any day now, Elton would surely lose his patience with my outings or the replacement teacher would be found. And truthfully, my presence was hardly crucial to the instruction of the Institute students. They could learn from anyone. But Anthony and Adelia—well, I was surely their only hope.

As Adelia continued working her way through the words of the page before her, I rounded her desk and stood behind her, as if to follow along. Truth be told, I feared that if I did not employ my eyes in a task, they might stray right back to Anthony.

When Adelia reached the end of the page, she handed the book to Anthony for him to take his turn. As he took hold of the book, I caught sight of the defect on his wrist, scar tissue puckered up around dead bone. I never asked about it, as the assumptions one could make were plentiful. He cleared his throat and began to read.

"How could you do so, Rebecca?" His pace was slower than Adelia's, but there was a melodic cadence to his words that prompted me to recall his interest in preaching. He glanced up at me, perhaps to ensure I was listening for errors. I nodded, and his eyes returned to the page just as a knock sounded at the door.

Before I could even think, I grabbed the text out of his hand, registering the sound of a page tearing.

"Just a moment!" I called.

Anthony hurried from his seat toward the wooden box, and Adelia moved herself to a back corner of the room, as if she might be awaiting some instruction from me. Anthony made himself busy with a ruler, like he was measuring the box for its next piece.

I turned the knob with trepidation, unsure the fate we were about to suffer.

There before me stood Reverend Black. He was still in his Sunday best, perhaps having just returned from the late service. His dark hair was combed over to the side as usual. His eyes moved past me to take in my company, and there was the tilt of something more than curiosity upon his features.

"Good afternoon, Reverend." I struggled to keep my voice steady even though my heart was nearabout pounding out of my chest. "I hope we haven't disturbed you. I'm having a display box built for the center of the room and hoped to complete it at a time that wouldn't disrupt teaching hours." I lowered my voice to a near whisper and added, "It's a surprise for the girls. I've ordered a substantial copy of Webster and Goodrich's for their use. Unabridged!" I forced excitement into my delivery.

"A dictionary?" he asked as his eyes traveled back to my face.

"N'est-ce pas génial?" I said, reverting to French in my alarm. "Not to worry," I corrected, hurrying on, "it's at my own expense of course. A gift to the Institute. From Mr. Randolph and me."

"A gift?" He said, his demeanor changing near instantly. "Well, isn't that lovely!"

I could hear Anthony behind me, banging now with a hammer, but I didn't dare turn round. Reverend Black seemed to remember himself then, and I could see him working through a thought. "This is not the first Sunday you've had this project underway, am I correct?"

I was unsure what he might know and ventured a vague reply.

"Just fixing to get the specifications right," I said as I forced myself to smile.

He crooked a finger then, motioning that I should lean in closer, as his eyes darted again to my companions.

"You best be careful," he whispered. I could smell the wine of the sacrament on his breath as he continued. "It hardly looks usual, having two Negroes inside a classroom like this. Might be best to make sure the display stand gets completed today. Or if not, maybe find another location to do the rest. The Institute endures sufficient talk of scandal as it is, simply for educating our own girls. You understand?"

Clearly, the ruse had been stretched as far as it could reach.

"Yes, Reverend." I nodded, unsure what else to say.

He pulled a pocket watch from his coat and added, "Certain parents will be returning their daughters to campus this evening. Best finish up within the hour." He nodded and turned down the hallway toward his own office.

As I closed the door, I heard both Anthony and Adelia release shaky breaths behind me, as though they hadn't dared to exhale the entire time the reverend was present.

"Well, that's the end of it then," Adelia said, looking from Anthony to me. It'd be no great loss to her, as she could continue her progress with me in my chambers at nearly any time. It was Anthony who would suffer from this development.

"Delly, you are too quick to accept defeat," I admonished her, thinking there must be another option that could allow Anthony to continue learning with us.

"You don't pay it no mind, Miss Colette," Anthony said as he turned the wood structure onto its side. "You've already done enough that I can just keep practicing on my own anyhow—reading the placards along theater row and the advertisements down Main Street. People be thinking I'm just staring off at the buildings."

"This is not the end, Anthony," I told him. "We will find a new place. I will come up with something," I said with a buoyancy I didn't feel. I was surprisingly disappointed by the idea of giving up time with Anthony. I had looked forward each week to our meetings for reasons I didn't dare consider. "We'd better have you finish that display stand though," I said, looking at the box he had crafted.

"I was thinking the same," he said as he reached for a fragment of glass paper meant for sanding. "Best to do it in the lot now that it's earnest work, else the dust is going to be something awful in here."

"Right," I answered absently as I began to collect my things, already distracted, wondering where else we could meet. It had already occurred to me that I could send Adelia without me, that she and Anthony might find a back room at the First African Baptist Church or some apartment near Shockoe Bottom, where it wasn't unusual to see groups of Negroes congregating on a Sunday. They could practice their reading and writing together, helping each other along. But I did not want to be excluded from the lessons, nor to relinquish the only two hours of the week that set my heart to racing and reminded me that I was still alive.

ANTHONY

Boston, March–May 1854

Anthony thought he settled in just fine to living as a free man. Hayti directed him to a passable boarding house near the waterfront in a part of town that folks called "Nigger Hill." White folk stayed far away from that neighborhood, thinking the area a breeding ground for vice and folly. That was fine enough by him, since all he cared about was being in a place that made it easier for a runaway to stay well hidden.

Hayti also helped him get set up with his first job, working on one of the dredging boats as a cook, just like his mama, who worked as a cook back home. Only, he never could get that bread to rise like his ma had done, and it wasn't more than a week before he got himself fired. After he lost that job on the barge, he walked himself all around Nigger Hill and beyond, looking for something new.

It was a bright morning near the end of winter when he passed by an iron works and saw a man outside washing windows. A short, fleshy Black fellow with eyes so big he had a constant look of surprise on his face, the man introduced himself as William Jones.

"But folks round here call me Billy," he told Anthony.

"Is there work enough for another fellow?" Anthony asked.

The man put down the rag and stick he was holding, dropping them into the bucket beside him as he studied Anthony.

"Might maybe be, maybe, maybe, maybe. If you're strong as you appear," he answered, studying Anthony and then glancing behind himself at the building. "Lots of windows, see?"

The window washer had a strange lilt to his voice that had Anthony wondering if he was in some way demented, but Anthony didn't much mind, so long as the man could help him find a job.

Anthony followed the man over to see a fellow in the office, and within the hour, he was washing windows just like his new friend, Billy. The place they worked was Mattapan, an iron works in South Boston, similar in kind to places back in Richmond.

Billy showed him how the boss liked the windows cleaned and which way to wipe to keep from making streaks. Anthony learned he would earn eight cents a window, but as he shivered alongside Billy in the cold that afternoon, he worried he wouldn't last long out of doors in the northern winter temperatures.

Such it was that he met Mr. Coffin Pitts and found where it was that he truly belonged in his new city. One evening when he and Billy were walking back from the iron works, they passed by Mr. Pitts's clothing shop on Brattle Street, and the door was propped open.

"How do, Mr. Pitts?" Billy called to the Black fellow inside the store.

Mr. Pitts looked up over his spectacles from where he was folding fabrics behind the counter, and his eyes settled near instantly on Anthony. "Who you got there with you, Mr. Jones?"

Now, the thing about Billy was that something wasn't quite right in his head. He was pleasant enough, but he didn't seem to understand so much about the world surrounding him. He never asked much about Anthony, and Anthony knew better than to offer secrets to him anyhow.

"This here's Anthony," Billy answered matter-of-factly, maybe not even realizing he didn't know Anthony's surname or anything about where he'd been.

"Well, just hold up there, gents," Mr. Pitts said as he motioned them inside. "I never seen you before, Mr. Anthony."

"No, sir," Anthony answered, feeling he ought to be respectful of this older fellow who operated his own store. "I'm new to these parts."

"That so?" he asked, and he made no secret of looking Anthony over, considering what he might be. While the man studied him, Anthony noticed the neat trim to the fellow's beard, the crispness of his collar, and his tightly knotted necktie. Everything about this Mr. Pitts seemed to be shipshape.

After the quick once-over, Mr. Pitts asked, "Well, why don't you come on down to Belknap Street on Sunday? Think you might enjoy meeting some others who came to Boston from places faraway too?" It felt like Mr. Pitts knew everything there was to tell about Anthony Burns.

"Yes, sir, I'd like that," Anthony answered. "Unless I have any work to do. Can't give up wages."

"You can't be working on the Lord's day," Mr. Pitts chided. "You'll come on down to pray with us at 12th Baptist Church."

"Mr. Pitts is a deacon there," Billy contributed.

"Well, yes sir, I wouldn't miss that then," Anthony smiled, pleased to have found Baptists there in Boston—maybe a whole new congregation where he'd be welcomed as a free man. He thought the invitation might mean he was finally settling in, getting himself fit to stay put. But in fact, he was barreling straight toward the moment when everything would change yet again.

WHEN SUNDAY ARRIVED, HIS THOUGHTS turned toward Miss Colette and their own weekly meetings, but he forced himself to push her from his mind. There was no reason to pine for anything down South, especially not her. Instead, he dressed himself as finely as he could and went over toward the north slope of Beacon Hill, searching for the building Mr. Pitts had described.

The 12th Baptist Church was in a temporary home until the new building over on Southac Street could be finished. Mr. Pitts said it had already been four years since they started building the new place, but after people heard about the new Fugitive Slave Law, construction stalled on account of so many church members running to Canada. Even so, Anthony found a large assembly of folks congregating near the place where he was headed.

The church was two stories high, looking like it could hold more than a hundred people. Wide windows filled the front walls and the sides, with more shining windows up top too. He'd never seen the likes of it for colored praying. He heard his name called as Coffin Pitts, wearing his Sunday best, separated himself from the crowd.

"Anthony!" Mr. Pitts reached out with a wide smile on his face. "Come, my brother," he said, putting an arm across Anthony's back, guiding him toward the door. And what he said next shocked Anthony most of all. "Welcome to the Church of the Fugitive Slave." Then he just gave a little laugh, like it was the easiest thing to say. As they reached the front of the crowd, Mr. Pitts said, "Here we come to the pastor."

Anthony looked ahead and saw a tall, light-skinned fellow about forty years old, shaking hands and checking in with each member of his flock as they passed.

"Coffin," Pastor Grimes said, reaching for a hearty shake of Mr. Pitts's hand. Then he smiled kindly at Anthony, curiosity in his eyes. Anthony could hardly have been aware then that the path of his life was changing forever in that moment. Instead, he just listened as Mr. Pitts asked after the pastor's wife, Octavia, and their children. Then Mr. Pitts directed Anthony inside, where they made their way to a pew near the middle of the room. It was the first time in his whole life being inside a real church and not being sent to the back or the balcony. He opened up his heart and thanked Jesus for all the good fortune raining down upon him.

COFFIN PITTS MUST HAVE TAKEN A REAL shine to him because after church that day, he offered up a room in his own home for Anthony to rent at a more than fair price. Anthony didn't have to think but a moment before shaking hands with Mr. Pitts and heading straight to the boarding house to fetch his things.

Aside from Coffin and his wife Louisa, only a barber by the name of Benjamin Bassett was lodging with them in that brick house, and Anthony found he had more space for himself in his new home than he might ever need. He also started working over in Coffin's clothing store, folding shirts behind the counter and thanking the Lord for saving him from more outdoor work. The weather in Boston could be something cruel, unlike anything he ever saw down South, that was for sure.

Each week, Coffin invited Anthony to come along again to church, where Pastor Grimes would be leading services. When the pastor learned that Anthony had done some preaching down in Virginia, he asked Anthony to give a sermon of his own to the congregation the following week.

"Oh, I couldn't hardly preach to so many," Anthony said as they stood just outside the church on a sunny Sunday morning. The air around them was still cool, as winter hadn't yet yielded to spring. "And Free Blacks," he said as he shook his head, "they'll be expecting better than I have to offer."

"Nonsense," Pastor Grimes said, taking Anthony's hand into his own like they were shaking on a deal. "I can tell you've got that special spark inside. It's just what the people need."

And so it was that he started meeting regularly with Pastor Grimes to talk about the lessons of the Good Book and plan some sermonizing of his own. Often times, they'd stray off topic and start prattling to each other about all manner of things. They'd talk about the pastor's wife and the herb garden she kept, or Anthony's Ma and what he knew about each of her three husbands. He told the pastor about the different places he'd been hired out over the years and the fateful day when his wrist had been injured at the Foote Mill.

He was feeling so contented to have settled in as well as he did that he thought it time to pen a letter to his brother, Carmen, back down in Richmond. His brothers would want to know how he was getting on, and Carmen was the only one of them who'd learned to read, thanks to a brash old lady he'd been hired out to as a boy. Anthony wrote out his letter, knowing it would have to be mailed from some place far off so as not to bear the postmark confessing his location. Any mail that arrived for one of Mr. Charles Suttle's slaves would surely pass by the master's hands first, and Anthony had no doubt that they would study the envelope and likely read the contents inside.

He was careful to leave out any information about the city where he was living as he told Carmen all about how he was working for a colored man at his clothing store and renting out a first-floor bedroom from that same man. He wrote about how Black folk could come and go around free as they pleased up there in the North. He confessed that he missed some people from his old life, but still, he encouraged Carmen that if he could find a way, he should try to get himself to freedom. Then he scratched that part out, running his ink over the words until they couldn't be read, as he knew Master Charles wouldn't like to see that. Instead, he focused for the rest of the message on the wonder of two thousand free Blacks living alongside him, how they could manage their own time or dress themselves up in elegant clothes. He thought the image of old Black ladies wearing hoops would make Carmen chuckle good. Then he quickly added the date, packed the letter up and brought it out to the front room to give to Coffin.

"It won't get there fast, mind," Coffin explained as he rose from the table where he'd been finishing his supper. But Anthony understood and wanted only for the message to reach his brother one day or another.

HE'D BEEN IN BOSTON GOING ON THREE months before the worst happened. The days had begun to warm, and he saw that springtime in the North brought with it air as pleasant as what he knew from time to time down in Virginia. The trees bloomed along Battle Street, sprouting pink and white and green, and he enjoyed his walk home from the store better each day. Folks had begun to know him as the fellow who worked with Coffin Pitts, and he reckoned he'd made himself some friends too. Many of the parishioners he met at church held jobs as good as his, working as waiters, hotel workers, stevedores, and seamen. It puffed up the soul to see so many Black folks making their own way.

Coffin liked getting home to Louisa in the evenings and began letting Anthony stay behind to finish business for the day and do the locking up. It was one such night in May when Anthony was securing the front door of the store that he caught a glimpse of three white men rounding the corner. They didn't make to approach him, so he just kept about his tasks. The evening sky still held its light, and he began his stroll, glad for the time to enjoy Boston in springtime. He took himself along Brattle up to Court Street and then headed over toward Hanover. Just as he passed in front of Brigham's drinking saloon, where jaunty piano notes floated out from inside, he felt a hand come down upon his shoulder as if from nowhere.

"Ho, boy!"

He turned to see that one of the white fellows was upon him, and his heart stuttered when he recognized the man as Asa Butman. With his fat ruddy face and pinprick eyes, that man was a US marshal with a reputation. Only just this morning, Anthony had noticed him fiddling about in Coffin's store like he was hunting for something. Or someone.

"Yes, sir?" Anthony asked, stopping in his tracks and fixing his eyes to the ground. The other two men came up alongside Mr. Butman, both standing rigid like they were ready to pounce if Anthony made trouble. He tried best as he could to act smooth and calm, like his blood wasn't racing inside his veins, like he was an innocent man.

Mr. Butman looked him over with brown eyes as sharp and mean as a black-footed ferret. "You been at the jewelry store, boy?" he demanded, and Anthony breathed a sigh so big it was nearly a laugh.

"No, sir." Anthony shook his head, as he added, "I been working all day with Mr. Coffin Pitts at the store."

"You telling me it wasn't you then," he said, his grip still tight on Anthony's arm, "that broke into the jewelry store, robbed the place?"

"No, sir, it sure was not," Anthony told him, well pleased that this was just a case of mistaken identity, rather than the end of his time living on free soil. He was readying to accompany the marshal wherever they needed to go in order to clear up the confusion, but then several men emerged from the shadows beside the saloon. Before Anthony could even argue, they were lifting him up, all of them with their hands on him. In a matter of seconds, he was positioned above their shoulders, as if he were a casket they were setting to carry at a funeral procession. It was such a strange way for them to move him, just as if he were a dead man. Almost instantly, they began marching him straight down the center of Court Street.

"I can walk; I'll come along!" he protested, but it was as if they heard nothing he said as he struggled to escape their hands. They held him firm as he tried to twist from their grip, and then he saw the courthouse come into view. He was relieved, thinking that once they arrived at the court, the confusion could be snuffed out.

By then, the sky had almost fully darkened. Even so, he could make out a man, a federal marshal, standing on the courthouse steps with his sword drawn, as though he was awaiting their arrival. The marshal looked as is if he were expecting the arrival of a very dangerous man. As they approached, Anthony arched his neck, trying to meet the marshal's gaze, but the captors didn't slow. Instead, they continued marching him straight up the steps and then climbing the stairs inside, all the way to the top of the building, to a place they called the jury room.

Only then did they finally set him down upon his feet.

He looked quickly about the room, ready to confront his accuser. It was a large space, empty except for a few chairs and a small desk at one end, and a mattress on the floor down the other side. Windows lined one wall, all of them covered up with iron bars.

"But where is the jeweler?" he asked Marshal Butman.

Butman huffed then, and Anthony was unsure whether he was annoyed by the absence of the accuser or by the question itself.

"Well," he said, as he walked closer to the door and glanced back into the hallway, "he was supposed to be here waiting for us." He looked back toward the other marshals saying, "Coolidge, Riley, see if you can't find where the jeweler's got off to."

One of those two men, the taller fellow, glanced at Anthony with a sneer on his pale lips before answering. "Sure, Marsh," he said looking back to his companion. "The jeweler."

It was then, with the cavalier twist to the word, that Anthony realized the worst. There was no jeweler. He was being held because he'd been discovered as a fugitive.

As he looked to the faces of the armed men who remained in that room to guard him, his vision began to dim. He was forced to grasp that this was the end. His time as free man was already over.

His legs became weak as he chewed on these thoughts. Surrounded by so many guards as he was, there was no hope for escape. He began to sink down to the floor, nearly ready to confess all, so defeated was he in that moment. Marshal Butman took a step toward him then, as though he could sense that Anthony had come to understand the reason for his confinement. Before the marshal could speak his mind, the door opened again.

What a mix of feelings Anthony endured when he saw who was entering their meeting. There were Master Charles and Master William Brent, all the way up in Boston. Master Charles looked weary from travel, his white hair disheveled and his necktie askew, but otherwise, he appeared much the same as Anthony was accustomed to. What's more, he seemed thoroughly pleased to see Anthony, even taking off his hat to greet him.

"Well, how do you do, Anthony?" he said as he approached, and Anthony could hardly understand his own thoughts, as he was nearly relieved to see the man—as if his old master were a familiar friend, who Anthony foolishly hoped might somehow protect him from the angry attackers.

Overcome as he was by the sight of Master Charles, Anthony failed to respond to his greeting.

Then Master Charles asked him outright, "Why'd you do it, Tony?"

Finally, at hearing the way Master Charles called him Tony, just as familiar as he'd always done, reason suddenly returned to Anthony's head, crashing down upon him.

"No, sir," he answered, already arguing against what Master Charles implied. "I fell asleep, down there in Richmond, helping out on one of the rigs. Time I woke up, we was already set asail."

Master Charles shook his head in disappointment, like he knew Anthony was telling fibs, trying to help himself. Then he asked a question Anthony hadn't expected. "Haven't I always treated you well, Tony? Given you special privileges and paid you favor?"

"Well, yes, sir," Anthony nodded, sure that he shouldn't say otherwise, no matter how little those paltry favors meant to someone who just wanted to be free.

"Tell me, how many times did I whip you?" Master Charles asked, running his hand down the front lapel of his coat.

"Well, none, sir," Anthony answered, surprised by the question.

"And didn't I give you money, Tony, whenever you asked for it?"

Well, Anthony couldn't help himself from answering forthright then, thinking on all the wages he'd earned over the years only for Master Charles to profit from his efforts. "I know you gave me twelve cents all of one time each year."

Master Charles's arm raised at that, like he was fixing to smack his hand across Anthony's face, but his eyes darted to the other men in the room and he kept himself contained. "I still can't figure," he said, shaking his head, "why you went to all the trouble of getting your envelope postmarked from Canada, when you'd already written your true location right there inside." His eyes went to the marshals again as he told them, "He put it right there beside the date, shouting it out clear as you please."

With a jolt worse than a blow to the head, Anthony understood the terrible mistake he'd made. He thought back to that day at Coffin's house when he wrote to his brother in Virginia. He'd gotten so deep into the habit of putting the word "Boston" beside any date he marked on paper that he didn't even realize he'd done it. He'd been hurrying to finish that letter, rushing some at the end. But how could he have made such a foolish mistake?

Marshal Butman stepped up and asked, "It's him then?"

"It's him," Master Charles said, decisive and cold as Anthony had ever heard him. Then he turned and left the room. Master William, to whom Anthony had been rented several times over the years, was likely there to support Master Charles's claims about Anthony. William Brent had not said a single word during the meeting and simply followed behind Master Charles without looking toward Anthony at all. Most of the guards left then too, their footsteps followed by sounds of the door being barred from the outside. Only Asa Butman and two others stayed behind to mind Anthony.

"Might as well get comfortable there, Burns," Marshal Butman said. "You're in for the night. Probably send you back South before the day's out tomorrow."

Anthony glanced toward the window. The iron rods showed there was no escape, and his failure and desperation settled upon him thick, a new confinement even worse than the first. The granite façade of the building surrounding him began to close in, and he suddenly felt himself struggling for air. Now that he had experienced life as a free man, commander of his own destiny, how could he ever survive in bondage again?

ANN

Boston, May 1854

The looking glass beside our armoire showed a woman not displeasing to the eye. Phebe had parted my dark hair at the center, looping it over my ears and then pinning it back. My simple dress of black silk with its white dickey was hardly the height of fashion, but it suited me. People might once have expected the wife of Wendell Phillips to adorn herself with more than a simple cameo pinned at the neck, but I'd been taught by my mother not to invest too much in possessions, whether with money or with sentiment. Plus, it was important to me to fit in with my peers at the Female Anti-Slavery Society. I was glad to be feeling well and was planning to attend the Society's meeting later that morning. We were organizing an anti-slavery fair to take place in autumn, where we hoped to raise even more than the $1,500 we'd collected at the last such fundraiser.

Wendell had left earlier for a meeting at the offices of Lloyd's newspaper, and I wondered why he hadn't yet returned to escort me as he'd offered. I found myself looking rather well that morning, my persistent aches and pains less prevalent of late, and I was anxious to brandish my improved appearance before my always dapper husband. Due to my chronic ills, Wendell was accustomed to viewing me in rumpled bedclothes and other less flattering attire, so I liked to make the most of the days when I appeared more well-assembled.

I was also on tenterhooks to inform him of the invitation I'd only just discovered in a stack of unopened mail. My brother had written, inviting us to pass the summer with his family at their residence in Milton, ten miles outside Boston. Although the country air never seemed to alleviate the many symptoms of my mysterious ailment, it was always possible that the next sojourn would be the one to make the difference.

"Ann!" The sound of my name was accompanied by the banging of our front door against the inner wall of the entryway. Oh, Wendell. As much as I loved my husband, how I detested when he bellowed for me as though we were children at play. I began making my way to the stairs, taking my time intentionally, if only to impress upon the dear man that hollering was not the most effective means of summoning me.

I was barely out the door from my bedroom before he was upstairs at the landing, his smooth face flushed and damp with perspiration.

"They've taken another fugitive!" he declared without preamble. "They've locked him up at the courthouse. Kept him there all night on the top floor before anyone even got wind of it. Leonard Grimes was made aware this morning, by one of his deacons. Grimes got word to Teddy, thank heavens."

"Arrested a fugitive?" It had been more than three years since an escaped slave had graced the inside of a Boston courthouse. "I was beginning to believe Boston had finally moved past the idea of apprehending refugees."

"I've been to the courthouse," Wendell told me as he took my hand and led me down the stairs. "They held proceedings this morning, and the arrested man was there without even a lawyer to represent him. Richard Dana had already arrived, offering to represent him, as you might expect. But when the matter was called, the captive declined representation."

Mr. Dana was well-known for appearing on behalf of refugees apprehended in Boston. In addition to Thomas Sims, the ill-fated fugitive who'd been sent back to Georgia three years prior, Dana was perhaps best known for his association with Shadrach Minkins, the runaway who'd been forcibly rescued from the courthouse some months before Sims's arrest.

"They've ruled then?" I asked, stopping on a step, afraid to hear the answer.

"No." Wendell tugged lightly at my arm, and I continued following him to the ground floor. "The fellow's name is Anthony Burns. It sounds as though he believes that fighting the charges will serve only to anger the man claiming him as property, that it will make his fate all the worse."

I stood rooted to my spot at the bottom of the stairs, dreading whatever else Wendell might reveal.

"After Mr. Dana gave up and stopped trying to convince Mr. Burns of the necessity of counsel," Wendell continued, "Teddy, heavens bless him, stood right up from the gallery and said, 'Well if no one else will represent the man, then I will!' At that, Mr. Dana seemed to get his hat on right again. He asked for a sidebar with Commissioner Loring."

"Loring again?" I interrupted, my chest tightening at the memories of how Commissioner Loring had ruled in the Sims case a few years prior. How was it that an unchanging cast of characters kept reappearing in these cases? How would we ever be able to make change if the same circumstances continued repeating themselves each time a decision was to be made?

The front door opened again and Phebe entered, along with her dear friend Emma, both of them holding baskets full of greens and fruits from the market.

"Come, girls," I called at them, "you must listen to the news. A man has been arrested as a fugitive slave."

Phebe's bright complexion paled as she set down her basket in the entry and followed me to the settee. Emma trailed behind her more tentatively. The daughter of John and Muriel Bathwaite, Emma also came from a family of committed abolitionists.

"You too, Emma," Wendell waved the slender girl toward a chair. Emma was only a month younger than Phebe, but with her petite frame and freckled nose, she looked so much younger. "Somehow," Wendell continued as we settled into our seats, "Mr. Dana convinced the commissioner to adjourn the proceedings in order to give the accused time to consider his rights and determine whether he might like to retain counsel after all."

"Why would he not want counsel?" Phebe exclaimed. "He sees himself defeated already?" she asked, striking at the heart of it.

"If they could only get the matter adjourned again tomorrow," Wendell said, as though a thought was occurring to him, "with the case postponed on a Friday, it would give us the whole of the weekend to complete a rescue from the jail."

I refrained from reminding Wendell about the iron bars that had been added to the windows during Thomas Sims's incarceration, though the words fought to slip from my tongue. Nor did I conjecture aloud about an increased presence of the guards and the difficulty of finding new ways to circumvent them. Wendell surely knew how onerous it would be for any escape plan to come to fruition.

"Perhaps you might convince the prisoner to accept Mr. Dana's services during that time," Emma suggested. "If nothing else."

"You must inform the others," I instructed Wendell. "Get a petition underway for the use of Faneuil Hall. The greater the number of outraged souls, the more chance there will be for success."

"Yes, yes, we must." Wendell seemed energized anew at

my words. He stood and regarded me then. "Birdie," he said, using my pet name, "you're looking well today. Your legs?"

"Yes," I nodded, perhaps overly pleased with myself. "I haven't felt a pinch or twinge since I awoke, not anywhere."

A strange look flashed across Wendell's features then. Before I could make sense of his expression, he'd moved on, losing interest in the topic it seemed. "I'll just take some bread and cheese along; I'll likely be gone the day," Wendell muttered, almost to himself, as he moved toward the kitchen. Phebe rose and scurried after him, fussing about making a package for him.

I could hear Wendell continuing to plot his next moves. He was talking about the imperative of getting word to Thomas Wentworth Higginson, another Unitarian minister and a leading member of the Vigilance Committee. Harvard-educated, just like my Wendell, but twelve years younger, he had been a central participant in the attempted rescue of Thomas Sims. Higginson was a man drawn to action, even violence if necessary.

"Wendell," I called as I followed behind Emma to the kitchen. Phebe was just pulling a hunk of rye bread for him from the loaf tin. "Let me join you today," I said, "I'm feeling quite well and up to the task."

"Join me?" he asked as he turned away from Phebe's outstretched hand. "But I'll be running all about town."

"Yes, I understand, dear. I am able. I'll help. Perhaps we should divide tasks, and I'll mobilize the women if that's more effective. I could start with Helen up the road, or Maria Chapman. I'll just grab my shawl." I was growing excited with the many plans blooming in my mind. I would make myself useful yet.

"Ann!" Wendell declared before I even escaped the room. "Feeling fit for the first day in ages is not a missive to go suddenly gallivanting like Paul Revere. You'll surely set back whatever progress you're making."

I paused as I considered his words, recognizing that if I caused myself any significant harm, it would only distract Wendell from helping the man at the courthouse. I noticed his lip beginning to curl as he awaited my response, and I understood then that whatever his reasons, he wanted neither my company nor my assistance.

"Very well." I released a defeated breath and added, "I will do what I can from the confines of our front parlor. As usual."

Wendell approached me and put his warm hands on either side of my face, suddenly full of affection again. "You must rest," he directed as he tucked a wayward curl back into place at my ear.

It only then occurred to me that perhaps Wendell loved me best when I was weak and helpless. I hated to think it, but he was a man who took nourishment from assisting others. Fugitives, young, orphaned Phebe, women fighting for equal rights, the poor, the hungry. I never imagined his affection for me might stem from the same place. I blinked hard, rejecting the idea. Wendell could not be one of those men who only cared for people he could save. And yet, now that the seed had been planted, I couldn't help but wonder.

SEVERAL HOURS LATER, MY HUSBAND had yet to return. I found myself glancing repeatedly out the window of our front room, hoping for some glimpse that might provide news of the goings-on in Court Square. Wendell had accepted Phebe's offer to help collect signatures, as the Vigilance Committee would be required to present a petition before they were permitted to use Faneuil Hall for their meeting.

But it was now well after dark, and I'd long since finished drafting a speech for Wendell to deliver at the night's meeting. His failure to return and retrieve it left me feeling utterly expendable. We hardly publicized the fact that it was I who wrote most of the speeches he delivered. We had agreed long ago that the words I drafted for him to speak generally proved most effective in influencing his audiences. We had discovered within me a knack for crafting statements that delicately balanced the need for both outraging and inspiring listeners. Once Wendell was armed with my words in his head, he could focus his energy on summoning the speaking skills for which he'd become so well-known. I fancied that our combined talents made us the perfect match, such that our efforts could galvanize whoever listened. But as I waited for him that night and he failed to return, I fretted.

Eventually I'd worn myself out so much that I was beginning to feel poorly again, just as he had predicted. With a sense of defeat surrounding me like a shroud, I walked myself up to bed.

SOME WHILE LATER, I WAS AWOKEN by the noise of Wendell moving about. The candle on my bedside table was still burning, and I could see him removing his shoes near the door. When he turned and saw me watching, he smiled, his features as startlingly handsome as ever, even in the dim light.

"Birdie," he whispered, affection seeping into just that one word. "I'm relieved to see you resting."

"You didn't use my speech," I said as I pushed myself to sitting.

"The meeting will be tomorrow night," he said. "We secured the signatures but thought it best to allow time to spread the word. We printed the handbills and spent much of the evening distributing them. There should be enough people in attendance to fill the entire hall tomorrow. Your words will be put to use, rest assured. But tell me of your health?"

"In truth, I did begin to feel poorly before taking myself to bed, but I am improved now that you've returned."

"My love," he leaned forward and wrapped his strong arms around me.

I relaxed into his embrace, relieved that whatever strangeness I had sensed between us earlier had now dissipated. Comforted by the feel of his hand rubbing circles on my back, I rested my cheek against his shoulder and thought of the fugitive. Faneuil Hall could hold thousands of people. If we could properly organize such a large crowd, perhaps there could be hope for the man yet.

Wendell shifted then, pulling at my nightgown. He pushed it higher on my legs and leaned in to kiss my neck. His intentions were clear, but I found myself too focused on the man being held at the courthouse to enjoy his attentions.

"Wendell," I took hold of the hand that was moving up my leg. "Not tonight, not while that innocent man is imprisoned only blocks away."

Wendell sighed and pulled away from me.

"I know," he answered quietly. "As usual, you are correct. I am just so full, to the very brim, with energy that needs an outlet. But we dare not enjoy such comfort while another who is suffering requires our immediate attention. It is best if I remain pent up until my time on the stage tomorrow. It may prove to be the most important address I ever deliver."

As I realized the truth of his words, my blood began to tingle. I thought of him reciting my speech to a full hall, of him mobilizing so many people to take action that might help Anthony Burns. Perhaps my utility was not fully spent after all, not quite yet.

ANTHONY

Boston, May 1854

As Boston came awake in the sprouting hours of morning, Anthony watched from the courthouse window, where he was still locked in, way up on the top floor. The commissioner said he could take the whole of Friday to consider if he wanted a lawyer, and they'd all get back together in the courtroom come Saturday.

His eyes followed the weekday traffic below, all the men and women heading wherever a Friday generally took them. Now that he'd tasted freedom, he felt the cruelty of his fate even deeper. He was troubled thinking of Master Charles too. What kind of punishments would be meted out once they were back in Virginia?

As he worried on the thought, he noticed three men on the street below, men he recognized. It was his friend, Coffin, along with Pastor Leonard Grimes, and a white fellow who'd been in the courthouse with them the day before. They approached the door of the building, and a US marshal stepped out to meet them. Anthony knew now that the guard who was greeting them went by the name of Watson Freeman. He thought that name, "Freeman," would almost be funny in another place, since he was the one keeping Anthony from being free.

From such distance, he couldn't hear what was being said outside on those steps, but it was clear the men were arguing. The white man who'd arrived with his friends seemed to be doing all the talking, gesturing about with his fingers pointed and then even a fist nearly raised. But the marshal stood firm, his hands stuck to his hips, shaking his own head over and over again. After only a few minutes, the men left, and Anthony's spirits slumped.

The guard across the room, a portly young fellow with pink cheeks and light hair curling at the collar, looked over at him just then, as if Anthony had spoken his disappointment aloud.

"You read and write, boy?" The guard asked as he put down the small piece of wood he'd been whittling at all morning. He'd been carving the thing to resemble a groundhog. Watching him with it made Anthony think of the wooden hawk, the one his father had carved, that was now left behind in his room back at Coffin's house.

"Yes, sir, I do," Anthony answered. As he watched, the guard pulled a fresh sheet of paper from the desk.

"I've been thinking about how you could help yourself out a bit," the guard said as he rose from his chair. "Why don't you have a seat here and write a letter of apology to your master?"

"Apology, sir?" Anthony asked, not sure he saw fit to apologize for seeking the very same rights that Master Charles enjoyed for himself. There wasn't justification needed for a person wanting to be in charge of his own self.

"Well, look here," the guard said, crossing the room and leaning to gaze out the window alongside Anthony. "I get why you done what you did, why you'd rather be living free up North. But now's you're going back to slavery, wouldn't it be clever to let on like you feel some shame? Maybe you take less on the chin if you say you got too big for your britches, say you won't try anything sneaky again. Tell your master he treated you good, things like that."

The only shame Anthony felt was for getting himself caught. He opened his mouth to say as much, but the guard interrupted him.

"I'm just saying it might help with how he treats you once you're stuck with him again is all." He placed the paper and a pencil down on the mattress behind Anthony before walking back to his chair in the corner.

Anthony turned and regarded that blank page. It was true that Master Charles was upset with Anthony for rejecting his small kindnesses. Anthony would surely be kept on much closer watch once they got back to Virginia; no more hiring out his time, for sure. And that would likely be true no matter how sorry he said he was. But maybe he could say some words sufficient to move Master Charles, add some scripture maybe, so Anthony wouldn't get sent straight to the whipping post on their return. He looked back once more at the scene outside the window, all the people below being free as anything, coming and going, carrying packages, traveling to jobs for pay. That life was being taken from him. If not for those iron bars, he might have thrown himself straight from the window rather than return to what he'd escaped.

With a loud sigh, he sat himself down on the mattress and rested the paper against his leg.

Dear Master Charles, he wrote. The words were wobbly with only his leg to rest against, but he kept on. *I'm sorry I ran from you when you were a better master than many.* But then he struggled with what to say next, how to explain the desperation, the fierce need to live free that drove him to take the actions he chose. He thought to describe the feelings he had that very first time he held wages in his hand that were his to keep with no one waiting for any accounting. The guard must have known from the way Anthony was staring at nothing that he was trying to find his thoughts.

"Here," the guard said, standing again, "Start with this, 'Master, forgive me for my grave mistake. You were the best master a man could ask for.'"

As Anthony put pencil to the paper and began copying down the dictation, the door to the jury room opened, and in walked Coffin and Leonard Grimes.

"Guard!" Leonard scolded, grabbing the paper from Anthony's hand. "You know better than that." Leonard shook his head, looking disappointed in the man as Coffin came up beside Leonard to read the beginnings of the letter.

"What is it?" Anthony asked them.

"It's a trick," Leonard said, as he tore the paper in two and then tore the pieces to half again and again. "He's looking for you to say that the claimant was a good master to you as a way of making you admit on paper that he was indeed your master and that you were indeed a slave. He's trying to win the case for the kidnappers." Leonard looked harshly one more time at the guard, who didn't argue. Then Leonard walked to the window, where he sent out the small shards of paper like flakes of snow to fall to the cobblestones below.

"We'd have come earlier," Coffin said, "but they blocked you from any visitors. Had to send a representative from the Vigilance Committee to get a special order from the commissioner allowing us in."

Anthony wasn't sure what to say then since it was strange talking to his friends with the guard standing right there, hearing their every word.

There was a knock at the door then and another man entered. It was the white fellow who'd been on the steps outside earlier.

"Mr. Burns," he said as he entered the room with a force, "I hope you'll forgive the delay. We've spent the morning hurdling obstacles in order to gain entrance to your chambers. Now that the cavalry has begun to arrive, I do hope you'll allow us to protect you and your freedom." He thrust out his hand to shake. "Wendell Phillips," he said, introducing himself. "I'm a member of the Boston Vigilance Committee and an admirer of your friends here." He motioned to Coffin and Leonard beside him.

Anthony considered the broad-shouldered white fellow—a tall, well-groomed man with a deep, warm voice. From his time working in Coffin's store, Anthony could tell that the man's clothes were well made and of fine cloth. If a fellow like this was intent on helping him, maybe it meant his case was not as lost as he'd thought.

"We will not let these kidnappers send you back to slavery," the man said.

The guard perked up then. "*Back* to slavery?" he asked. "I'm thinking that there proves a point, don't it?"

"The only question at issue is whether Anthony was ever owned by that man from Virginia," Leonard answered pointedly. "And he was not. It's mistaken identity or a blatant attempt at kidnapping."

"Come," Mr. Phillips said then, shushing Leonard, "There's no need to argue his case to the guards. As it happens, gentlemen, Lewis Hayden sent lawmen over to the Revere House hotel this morning to arrest the visitors from Virginia on charges of conspiring to kidnap."

"The owner and his agent?" the guard asked then, unable to hold back.

"Indeed." Mr. Phillips smiled. "I'm told that both Charles Suttle and William Brent were promptly bailed out, but at a price of more than $1,000. Small victories," he said, looking from Coffin and Leonard to Anthony. "Correct, my friends?"

Then Mr. Phillips got to business, telling Anthony that he needed to make a decision about whether he would accept representation from the lawyer, Richard Henry Dana. Anthony worried still that fighting the charges would only make his circumstances worse once he was returned to Master Charles. But listening to Mr. Phillips talk all about his rights to liberty and self-determination, Anthony found he was not yet ready to surrender to the worst.

He signed his name to a paper Mr. Phillips called a power of attorney, which would authorize Mr. Dana to be his lawyer and to work on his behalf. As Anthony handed back the pen, he saw Coffin and Leonard exchange pleased glances, marking that they were satisfied with his decision. He felt a flicker of hope then that they might yet find a way for him to continue living as the free man he was meant to be.

ANN

Boston, May 1854

There must have been close to five thousand bodies crowding Faneuil Hall as I snuck myself into the back of the room. I had been feeling well for the entire day, but I knew Wendell would protest if I told him I planned to accompany him to a Vigilance Committee event as potentially tumultuous as this one.

I was still perseverating on the thought that what drew Wendell to me might be my physical weakness, my need for his continuous support. All those years wondering what a man like him was doing with me, an invalid for a wife, seemed suddenly explained. After all, it was only when my family was sure I was going to succumb to my illness, when I lay abed waiting to die nearly two decades earlier, that Wendell had proposed. But this was not the time to focus on such memories.

Instead, I pulled my bonnet in closer around my face and pushed into the crowded space. I could see George Russell up front, already speaking to the crowd. The man was a wealthy merchant and the former mayor of West Roxbury. He seemed to be doing just what the Vigilance Committee would have intended by his presence, riling up the audience, inflaming their emotions. His words rang throughout the hall as he described the arrest of Anthony Burns as an act of Southern aggression against all Northerners and declared that slave hunters were polluting Northern land.

I scurried into a corner near the wall, where I was almost completely concealed behind the shoulders of two tall men. The crowd was thick enough that those men would not think it odd the way I settled in behind them. I could stand and listen to the speeches while availing myself of the small openings between the bodies beyond me to catch glimpses of the speakers at the podium.

After Mr. Russell finished his address, we listened to remarks from the lawyer Samuel Sewall and a physician named Dr. Samuel Gridley Howe. Next came the Freesoil leader Francis Bird. As was his way, Bird attempted to appeal to the baser nature of the crowd, advocating for physical counteraction to the travesty of Burns's capture. Then young attorney John Swift spoke, focusing on religion and calling the potential release of Burns a "resurrection." He decried the Kansas-Nebraska Bill, which allowed settlers in new states to determine for themselves whether slavery would be permitted in their borders. There could be no such compromise, he shouted to the audience, when liberty was at stake. After Swift, Dr. Henry Bowditch, another physician, made similarly rousing remarks.

The stage thus set, finally, Wendell strode to the dais. Here he was in his element. His ability to impassion an audience would have been evident if he were to deliver a speech on something as mundane as polishing shoes. Speaking to this crowd, where so many were already vibrating with anger over the idea of Boston citizens surrendering to a Southerner's bidding, he was poised like a lit match, ready to set fire to acres of wheat chaff before him.

I held my breath as he straightened his shoulders and surveyed the crowd. He nodded once, as if to himself, and then began to speak.

"The city government is on our side." His rich, robust voice rang out. "There is now no law in Massachusetts. When law ceases, the people may act in their own sovereignty. I am against squatter sovereignty in Nebraska, and against kidnappers' sovereignty in Boston."

The intention of those words was to alert the audience that if they acted out against the federal marshals, local police might not stand in their way. If civilians knew the police were unlikely to arrest them, many here would certainly be more apt to help.

"If Boston's streets are to be so often desecrated by the sight of fugitives being captured and returned," he declared as he stepped out from behind the lectern and moved closer to the audience, "let us be there, that we may tell our children we saw it done. Faneuil Hall is but an extension of the courthouse, where tomorrow morning, we, the children of Adams and Hancock, must prove that we are not bastards. Let us prove that we are worthy of liberty."

I watched him pause and look from listener to listener, meeting the eyes of many and making sure he had their attention. When he recited his next words, my lips moved silently along with his. "See to it," he told them, "that tomorrow, in the streets of Boston, you ratify the verdict of Faneuil Hall: that Anthony Burns has no master but his God."

Cheers erupted throughout the room, as those on the floor chanted Wendell's words, "No master but his God!" Wendell then put forth a directive, that all members of the audience should assemble in the morning at Court Square to stand between Anthony Burns and any decision to return him to slavery. Vibrations thrummed through the crowd, the calls of "Save Anthony Burns!" revealing the people's agreement.

Wendell stepped away from the podium then, making room for Teddy Parker to finish out the meticulously choreographed program of the eve. Where Wendell was a handsome and educated gentleman with a propensity toward dialogue, Teddy was, well, different. He was a clergyman, but one of ever-shifting religious assertions and congregants. Despite his small physical stature, he gave off the air of ruffian through his belligerent gait and shrewd dark eyes. Fierce, determined, and direct, he was the perfect contrast to Wendell's more refined demeanor, and the ideal clincher to win this moment.

"Fellow subjects of Virginia," he began, and boos erupted at his inflammatory statement. But I agreed with his point. Weren't we, up here in Boston, simply subjects of the slave states, if we were forced to do their bidding?

"Gentlemen, there is no Boston today. There was a Boston once. Now, there is a north suburb to the cities of Alexandria and Richmond. And you and I, fellow subjects of the State of Virginia."

The audience cried out in response, "No!" and "Take it back!"

"I will take it back," Teddy countered, "when you show me the fact is not so. Men and brothers, I am an old man; I have heard hurrahs and cheers for liberty many times; I have not seen a great many deeds done for liberty. I ask you, are we to have deeds as well as words?"

Men, and even some of the women, hollered back at him, "Yes! Yes!" and there were cries of, "To the courthouse!"

But Teddy was not finished.

"Gentlemen, I am a clergyman and a man of peace. I love peace. But there is a means, and there is an end; liberty is the end, and sometimes peace is not the means towards it. Now I want to ask you what you are going to do. There are ways of managing this matter, without shooting anybody. Be sure that these men who have kidnapped a man in Boston are cowards, every mother's son of them; and, if we stand up there resolutely and declare that this man shall not go out of the city of Boston, without shooting a gun, then he won't go back. We must gather at the courthouse in the morning!"

"Now! Now!" listeners called. The chanting from the crowd was growing ever louder.

As I noted the flushed faces and bright eyes of the people surrounding me, many seemed too worked up to wait until morning. Now was the time for me to leave, before the trouble brewing escalated to actual violence, and certainly before Wendell discovered that I had been skulking in the back of the hall rather than waiting for him at home. I pulled my bonnet tight again and bent low before pushing myself through the crowd, back to the exit.

I hurried through the warm streets, relieved when I finally reached the door of our Essex Street home. I made my way quickly to my bedroom and began removing my street clothes, thinking frantically what I might tell Wendell upon his return. I pulled on my nightshift and hastened to settle myself under the bedsheets. As I lay my head back on the pillow, attempting to arrange myself in such a way that would suggest a long repose abed, I realized only then that even after my evening of rather extreme excitement, I was still feeling miraculously comfortable within my body. It was just as Wendell and I had prayed together for so many years. How odd that when I was finally beginning to see improvement, I was too much a coward to share the news with my husband.

As I settled in, my gaze strayed toward the window and the dark night beyond. There had been a solar eclipse earlier that day. Phebe had been reminding me the whole morning long that I must watch from the window at the appointed hour. But indeed, as we shielded our eyes to watch the moon pass over the sun, the final effect had been rather disappointing. I worried then with a jolt that the meeting at Faneuil Hall would be like the eclipse—much fuss, but to little effect.

Less than an hour later, I heard Wendell and Phebe. Wendell moved swiftly up the stairs, climbing two risers at a time, as he was wont to do, as though his long legs left him no other choice.

"I'm awake," I called out.

His form filled the entryway, and he stopped to take my measure.

"Well?" I asked, feigning suspense. "Will you not fill me in at once?"

"You're pale," he answered, moving toward the bed and placing the back of his palm against my forehead. "And a bit warm, I think. Let me get you a cool cloth."

I was quiet a moment, as if to accept his ministrations, but then I thought the better of it. I was generally resistant to his caretaking until he persuaded me to allow it. Should I suddenly become docile, it would only arouse suspicion.

"Darling, please," I protested. "Won't you tell me of the meeting?"

"I fear there may be an attack on the courthouse as we speak."

"No!" I sat up in spite of myself.

"I thought we had quashed the violent intent after Teddy finished speaking, but just as the audience was readying to disperse, men ran in and shouted that a mob had already descended on Court Square."

"But I thought everyone was at the hall?"

"Apparently a group of Negroes assembled earlier at Tremont Temple. They began it, and then so many of the crowd from Faneuil Hall rushed to join. I fear they will ruin everything. The unplanned attack will only make it more difficult to extract Mr. Burns. They are not organized, nor have they any cogent strategy beyond force. They will seal his fate."

"No," I began to argue, "perhaps it will do the opposite! If the number of protestors is sufficient, they might breach the courthouse door, overtake the guards. They may save him!"

Wendell only shook his head in response, as though my optimistic suggestions were utterly infeasible. Still, as I thought of that fugitive locked in the jury room, I prayed with all my might that the mob would surpass my husband's expectations.

ANTHONY

May 1854

Anthony stayed in the jury room all the rest of that Friday, watching the same guard whittle away at another stalk of lumber, turning the wood this time into the shape of a weasel. The man glanced over toward Anthony from time to time in the quiet, but nothing more. Anthony wondered if the guard even felt any shame at all about trying to trick him earlier.

Eventually, another guard came, stepping into the jury room to put a dish down beside Anthony and then leaving again. Potatoes and boiled oats.

As the loamy scent of warm potatoes filled his nose, Anthony could hardly eat—thinking of Master Charles over there at his fine hotel, surely feeling so cross. Since the time Anthony arrived in Boston, he'd come across plenty of other refugees, and he'd heard about masters meaner than his own. Maybe he should have taken comfort in the knowledge that Master Charles wasn't the worst out there. But even when there's worse horrors to endure, misery is misery just the same. And being captive for all time was the worst misery of all. He didn't expect that Coffin Pitts, Leonard Grimes, or any of their white friends would manage to save him from the yoke of slavery coming back round his neck.

He forced down a few spoonsful of the watery oats. The paste slid down his throat like the despair creeping into his whole being, and he left most of the food untouched. Instead, he just laid down on the pallet, his eyes turned toward the windows. He tried to keep his thoughts from running wild as he watched the sky outside turn to dark.

That was how they stayed then for some time, the guard and Anthony, the quiet and the sorrow. Anthony was just starting to doze when there was a rumbling from somewhere down below them. It seemed he felt it first more than he heard it.

The guard jumped from his chair to peer out the window. He uttered an expletive and then ran to the door, turning back and pointing an accusing finger at Anthony.

"You!" he nearly spat. "Don't you try anything." He fiddled with his keys until he got the door to open, and then he raced from the room. As the lock clicked back into place, Anthony rose and hurried to the windows to see for himself what was causing the disturbance.

He heard the shouts clearer before he saw the many bodies moving toward the courthouse. People were chanting "Liberty!" and "Release him!" It was then he realized there was a mob outside, and it seemed they were coming for *him*—he might yet be saved!

Pushing his face against the iron bars of the window, he stared out at the picture below. The lanterns in Court Square were still burning, and he could make out a crowd of men in the glow, coming up State Street and charging toward the west side of the Court House. It looked to be mostly Negroes in the crowd, but then he saw white men coming up behind them too.

He wrapped his hands around the bars, his body shaking with a wakened energy. His eyes maybe deceived him, but it seemed the crowd continued to grow. They looked to be as many as five hundred strong. So many men shouting and disrupting the quiet of the night.

And ho! Then came some men holding a long beam of wood level across their arms. As he stretched his own mind to wonder at their intent, they attacked the door on the south end of the building, using the wood as a battering ram. The thump and clang came loud and strong, such that he could hear it clear all the way at his perch. And then a shout went up among the crowd, and he hoped that meant they'd broken through the entry. He swung his eyes back toward the door of the jury room, wondering if the bandits might come bursting through any moment. If the mob could beat down one barrier, why not the next?

He stood waiting at the ready so he could run with his rescuers as soon as they got the door opened. His mind started racing about where he would go once they freed him. Would he hide back at Coffin's? No, that was the first place they'd look. It'd be better if he found a way to carry himself to Canada, like so many others had done.

He looked back out the window, but he could no longer make out what was happening below, only that bodies were swarming against bodies. But then shots rang out. And suddenly, men were pouring out of the courthouse instead of coming in. He thought it must be Marshal Freeman and his guards fighting back the attack. As the shouts began to build again, police seemed to be arriving from every corner of the common.

He watched them begin weaving their way through the mob. He couldn't make out the words being hollered in the chaos, but he was certain enough that people were being threatened with arrest. Some officers had clubs raised high in the air, and several rioters shrank from their presence.

In only a matter of minutes, the square began to empty and the noise outside got quieter and quieter. Before long, just a small group of men remained, lingering outside in the clear night, relaxed postures suggesting they were there for the spectacle more than anything else. Anthony felt stunned, unable to pull his fingers off those iron bars holding him in. Watching the mob dissolve, he felt the weight of defeat all over again. His hopes had risen too high and feeling them crushed again stung him fierce.

AFTER A SHORT WHILE, ANOTHER GROUP came out from the building, four of them carrying a man on a stretcher to a waiting cart. Anthony wondered who that man had been defending, the rescuers or Master Charles, and he didn't know how sorry he should feel.

It wasn't too much longer, probably near midnight, when Anthony heard a key in the door outside the jury room. When the door opened, he saw his keeper had returned. Behind the guard followed that scoundrel Marshal Freeman, who sauntered in with his hand on the pistol at his waist. He was a tall man with a dark beard and eyes the color of a robin's egg. The way his lips turned down at the corner had his face looking haggard and mean.

"You must be thinking you're something damn special," he said as he let his eyes roam over Anthony. "They weren't very effective, those agitators." The marshal pointed with his chin toward the window. "Guess they didn't care as much as they thought, scurrying off like the rats they are." He pulled his coat in on himself then, like he was readying for business. "One of my guards was shot though, and somebody's going to have to pay for that."

Anthony kept quiet, knowing whatever he could say in response would be wrong to the marshal.

"No matter," the marshal continued as he glanced over at the young guard beside him, as if to include him in the conversation, like they were all three having a chat together. "I sent word on over to my men in East Boston, chartered a vessel to fetch a company of marines over from Fort Independence. They'll be here by sunrise, latest. And a group of marines is coming from the Charlestown Navy Yard. I've got it on good authority that President Pierce will approve any expenses to protect his laws." He shifted his gaze to stare solely at Anthony, hatred taking over his face. "And those laws *will* prevail."

WHEN THEY FETCHED ANTHONY THE following morning, they affixed irons to his wrists and then pushed him into the hallway, where several armed guards moved into a formation to encircle him. As they made their way toward the stairwell, Anthony saw that a swarm of militiamen lined the steps, awaiting them. He swallowed hard before stepping closer, not liking to move so near to all those weapons. But a guard shoved him to get going, so down they went. When they reached the ground floor, Anthony saw it was only worse. Marines with shining bayonets filled the hallways, choking the path for anyone who might wish to pass. He had never seen so many guns all in one place. That display of weapons must have been putting everyone present real on edge.

As they stepped through the wide doors into the court-room, the man from the last court meeting, the lawyer Mr. Dana, was waiting there. He showed Anthony that his own pockets were empty of weapons and said the defense attorneys were making it a point to be unarmed.

"Attorneys?" Anthony asked, surprised he might have more than the one lawyer there to argue on his behalf.

"Yes," the man said, pointing out a light-haired fellow across the room with his back to them. "That's Charles Ellis, who will be representing you alongside me." When the man turned and Anthony saw the youth of his face, he understood that having two lawyers wasn't such a big fuss after all—not when one looked barely old enough for the whiskers on his chin.

They sat around a long time in the courtroom that morning, just waiting for things to get started. All the while, Anthony's hands were cuffed behind his back, the metal bracelet rubbing against his old wound from the sawmill. Once, he might have considered the scuffing of his wrist a reminder from the good Lord about where a man such as himself belonged. Yet now he knew better. The Lord never meant for him to live any way other than free.

He caught sight of that white fellow, Mr. Phillips, weaving through all the bodies at the back and making his way up to where they sat. He was dressed again in a tidy suit and he met Anthony's eyes with a brisk nod.

"Let's see if we can get those shackles removed," Mr. Phillips said, shaking his head at the way Anthony's arms were twisted behind his back and then looking toward Mr. Dana.

"They won't yield," Mr. Dana answered. "We must keep focus on the larger issue."

As Mr. Phillips began to argue, Mr. Dana matching each of his points, Anthony stopped hearing their words, his attention turning back to his own thoughts. The darkness in him had been growing steadily since his arrest as he imagined the rest of his life a slave. Sitting there in the courtroom, looking around at who was there, the newspaper reporters in back, the onlookers, the officers of the law, and Master Charles with his posse of lawyers across the way, the weight inside him grew only heavier.

Finally, the same white-haired man from the day before entered the room through a side door; the commissioner, they called him. Anthony didn't know how that was any different from a judge, but with the man's entrance, people started hushing themselves. Anthony looked toward Mr. Dana sitting beside him in a pressed coat of dark gray. He wanted to hear what the man might say on his behalf, but it was Mr. Ellis who rose and began to speak.

"Your Honor." He had a deep, commanding voice, with greater power than a person would expect from a fellow with his smooth cheeks and slight frame. "We request an immediate adjournment on behalf of our client, as he was able to secure our representation officially only last night. As such, we have been permitted inadequate opportunity to prepare his defense. Moreover, Your Honor," he added, as he walked out from behind the table and strode closer to the commissioner, "this overwhelming show of military force in the courtroom today is naught more than intimidation tactics directed at my client, and perhaps at counsel as well. There can be neither a fair nor productive judicial proceeding under these conditions, and we respectfully add these grounds to our request for an adjournment."

Pushing his shoulders back, like his next point might be the most important of all, Mr. Ellis added, "If the court sees fit to adjudicate a man's freedom or his sentence to perpetual enslavement, I would submit that such a determination must be made under the fairest circumstances possible, and the conditions here today, Your Honor, are not it." He held his pose in silence for a moment, as if to let his words sink in for the commissioner. The statement certainly hit its mark inside Anthony's own heart.

The lawyer for Master Charles, a man named Edward Parker, wasted no time when Mr. Ellis sat back in his seat.

"Your Honor," he declared as he burst out from his chair, "we must object to the defense's request. My clients have traveled to Boston from a great distance, and they have already been subject to delay. They are enduring great expense for their extended lodging, as well as suffering the inconvenience of hecklers, who have chased them from their first hotel to the second one where they are now staying. Moreover, they fear for their safety at the hands of those who oppose the law they seek to see enforced, and they've been forced to keep themselves armed at all times. They must be permitted to resolve this matter expeditiously so they may return to their home state and the relative safety it offers them all the sooner. There is no amount of time, Your Honor, that could produce an effective challenge to the evidence in this matter. As is clear from a simple review of the record, the documents and evidence at hand are conclusive."

Mr. Parker sat down then, but another lawyer for Master Charles stood. The fellow, who Anthony later came to learn was Seth Thomas, was the same lawyer who represented the owners of Shadrach Minkins and Thomas Sims. The lawyers on both sides of the room had done this very same fight with each other more than once before. Mr. Thomas was a small man, but he stood straight and proud with his chin poked up toward the ceiling, like he didn't want to view anyone eye to eye. He set to detailing for the commissioner the events of the previous evening, telling how the mob stormed the courthouse.

"Your Honor," he continued, looking for a moment toward the windows in the courtroom, "the unrest in our fair city is hardly a reason to delay, but is in fact, reason to expedite these proceedings and put this matter to rest. Might I remind Your Honor that last evening, a United States Marshal, James Batchelder, was mortally wounded outside the jury room where the defendant was being held. Today his wife and children are grieving the loss of their hero and provider. Let us not provide any excuse for the ruffians of this city to deprive any other Bostonians of their rights to protection and security. Let us move this case quickly to a finish and send the petitioner, Mr. Charles Suttle, back to Virginia where he may deal with his chattel as he sees fit. Opposing counsel does not even have a defense."

When Mr. Thomas finished, Anthony's other lawyer, Mr. Dana, finally arose.

"Your Honor." He buttoned his waistcoat as he walked to the room's center. "How can opposing counsel assert we lack a defense for our client when we've not even had the time ourselves to make such a determination? Furthermore, counsel's assertion that the status of Mr. Burns might be adjudicated once he returns to Virginia is patently erroneous. This is not a case for extradition in order to allow another state to make a final decision. No, this is a moment to litigate upon securing one man's right to liberty or handing him over to another man as the latter's personal property. A lawsuit over a $25 debt would last at least two weeks in this city, between the filing of papers and answers between parties. Certainly, the permanent fate of a human being is worth at least as much."

The commissioner stared back at Mr. Dana from above the circular spectacles resting on his nose, and Anthony sensed that his lawyer had done his part to convince the man.

"We will meet again Monday at 11:00 a.m.," Commissioner Loring said, as he banged a small hammer against his desk and then pushed himself up from his chair.

Anthony wanted to feel elation at this small triumph, but he reckoned his lawyers were only prolonging his fate. He looked over at Master Charles, the man's jowls sagging with frustration over the delay, and Anthony thought of all the ways his master might make him suffer in the future, all the punishment he'd endure for the bother he'd caused.

As his mind ran away with itself, thinking on whippings and floggings, he noticed Pastor Leonard Grimes making his way toward the front of the courtroom, not to him, but toward Master Charles. The pastor addressed Mr. Parker, the younger of the two attorneys, but too quietly for Anthony to make out.

Mr. Parker's response was perfectly loud and precise, and Anthony's heart jumped and stuttered at the words.

"Yes," the lawyer answered, "Mr. Suttle would be willing to sell the slave for a sum of $1,200."

Anthony glanced over at Master Charles, meeting his eyes for the first time since they walked into the courtroom. Master Charles glared back, showing Anthony just how displeased he felt, how much damage had been done to their association.

Anthony thought then that maybe he should feel the same in return, riled at Master Charles for all the man was putting *him* through. But some old part of Anthony couldn't help despairing over the master getting cross with him. Master Charles turned away then and added to what his lawyer had declared.

"So long as the funds are collected and delivered before the end of business today," he said as he removed his spectacles and folded them to put in his coat pocket.

Now Anthony knew Pastor Grimes had been raising funds for various causes, like the building of the new church, ever since he arrived in Boston years earlier. He also knew the pastor wasn't afraid to put his own safety on the line for the liberty of other Negroes. He'd learned only a few weeks earlier that Pastor Grimes was once sent to prison for working with the Underground Railroad, using a stagecoach business as a ferry for slaves on the run. Even so, collecting a whole $1,200 in only a matter of hours seemed an almighty task.

Before Anthony could hear any more spoken on the matter, the guards were there, collecting him. As he rose, he felt again the chafing of the cuffs against his wrists, and he pushed all the prayers he had toward hoping his Boston friends would be successful in liberating him.

COLETTE

Richmond, May 1854

Adelia was almost finished plaiting a slender lock of my hair. She'd already fastened most of my tresses in a full, round chignon at the base of my neck, pulling several blonde tendrils loose to soften the style and frame my face. The small braid was to be wrapped round my head like a garland. I had made plenty clear to her that I was not to be outdone by Sara Anderson nor Anna-Marie Cowardin, who would be joining us that evening.

"Up now, Mistress," Adelia directed me. It was time to fasten the final closures of my gown. I shifted my gaze away from the window and the pink leaves of the dogwood outside to push back my chair and stand.

I had chosen a powder blue taffeta costume for this occasion, cut to show off my shoulders. The bodice was trimmed with a fine white lace, and there were small rosettes decorating the flounces of the skirt. The dress was cumbersome, with wide hoops and so many layers of crinoline surrounding them, but I knew it looked well on me. It was Elton, not I, who cared so much for appearances, but whether I pleased or disappointed him would carry implications for my own fate. And so it was that Adelia and I took great care.

I was struggling still to return to my husband's good graces, and I hoped that if I pleased him that evening with our guests, he might relax the restrictions he'd placed on me these last months. If only I could conceive a child, grant him the heir that continued to elude us, perhaps my other transgressions would be forgotten.

When I arrived in the drawing room to await the arrival of our callers, Elton was already settled in a velvet wing chair, his eyes focused on the newspaper in his lap.

"They found him," Elton said, hardly sparing me a glance before his eyes returned to the document.

"Found whom, darling?" I asked, moving closer and glancing over his shoulder at the paper. The *Richmond Daily Dispatch* sat splayed across his corpulent thighs. It was no surprise that Elton would be reading that particular paper prior to the arrival of our guests, as the *Dispatch* was owned by Anna-Marie's husband, James. Elton liked to tell me that James Cowardin, who was nearly a decade my husband's junior, was singlehandedly responsible for transforming the way news was delivered to the people of Richmond. Whether that was true or not, I couldn't say, but Elton surely seemed awed by the man and his accomplishments.

My eyes landed on the article Elton was reading, and I saw it was titled, "Fugitive Slave Case in Boston."

Before I could read any further, we were disturbed by Gabriel, Elton's favorite house slave, coming to announce that our company had arrived. Elton quickly folded the four-sheet paper, resting it deliberately atop the console table just adjacent to the settee, where James Cowardin would be sure to see it. I was desperate to learn more, to determine whether Elton had been referring to Anthony and what had become of him, but my curiosity would have to wait.

As the Cowardins and Andersons entered the room, Elton transformed, his eyes flashing like firelight and his entire affect shifting instantly toward vigor and warmth. I found the sight of Anna-Marie and Sara surprisingly welcome. I had only a polite relationship with each of them, but I'd been deprived of company for so many weeks that any fresh faces were a blessing. The women wore dresses similar in style to my own, Anna-Marie in a cranberry silk and Sara in a pink organdy. They had open necklines as well, but I daresay that the effect of their décolletages was significantly less pleasing than what I myself possessed to display, on account of their more matronly figures.

Joseph Anderson was first to speak. Tall and slender with full hair and a thick mustache, he was the man at the helm of Tredegar Iron Works, the company responsible for providing iron steam engines to sawmills, gristmills, bridges, and the like throughout Virginia and beyond. As Elton had reminded me only hours earlier, Joseph was amongst the wealthiest citizens of Richmond. I suppose the same could be said of my own husband. He was, after all, the most successful tobacco manu-facturer in a city full of tobacco manufacturers. Though I was only mildly acquainted with Joseph, I couldn't help but envy Sara her attainment of a husband so much more pleasing to the eye than my own.

After shaking hands with Elton, Joseph turned to me.

"And the magnificent Colette," he said cheerfully as his eyes swept over my person. "As bewitching as always."

My eyes flashed toward Elton, but I could tell it suited him just fine to see Joseph ogling me. It was a source of pride to Elton that his own wife was invariably the most fetching woman in any room. He especially enjoyed occasions such as this, where my appearance so far eclipsed the wives of other men who were near his equal in business. I could hardly say why he felt such competitiveness, but I had come to expect it.

Of further mystery was why a man who cared so deeply about my appearance paid so little heed to his own.

James Cowardin, our other esteemed guest, was not only the owner of the *Richmond Daily Dispatch*, but had also recently served in the Virginia House of Delegates. Elton was a proponent of James's Whig philosophies, and my husband seemed set as ever on impressing the man. As I watched Elton playing up to James, it was difficult to feel anything other than revulsion. James's perfect posture and sculpted features, his neatly-trimmed dark beard, and his kind eyes only emphasized my own husband's flaws. I saw afresh the cascading layers of fat beneath Elton's small chin, the sheen of perspiration forming between the few white hairs decorating his freckled head.

We walked as a coterie to the dining room and found our seats. Elton took his usual place at the head of the table, motioning for James and Joseph to settle into the chairs at his left and right. I sat opposite my husband, with the ladies flanking me in kind. Following the detailed schedule I'd laid out, Gabriel commenced filling our thick, cut-crystal glasses with vibrant burgundy wine. Platters full of inviting cuisine were set down before us, and I allowed myself a moment to revel in the success of the tableau. Dishes continued to appear, bursting with brightly colored vegetables and glorious meats, just as I had directed. Conversation was flowing freely about all manner of trivial topics, and I was hopeful that the evening would continue unfolding with elegance. I was desperate to return myself to Elton's good graces, so fatigued was I by the punitive constraints he'd placed on me.

As we moved onto our main course of stuffed turkey served with scalloped potatoes and blanched greens, Elton saw fit to begin asseverating on his favorite topic. It was all I could do not to roll my eyes heavenward when he began ranting about "saving the South" from dependence on the North and going on about the importance of developing Southern cities.

Luckily, our guests seemed more tolerant of his pet topic than I.

"Indeed," Joseph piped in as he lifted his napkin to wipe at his moustache. "Urban slavery shows the adaptability of the system and the flexibility of the slave to develop new skills. It's hardly a meaningful invective to say that our system would be unable to survive modernization; we've already begun."

"And Richmond is a beacon to cities farther south," James added, turning his dark eyes in our direction, as if to include the ladies in the discussion. "We have become a model of the manner in which to proceed." He sipped from his wine and seemed as if he would say more, but Elton interrupted.

"You ought to send that penny paper of yours down to some of those southerly places," he told James. "Cities in Louisiana, say, or Alabama. Let them see what we're accomplishing up this way. Readership here in Richmond hovers at what, fifteen thousand? Why not let people far and wide read about our successes?"

"No need, my old-fashioned friend," James answered with a self-satisfied gleam to his eye.

Elton's face reddened, detesting as he did when others referenced his advancing age, but thankfully, he kept quiet, allowing James to continue.

"With the telegraph lines and rail systems expanding by the day, those due south of us are already hearing all about the marvelous success of Richmond. Just as we can follow the case of that fugitive up in Boston."

"Yes," Elton answered without sparing a glance my way. "I was just reading about it in your latest edition. Don't mind if I say I'm tickled they found him."

I was still hoping against hope that it was a different fugitive who had made his way all the way to a Richmond newspaper. That was when Anna-Marie turned to me and said in a mock whisper, "It's enough to spoil your appetite, ain't it? When the men talk only of news and politics?"

James and Joseph both laughed at that, as though Anna-Marie's comment had well and truly hit the mark. *Hush*, I wanted to tell her. *Let me listen.* How desperate I was for news of Anthony and his whereabouts. Ever since he'd disappeared three months earlier, I had been praying daily that he reached safety in the North. I shuddered remembering the day that the elderly pharmacist, Mr. Millspaugh, appeared at our doorstep. He had wanted to speak to Adelia, to see what she might know about where Anthony had gone. Elton was not the only one who believed that Anthony and Adelia had been courting. That ploy of ours, the subterfuge as to why Anthony was spending time in my vicinity, accounted for why that fellow William Brent had also come by the house a few days later, asking all the same questions as Mr. Millspaugh all over again. Brent had been sent on behalf of Charles Suttle, the man who claimed ownership of Anthony.

I still winced, these months later, thinking about what happened after Elton closed the door on William Brent that cool March afternoon. With a swift and sudden force, he slapped my cheek so hard that I fell to the floor. He was outraged that we were in any way connected to a slave who ran from his master. He roared that I'd brought shame upon our household, and that neither Adelia nor I was to be seen outside until the entire scandal had been forgotten. Yet now, if Anthony was appearing in the papers, it seemed our seclusion might be only beginning. Worse yet, what of Anthony? I pictured his smooth dark skin and easy smile with sharp longing. When I remembered the way he listened as I spoke, as though my words were of actual consequence, I felt a tightening in my chest. Those scarce moments were everything to me.

"Such unlikely odds, wasn't it," James continued, "that the very same Negro who y'all were familiar with would be the one making the papers right back where he left?"

The water glass in my hand began to shake, and I placed

it quickly back atop the table before anyone might notice. I couldn't bear to think what might happen to Anthony if he'd truly been found, what they would do to a man such as him, someone clever and defiant, when he returned to the South. His very existence undercut so many of the stories slaveholders liked to tell themselves about what it meant to be a Negro.

As I braced for Elton's response, he stared into his nearly empty wine glass but said nothing. James seized the opportunity to charge on with the information he possessed.

"He's causing quite a hullabaloo up in Boston, riots and such. And now eight men being held for the murder of a US marshal."

I wished James would stop talking for the safety of my own hide, and yet, I was desperate to know what-all Anthony was suffering. Perhaps as a newspaper man, it was simply James's habit to share all that he could about events and goings on, and so he kept at it.

"Most of the men being held are whites!" he said. "Those clodhoppers can't figure who's responsible, so they went and collected as many from the mob as they were able."

Joseph spoke up then, turning to his wife Sara, who was seated beside him. "Come, Sara, why not tell the ladies about your recent work with the Benevolent Society? Then y'all don't have to listen in while we discuss mobs and murder over this side."

"Bother that." Sara shooed away his idea with a flick of her hand, but still, she did just as he bid. "I have to tell them about what Archer has gotten up to in his schooling." And just like that, I became a new kind of prisoner, forced to listen to Sara talk first of her eldest son, Archer, and then each of Archer's two younger brothers and his three sisters in turn. Sara's detailed account of her children predictably inspired the same from Anna-Marie, who also saw fit to wax poetic about each of her six children with agonizing specificity. All the while, I strained to hear what the men were saying, but the volume of my female companions left no quarter for wayward sentiments from across the table. How I wanted to run back to the drawing room that very instant to grab the newspaper Elton had been reading. As Anna-Marie moved on to tales of the young Mary-Alice and her excellent singing voice, her hand suddenly flew to cover her mouth.

"Oh dear," she gasped, "how thoughtless of us, to carry on about our children so." She shared a contrite glance with Sara. I had become somewhat conflicted about my continuing childless state, as Elton was not a father I would seek to foist on any child. Recently, he was so often teetering on the edge of violence or shoving his mysterious tablets into his mouth. He'd also tasked Adelia with so many duties in the property's outbuilding. I was certain he was simply being vindictive, aiming to limit my time enjoying her company. There was no valid reason to send a lady's maid to do work in the kitchen.

When finally the evening concluded and we closed the front door behind our guests, I thought to retire to my chambers and then sneak back to the drawing room to fetch the *Dispatch*.

"Colette." Elton stopped me while we were still in the foyer, wrapping his wide hand around my wrist.

I glanced longingly up the curved staircase and braced for whatever might follow.

"You did well tonight," he said, surprising me. "Even with all that chatter about the runaway, you kept your place." His gaze slid down to my bodice and across my hips before coming back to my face. "So much younger and fresher than the others," he said, as his eyes grew hungry. "It's almost enough for me to keep you without child simply to preserve your superior figure. Almost, but not quite," he concluded, as he reached out and took my arm, indicating I should follow him to his chambers.

ANTHONY

Boston, May 1854

Not long after the sun rose that Monday morning, Anthony heard commotion coming from outside in the square. He'd been awake already, lying on the pallet and staring up at the room's painted ceiling, just trying to keep his mind from running wild. He rose at the noise and looked out through the thick bars on the closest window. Groups of people had gathered below, and they appeared to be organizing themselves in protest. Some folks were heckling the guards around the courthouse steps while others were holding up signs demanding Anthony's release. They had begun chanting, though the only word he could make out from up inside was "liberty."

As he watched, more people arrived, filling the square until it became like a sea of bodies. He stared down at one particular sign someone held, a painted cloth bearing the words "Worcester Freedom Club," and he thought how nice it must be to participate in such a thing, a freedom club.

But as the crowd grew, it seemed the number of officers continued to grow along with it. Anthony couldn't say whether the uniformed men were federal marshals, militiamen, or Boston's own enforcers, but what he could see for sure was the shine of their weapons glinting in the sunlight. Then he noticed the others, the people shouting back at the protestors, and he knew those were folks who wanted to see him condemned. Shifting his gaze away from that group and their nasty placards, he let his eyes roam over the other men and women who were still piling into the square. While some folks hooted and hollered, others simply stood about, watching the ruckus unfold, as if they'd come for entertainment and that was all.

He watched and he waited for some time, thinking he'd soon be carried by the guards back to the courtroom. The morning grew brighter, but still no one showed up to fetch him. The crowd outside didn't like the waiting either, and as the minutes turned into hours, they became progressively rowdier.

It must have been close to ten o'clock before anyone finally saw fit to collect him. Two guards burst into the jury room, all in a hurry now, and wrapped shackles back onto his wrists. Then they pushed him out to the hallway toward the stairwell. As they descended the stairs, Anthony was surprised to find even more soldiers inside the building, waiting there on the ground floor. The uniformed men were armed with bayonets, lining the path through the hallway as though they were guarding a very threatening man. With his hands locked together in those irons, there was hardly a chance he could hurt anyone, even if he'd thought to try it.

When the guards lifted their weapons and opened the doors to the tribunal, Anthony saw a room so tightly packed, it seemed they might scarcely have space for him to join. Even so, he was pushed inside, where the mass of bodies began to part for their passage. Anthony expected they'd lead him to the same table where he'd sat on Friday and Saturday, up there across from the commissioner. But instead, they brought him to a different seat, farther back in the crowd. Once he sat down, the guards put manacles on his ankles, too. Then those guards sat themselves so close around him, encasing his every side, it was a wonder he could see beyond them to make out what was happening up front.

He leaned to the side so he could glance round the room. As his eyes traveled over the others in attendance, he found one man after another holding some sort of weapon. Pistols and cutlasses seemed near as plentiful as the number of people present.

Then he spotted Mr. Phillips, attired again in a trim dark suit and making his way toward them. Reaching the circle of men surrounding Anthony, Mr. Phillips addressed the guards as a group.

"Gentlemen," he said, his tone stern as he looked from one to another of them, "If you would be so kind, I'd like to sit beside my friend."

The marshal closest by stammered a moment, and Anthony thought that Mr. Phillips was the kind of person who somehow made others want to grant his requests, maybe by the way he spoke with his shoulders so straight and his head held high.

Then from the other side of their circle, another guard answered. "Can't allow it. Marsh's orders."

Mr. Phillips twisted his lips and went quiet a moment, maybe waiting for a different answer, one that he liked better. When none came, he looked round the room a moment and then nodded slowly.

"Well then, Anthony," he said, "I'll be just there then." He pointed with his chin toward a spot right behind the tight cluster of guards. "And I shall stay close at hand until we have seen this through."

Finally, when the bailiff called everyone to order, the young lawyer who was helping Mr. Dana with the defense shot out from his seat to address the commissioner.

"Before we can proceed, Your Honor," Mr. Ellis's voice rang out strong into the quieting room, "I must object to this extreme and offensive show of force by the government in the courtroom—a display even more egregious than at our last meeting. We cannot conduct a fair and impartial proceeding while the walls of this room are lined with armed men and the military stands guard at every entrance. These blatant intimidation tactics will cow neither me nor my co-counsel, but the disadvantage to my client, whose testimony cannot help but be influenced by this extreme demonstration, is patently unfair. As such, I believe it is also incumbent upon this court to remove the shackles from my client unless and until such time that this case is decided against him."

When Mr. Ellis ceased speaking, the commissioner sat silent for a moment, and the shouts of the protestors outside grew all the louder in the quiet of the courtroom. As if his wrists knew they were the subject of current discussion, the skin around Anthony's old injury began to smart, and he hoped the commissioner might agree with Mr. Ellis.

"I have noted your objection, Counselor," the commissioner said as he looked down over his spectacles at Mr. Ellis, "and should removal of the manacles become necessary during the accused's examination, I will consider it then."

Words erupted from the other side of the courtroom, near Master Charles.

"Shame, shame!" called a man sitting near Master Charles's attorneys. "How dare the fugitive's counsel question the necessity of securing the courtroom with force. Has he not himself seen the violence that these abolitionists engender? Might I remind everyone that only yesterday, there was a funeral for a federal marshal held in Charlestown?"

The commissioner seemed to find the little man an annoyance, waving a hand and answering, "Yes, yes, Mr. Hallett, but these points have already been decided. There is no need to persist."

"Indeed!" the man called Hallett retorted. "Marshal Freeman wired the White House, and President Pierce himself responded to endorse our approach. I can produce the telegram."

"No need, Mr. Hallett," the Commissioner answered in a tired voice before looking back toward Anthony's lawyers. "Mr. Dana, are you ready to present the case for the defense?"

Mr. Dana asked Master William Brent to take the stand.

Master William, who had rented Anthony for two years during his boyhood, seemed like he felt real important as he took his time making his way to the front of the room near the commissioner. He was wearing a fine wool coat Anthony had never seen before. Mr. Dana asked Master William lots of simple questions at first, like what was his name and how was it that he came to know Colonel Charles Suttle and Anthony.

"And tell me, Mr. Brent," Mr. Dana said as he walked back and forth, "when was the last time you saw the man you call Anthony Burns?"

Anthony knew that Master William Brent had a long business relationship with Master Charles. Sometime after Anthony finished his time working for the Brent family, Master William had begun working as agent for Master Charles, handling the hiring out of the Suttle slaves each winter. It was Master William who'd arranged for Anthony to go to work for the apothecary, Millspaugh, so maybe that made it Master William's fault too that he'd run.

"Well," said Master William, as he rubbed his hand against the whiskers of his chin and looked over at the commissioner. "I reckon that had to be on a Monday; it was 20 March."

Anthony almost jumped out of his seat at that. He knew for certain that he'd climbed aboard that vessel in Richmond when it was still the month of February. By the twentieth of March, he'd long been well and truly gone. Maybe Mr. Millspaugh hadn't wanted to confess that he'd up and lost the slave he rented from Mr. Brent, and so he'd delayed in announcing Anthony missing, but no matter. With that testimony, Anthony's case should be saved. By the twentieth of March, he was already settled in up North, washing windows over at the iron works.

As Mr. Dana finished with the questions, Anthony was bursting to tell him of the big mistake that Master William had made. But Mr. Dana sat back at the table up front, too far for Anthony to communicate with him at all. Then one of the lawyers for Master Charles, Mr. Thomas, stood to begin asking more questions of Master William.

"Your Honor," the other lawyer said shortly after he began, "I'd like to submit now the admissions of the accused himself at the time of his arrest, where he explained to Mr. Suttle why he ran away, effectively confirming his identity as claimant's property."

"Your Honor!" Mr. Ellis shot out again from his seat. "I object to the use of these statements, as they were made by my client either while he was under duress or in a situation that he was unable to understand. I thought we already concluded these statements constituted hearsay. The witness cannot testify on my client's behalf."

The commissioner looked unsure for a moment but then shook his head at Mr. Ellis. "We can revisit this at a later time, if need be, but for now, I will allow Mr. Thomas to proceed with this line of questioning."

Mr. Thomas proceeded to ask Master William all manner of questions about what Anthony said to Master Charles on the night he was arrested, like when they spoke about how much money Master Charles gave to him each Christmas Day.

"And did the fugitive say—"

"Objection, Your Honor!" shouted Mr. Dana. "Counsel may not refer to my client as 'the fugitive.' It is prejudicial as the matter has not yet been decided."

Mr. Thomas's face turned red as he looked to the commissioner. "How then shall I refer to the Negro in the courtroom?"

The commissioner looked back and forth between the two of them and finally said, "Counselors, approach the bench."

Anthony couldn't hear even small scraps of what was being said after that. They were arguing in hushed tones, and all the while, there was still a commotion coming from the mob outside, a ruckus that made it hard to even hear his own thoughts.

While he watched the men up front continue to bicker, he started wondering again if he might be able to find a way to die. As different ideas flitted through his mind, he wasn't sure he could call up the bravery he'd need, but he knew also that he could not go back to the life he'd left behind. When the men finally stopped their squabbling, Anthony still hadn't settled on any sort of plan.

Mr. Thomas set back to asking Master William more questions. He wanted to know about Anthony's mother down there in Stafford, his sister the nursemaid, and even his brothers still in Richmond. He asked about times Master William had seen Anthony at Master Charles's home, about the hiring out, and in particular, the years that Anthony was hired out to Master William himself. On and on went the questions, all the while, the soldiers with their weapons, and Anthony with his shackles, just listening in.

Finally, the lawyer finished, and Mr. Ellis stood. After he got Master William to say he was thirty-five years of age and that he did business as a grocer in Richmond, he set to asking him about Anthony and the arrangement with Mr. Millspaugh. Anthony learned that Mr. Millspaugh had visited Master William sometime after the escape to report Anthony missing. Master William then sent a letter to Master Charles to let him know the news.

Next, Mr. Ellis wanted to talk about how Master Charles had taken a mortgage on Anthony and certain of his other slaves.

"Yes, yes," Master William answered, while Anthony wondered at the white men and why Master Charles's finances might have anything to do with whether Anthony had the same right to liberty as all the other people living free in Boston. "The assignee was John Tolson of Stafford County, though I couldn't say the amount mortgaged."

"So then if anyone were to have a claim on this man," Mr. Ellis said, "wouldn't it be Mr. Tolson, who is technically the owner of any property mortgaged, is he not?"

Anthony could see Master William didn't know how to answer that. He eyes shot to Master Charles sitting at the table across from the stand, and then he looked over at the commissioner.

Mr. Ellis spoke up again. "Your Honor, I have no further questions for this witness, but I would like to call to the stand a Mr. William Jones."

Anthony's heart soared at that. His old friend Billy Jones would swear to the dates Anthony started his employment in Boston. He would surely tell the lawyer that Anthony was over there at Mattapan Iron Works washing the windows well before Master Brent claimed to have seen him last.

"Counsel," the commissioner said, "it's late." Anthony almost sprang from his seat. This was the witness who could save him. Billy Jones must be heard! "We will reconvene in the morning," the commissioner said. It took a moment for the words to settle on Anthony, but as he realized the trial was only on break until the next day, the air began to come back to his lungs. All was not lost. Not yet.

THE NEXT DAY STARTED MUCH THE SAME as the one before, with the same large crowd outside, the same guards standing sentry everywhere a person might turn to gaze, and that same white-haired commissioner up on his seat, waiting to decide what would become of Anthony.

When Mr. Dana called Billy Jones to the stand, Anthony's body prickled with excitement. Even though Billy was a man of a certain foolishness, the facts the lawyers needed from him would be easy enough for anyone to grasp. As Billy walked to the stand, that familiar lilt to his steps, almost like he was fixing to fall over with each stride, it made Anthony long for those days back in March, when he was newly arrived and had only the brightest thoughts of his future before him.

He was disturbed from his remembering when that irksome Mr. Hallett called out from across the way.

"Let's get set to watch a fellow perjure himself," he said to the room at large. "No doubt this man was commandeered by Theodore Parker or some other friend of the darkies."

"Mr. US Attorney," the commissioner looked down at Mr. Hallett, "decorum."

Mr. Hallett's lips twisted at that, like the commissioner was being too fussy. But still, he piped down.

And then Mr. Dana set to asking Billy all about how he came to know Anthony.

"Well, the first time I saw him, he was sick with the cold, but looking for work," Billy said nice and loud. "I had myself a job washing windows for Mattapan, and I brought Mr. Burns right along with me from that very day, I did."

"And what was that date, if you recall, Mr. Jones?" Mr. Dana said.

"Well, sure I recall," Billy said. "I have a book I always carry with me, where I like to keep track of certain things. And there's a mark right in my book saying that it was on March 1, 1854, that I met a kindly fellow named Anthony, and I got him set up along the job with me. And then we started window washing together on the date of March the 4th. Me and my new friend."

When the other lawyer, Mr. Thomas, started asking Billy questions, trying to get him to say he was mistaken or that a white man was paying him to lie, Billy couldn't be shaken. Anthony started to feel a little hopeful for himself. That hope grew even bigger when he saw that the next witness to come up would be Mr. George Drew, the bookkeeper over at Mattapan. And he was a white man! He said that yes, Billy was most certainly correct about it being March 4 when Anthony started the job at Mattapan, and the man even had an account book showing that he paid $1.50 for Anthony's work on that very day.

From there, it seemed things only got better. Mr. James Whittemore, another white man who was part in charge over at Mattapan got on that stand and told the room that he remembered seeing Anthony on March 8 or 9 at the iron works, which was the day that he first got back from some traveling. They just kept bringing up man after man, such as Mr. Pitts who first saw Anthony outside the clothing store on March 1, a blacksmith who'd seen him at the iron works, a carpenter, a machinist, even a policeman who used to work at the iron works and had seen Anthony there well before the twentieth of March.

After all the witnesses finished telling their stories, Mr. Dana got up and began his final argument. He started out by praising all sorts of people. He congratulated the commissioner on being almost finished with the business of having to listen to all the evidence in the trial. He congratulated the government and that nasty Mr. Hallett on being set almost to return to their usual enterprises. He congratulated those in attendance in the courtroom and even the city of Boston itself on being near rid of all the federal men in arms who had appeared since the time of Anthony's arrest.

Then he began to focus on the issue of mistaken identity.

"It is incumbent on the claimant," he announced to the room, "to prove all that he asserts. We have before us a free man. Colonel Suttle says there was a man in Virginia named Anthony Burns; that that man is a slave by the law of Virginia; that he is *his* slave, owing service and labor to him; that he escaped from Virginia into this state, and that the prisoner at the bar is that very same Anthony Burns. He says all this. Let him prove it all! Let him fail in one point, let him fall short the width of a spider's thread, and the man goes free. What we have here today, gentleman," he paused to look the commissioner in the eye, "is a case of mistaken identity. Aren't such cases nearly as old as time itself? One need only look to the Holy Scripture to the story of Jacob and Esau. Their very own father, Isaac, confused their identity. Surely a man who saw his slave only intermittently each year might make a similar mistake more easily."

Mr. Dana was getting well and truly worked up by then, but it turned out, he was just getting started.

"I'm sure most of us here remember the first case that was brought under the Fugitive Slave Law. In that, the Gibson case, a man was arrested in Philadelphia and adjudged to be a fugitive slave. Yet, when the alleged fugitive was sent back to his purported master in Maryland, the master refused delivery, as he'd never before seen the fellow who the law had sent him!"

"The evidence in this case comes entirely from Mr. Brent, who, like Colonel Suttle, saw the missing slave only sporadically. The time when the missing Anthony Burns actually worked in Mr. Brent's own employ was seven years ago, when the fellow would have been but a boy, and we all know the appearance of a young man can change drastically as he settles into his adulthood." Now Mr. Dana stopped speaking for a moment and turned toward the back of the room to look at Anthony. As Mr. Dana gazed at Anthony, where he was squeezed between all those guards, others in the room began to turn toward him too. Anthony supposed that was Mr. Dana's very purpose, as the lawyer next began to speak at length about Anthony's appearance.

"Had Colonel Suttle intended truly to identify this particular prisoner," he said, pointing a finger in Anthony's direction, "he would not have said simply that the man possesses a scar on his right hand. Does it look to anyone in this room like the prisoner is endowed only with a scar on his right hand?"

Anthony felt then like he ought to hold up his arm to let people better see his mangled wrist as they listened to all that

Mr. Dana might say about it. With the manacles firm, he was saved from considering what conduct was called for, and he just kept himself still as he already was.

"A scar! The prisoner's right hand is broken, and a bone stands out from the back of it, a hump an inch high, and it hangs almost useless from the wrist, with a huge scar or gash covering half its surface. Now, sir, this broken hand, this hump of bone in the midst, is attached to the most noticeable thing possible in the identifying of a slave. His right hand is the chief property his master has in him. It is the chief point of observation and recollection. If that hand has lost its cunning or its power, no man hears it so soon and remembers it so well as the master. Now, it is extraordinary, sir, that neither the record nor Mr. Brent say anything about the most noticeable thing in the man." He gave the room a long look then to let his words sink in. Anthony didn't mind the sharpness of how his lawyer described the wrist. If Mr. Dana could get the case won with hard words, Anthony was content to listen to it all.

"If Mr. Brent does know intimately Anthony Burns, of Richmond," the lawyer continued, "and has described him as fully as he can, then this prisoner is not the man. Emissaries are sent out with the description in their hand, and they find a Negro, with a brand on his cheek and a broken and cut hand, and that is near enough for catchers, paid by the job, to find a 'dark complexioned man,' with 'a scar on the cheek and on the right hand.' Mr. Brent knows, and does not swear otherwise, that the Anthony Burns he means had only a scar or cut, and he distinctly said 'no other mark.' But still he swears to the man. Identification is matter of opinion. Opinion is influenced by the temper, and motive, and frame of mind. Remember, sir, the state of political excitement at this moment. Remember the state of feeling between North and South; the contest between the slave power and the free power. Remember that this case is made a state issue by Virginia, a national question by the executive.

Reflect that every reading man in Virginia, with all the pride of the Old Dominion aroused in him, is turning his eyes to the result of this issue. No man could be more liable to bias than a Virginian, testifying in Massachusetts, at this moment, on such an issue, with every powerful and controlling motive on earth enlisted for success."

At the mention of newspapers in Virginia, Anthony thought again of Miss Colette. Had she gotten word of his trials up there in the North? Was she at home following along, or still wondering where he'd gone? He liked to think of her back there in Richmond, sitting on a rocker in a quiet room, a cup of sweet tea in her smooth hand, telling Adelia what she read in the penny press. Maybe the two of them were applauding him, hoping for his victory. His attention was pulled back from the thought as Mr. Dana continued speaking.

"There is, fortunately, one fact, of which Mr. Brent is sure," he said, with his voice rising. "He knows that he saw this Anthony Burns in Richmond, Virginia, on the twentieth day of March last. To this fact, he testifies unequivocally. After all the evidence is put in on our side to show that the prisoner was in Boston on the first and fourth of March, he does not go back to the stand to correct an error, or to say that he may have been mistaken, or that he meant only to say that it was about the twentieth. He persists in his positive testimony, and I have no doubt he is right and honest in doing so. He did see an Anthony Burns in Richmond, Virginia, on the twentieth day of March, and that Anthony Burns did go missing soon thereafter. But the prisoner here was in Boston, earning an honest livelihood by the work of his hands, through the entire month of March, from the first day forward. Of this Your Honor cannot, on the proofs, entertain a reasonable doubt."

And here, Anthony thought his case should be won, but then Mr. Dana marched on, getting deep into issues about the law they were arguing under and whether this trial should be happening here in Boston or back down in Virginia. He talked about whether Anthony should have been given a jury to decide his rights. He spoke about the nature of a lease, saying that even if the accused were the same Anthony Burns as the escaped one, that maybe Mr. Millspaugh should come collect him, as the druggist was the one who had rented the missing slave.

Finally, finally, after Mr. Dana had talked so long Anthony wondered how the man's throat still had the will to work his voice, it seemed like he was coming to a close. He stopped his pacing and stood near frozen. Anthony knew from the hours of watching the lawyer perform already that this meant it was time to sit up and listen good.

"You recognized, sir, in the beginning, the presumption of freedom. Hold to it now, sir, as to the sheet anchor of your peace of mind as well as of his safety. If you commit a mistake in favor of the man, a pecuniary value, not great, is put at hazard. If against him, a free man is made a slave forever. If you have, on the evidence or on the law, the doubt of a reasoning and reasonable mind, an intelligent misgiving, then, sir, I implore you, in view of the cruel character of this law, in view of the dreadful consequences of a mistake, send him not away, with that tormenting doubt on your mind. It may turn to a torturing certainty. The eyes of many millions are upon you, sir. You are to do an act which will hold its place in the history of America, in the history of the progress of the human race. May your judgment be for liberty and not for slavery, for happiness and not for wretchedness; for hope and not for despair; and may the blessing of Him that is ready to perish come upon you."

ANN

Boston, June 1854

A fierce pang in my lower leg startled me from my sleep. I'm ashamed to admit that my first reaction was one of relief. Finally, I could stop pretending to Wendell that I was feeling shadow ailments of my own design. It seemed I was still the sickly woman who required so much care and dependability from my husband. It was a strange sensation to relish my own suffering, knowing that this resurgence of pain would lead to joy, a bolstering of Wendell's affection for me.

I imagined that Phebe was already down in the kitchen preparing some version of a morning meal for my Aunt Caroline, who had come from Weymouth earlier in the week. Barely another moment passed before I heard the girl's light footsteps trotting up the stairwell toward my quarters.

Although the scent of cornbread had traveled upstairs along with her, she was holding a piece of paper, not a tray of food, as she opened the door.

"Lloyd's been by," she said. "He dropped this." Her voice was timorous, which I presumed was a lingering effect of the reprimanding she'd received from Wendell and me the prior evening. Late Thursday, while all of Boston and the world beyond awaited the decision in the Burns case, Wendell had discovered Phebe in Court Square, sandwiched within a large group of protestors. Though we generally encouraged her activist behaviors, there had been such violence erupting about town that it hardly seemed safe for her to participate without at least a chaperone. Her poor judgment required redress, and we did exchange cross words after Wendell brought her home. Even so, it was exceedingly difficult to hold anger at Phebe for any length of time, and we had forgiven her transgressions rather quickly.

She held the paper out for me to take, and I pushed myself up with a grimace. I saw it was a reprinted proclamation from Jerome Smith, the mayor of Boston. I commenced reading the document aloud to Phebe in its entirety, unsure how much she'd already seen.

"To secure order throughout the city this day," it announced, "Major-General Edmands and the Chief of Police will make such disposition of the respective forces as will best promote that important object; and they are clothed with full discretionary power to sustain the laws of the land. All well-disposed citizens and other persons are urgently requested to leave those streets which it may be found necessary to clear temporarily, and under no circumstances to obstruct or molest any officer, civil or military, in the lawful discharge of his duty."

When I looked up from the document, I saw Wendell standing in the doorway listening. He was dressed in his suit for court.

"He's declaring martial law," I said. The *Burns* decision was to be announced later that morning, and it appeared law enforcement was preparing to encounter even greater unrest.

"Does this mean they're sending him back? He's lost his case?" Phebe asked, giving voice to what was worrying us all.

We had grown optimistic in the few days since testimony

at court had concluded. Counsel for Burns had put on a convincing case. But this decree seemed to imply otherwise.

When I didn't answer, Phebe turned toward Wendell. "Can he do that?" she demanded.

"I'm off to the courthouse now," he said. The lines of his face were taut as his eyes traveled between the two of us. "The streets will undoubtedly fill with both friends and foes. If you feel you must go to the square, at least take the carriage. Your aunt Caroline's already gone on foot. Perhaps find a spot inside the Commonwealth Building where you might have a chair and a view from a window. It just seems"—he paused, rubbing a hand across his brow as if to collect himself—"we ought all to be there, so that we might bear witness to . . ."

We knew the thoughts he couldn't bear to utter.

"I refuse to relinquish hope yet," I declared. "It was only days ago, Wendell, when you returned from the courthouse feeling triumphant. The conflicting evidence about the accused's identity, the force of Mr. Dana's closing argument. The mayor's precautionary behavior does not negate it all."

"That may be," Wendell said, "but we must remember too Commissioner Loring's Whig affiliations and his political aspirations."

I did indeed feel a personal obligation to stand myself up for the young man, for the importance of his own case as well as what it represented on a grander scale. Even if the outing resulted in weeks of bedrest for me, certainly there was no choice. In the meantime, I would not allow myself to think too long on that day three years prior when I had gone to bear witness in the Sims case. I pushed away the awful memory of Thomas Sims being marched away from the courthouse back to a life of bondage. Since the decision on Mr. Burns was still pending, I would not equate those cases. Not yet.

"The carriage will be good. Either which way," I answered.

A SHORT WHILE LATER, AS WE TRAVELED to the federal courthouse, we found Court Square so congested with people that we had to abandon the carriage and walk the final portion of the journey. The pain in my leg had not abated, but it had not worsened either, and that was a bit of good news. Hopefully there would be more good tidings to report this day. I found that despite the burn in my muscles, I had sufficient strength to maneuver through the bodies crowding the sidewalks.

"You're sure you're all right?" Phebe asked for the third time as we made our way closer to the square.

"Enough, child!" I scolded in exasperation. My own comfort could not be our primary concern today.

As we proceeded through the morning heat, we saw many storefronts and office buildings displaying signage announcing closure for the day. This was true especially of the establishments known to be owned by abolitionists. Several of those windows and doors were draped in the black cloth of mourning. It seemed Wendell was not the only one expecting the worst.

"A cannon!" Phebe exclaimed, and I followed her gaze to the eastern door of the courthouse, where a brass cannon had indeed been stationed.

Wendell, and several other members of the Vigilance Committee, were now inside the courthouse, awaiting the decision along with Mr. Burns, and I wondered whether they had been forced to walk past that imposing weapon. Surely, I thought, the display had been meant for intimidation and nothing more. Surrounding the cannon, as if to guard the weapon itself, was a group of US marines armed with muskets and bayonets.

At the sound of my name, I turned to see Samson and Priscilla Gates dressed in black funereal garb and weaving their way through the growing crowd of spectators as they pushed toward us.

"The militia has been here since seven!" Samson said when they reached us, his plump cheeks ruddy with exertion.

Priscilla's face was flushed as well, and small droplets of perspiration showed beneath the dark ringlets framing her forehead.

"You've been here since then?" I gasped in surprise as I stepped closer to them to make way for three businessmen rushing past us. It was now after ten, and the crowd appeared to be growing ever larger.

"The police arrived earlier to clear everyone from the square, so we've been a part of this group surrounding the outskirts since, oh," Priscilla said, glancing at her husband, "I can't even say quite how long."

"And now the soldiers have started practicing loading and firing that dastardly weapon," Samson huffed.

I looked back toward the cannon, which was obscured now by the crowd. It seemed that in addition to the civilians, the military presence was growing minute by minute too. I stood on tiptoe to get a better look and was able to identify uniformed troops from the 1st Battalion Light Dragoons, an artillery regiment, another battalion of Light Infantry, as well as other Divisionary Corps of Independent Cadets. There were still others whose uniforms were not familiar to me.

Suddenly, there was new commotion around us: people of all sorts suddenly hurrying past.

"What's happening?" Samson asked of a young fellow dashing by.

"They're clearing us out," the man answered. "Everyone's taking stations inside buildings along the path to the wharf." We would learn later that using the military to clear the entirety of the route to the waiting ship was but one of many measures specifically sanctioned by President Pierce.

"You'll come with us to the Old State House," Priscilla said, grabbing firmly onto my elbow and nodding at Phebe to follow.

As we moved toward the corner of Washington and State Streets, there was such force from the bodies around us, all of us proceeding in the same direction, that I wondered whether we were even responsible for our own movements or simply being propelled by the energy of the crowd.

Samson pushed open the door to the Old State House. People inside were already gathered at the many paned windows along the ground floor. We followed him into the packed space, and I saw that the businesses and shops inside this building had also locked their doors for the occasion. We made our way immediately toward the stairwell, hoping for less congestion on one of the higher floors. Phebe was concerned for my legs, but my fervor propelled me up the stairs.

As we moved through the hallways looking for an open spot on the third floor, we finally found an area where the crowd was slightly thinner. Samson directed us toward one of the large rectangular windows and then positioned himself directly behind us, where he would be able to see above our heads and also shield us from jostling as others continued to cram into the building.

I turned my focus back to State Street outside. Across from us faces gaped out from every window. On every balcony, every roof and terrace, as far as I could see, people gathered and peered down, straining to see what would follow. Perhaps the crowd was so large because it was Anniversary Week in Boston, when members of various religious and moral societies from around the country convened to celebrate their causes. Or perhaps, it was simply the naked horror being perpetrated before us, the blasphemy of shackling an innocent man here, in a free state, and sentencing him to a life of captivity. Maybe those around us were finally awakening to their outrage, or they had discovered within themselves a deeper love of freedom than they ever before realized.

If the decision should come down against Burns, then all those dark shawls and scarves, which people had draped down from open panes, would be appropriate, as today we would witness the death of freedom and the demise of decency. For all the anti-slavery conventions I had attended in my life, I had never yet been a part of a crowd this staggeringly large. As I watched, additional soldiers continued to appear, as if a steady supply of men were being shipped from all across the country to come display their weapons for the people of Boston. The attempt to clear the streets was clearly failing, as every available spot on the sidewalks remained occupied. The soldiers began to form columns along the street regardless, presumably to prevent protestors from pushing forward.

On one of the rooftops across the way, several men began unfurling a large black sheet. After a moment, they draped it over the side of the building with a flourish, and I could see the word "Shame!" painted across the fabric in bright white letters. Cheers rang out from windows and the street below, applauding their statement, and then, almost immediately, naysayers elsewhere within the crowd began throwing trash at the banner, bits of food and scraps. Had I wondered whether all members of the horde were hoping for the same outcome, that question was now firmly answered in the negative.

As the hour approached eleven o'clock, a new kind of energy began to rise amongst the spectators. Something was happening. From window to window and building to building, some word was being passed. A young man standing just down the hallway from us shouted out that Commissioner Loring was back on the bench to announce his decision. After this, silence descended, as if we were all collectively holding our breath.

Despite the mourning imagery everywhere, I found myself still hopeful. Although so many seemed to consider Burns's fate a foregone conclusion, I couldn't help feeling this continued flicker of optimism in my heart. Surely the commissioner would be driven by righteousness. How could he, a lifelong Northerner, do anything other than rule in favor of the fugitive, in favor of liberty and decency? Hadn't Mr. Dana proven the case as admirably and conclusively as Wendell told me? I grabbed hold of Phebe's hand, grasping tight to her smooth skin as I willed my thoughts to be true, for justice to prevail.

I cannot say how many minutes passed like this, but suddenly, we heard the tolling of church bells, sounding first from one church and then almost immediately, echoing from other churches across the city. My heart leapt. Were they ringing in celebration?

I looked to the faces of those surrounding me. Was there cause to rejoice? The expressions I saw mirrored the confusion that I felt. But then there was a murmur, growing into a rumble throughout the crowd.

From somewhere down the hallway, a man's voice rang out.

"He is condemned!"

"No!" I heard myself shout. Almost immediately, my legs felt too weak to hold me. The strength I'd found earlier in the day left me in an instant. The tolling outside was a death knell crying out into the air. Here I stood in a building erected almost directly atop the site where Crispus Attucks was killed during the Boston Massacre, when our entire nation was fighting for freedom. And yet, it seemed we had made no progress, none at all. How could it be?

"Mother!" Phebe shouted, grabbing my shoulder and holding me upright. There was commotion as I struggled to stand, to find breath, to fight the blurriness now encircling my sight. After another moment, someone produced a chair. I cannot say even from where, as I was in such a state of despair that I felt I was only marginally conscious. Priscilla was there, helping to settle me onto the chair. And then the three of us were embracing, crying softly with each other, as all around us, we could hear women wailing and people again crying, "Shame! Shame!"

But the crowd did not disperse. We braced for the horrid sight that we knew was to follow, where Anthony Burns, the symbol of our country's greatest struggle, would be marched through the streets to the dock where a vessel awaited. The path from the courthouse to the wharf, though only one third of a mile, would mark the longest walk imaginable, the procession from liberty to eternal bondage.

I forced my eyes back to the street outside, and the minutes began to creep by. Eleven o'clock slowly became high noon, but still, there was no movement from the courthouse. While we waited, we wiped tears from our cheeks, alternately crying and consoling each other. The sun moved even farther across the sky, as the hour passed one. The crowd was growing restless, intractable even, but no one dared leave. Every now and then, a group of young men would rush at soldiers in the street, pushing toward the courthouse, only to be held off by bayonets.

Finally, near two o'clock, there was new movement in the square. US soldiers began to shift into formation. Marines and artillery corps commenced aligning in columns, and then a group of federal marshals joined. I thought I spotted a group from the Boston Lancers, as well. There were soldiers on horseback assembling at the front, and others on foot, with gleaming silver blades, readying to take up the rear. At the center of the formation, upwards of fifty men stood with swords and pistols. The sheer number of armed forces in attendance was astounding. I could not begin to guess how much this display was costing the federal government.

Only a few minutes later, the east door of the courthouse opened, and Anthony Burns emerged into the bright sunshine and one of the worst moments in our nation's history.

ANTHONY

Boston, June 1854

The guards gave Anthony a new suit that morning. After so many days wearing the same rank outfit all the time, he was glad for something clean to put on. And the clothes they gave him were fine. The only time he saw Black folk dressed so costly was when they were being sold at auction for house slaving. He took his time putting on the trousers and the sharp coat, and he found himself still hoping. If they gave him all those fine fabrics and even a top hat to wear, that maybe signified more good was to come.

But it turned out those clothes were meant just to show folks outside that he'd been treated well, that maybe the slave life wasn't so bad after all.

When the commissioner announced his decision, Anthony could scarcely believe it, even though he heard it clear with his very own ears.

Pastor Grimes stayed with him all the time that day. After the court session was over and they knew the worst was yet to come, a group from the Vigilance Committee waited in the courtroom with Anthony and the pastor. Men Anthony hadn't even met before just kept coming on over to shake his hand, like they were paying their respects. While each one came and went, there was Pastor Grimes for all of it, just talking, talking, trying to use his words to hold Anthony up.

When it came time for him to return to his cell, the lawyer, Mr. Dana, followed them back, explaining that the prison room was where Anthony was to wait until it came time to leave for the wharf. Pastor Grimes kept saying that the commissioner maybe didn't have much choice in making the ruling. It was a matter of preserving honor for the US government, the pastor said, that Anthony had to be sent back so the government wouldn't be disgraced.

"Don't forget," Pastor Grimes said, putting his meaty hand atop Anthony's shoulder, "we nearly persuaded Mr. Suttle already to sell you. But that Mr. Hallett . . ." He shook his head remembering.

Pastor Grimes already explained how they'd tried and failed to buy Anthony's freedom. Master Charles had agreed to part with Anthony for $1,200, but then everything went sideways. First the district attorney, that Mr. Hallett, he worried that if Master Charles went home without the slave he'd been chasing, the government would refuse to pay back to the city what it cost to capture and hold Anthony. The commissioner promised Mr. Hallett the city would still get paid. Then Mr. Hallett complained that the buying and selling of human property was prohibited in the state of Massachusetts. Pastor Grimes finally offered himself up to be arrested for making the purchase. But then came the Sabbath, and the sale was prevented because of rules about doing business on the Lord's day. By the time Monday morning arrived, Master Charles had changed his mind and was refusing to sell at all, and that was that.

"We have to feel hope in our hearts," the pastor kept on, "that after Mr. Suttle gets settled back in Virginia, and the newspapers move on to reporting something else, he'll be willing to complete the sale. Wouldn't he rather have the $1,200 than a slave who knows how to run? The worst kind of slave is one who's tasted freedom. Especially one as sharp as you."

Pastor Grimes was trying to be kind, but he didn't know Master Charles like Anthony did. Master Charles cared about his reputation too, just like the government did. Even after the newspaper tired of talking about Anthony and his case, Master Charles wouldn't be selling him North. That'd mean letting folks around town see Anthony get away with what he'd done. Even if Anthony's Boston friends offered enough money for Master Charles to close all the loans on his slaves, or enough even to buy himself a brand-new quarry, he'd care more about his good standing with the folks of Richmond and Stafford to ever do a thing like that.

"He'd sooner sell me down river," Anthony said. He was thankful to Pastor Grimes for his care, and so he tried to keep the mean-spiritedness from his voice, despite his feelings. He was angry at everyone and everything, feeling ready to claw at the iron bars of his holding pen, bite through them with his teeth if he could. But Pastor Grimes didn't deserve any of the ire.

"We're not going to let that happen," the pastor answered, patting Anthony's hand. "Say my address to me again now, and you keep practicing it at least once every day."

Anthony was tired of repeating it and let his lips twist at the pastor's nagging.

"I mean it now," Pastor Grimes said, "like it's a part of your morning prayers."

They were interrupted by sounds of talking just outside the cell, and then there was Mr. Wendell Phillips coming to see him again.

"Anthony," Mr. Phillips said as he hurried over to shake hands. All the pink vessels in his eyes were on show, like he hadn't slept at all through the night. "There are no words I can say to render Commissioner Loring's decision anything other than the worst travesty," he said as he continued to grip Anthony's hand, then adding his second hand too. It seemed the man's whole body was vibrating with rage, and he was holding onto Anthony to keep himself stable.

Mr. Dana came closer then, greeting Mr. Phillips, and then turning his attention to Anthony.

"Pastor Grimes and I will be on our way now," Mr. Dana said, "but I'll return shortly to escort you to the cutter so you do not walk alone."

Anthony knew he should have thanked Mr. Dana for his kindness, but the fear and anger inside him were both so sharp, he found he couldn't say anything at all.

As the men left the cell, Mr. Dana told the marshal outside that he'd be accompanying the prisoner to the wharf. Anthony couldn't make out what the marshal said in response, but sounds of arguing followed. He supposed they didn't want him to have even one friend with him, even in his very worst moment.

Mr. Phillips turned then to the tall guard who had followed him inside and was still standing just behind him.

"Can we not have even a moment to converse in private?" Mr. Phillips snapped at the man.

The guard blinked hard, showing his offense at Mr. Phillips and his tone, but he turned back toward the door all the same.

Anthony asked then what he most wanted to know. "Have we really done everything we can, Mr. Phillips? Isn't there something more, some way to keep me here? Must I really march off in stride with them?" He thought of their Lord Jesus walking to his crucifixion, but he didn't figure there was any larger purpose for himself like that here.

"I'm afraid you must," Mr. Phillips said, as he hung his head, looking for all the world as though he was shamed to say it. "But you listen to me," he said, raising back up with an insistence to his tone, "we will keep fighting for you from here in Boston."

Anthony shook his head before Mr. Phillips could say more. "No, Mr. Phillips, y'all up here in Boston are going to forget me real quick once I climb on that vessel down in the harbor."

"No!" Mr. Phillips said with such force that Anthony sat himself up straighter. "To think of all the effort it required for you to reach Boston, and then to enjoy the fruits of your labor only a matter of months before your struggles began again."

As Mr. Phillips talked on, the tempo of his voice rose higher, like angry sparks on a windy day.

"No, Anthony," he said, "we will not soon forget you. I've been thinking all this morning of the history of Massachusetts, the very soil on which we stand having represented freedom for decades. And yet, here our government sits, forcing you back into bondage. Clearly, we have not yet achieved the humanity, justice, or Christian goodness that were meant to be foundational to the very creation of this state. I will not forget you. No, I will lie awake night after night, shuddering in shame at your hardship and the behavior of this nation."

Anthony wanted to be grateful about the man caring so deeply, but what he heard the most was that there was no hope, nothing to cling to, no evenness to the way of the world, no mercy.

Mr. Phillips kept talking for some time longer, but Anthony's mind was busy thinking on what would happen next. He wondered again whether it wouldn't be better to die than to surrender himself back to slave life. He couldn't say how many minutes passed before the marshals told Mr. Phillips to leave so they could get ready to go to the wharf. Anthony didn't feel really like he was in his right mind, just too busy despairing.

Eventually, they brought him down to the vestibule just inside the east doorway of the building. When they reached the door, Marshal Freeman spoke up.

"We wait," he said to his men, "until we receive the signal."

It was just Anthony and the guards then. Again, there were plenty more than necessary to guard one man. Each wore a pistol holstered on his left side and a cutlass hanging from the right. He turned to the man nearest him, a shaggy-haired fellow he'd seen outside the jury room several times during the week.

"Sir, won't you please remove the shackles from my hands?" he asked. "I'm not going to run nowhere, not with half the United States army out there."

"It's procedure," was all the guard said. He didn't meet Anthony's eyes, as if he at least seemed to feel sorry about it. Anthony reckoned then maybe that was the reason they gave him the new suit and the shiny shoes too. Shame.

"Please, sir," he begged again. "If I'm to look no better than a felon, why bother with the fine clothing y'all gave me? These irons will disgrace the whole of my appearance. For my last minutes on Northern soil, please set me free of them." He wouldn't let his mind go to the places it was still trying to wander, thinking on what might await him back down in Richmond. His only thought now was that he should be free as possible for his last minutes there in Boston.

The guard looked to Marshal Freeman, who was peering out the window with his nose near pressed to the glass, waiting on the right moment for them to walk. "Marsh?" he asked.

The marshal gave Anthony a quick glance. "Fine," Marshal Freeman snapped, maybe exasperated by the repeated requests. "Just quickly," he told the guard. "Where is that damned Edmands?" he added, mostly to himself.

With the handcuffs off, Anthony shook out his chafed wrists, knowing the respite wouldn't last long.

Something must have finally happened beyond the window, out there in the square, because suddenly Marshal Freeman started to command the men.

"Formation!" he ordered, and the officers came to surround Anthony. Then Marshal Freeman swung open the doors.

A blinding sunlight assaulted them, and while Anthony's eyes accustomed themselves to the brightness, the men moved in even closer around him.

"Quick step!" the marshal commanded, and then Anthony was being pushed forward into the light. A clamor of commotion burst forth when the people outside caught sight of them. Shouts and hollers erupted from a crowd that he could scarcely see through the bodies surrounding him.

They kept him so closely surrounded that he had to peer between the bodies in front of him to see that they had taken their place behind a regiment of soldiers. The soldiers wore blue jackets with brass buttons and matching caps on their heads. They stood in tight formation, as if they were readying for battle. Ahead of them looked to be other groups in uniforms of different colors. And beyond the foot soldiers, there was a band of men on horseback, who Anthony supposed would be leading their procession. It seemed almost a mockery to him that so many officers and infantrymen had been brought out to escort just one Negro to a ship. He looked round for Master Charles and Master Brent, or even Mr. Dana, but instead, he saw only strangers, dark and light-skinned alike, staring out at him from the endless, hollering crowd.

There were cheers and hisses from the mob, and he couldn't say for sure which sounds were meant to encourage him and which ones to condemn. It didn't much matter, he decided, as his fate was already sealed. He looked away and tried to fill his mind with thoughts of easier times. By going back to Virginia, he might see his mama again, at least, or his brothers. But first he would see the whipping post. Mostly, he was thinking on how he had a lifetime ahead of himself of being a slave, with no more say-so in the keeping of his time or anything else about his life.

The marshal called another command, and they started down State Street, all the bodies tight together, feeling to

Anthony like they were one giant animal. It seemed the entire city had been shut down. With so many folks there watching in the streets, there couldn't hardly be anyone left to go to business anyhow.

As they passed by the Commonwealth Building, the guards started shouting. Anthony looked up and saw people peering out from all the windows inside, and even people on the rooftop, jammed up all along the edges. Then he saw it wasn't just the Commonwealth Building holding so many folks, but all the buildings were full-up with onlookers, all there to witness his undoing. Some men had draped a wooden coffin out from a window above them. It was painted all in black with words written upon it. "Death to Liberty!" it said.

A guard somewhere ahead of them jumped out of formation and aimed his pistol up toward the roof of the Commonwealth Building. "They're throwing pepper!" he shouted.

"Back in formation!" came a shout from another commander in the crowd, and the solider returned to his place. They'd surely all been told to let nothing lead them off course.

From along the sidewalk, groups of men began pushing forward, shouting and spitting at the soldiers. Men and women were crying, "Shame!" Anthony had the urge to hold up a hand and tell everyone they could go on home. There was nothing they could do for him now, even with all their fussing. This was the end of hope so he turned his eyes ahead and just kept on walking.

It was hardly a long walk from the court to the wharf, and soon they were nearing the Merchants' Exchange. The militiamen who'd been posted there saw them approaching and began to sing. First, Anthony thought it was a song meant to comfort him. But then the cruel words came clearer, and he recognized the tune as "Carry Me Back to Old Virginny."

As they made their way closer to the docks, marching down Commercial Street, the crowd grew more raucous.

Dockworkers were known as rougher folk, and this day didn't seem any exception. They called out new insults at the soldiers, using nasty words and pushing even harder toward the officers. Up ahead, a truckman suddenly moved his horses and began driving his wagon straight toward a line of troops. The soldiers saw him coming and brandished their swords. Anthony couldn't see who, but someone's blade struck an animal in the chest. As the horse reared and squealed, all the people jumping out from its way, the soldiers called new commands.

"Face about!" hollered a man in front of Anthony. "Present arms!"

It seemed there might be a true skirmish then, and Anthony's heart quickened. The soldiers lifted their guns, readying to shoot into the mob.

For a moment, everyone on both sides seemed to hold their breath. But then the one slashed horse fell, and the people just stepped farther back, away from it. Everyone began quieting down as they retreated to their places.

The procession picked up walking again.

When they reached T-Wharf, the officers kept their positions all the way up until the steps of a steamer called the *John Taylor*, which would carry them to a cutter waiting farther out in the harbor. As Anthony started up the gangplank, he remembered his first steps on Boston soil, less than half a year earlier, and he had to swallow down the bile that rose up from his gut.

They made their way down below deck. The guards followed along behind Anthony as they filed into a small cabin. There were so many men present that the group could scarcely fit inside the small quarters. They stood quiet, crammed in like that, and waited. Nobody made to talk to Anthony then, and he stood himself still as he could, wondering where to put his anger.

Soon there was rocking as the boat began to move, and Anthony shut his eyes hard to prevent tears from falling.

It felt like only a few minutes before the steamer approached Minot's Ledge Lighthouse. There it would be setting tow alongside the cutter *Morris*, the vessel that was to carry Anthony all the way to Virginia. They ushered him back to the deck, where six of the guards transferred him onto the new ship. At the front of the group was J.H. Riley, then Marshals Coolidge, Wright, Black, and Godfrey, and finally Asa Butman, who it seemed would plague Anthony until the very last.

Once they boarded the cutter, the guards brought him down to a cabin. They shoved him in through the door, and as his eyes adjusted to the dim light, there he saw Master Charles waiting inside.

"Aha! Deputy Marshal Riley, it took y'all long enough now." Master Charles rose from a leather chair. He was dressed extra fine that day, likely to celebrate his victory. His light morning coat was decorated with fabric fasteners, and it was cut low to the waist to show the delicate silk of his gray vest beneath.

"Apologies sir," the guard answered with a respectful voice. "We had some trouble stowing the cannon."

"You can leave Tony here with me," Master Charles directed them. "Just a word, Deputy Marshal, please before you go." He pulled Marshal Riley aside while the others left the cabin. Anthony looked down at the shiny new boots the guards had given him just that morning and let himself wonder how bad things were about to get for him. The door to the cabin was still open, and he jumped when he heard a single gunshot ring out from above. Master Charles and the guard made no move to take cover, and Anthony realized it was probably just a salute as the *John Taylor* set itself free from the cutter and turned back to Boston. How he wished with all his soul to have been aboard that other vessel heading back to shore instead of the one where he stood.

The men finished whatever they were whispering about and came back toward Anthony.

"You want me to shackle him?" Deputy Riley asked Master Charles.

"That's fine; that's fine," Master Charles said shaking his head. "Tony's not going to hurt me. You go ahead and find Mr. Brent. Let him know we're starting."

As Deputy Riley left the cabin, Master Charles sat back down in the padded chair, making himself comfortable as you please across from where Anthony stood.

"Now Tony," he said, "I know it wasn't you who thought to double cross me the way you did. There must have been others who set you up as a pawn. Now I'll tell you what." He looked Anthony over, thinking on something for a moment. "I never wanted you to be unhappy during your time with me. We were family, weren't we Tony?"

"Yes, sir," Anthony said, with no real choice on how to answer.

"How about it, Tony, if I find a way to give you back your freedom?"

"Sir?" Anthony knew better than to expect as much from Master Charles. That man didn't give away anything for free. "You go ahead and tell me the name of the captain that brought you to Boston over the winter, and I will find a way to make you free."

ANN

Boston, June 1854

As I finished dressing, I regarded myself in the narrow looking glass. My cheeks were pink and smooth, the whites of my eyes snowy and pristine. No one would guess from looking at me that I was suffering an ache in my back or incessant dryness of my mouth, nor would they suspect the throbbing tenderness in my joints. The doctors had begun to conjecture that perhaps I suffered from some form of rheumatism, but they offered no effective treatment, only patronizing reminders that I should try to keep calm. Certainly, the deep melancholy in which I landed after Burns's rendition could hardly have been beneficial to my health. Even at a happier time, the physical exertions in which I engaged the day before—the walking, prolonged standing about, elbowing through crowded streets—would have left me especially achy and tender the following morning. So there I was, stiff and rather wretched.

Firm up, I chided myself. Certainly, Anthony Burns was suffering greater discomforts than I.

As the first notes of accordion music reached my ears, I remembered it was Saturday. I made my way slowly across the room to open the window. There on the sidewalk below stood Bob Looster, the musician Wendell had retained years earlier. Each week, Mr. Looster tarried outside my window to play a few songs before continuing on to his other engagements. Since I was nearly always confined to our home, the music was generally a welcome diversion. As much as I appreciated my husband's thoughtful gesture, it felt wrong just then to listen to the cheerful notes of the staccato tunes.

Mr. Looster was looking up at my window as he opened and closed the instrument's bellows. Likely, he was wondering why the glass was not ajar already in anticipation of his arrival. As I pushed out the pane, I waved a hand in greeting. He smiled back at me from under his dented hat, whereupon I held up a finger, indicating I wished to interrupt him but a moment.

"Good day, Mrs. Phillips," he called with a question on his face.

"Only quiet songs, today, please, Mr. Looster. Songs for thinking, if you would."

He nodded with something akin to relief, and I wondered if he too had been in the crowd the day before. "Understood, Mrs. Phillips," he called back, and his fingers began moving again, this time putting out a ballad.

The new song, full of keening, haunting notes, indeed felt more appropriate for my mood. I lowered myself down on the cushion beside the window, ready to think about Mr. Burns. I was struggling greatly with my attempts to digest what had occurred in my home city, the kowtowing to Southern laws, the lack of justice for a human soul. Boston was supposed to be the Athens of America, not Hades. When the attendees of Anniversary Week departed for their homes in Providence, New Bedford, Worcester, and beyond, how glad they must have been to see Boston fade into the distance. How shamed I felt.

Mr. Looster commenced with another plaintive tune, and as the notes floated toward me, tears began to cloud my vision.

I reached for no handkerchief, but simply allowed the tears to fall, finding a strange solace in the depth of my grief, relieved by my own humanity. The more sodden became my face, the more resolved I grew. We would not soon surrender the fight for freedom, but we would begin afresh, with Anthony Burns as our newest beacon. I sat listening and ruminating for the remainder of Mr. Looster's performance until Cara, our new nurse, peeped her head into the room.

"Ah! Good to see you're up and risen, Mrs. Phillips." She smiled brightly at me. Cara was a solid young woman with ruddy cheeks and crimped russet hair, recently arrived from Ireland. Her words resounded into the room, thick and bouncy, making it nearly impossible for me to do anything other than smile in response. Wendell had brought Cara to the house three weeks prior, after being introduced to her by the Garrisons' washerwoman. I tried to convince Wendell I did not require constant tending, but truthfully, I did enjoy having Cara with us at Essex Street, especially now that Phebe was so often occupied with her own engagements.

"Nice, weren't it, having the music today?" she said, as she entered the room and began pulling up my bedsheets. "A trifle sad though, weren't it? Looks like you felt the same."

"Indeed," I nodded along, still too desolate to explain.

She made up the bed with hearty efficiency, pulling the coverlet into place and fluffing up the pillows. Motes rose into the air around her, glistening in the sunshine, their shimmering somehow rendering me even more despondent.

"Come now, Mrs. Phillips," she said as she held out her thick arm out for me. "Time to bring you down below. There's better things for your time than moping about. Mr. Phillips will be getting back soon, and he'll like to see you sitting up with a cuppa."

I glanced at the clock.

"But it's only just two in the afternoon," I answered, thinking that Wendell would be busy at his meetings, especially in light of the many signatures the vigilance committee was seeking. In addition to petitions for use of the halls for anti-slavery meetings, there was now a petition to remove Commissioner Loring from his post.

"He's got himself something else planned for tonight now, he does. Said he'd be wanting to check on you afore evening. Might as well let him see you looking blithe and bonny, even if you're not truly feeling it."

Well, she was right after all, wasn't she? I wondered if she could sense how dearly I held my attachment to Wendell, how even after all these years, I wondered if he might, at any moment, suddenly lose interest in his sickly wife. I nodded and pushed myself up from my seat. Cara wrapped her arm around my back for support, and I leaned into her, grateful.

After a careful walk down the stairs, she settled me onto the divan in the parlor. I eyed the newspaper where she had rested it on the small table beside me. There would be a recounting of Burns's procession down Court Street, surely with long lists of the military outfits that had been in attendance. Worse would be the editorials, some lamenting Boston's commitment of atrocities in subservience to Southern ideas, but surely there would also be letters from readers praising the return to law and order, the prioritizing of the Union above all else. I could hardly stomach the thought.

Cara was already back in the kitchen, banging pots and pans about, and I was reluctant to disturb her with requests for alternate reading material. My indecision lasted only a moment before the front door opened and Wendell walked in holding a disorderly pile of envelopes.

"Mr. Phillips," Cara said, rushing to meet him. "Give me the lot of that, won't you?"

"So many letters, Cara," he said, his tone weary as he handed her the stack.

Cara paid no heed to his exhaustion as she attempted to

engage him. "Friends and foes, both, ain't it?" She waved the letters in the air.

Her words elicited a small chuckle from him, and I could see that he found her as delightful as I.

"Isn't it always just that way, Cara?" He smiled politely as he turned toward the parlor and she returned to the kitchen. When he caught sight of me seated on the divan, his cheeks instantly rose with joy, gladdening my own heart. "My little Birdie." He walked into the room and kissed the crown of my head. "You are a sight to behold," he said looking down at me. "But," he hesitated a moment, studying my face, "you are in added pain today."

I wondered what it was about my bearing that had given me away. "It is not so much worse than usual," I answered. "To what do I owe the pleasure of your afternoon return?"

He appeared to waffle then, glancing away toward the window behind me, as if he was unsure whether to share whatever had sent him home midday. It was the gesture of a gentleman reluctant to burden a delicate lady with unpleasant news. But then his eyes were back upon me with me purpose. We both knew that withholding any news would only cause me more distress.

"They say Higginson is to be arrested." He pulled a side chair from its place and moved it closer, catty-corner to where I sat. "For his part in the Friday night riot at the courthouse, the murder of that marshal, Batchelder. They won't have enough evidence to convict," he added without worry, "but the rest of us must seize the opportunity to publicize whatever we can."

Of all those who could provoke bystanders and cause a stir, Thomas Wentworth Higginson was certainly at the front of the group. He was one of the more outspoken abolitionists in our circle, militant really, and overtly aggressive.

"His arrest may actually be a boon for the Cause," I agreed.

"Yes, and I had been thinking of touring about later to drum up support," he said.

"And you came to see me so we wouldn't pass the day without laying eyes on each other? You can't manage without me for even a single day, Gra?" I was surprised to find myself resurrecting my old pet name for him and teasing him despite my downcast state.

He reached for my hand, covering it with his warmer one. "I've just come from Richard Dana's," he said, rubbing his free hand against his forehead. "He was attacked yesterday."

I gasped at the news, my hand leaping to my mouth in surprise.

"He departed for his office following the court's decision," Wendell said, "figuring to avoid any adversity from the mob and to transcribe the contents of his closing statement for the *Evening Traveler*. He was passing Allen's Oyster Saloon when he caught movement from the periphery of his vision. The next he knew, he was lying on the pavement with pain in his head. It's lucky some concerned passersby arrived to assist him."

"How hideous," I exclaimed. "To think of additional distress suffered yesterday for any good man is nearly unbearable."

"Indeed," Wendell agreed. "Lloyd believes the culprits were off-duty marshals. In all likelihood, they were celebrating Burns's return to slavery at the saloon when they saw Mr. Dana walking past the window. It was a perfect opportunity for them to show Mr. Dana precisely what they thought of his assisting the fugitive."

"He'll be all right then?" I pushed, desperate for reassurance about anything at all.

"It will take some time. A couple of his teeth have been chipped, but the head will mend."

"What is next for us all, Wendell?" I asked, wondering if we would ever win this fight.

"Oh!" he answered, as if remembering something. He reached into his breast pocket and extracted two slender rectangular papers. "I wanted to bring you these."

"What is it?" I asked.

He sighed, adding to my confusion. "I bought them weeks ago. Theater tickets—to surprise you. But the performance is tonight, and clearly there is too much to be done for me to attend. I thought that with great care, you might attend and take Phebe."

"The theater? I cannot go to the theater!" I was appalled by the suggestion. "There is work for *you* to do," I scoffed. "While, what, I fritter about seeking diversion and entertainment?" I was sorry to have grown snippy, but he should have known better than that.

"No. Of course I am aware. It's just," he looked down at the tickets in his hand. "It's that actress, Anna Cora Mowatt."

"The tickets are for *Ingomar*?" I asked, thinking of the production at the Howard Athenaeum. "Oh, Wendell."

It was a lovely gesture indeed. Wendell knew my admiration for Mrs. Mowatt, the first American woman to write for the professional stage and one so bold as to cast females in various male roles. She was a young widow soon to be married again, and she was on her farewell tour. That evening, I realized, was the one meant to be her very last performance.

"Oh, Wendell," I said again, "the tickets must have been dear." They would have been charging extra surely, for that night. "I would have been thrilled under different circumstances, but I can hardly go watch her portray Parthenia while our nation, our beings, our very existences, are in crisis."

"Yes, yes," he said, nodding along with me, "I somewhat expected as much."

We were interrupted then by a pounding on the front door.

Cara emerged immediately from the kitchen, rubbing her hands with a rag.

"I say, someone's anxious to see you today, ain't they?" She looked back at us and then pulled at the door.

In bounded William Lloyd Garrison and Edmund Quincy behind him.

"So sorry, Cara!" Lloyd said as he hurried past her and came at us in the parlor. "There's talk of a mob," he declared. "Coming here, to your house, Phillips."

"A mob?" I demanded. "What for? The beastly slavery sympathizers already won the day, haven't they?"

Edmund stepped in then. "It's the truckmen," he explained. Edmund was an editor of *The National Anti-Slavery Standard* and also assisted Lloyd in editing *The Liberator* from time to time. Wendell had known him since their days at Harvard. As a result of Edmund's journalistic interests, he had become well-acquainted with a vast array of Boston's less-savory individuals, and I was inclined to trust his information.

"Ah, yes," Wendell responded with pointed calm, rising to shake hands with each of the men. "That was the other rumor I was just planning to mention to Ann. I was hoping I might convince her to vacate the premises for the evening."

"Vacate?" I asked.

"It's about Batchelder," Lloyd explained as he turned toward me. "When Wendell left the court yesterday with Higginson, it created the impression that they were in cahoots. Now mischief-makers are saying Higginson and Phillips together were responsible for the marshal's death. And," his eyes were back on Wendell, "your speech from Faneuil Hall is the one best remembered from the meeting the night that he died."

I began to wonder if Wendell had truly purchased the theater tickets weeks earlier, or if he knew how difficult it would be to persuade me to abandon my home in the event of unrest.

"Let them come," I responded, looking up at the three of them. "I will not be cowed by their bullying."

Edmund lowered himself beside me on the divan.

"Please, Ann," he said as he pushed his eyeglasses higher on his narrow nose. "Batchelder held a second job as a truckman, and his employer, Peter Dunbar, is causing a stir, rallying up the others. But if the house is empty when they arrive, there will be no cause for violence."

"With apologies," I told my friend, "I understand your nonresistance position, and you, too, Lloyd, but I will not be run out of my own home. Let them come," I said again.

I realized then that Cara was still standing in the small foyer, watching us anxiously.

"Take Cara," I said. "Perhaps bring her to Mrs. Gwynn's."

Cara nodded vigorously at the suggestion, her eyes wide. Perhaps this was her first indication of what she'd gotten herself into, coming to work in the home of Ann and Wendell Phillips.

"But Ann," Wendell said, "I cannot stay."

"Then do not stay." I shrugged with bravado I did not feel. "As you said, there is work to be done. I will be fine." My heart pounded at the idea of what might unfold, but I was on the side of righteousness, and I would not be daunted. That we should be victimized because Wendell gave a powerful speech was an outrage. If I left the house that night, how many more times would I be wrested from my home by those who would see us fail?

Wendell released a loud breath. He knew I would not be swayed. "I shan't leave Ann." He glanced at me with a fondness in his eyes, his admiration settling me more firmly into my position. Turning to Lloyd, he added "I will make new arrangements so I might do what work I can from the house. Collect some of our men as guards, if you would."

"Indeed," Lloyd answered, pulling a small folio from his breast pocket and flipping pages in search of an entry. "Ah!" he declared, landing on whatever he'd been seeking.

Another knock at the door. Poor Cara nearly jumped to the ceiling at the sound.

"It's fine, Cara," Wendell said, making his way to the entry and smiling kindly at her. "Mobsters rarely knock," he had the audacity to joke.

He opened the door to reveal Theodore Parker with Francis Hart, another member of the BVC.

"We've been to the police," Theodore said as he and Mr. Hart strode inside, each shaking hands with Wendell. "They're aware of the situation and will be sending a man to watch the house."

"Francis!" Lloyd declared in delight. "I'd only a moment ago been looking for your address. Perfect."

It was easy to see why Lloyd had thought of Francis Hart as a guard for the evening. He was young and broad-shouldered and so tall that his head rose several inches higher than even Wendell's.

Lloyd began barking directions then, always most at home in the role of commander. "Teddy, you'll drop Cara down the road and then round up the others. Edmund, find some dark cloth and start covering the windows."

"Come," Wendell said, beckoning Edmund toward the stairs and the extra linens that we kept in a closet on the second floor.

"Francis," Lloyd called, "you have a pistol on you?"

"Always," Francis nodded, reaching toward his waist.

"Good, good," Lloyd said absently, glancing again toward the window. "Teddy will make sure the others arrive prepared as well. This house will be a fortress tonight. But now," he said, looking toward me, "let's get you some ink. Whitsunday comes but once a year, and we must take advantage of the full churches. Those sermons aren't going to write themselves."

AS THE HOURS TICKED ON, VIGILANCE Committee members came and went from the house, taking turns acting as our own small army against possible intrusion. Each man who entered came prepared with a weapon. Meanwhile, by the evening's fading light, we drafted sermons that would be put forth the following day.

Higginson would be speaking at the Free Church at Brinsley Hall, home of Worcester Freedom Club, provided he was not yet arrested. His speech would advocate making Worcester truly free by commanding that the populous cease hiding fugitives and rather bring them out into the open. Instead of helping refugees onward to Canada, Higginson would declare, residents must openly refuse to comply with the Fugitive Slave Law and make any runaways free right there in Worcester for all to see. Theodore Parker would deliver an address called "The New Crime Against Humanity" at the Music Hall, campaigning for the creation of organizations to preserve personal liberty and states rights. James Freeman Clarke would perform something similar at the Church of the Disciples, Octavius Brooks would do the same at Frothingham, and so on.

It turned out that Peter Dunbar's mob never quite materialized. There was some shouting in the street after dark, the hurling about of epithets. Perhaps there were a few bodies more than usual milling about in the nighttime shadows. But the house was all lit up from the inside, near bursting with the energy of our collective ideas as we put our minds together to push for better times. I like to think the naysayers could see the force of it all from well down the road, that even they, in their ignorance, knew better than to come and interfere. If it was simply the presence of many able-bodied men weakening their resolve, so be it. But I choose to believe the former. And so it was that we were able to return to our plans about how to save Anthony Burns and all those in similar straits.

COLETTE

Richmond, June 1854

Adelia was standing behind me, pulling and grunting, struggling to fasten my day dress as it strained atop my corset. Neither one of us said what we were both thinking. Confronted by my reflection in the looking glass across from me, I could see plain as day the way the rose-colored fabric strained against my bosom.

Ever since that night with the Cowardins and Andersons, Elton had recommenced nightly visits to my chamber. I could do the math as well as anyone. It wouldn't do to mention anything of course, not yet, as I had only missed one monthly. Meantime, I knew to continue being sweet as locust honey, doting on Elton to save myself the consequences of my husband feeling anything less than adored.

Since the resumption of our nightly coupling, I had begun making inroads with him. How agreeable he would become once sated, so long as he had his tablets with him. He would not speak to me about the purpose of his new medicine, and so I stopped asking. Instead, I focused on my own circumstances.

On one of our first nights reunited, I convinced Elton to allow Adelia additional time attending to my wardrobe, rather than forcing her to toil away the afternoons in the kitchen as she'd been doing. I was near dying from boredom each day, being kept so isolated, but what I told Elton was that her increased presence was required for my aesthetic upkeep. Next, I persuaded him that I should be permitted brief walks out of doors, provided I remain on our own property. And owing to my strong negotiation skills, or perhaps the three tablets he had swallowed a few minutes prior, he even agreed to allow a visit from my *Maman* and my sister, both recently returned from France.

"That will do," I finally told Adelia, when I could hardly take more of the squeezing and yanking coming from behind me.

"But Mistress," she protested, meeting my eyes in the looking glass, her hands still holding the back of the dress. "These eye hooks won't close."

"Let it alone. Just pass me a sash so it won't show."

She did as I bid, clucking her disapproval even as she carefully arranged the fabric across my upper back.

"Better yet, if you don't mind . . ." She held up a finger and hurried to an armoire in the corner where she extracted a cream-colored shawl. "That be just what you need," she told me, pulling up her chin in satisfaction as she evaluated my reflection, and I daresay, it did just the trick.

Adelia followed me down to the parlor, where I planned to await the arrival of Maman and Fay. They were not due for another hour yet, and I felt almost childish in my excitement, racing into the room to stand by for their appearance. They'd been abroad near a year, visiting with Maman's sisters and the family of Fay's new husband. In my recent seclusion, my longing to see them had grown intense.

"I best be checking on the luncheon," Adelia said, turning toward the back of the house and leaving me to myself as I settled into one of the room's upholstered chairs. The day before, I had abandoned a book of poems on the marble turtle-top table, and I retrieved it to help pass the time while I waited.

I was onto the third sonnet in a series when there was a knock at the room's open door. I looked up to see the house boy, Tandey, awaiting my attention.

"If Mistress don't mind," he said, "I've been to the post." He held up the collection of parcels and envelopes in his hand.

"That's fine, Tandey." I beckoned him into the cavernous room. "Go on and leave it on the console there for Master Elton," I told him, returning my attention to the poetry. It was only after another few minutes of reading that I remembered Tandey often collected a newspaper for Elton. The thought propelled me instantly from my seat, and I hastened toward the console. Ever since our last dinner party, I'd been undertaking to find that article Elton saw about Anthony. But it was to no avail. Elton likely used the pages as kindling once he finished reading it, frustrated that the matter was resurfacing and making headlines. I'd been stewing in my own desperation ever since, wondering how I might learn of Anthony's fate. Yet, for the many days that elapsed since, I failed to collect any news, surreptitiously or otherwise.

But *ça y est*! There at the bottom of the pile sat the day's issue of the *Richmond Daily Dispatch*.

My eyes quickly roved over the paper. I saw James Cowardin's name, as editor, at the top, followed by advertisements for Kent, Paine & Kent dry goods. There were offers of rewards for missing slaves, announcements of houses for rent, an article about the French consul, another about Spanish troops bound for Cuba. I grew frustrated as each passing headline failed to mention the news I sought. But then there it was, the header same as the last, "The Fugitive Slave Case."

My heart raced as I read on. The article explained that the fugitive at issue was indeed Anthony Burns. He had been apprehended in Boston, and his entire case had already been adjudicated. The claim of his master, Charles Suttle, had been granted, and Anthony had already set sail upon a vessel to carry him back to Virginia. He would land first in Norfolk, and then would be loaded onto another vessel to finish the trip to Richmond. The Northern commissioner's decision, along with testimony from the case, had been reported in the *Boston Post*, and the *Dispatch* announced it was reprinting the very same material.

My eyes hurried on in a fever to learn more. I waded through the judge's lengthy ramblings, grumbling as I realized he talked more about the purpose of the laws being applied than about Anthony. My dread was replaced by horror as I read the text that followed the court's opinion.

The good people of Boston upheld their end of the bargain between slave states and free. Although a mob approaching 50,000 people assembled in the streets to spectate as the Negro was carried off, no violence erupted. Despite some insults to police and minor scuffles, the Federal Government was successful in demonstrating its power sufficiently to control the crowd. William (Billy) Jones, a witness at trial, was arrested for using forceful, inciting language. In attendance was the entire First Brigade, including Lancers and Dragoons, all on parade with the Marshal's guard. Citizens of Boston also came forward to assist in maintaining the enforcement of the law. This turnout of militia showed that any rescue attempt would have been in vain. The fugitive was placed on the steamer Morris, the people of Massachusetts having done their duty to the Union and the Constitution.

The fugitive perked up with delight after being told he was to be sent home. Reports state that until the decision was rendered, and in the days leading up to it, Burns had appeared sullen and in despair. He was likely terrified by the notion that he might be left to fend for himself amongst the rabid abolitionists of the North. His demeanor was quiet and concerned for days, but not so once he discovered he would be journeying home. Dressed in a fine new suit of clothes, paid for by funds raised by the Marshal's guard, he walked out into the crowded streets toward the wharf and declared himself "de star ob de 'casion." Burns was outfitted also with a new breastpin, hat, and boots. The escort he received to traverse State Street was like none ever enjoyed by Sambo. After the steamer departed, he must have been elated to watch Boston fade into the horizon, along with whatever terrible fate might there have awaited him.

As the journey continued, Burns complained of some seasickness. Likely his stomach was upset from the candy and oysters he had been fed by the Marshals prior to his departure.

The Marshals have described the fugitive as a Negro of "advanced intellect for his kind," so it is of little surprise that he felt relief at the prospect of returning to his life in Virginia. They reported that Burns is a religious man who did not employ profane language.

Burns is expected to arrive in Norfolk by Friday. The papers in Norfolk recommend that the officers traveling from Boston be shown appreciation at the time, perhaps in the form of a fine Virginia dinner.

I read the entire article over again, wiping at the tears beneath my eyes. I hardly even knew which outrage to focus on first. To think of Anthony, having made it all the way to Boston! I imagined him up there in the North, with a paying job and rooms of his own to rent. I thought he must have found a church he liked, and friends. Maybe a special woman, I considered with a foolish wince. But then, only to be imprisoned for days, studied like a curiosity, a matter for entertainment of onlookers from North and South—how he would have hated that.

I shuddered to think what would await him upon his return to Richmond. I was not acquainted with his master, but I didn't doubt the man would do his level best to make an example of Anthony.

I scanned over the article yet again, my indignation growing as I reread the quote they attributed to Anthony, saying he called himself "de star ob de 'casion." He would never have said that. Certainly not with that rough country diction. The papers surely created that picture of a happy-go-lucky, dim-witted Negro intentionally, so intent were they on maintaining the fiction that we Southerners somehow lifted up the colored population through slavery, providing them with life's necessities in ways they surely could never achieve for themselves. We could all keep patting ourselves on the backs down here, so long as we could hold onto the idea in our minds of the Negro as simple and helpless, couldn't we?

Before I had time to ruminate further, I heard the knocker banging against the front door. I shoved the paper back beneath the pile of letters, knowing Elton would be looking for it when he returned from his day at Shockoe Bottom, and then I hurried back to my chair.

It was only a moment before Tandey lead my visitors into the room and Maman was exclaiming with her usual exuberance.

"Coco!" She held her arms out to me. "*Ma fille*, come to me!" she called, her accent more pronounced now that she'd spent an extended period with her family in Paris.

It had been so long since I'd seen her that for once, I welcomed her theatrics and sentimentality. I nearly fell into her arms, allowing myself to be enveloped by her floral perfume and the many layers of yellow silk surrounding her petite frame.

"Maman!" my younger sister reprimanded from behind her, "You'll suffocate her!"

"Nonsense." My mother waved a hand dismissively and then squeezed me once more before stepping back to hold me at arm's length. "This face. I have missed it, eh?"

We regarded each other for a moment. It was comforting to see that Maman was her usual self. Her skin was still smooth and dewy, her rich caramel hair coifed just behind her head with tendrils falling on either side. I watched her blue eyes sweep over me and wondered what she would notice.

"You were all she talked about with Aunt Marie and Aunt Therese," Fay said, coming forward to give me a quick embrace as well. Fay was as fetching as always, her hair the same shade of yellow as my own, but always so much fuller, as if she'd been given a double portion. She was outfitted in a flattering blue day dress, and her cheeks were just slightly flushed.

"'You must hear about *ma fille* Colette,'" Fay said, imitating my mother's accent, "'*trés magnifique*, the face of angel. And her husband,'" she continued, waving her hands about and parodying my mother in that good-natured way that always allowed her to say what-all she pleased. "'*Ooh lá lá*, so 'andsome,'" she finished, dropping the H just like my mother would.

"Please," I quipped as I roll my eyes heavenward. I knew better than to comment on Elton's appearance, even with my own family, but we were all well aware the match hadn't been based on his physical attributes.

"Coco!" Maman clicked her tongue behind her painted lips, reminding me of my manners.

"And how was it with Henri's family?" I asked my sister, hoping her marriage was still serving her better than my own was me. Henri's personal wealth was far less than Elton's, but he did well enough as a merchant that my persistent sister had been able to convince our parents to allow the match.

"Pfft." She waved a hand in the air. "Let's just say I under-stand even better now what drove my dear husband away from his home country."

"And where is Delly?" my mother demanded, her attach-ment to Adelia almost as strong as my own.

"Here I am, Mistress Élise," Adelia said, entering the room with a tray of lemonades. "Thought y'all might like refreshment."

I was bursting to tell Adelia what I learned from the paper about Anthony, but Maman would never have abided it. Heaven forbid I jeopardize any part of my hard-won social status.

"You look well, my girl," Maman said as she approached Adelia and helped herself to one of the full glasses on the tray. Had Maman been in the safety of her own home, she might have embraced Adelia the same as she had me, but not here.

"Thank you, Mistress," Adelia said, and I could detect the strain on her features in seeing Maman and Fay. She missed our old life outside the city. Living in this house hadn't been easy on her either.

Maman let out a soft sigh, as though she could hear my thoughts. It hardly mattered anyhow, as she was powerless to do anything in my favor, or Adelia's.

When we finally made our way to the dining room for luncheon, everything had already been set out. But the beauty of the meal did little to allay my distraction. All I could think of was Anthony. *Where would they send him? Would he be badly hurt? Would I ever lay eyes on him again?*

"What is it, Coco?" Maman demanded halfway through the meal. She had always been attuned to my moods.

"Forgive me, Maman. I've just missed you and Fay both so much."

"Nonsense," she responded as she set her fork down. "You must enjoy this beautiful life. So much grace and elegance." She spread her arms wide, gesturing to the room around her, the chandeliers, the crystal glasses on the table. "It is not duty alone," she said, "you must learn to enjoy. Once a baby comes, it will be better. You will find joy again."

"Maman!" Fay snapped, "You're like to make her feel worse, talking about breeding and what-all."

I put down my fork then. "Well, in fact," I started, looking toward the doorway and then back to Fay, "it's only been a couple of weeks yet, but I do suspect . . ." I trailed off to let them figure out the rest.

"*Ma chérie!*" Maman exclaimed. "What wonderful news!"

She made as if to say more, but I cut her right off. "I've not told Elton yet."

"No, of course!" She appeared affronted at the very idea. "It is much too soon! But we must do all we can to assist the *bébé*. You are taking tonics?"

I shared a quick look with Fay at Maman's faithful reliance on tonics for every possible condition. Fay simply smirked and lifted her water glass as I responded, "Not yet, Maman, but I do believe that's about to change?"

"*Absolument,*" Maman agreed.

LATER THAT AFTERNOON, THE THREE OF us visited the apothecary so that Maman might advise me on the tonics and such. Truth be told, it had taken so long for a seed to settle inside my womb that I was willing to do whatever Maman, or anyone else, might suggest to keep the little babe thriving.

It was my first trip to town in months. I worried I would suffer repercussions from Elton for participating in this excursion, but I couldn't very well tell Maman I'd been under house arrest. Thankfully the druggist closest to the house was not the elderly Mr. Millspaugh, who had employed Anthony, but Mr. Hedgewood, just down on Main Street.

Maman was holding bottles of Ayers Cherry Pectoral and Lucien's Ginger Tonic as she interrogated Mr. Hedgewood.

She was fixated on a vial of Dr. Townsend's Sarsaparilla and whether it was the genuine article. Fay was busy browsing the shelves, so I took the opportunity to walk back out to the street. The sidewalk was crowded with all manner of people, slaves out marketing for their masters, women in fine dresses dallying outside the milliner's, merchant men hurrying to and fro with various goods. Then I saw a paperboy. He was making his way toward me, holding a thick stack of newspapers. The sign hanging from his neck said he was selling the *Enquirer*. I wondered if the *Enquirer* might contain information not reported by the *Dispatch*, perhaps more recent news.

I flagged down the boy and reached into my coin purse for a penny. "Paper! Paper please!" I called to him as he approached.

Just as he reached me, Maman and Fay emerged from the apothecary. "There you are!" Maman said as she presented a basket with three bottles inside, shoving it into my hands. Then she turned to the paperboy. "No, no, thank you, young man," she said, waving him away and looking back at me. "You mustn't read the news or anything else that might distress you. Only the most peaceful and delightful reading, if any at all. We will take no chances, hmm?"

As usual, I found myself listening obediently to whatever Maman commanded. I would have to wait to find out more about what was to become of Anthony.

ANTHONY

At Sea, June 1854

Anthony didn't have a name to offer Master Charles. Even if he did, he would have kept it to himself anyhow. He wasn't fixing to betray the captain who sailed him north from Richmond for a kindness the man didn't even know he'd done. Anthony figured Master Charles was telling tales anyhow and wouldn't truly let him be free, no matter what he said.

Master Charles finally quit asking and just left Anthony locked in the cabin. All that first day on the cutter, he stayed there by his lonesome. The next morning, Marshal Coolidge came and said Anthony could have a moment to walk on the upper deck. The marshal brought him up the narrow stairwell toward the bright sunlight and the salty June air. Soon as the man released his arm, Anthony marched clear across the wooden decking to the ship's rail. The water below was a deeper blue than he'd expected, with white capping off the waves. Out in the distance, he spotted land, just a hazy lump of gray against the clear sky. The ocean air was ripe in his nose as he squinted against the sun and looked back down to the water. He wondered how long it would take a body to sink down under those waves. Would death come suddenly, or would there be fierce suffering in the minutes that he struggled for air? He searched for the courage to throw himself over the edge, to do one last act of freedom. But now that he was there, with opportunity to climb up and fly away, he couldn't call up the bravery.

"Don't even think about it," Marshal Coolidge said, taking a step closer.

Anthony glanced up, surprised the man knew his mind. The marshal needn't have worried, as it seemed that both Anthony's fear and his Christian duty had his feet planted firmly on the creaky deck anyhow. Coolidge, the youngest marshal in the group, was the only guard who had showed him any kindness, making sure he had enough to eat and suggesting the fresh air. Anthony nodded back at the man so he wouldn't worry none.

Then walking up from the other side of the deck came Master Charles.

"Tony!" he shouted, like he was filled with delight. He was holding a half-eaten biscuit in his hand, and he bit off a wide hunk as he approached. "Just taking in a spot of sunshine?" he asked, making it sound as if they were just two white gentlemen friends.

As Master Charles talked, Anthony could see the lumps of dough churning round in his open mouth. He remembered his mistress from one of his hirings so many years ago, Miss Horton, always telling her children to swallow their food before they spoke. He wondered if old Mistress Suttle ever told the same to Master Charles before she died.

"Yes, sir," Anthony answered, looking down to the wooden planks beneath his feet and wondering how his mind could wander to something as slight as table manners at a time where his whole life was uncertain. As Anthony waited to see what else Master Charles would say, he hoped to learn something of the man's plans for him.

Master Charles just stood there across from him though, considering. He took his time about it, rocking back on his heels and looking long at Anthony. Finally, he tossed the last of the biscuit into his mouth and wiped his hands together to rid himself of the crumbs.

"Tell me, Tony," he said, his voice still friendly as he stepped closer and put a hand to the railing. He turned his light eyes toward the land in the distance. "What do you think I ought to do with you?" he asked.

Anthony couldn't help himself from speaking his honest thoughts, like he'd near always done when Master Charles asked. "I suppose you're fixing to sell me south, on account of what I done, sir."

"You've caused me great expense," he said, with disappointment on his leathery face. "You know that, don't you?"

"I do now, yes, sir," Anthony answered.

"The lawyers' fees alone, Tony," Master Charles said, as he pulled on his beard.

"Yessir."

"More than $400," he kept on. "How do you suppose I'm going to make up for that? I'm not a rich man, Tony."

"No, sir."

"We're almost to New York," he said next.

"Sir?" Anthony couldn't think why Master Charles would want to take him to New York.

"Not for you, Tony," he said with a little laugh. "Mr. Brent and I will be departing there and leaving you in the good hands of the marshals. It seems sea travel doesn't much agree with my constitution. Nor William's."

Anthony glanced at Marshal Coolidge, who was still standing off to the side, listening in on them. He wondered what the other guard, Marshal Butman, might like to do to him without Master Charles there. Marshal Coolidge turned his eyes away then, like he knew why Anthony was worried.

Master Charles followed Anthony's gaze to the marshal. "Tony here won't give you boys any trouble," Master Charles said. "Ain't that right, Tony?"

"No sir," Anthony answered again. "No bother."

"They don't tell you about it being so hot in the North," Master Charles said, pulling a kerchief from his pocket to mop his brow. "I'll see you back in old Virginny," he said, raising an eyebrow for a moment before he turned to walk away. He was whistling that same song, "Carry Me Back to Old Virginny," the one the hateful army men sang in jest when Anthony boarded the *Morris*. If he needed any warning that Master Charles intended to punish him good, well, he had it now.

IN ONLY A FEW HOURS, THEY REACHED New York. Anthony was locked back in the cabin by then, but even from inside, he could feel the slowing of the vessel and the clanging about as they anchored. Being again so close to free soil with no possibility of reaching it was almost more than his sorry soul could bear.

There was no chair in the ship's cabin where he was being kept, only the pallet on the floor, covered with a rough blanket, and a fancy standing clock that didn't seem to belong in the room. The ship didn't tarry long in the choppy seas near New York, waiting only long enough for Master Charles and Master William to board another vessel that would carry them to shore. It felt like only a short breath before the vessel started up again, as though the captain couldn't ferry them south fast enough. Anthony sat there on the pallet inside, his legs stretched out in front of him, and he thought hard about how alone he was. As his stomach roiled and rebelled against the rocking and swaying of the boat, he hoped he wouldn't grow as ill as he'd done on the journey north. At least then, there had been reward waiting on the other end. With the way his insides still churned in response to the ship's movements, it seemed he was no more fit for sea travel than Master Charles.

With his eyes closed in a weak attempt to shut out the rocking, he wondered if his friends in Boston had already forgotten him. But he didn't get to ponder long before he heard a key in the door, and then in came Marshal Butman, just as he'd expected, charging forward with Marshals Godfrey and Black behind him.

"On your feet, boy!" he shouted.

Anthony shot up off the pallet and stood at attention with his heart pounding in his chest. He hoped the marshal wouldn't do enough damage to anger Master Charles, but his blood ran cold just the same. There was plenty a man could do that wouldn't leave a mark.

"Now, Anthony," Marshal Butman started, and Anthony's fear grew bigger in spite of himself. He backed so close to the pallet that there was no farther to go. Seeing him bump against the bed like that, the marshal laughed. "You scared of me, boy?" He took another step closer.

Anthony didn't know how to answer. Say yes and make him angry. Say no and make him angry too. Some men always just looking to find their fury howsoever they can.

"Finally showing some respect, ain't he?" Marshal Butman said, turning to his friends. "We're not here to rough you up, boy. Not yet." He stepped even closer then, and Anthony stood still as he could. With a man like Butman, you never knew for sure whether he was speaking the truth.

Marshal Black moved forward then, putting his hands on his hips. He was slimmer than Marshal Butman with small dark eyes, sharp like a weasel's.

"You can save yourself a lot of trouble, boy," Marshal Black said, "if you tell us who helped you get to Boston, who met you there once you arrived, where they hid you."

There wasn't a single fact Anthony saw fit to share with those men.

"Maybe," Marshal Butman said, like he'd had a new idea, "we can get you set free if you tell us what we want to know." He looked back and forth to the other marshals and then pulled a snuff tin from his pocket. "Don't you think, fellows?" he asked, opening up the tin. "We could make something of a trade. If you start sharing your secrets, why then your freedom would be a matter of national importance. All you'd have to do is come back to Boston and help us find more fugitives like you. You'd like that, wouldn't you, living in Boston permanently?"

Anthony knew better than to put stock in what the men were saying. He'd never betray those who'd helped him, no matter what it'd get him. And anyhow, he could guess pretty easy what would happen to him if he started sharing what he knew. He'd be prisoner all the same, except now with plenty of his friends being prisoner too. Well, no sir.

When he hesitated to answer, Marshal Black started again.

"You know, we made an arrangement with another Negro like you. He's become a real rich darkie back in Boston. Wouldn't you like to be like him, Anthony?"

Anthony was quiet a moment, trying to figure how to refuse without waking the monster inside any of them. "Well, sirs," he finally said, playing the fool, "I do wish I had something to tell y'all. I sure did enjoy my time in Boston, but it looks like it's just my time to go on home."

Marshal Butman sighed long and loud at that. He kept on with his staring though, silent, like if he waited long enough, maybe Anthony would change his mind and start double-crossing all his friends. But no, Anthony would not, not after how hard those friends had tried to help him. Finally, Marshal Butman turned to the others.

"Forget him," he said to the men. "Let the bastard get what he deserves."

Anthony made the mistake then of beginning to relax. After the other marshals walked from the room, Marshal Butman turned back.

"You think you're so smart," he said, pulling a club from where it was fastened at his belt. "With your book learning and your fancy city friends. Don't kid yourself that they'll save you. You're just one more Negro, and you're not fooling a one of us."

Then he raised up that club and before Anthony could even cower, the marshal thrashed it hard against his arm. Anthony fell backward onto the pallet, the pain smarting all the way up into his shoulder.

"That's all you got?" Marshal Butman looked down at him, disappointed, it seemed, that his victim had fallen so fast.

He raised the club again, and Anthony felt himself curl right into a ball, waiting for whatever blows were to come. Butman made a noise in the back of his throat, like a sound of disgust.

"Gutless," he said. "Like all of them." And then he turned for the door.

He locked Anthony in the cabin, leaving him with only a throbbing arm and his own despair.

COLETTE

Richmond, June 1854

I was just finishing my eggs and bacon when I had to leap from my seat and run from the dining room. I reached only as far as the corridor before I began retching right there, my breakfast reemerging atop the polished floor.

"Oh, Mistress!" Adelia appeared from behind me and hurried to where I was crouched over the mess. She took hold of my loose hair and held tight as I continued to forfeit my meal.

"Get a basin," I begged raggedly between heaves, not wanting to further befoul the floorboards.

"Come, now," she said, rubbing my back and ignoring my request. "You just let it out. You'll see it soon pass." Adelia had helped enough expectant slave women back at my parents' home, so she knew a bit about pregnancy.

We stayed like that a few minutes more, she and I, staring down at my regurgitations. And then just as suddenly as it began, my stomach seemed to settle itself.

"I think I'm all right now," I said as I stood and wiped the back of my palm across my mouth.

Adelia's lips twisted in disapproval of the gesture. "Mistress," she said glancing down at my wet hand, "let me fetch you a cloth."

"It's fine. Just tell Tandey to come for the mess if you would." I was glad Elton had left for Main Street already. He was so full of joy at the pregnancy, and I hardly wanted to damper his emotions by letting him see the uglier sides of growing a baby.

It had been only three days since I'd told him. Perhaps it was uncouth to share the news so early, but just as I'd predicted, revealing my condition had the near immediate effect of reinstating me to my former esteem within the household. Adelia's kitchen chores were abolished *tout de suite*, as Elton insisted I be kept contented at all times. He only wanted to know how else he could cater to my needs. The list inside my head was plenty long, but I shared only a few requests—the very first of which resulted in permission for me to come and go from the house just as I pleased.

"I'd like to change my dress and head to town," I told her. I could hardly stand to be inside that house one minute more than necessary.

AS WE APPROACHED THE DRY GOODS, I caught sight of the newspaper cart just beyond the cobbler's shop and marched through the blazing sunshine straight toward it.

Each day the papers held some mention of Anthony, but mostly to discuss the politics of the situation, rather than reporting on where he was or what was to become of him. The papers were saying that the whole affair proved why it was high time for the South to secede from the Union. There was the usual boasting about the South being more wholesome than the North, claiming the North was all full of crime, disease, intemperance, vice. But there was a new sense of panic to the articles, as well, a worry about the North fixing to destroy the

Southern way of life, the luxuries and privileges. Anthony's case had increased public outrage up North about slavery, and any more cases like his might inspire changes to the law that would put limitations on slaveholding. One quote in particular from the *Enquirer* kept repeating itself in my head: "We rejoice at the recapture of Burns, but a few more such victories and the South is undone." Indeed.

I was still rather amazed that the Virginia-born man I'd been secretly educating only a few months earlier was now a national sensation. His name had become shortcut for declaring a political position. People couldn't hardly stop talking about his escape and the rendition and what-all it meant for our nation.

The article I'd seen in the *Enquirer* days earlier had reported he might arrive in Richmond any moment, and I was desperate for an update. I lifted a copy of the *Dispatch* from the pile on the cart and handed my penny to the young man behind the cart. Adelia and I then hastened toward the benches in Capital Square. Under the blessed shade of an oversize oak, I passed Adelia my parasol and sat myself down on a bench to read.

The Fugitive Burns

Burns arrived in the city of Norfolk yesterday. The papers of Norfolk report that the fugitive is heartily ashamed of the bad company he fell into in Boston. Genteel negroes in Virginia lose caste among their own class when they become intimate with such trifling characters as Theodore Parker, Wendell Phillips, etc.

I noticed from the corner of my eye that Adelia was looking over my shoulder, anxious too, for news of our friend.

"Delly," I scolded. It wouldn't do for passersby to see her reading the paper over her mistress's shoulder.

She stepped backwards from the bench, allowing herself an annoyed huff, and I returned my attention to the article.

The revenue cutter Morris, *helmed by Captain Sands, arrived in Hampton Roads Friday night. Towed up Saturday morning by steamer engineer, Burns was brought ashore under charge of the officers who accompanied him from Boston and presented at the offices of Simon S. Stubbs, mayor of Norfolk. The mayor ordered him into the custody of the Jailor. There he stayed until last evening, when he was put aboard the streamer Jamestown. The deputies from Boston were treated to a fine dinner with the mayor in recognition of their effort and exemplary behavior on behalf of the South.*

Upon reaching Richmond, Burns will be presented to Mr. William Brent, his owner's agent, and the man from whom he escaped. There was significant interest amongst the people of Norfolk to get a look at the fugitive, and crowds assembled. No violence or unrest occurred. Burns is reported to be a comely specimen, about twenty-seven years old and very dark skinned. He said he would like to spend the rest of his days in Virginia, but he suffers such shame at his behavior that he can no longer walk with his head held high in front of his owner, his friends, or any who formerly held him in any positive regard. He said he knows he will never again be as happy as he was before he ran away.

"We have to go home," I said, standing before I had even folded the paper.

"Mistress?" Adelia asked.

"Not now. *La discrétion est requise*," I said, reverting to French in my agitated state. We could hardly be discussing the contents of the article out here on the street.

We walked the remainder of the route back to Fifth Street in silence. Normally Adelia and I were rather chatty with each other, but I supposed then that we finally appeared a more typical Richmond sight, just a mistress and her slave, and not the two friends I liked to think we were.

When we finally reached the house and Adelia closed the door behind us, I explained.

"He'll be in Richmond anytime now," I said as I handed her my parasol to be put away. "It may be that he's already here. They made him stay in prison in Norfolk, but I don't reckon it'll be the same here. Seems it'd make the most sense to return him to his owner directly or the agent. That's what the paper said, that the agent would come to collect him."

We were both quiet a moment, still standing there in the foyer. Adelia had a faraway look on her face, and she just kept on shaking her head slowly.

"That'll be some whipping on him," she finally said. "Here," she held out her hand. "I'll take your shawl and reticule on up."

I watched her climb the curved staircase and couldn't miss the way her shoulders hunched as she continued shaking her head. She was making little sounds, like she was talking to herself, or maybe to God, as she went.

Meanwhile, the newspaper was still hot in my hand. I could leave it for Elton, but the pages were crinkled enough to show they'd been read through. Though the pregnancy had placed me back into my husband's good graces, I needed still to take heed, lest I bring his inner bear back from wherever it'd been hibernating.

I hardly had to deliberate long as the front door suddenly opened, and in walked Elton, along with another man.

"Ah, perfect!" he exclaimed with delight at meeting me in the entry. "Let me introduce you," he said, as the other man shut the door behind himself.

"Well, isn't this a pleasant surprise," I answered as brightly as I could manage. Elton's arrival in the middle of a working day was a rare occasion, and I worried what his presence might signify.

"This here," he said, motioning to his companion, "is William Foushee Ritchie, esteemed editor of the *Richmond Enquirer.*"

"Mr. Ritchie, a pleasure," I answered, extending my free hand. The gentleman appeared to be a few years older than my husband. His hair was thick, and his bushy beard showed only a smattering of gray, but his skin was deeply creased and weathered, and his eyes, raw around the edges, signified his more advanced age. Meanwhile, the newspaper I was holding felt increasingly conspicuous.

"Please," he said as he took my other hand, "call me Foushee, as all my friends do."

"Foushee," I repeated, and then looked toward Elton. "Have you eaten? I can have Cook warm some turkey."

Elton waved a hand dismissively. "Nothing, no. We've just come from the Arbour," he told me, referencing the restaurant on 12th and Main where he often met business associates. "The owner, Mr. Allen, advertises with Foushee here, and he was rather keen to spoil us with a number of dishes we didn't even request. Can't say I minded," he added as he rubbed a hand over his rounded middle. "The broiled sora was particularly choice," he added, nodding at Foushee.

"Your husband was kind enough to invite me back for a tour of your beautiful home," Foushee told me as his eyes strayed above my head to the vaulted ceilings and the curved staircase. "I've recently married, and I will be making some improvements to my residence in hopes of satisfying my bride."

At the mention of nuptials, I realized why his name was so familiar. The articles about Foushee's recent wedding to the actress Anna Cora Mowatt had been all over the papers. I'd had to jump past the lengthy accounts day after day, as they detailed the menu, attire, and guest list of the extravagant affair that occurred in New York, or somewhere thereabouts. I was utterly uninterested in the particulars of the party, even if the bride was a well-regarded actress. The incessant reporting on the affair had been noteworthy to me only insofar as it created an additional impediment in finding news about Anthony

"Congratulations," I offered with a smile. "I'll leave you to it then." I hoped I might take my leave without either of them noticing the *Dispatch* in my hand.

"I hope we'll have occasion to meet again," Fosuhee said. "You and my wife have much in common."

"Oh?" I asked, curiosity getting the better of me. I couldn't imagine how I might be similar to the famous actress who had traveled the world writing plays and starring in them. With the exception of a childhood visit to Europe, I'd been stuck in Virginia most of my life.

"Certainly!" he answered. "If your husband will forgive me for saying so, both you and my wife are far too attractive for the old men you married. And I'm sure that's just the beginning of your commonalities."

"Well," I said with a smile, "then you mustn't be surprised when you receive an invitation to dine with us soon."

"Lovely," Foushee answered, while Elton looked on with an affable smile, like I'd done him proud. "And I'll make sure to bring you some better reading material than that drivel." He dipped his head, looking pointedly toward the paper in my hand.

"Oh!" I gasped, as my cheeks immediately heated. "I, well, we were in town, and it just, well, it was the first paper we passed." I was embarrassed to be stumbling over my words and unsure of what I could even say to make this moment less graceless. I couldn't even bring myself to look at Elton.

But then Foushee guffawed. "Ha! I'm just teasing, Mrs.

Randolph. You poor dear. If we are to be friends, you'll have to grow accustomed to my humor."

Elton cleared his throat, growing restless to show off his impressive home to his new friend.

"I look forward to it," I answered as politely as I could, and then I looked over at Elton. "I'll just be in the parlor."

"Good, good," he nodded with a certain deliberateness, as if to reassure me that our recent reconciliation was still in place. Unfortunately, there was little he could do to diminish the fear I'd felt toward him ever since the first night he hit me. I believed I was safe while carrying his child. After that, who could rightly say?

ANTHONY

Richmond, June 1854

When they docked in Richmond, Anthony expected Master William Brent would be waiting, but no one was there to retrieve him. The marshals had plans to stay in a fine hotel for the night, and they got tired of waiting on Master William. After only a short while, they left Anthony with a local officer who brought him straight to the city jail, and there he stayed waiting for ten days.

Finally, Master William did show up, and he brought with him a man named Mr. Robert Lumpkin. Anthony was relieved to see Master William, but the presence of Mr. Lumpkin had him worried he should feel otherwise.

Anthony had never had dealings with Lumpkin directly, but everyone knew him by sight around Richmond parts. With a pockmarked face and a belly that strained the buttons of his shirt, he was not a comely man. His hair was a red-brown that brought to mind the clay in the Virginia soil, though not as smooth. Folks in Richmond called Lumpkin a bully trader for the way he traveled around the country picking up slaves all along the way and keeping them in irons to sell when it suited him. He also ran the slave prison, down there in Shockoe Bottom.

"Don't be expecting any kindness from me, Tony," Master William said as he walked to where Anthony had been collecting rocks in the prison yard. "You've disgraced us all."

"Put your hands behind your back," Lumpkin said, and then he spat on the ground beside Anthony's feet. Anthony did as Lumpkin said, and the officer standing beside them stepped forward, fastening iron cuffs to his wrists. Master William didn't say anything else but just watched Mr. Lumpkin as he pushed Anthony toward the street and a wagon that awaited.

When they arrived at Lumpkin's jail, the officers didn't bring Anthony to the rooms with the other slaves. They put him in a different space that was just for himself. It was on an upper story of the building, and it was more a small nook than a room, only about six feet wide. There wasn't even a real entrance, just a trapdoor to open before climbing inside. Instead of a bed, there was only the crudest bench, taking up nearly the whole space. Anthony thought they'd at least remove the cuffs now that they'd be locking him in. Instead, the guard added shackles to his ankles and left his arms locked behind his back, twisted tight, just as they were.

He could feel the iron rubbing against the bone that bulged from his long-wounded wrist, but worse was the numbing and strain that his arms felt from being pulled into that unnatural position.

At least there was a small window, about the size of three ears of corn, cut into the wall. It didn't do much to ease the stifling summer heat, but leastways he could see daylight. Back when he was hired at the grist mill, he used to walk the portion of Wall Street near Shockoe Creek on his way to work each day, and he'd pass by this jail. "Devil's Half-Acre" is what they all called the parcel of land and the four buildings that were set upon it. There was a tall wire fence surrounding the entire property, with spikes on top, meant to scare anyone who looked up that way and imagined getting out.

There was a two-story brick building on the lot known as the slave pen, about forty feet long, and that's where they put Anthony. From the outside, that slave pen looked just like a chicken coop, and the stench that came off it wasn't that different either. He used to fuss over the fact that they were holding people in a place that barely seemed fit for farm animals. He didn't like to imagine back then that it might be the smell of human waste reaching all the way to the street. But once he was brought inside the jail, he knew two things for certain: that smell was from cruelty alone, and any farm had to be better than where he was.

They left him inside that room for days on end, only bringing one meal each day. The first time they brought food, he begged the guard to remove the shackles so he could eat proper, but the man didn't even turn back to answer before locking the door. So he lowered himself to his knees and bent his mouth down toward the bowl. It turned out that if he didn't want to fall over, he had to lie all the way down to eat. He would lay on his belly, feeling worse than a stray dog, licking at the bowl of scraps they brought. They left a bucket of dirty water where he had to do the same. Nobody came in to help in any way, and so he was forced to relieve himself inside his clothes, and then lie in his own filth day after day.

At some point, lying in all that waste and drinking the dirty water, it got him too sick to even eat the slop they brought. One day, the guard who opened up the small trapdoor to give Anthony his daily rations found him lying belly down on the bench, too weak to move. He opened his eyes halfway and watched as the young guard stepped into the space to take the bowl he'd left the day before. Instead of rushing back out like he usually did, the man stalled.

"Boy!" he barked. "Why's this dish still full?"

Anthony opened his mouth to answer, but the sound he forced out wasn't more than a whimper. He closed his eyes again, too limp to respond. He could sense the guard still there, lingering. After another moment, the man muttered an expletive and left.

Anthony lay there imagining that he would soon pass on, and then at least his suffering would end. He remembered his days preaching down in Alexandria and the things he used to say when there was a slave funeral. The Lord would be his shepherd. The Lord would take him to green pastures.

He couldn't say how much time passed before the door opened again, but the next time it was Lumpkin himself, with the same guard behind him. Anthony forced open his eyes, but he couldn't lift his head.

The men stood there at the doorway studying him.

"Well, boy?" Lumpkin near shouted. "We can't have you dying on us. Brent won't hold with that. Get him some fresh clothes," he told the young guard. "And broth until he perks up."

The next time that door opened, the guard was there with a steaming bowl of soup. He came to where Anthony was lying on his stomach and unfastened the irons from his wrists. Anthony's arms fell straight away to his sides, heavy, like they didn't belong to his body.

"Well, boy," the guard said when Anthony just stayed there face down. "You gonna eat this broth or should I take it away?"

Anthony used all the energy he could find to force his body to sitting. He reached out for the bowl, his arm stiff and unsteady. The guard handed it to him, but Anthony was too weak, and when he tried to take hold, he spilled it all to the floor.

"Damn it, you worthless rat!" the guard shouted and left the room. Anthony figured he wouldn't have another chance at any more broth. But before long, the door opened again, and the guard returned. He had a slave boy with him, probably about eleven years old. The boy was holding a fresh steaming bowl in his hand. Both he and the guard just stood there looking in at Anthony while he lay there with his eyes half open. Each one had put a hand over his nose at the stench of the room, and Anthony could hardly blame them. He could feel spittle dripping down his chin from his open mouth, but he didn't have the energy to wipe at it.

The guard hollered at the boy. "What are you waiting for, boy? Go on and feed him!"

The boy came in and crouched beside Anthony, putting his knees down on the wet floor. By now, there was little contrast between his different excretions, everything just coming out as foul fluid, and Anthony felt sorry that the boy had to suffer the feel of it against his legs. The child's hand shook as he lifted the spoon toward Anthony's mouth, and it was unclear whether the boy was scared of the guard or of Anthony. To make it easier on the boy, Anthony stayed still as he could as the child put the spoon to his mouth, tilting it down to let the broth drip in. When Anthony tasted the warm salty liquid, it was near like heaven sitting on his tongue. He swallowed it down and prayed for more.

After the sky darkened that night, the boy and the guard came back to feed Anthony again. They kept on coming two times a day for enough days that eventually Anthony was able to sit himself upright. He tried to hide his strength as it grew, afraid the broth might stop, and he'd be back on that other slop they gave him from the start. He couldn't hide his improvement all that long though, and one morning when the door to his cell opened, it was the guard alone, without broth or boy.

"Put these on," the guard said, throwing a pair of pants and a shirt onto the bench beside Anthony.

The guard started to close the door again, but Anthony called out to stop him. "Sir," he said, his voice still weak, "my feet."

The guard did some sort of groan, but he reached for a circle full of keys at his waist and stepped toward Anthony to undo the irons. Without giving him even a moment to enjoy the free movement of his legs, the guard barked at him again.

"Get on with it!" he said, waiting there for Anthony to do as he was bid. Maybe now that the irons were off, the guard had decided it was best he stay.

Anthony's heart began to thump hard as he wondered how he could save the items he'd snuck into jail along with the pants he was still wearing.

"Sir, sorry, sir," he started, "you ain't gonna want to see when I remove this pair. You might be wanting to turn roun' sir."

The guard snorted out a laugh. "If that ain't the truth," he said, shaking his head, and turning toward the door.

Anthony reached quick for the pen that was still inside his pocket and the few coins. He wiggled out of the foul pants, still wet in some places, crisp and caky in others. He threw them to the floor and grabbed the fresh pair, shoving his goods right into the pocket before even putting in one leg.

Once he got on the pants, it was quick work to change his shirt. The new one was a coarse, scratchy material, but just from it being clean of his sickness, it felt like luxury all the same.

"All done, sir," he said, expecting the guard to leave then, but the man turned back round and surprised Anthony.

"Come on then," he said, motioning for Anthony to follow.

Anthony couldn't guess where they were going. He thought maybe he was being moved to the area where the other prisoners were held all together. But after reaching the bottom of the stairs, the guard kept walking past all the big rooms that held large groups of slaves. He continued straight until he reached the back door.

Anthony's heart jumped then, thinking that maybe it was time for him to go back to Master Charles or Master William. Maybe they'd seen now he'd been punished enough. He'd never find success running again; he knew that. But at least if he was outside this place, there was hope for his Northern friends to try buying him—unless Master Charles was just protecting his investment in Anthony and was ready now to sell him south after all.

The guard opened the door to the blazing sunshine outside and shooed Anthony to go on out. "Get," he said.

Anthony stepped into the dusty yard, squinting his eyes at the light. He heard hollers and catcalls from down the other end of the yard, and he saw then that there was a crowd assembled outside the fence.

"Well, don't make them wait," the guard said. "Now that people have learned you're here, they want to see the famous coon boy who proved there's no escaping."

Anthony looked from the guard back to the crowd, unsure what was expected of him.

"Go!" the guard hollered.

Anthony walked toward the other end of the lot, his legs still feeling weak after so long lying tight. Beyond the large group of white folk standing outside the yard, he noticed a few Negroes standing back, across the street, looking on too.

As he got closer, he started to make out some of what they were saying, and he stopped stepping then.

"There's the sinner!" came one shout.

"Boy thinks he somethin' special!" came another.

Someone started hooting, making ugly sounds meant to mock him. He looked back toward the guard, but the man was just standing near the door, resting himself against the building, slicing at a bell pepper with a knife and bringing the pieces to his mouth.

More shouts and threats came from the crowd. Anthony tried not to hear them, but just to stand still until it was time he could go back inside.

"I could show that coon boy what's what!"

"Look at his wrist!"

"Put him in a barrel of nails and roll it down a hill!"

"String him up!"

He couldn't say how long he stood there while they shouted insults at him, but the guard must have gotten bored just listening because finally, he came and got Anthony. The guard yanked him by the arm and pushed him to walk back toward the door. When the people realized Anthony was leaving, the shouting got even louder.

"They been coming every day trying to get a look at you," the guard told him. Then a sneer appeared on his face. "Maybe tomorrow we'll make you do a dance for them."

Anthony glanced back at the mob in spite of himself. He saw angry men spitting and sneering and even a few ladies looking on. He wondered again how just one Negro could create such a commotion all up and down the country. As he began to turn back toward the prison door, he caught a glimpse of something else—a shock of blonde hair on one of the ladies, peeking out from beneath a parasol. She and a Negro woman behind her were walking away, their backs to the prison. He couldn't be sure, but he was jolted by the set of the shoulders, the quickness of their steps. He felt the urge to weep then, thinking of his friends seeing him that way. But he told himself to feel hope instead that they might somehow find a way to help him.

ANN

Framingham, July 1854

It was a sweltering day in Framingham as I waited under the meager shade of a birch tree at Harmony Grove. The temperature felt hotter than one hundred degrees, even in the shade. I stared down at the broadside in my lap, hoping we were taking the correct approach in holding this meeting of the Massachusetts Anti-Slavery Society. Instead of celebrating the birth of our country this July Fourth, glorying in the achievements of generations past, we would spend the day focused, as the broadside promised, on the country's "Humiliation, its Disgrace and Shame, and in resolute purpose—God being our leader—to rescue old Massachusetts from being bound forever to the car of Slavery."

There had been special trains running all morning from Milford, Worcester, and Boston, and a large crowd had assembled, descending on the Grove with their picnic blankets and baskets full of summer foods. Although the Anti-Slavery Society had been conducting Independence Day gatherings here on the shore of Farm Pond since as far back as 1846, this year's was looking rather different from the usual.

For this mass meeting of the Friends of Freedom, the organizers had arranged a speaking area, a sort of amphitheater, with a stage at front that was bedecked with multiple flags. There were white flags printed with the names "Kansas" and "Nebraska," a reference to the horrid Kansas-Nebraska Act that repealed the Missouri Compromise, thereby allowing western settlers to legally establish slavery in expanded territories. One banner read, "Virginia" and another declared, "Save Massachusetts." At the center of all these streaming cloths hung an inverted US flag, draped in black crepe.

A murmur started within the crowd, and Helen Garrison nudged me from where she sat beside me with a bowl of cherries in her lap.

"They're starting!" she exclaimed as she put aside the cherries and jumped to her feet. She reached out her hand to help me up, and I was glad for the support as my legs were already tender from the journey to Framingham earlier that morning. Though we'd traveled only sixteen miles from Boston, my physical health had hardly improved of late. Even brief journeys could prove taxing. But I allowed myself to be yanked upright, as I was intent on viewing the stage.

"Mother," Phebe said, coming to stand flush beside me and taking my arm so I might rest some of my weight on her.

"Too hot for that," I said, though I made no effort to move away from her.

The crowd cheered as Lloyd climbed to the stage. Suddenly the entire Grove was singing a hymn. I cannot say whether the tune was started by Lloyd himself or one of the other members in the crowd. I looked around at the faces of my fellow picnickers, and I saw such hope as we all sang together. There were nearly as many women as men in the crowd, with everyone dressed for a summer excursion to the country. Children ran about too, pushing toy boats on the lake and holding kites that refused to fly in the stagnant air. They happily ignored the adult activity surrounding them, allowing the parents to focus on the spectacle up front. Several well-known abolitionists were also in attendance. In addition to Wendell's usual circle, I'd already spotted Henry Thoreau, Sojourner Truth, Charles Redmond, John Pierpont, and Lucy Stone. With so many of us clearly on the side of liberty, I had to believe that sooner or later, we *would* rid this nation of slavery.

As the singing came to conclusion, Lloyd held up a large, scrolled document, which he made great show of unfurling. Then he began to read from it.

"We hold these truths to be self-evident . . ." he began, and there were simultaneously cheers and hisses as people recognized the opening words of the Declaration of Independence. How sad, I thought, that our countrymen were unsure whether to censure or exalt a document meant to inspire unity and greatness. As Lloyd read ". . . that all men are created equal, that they are endowed by their Creator with certain unalienable Rights . . ." a certain crossness seemed to grow among the people around me, a reminder of our collective horror at the state of our country.

Lloyd began to discuss the disassociation of these principles from the Fugitive Slave Law and the recent decision in the *Burns* case. People shouted and booed again as he read from Commissioner Loring's decision remanding Burns to Virginia.

"Ladies and Gents!" he shouted with increased agitation as he lifted another document. "The Constitution of the United States." He began reading again, starting straight away with the portions of the document that provided for slavery as an allowable enterprise in the country. As he read out the words from Article I, stating that, "Representatives and direct taxes shall be apportioned among the several States which may be included within this Union, according to their respective numbers, which shall be determined by adding to the whole Number of free Persons . . . three fifths of all other Persons," the crowd thundered its disapproval.

"No!" he shouted from the stage. "No! We in Massachusetts will tolerate it no longer!"

Shouts of "Amen" rose from the crowd.

"Today," he said, "we are called to celebrate the seventy-eighth anniversary of American Independence. In what spirit? With what purpose? To what end? The Declaration of Independence declares that all men are created equal. It is not a declaration of equality of property, bodily strength or beauty, intellectual or moral development, industrial or inventive powers, but equality of right, not of one race, but of all races. And yet! We have been misled! This document is a covenant with death, an agreement with hell!"

And then he lit a match. I could hardly believe my eyes as he brought the flame close and ho! He set fire to the Constitution!

I gasped at the audacity of it, but the audience erupted, cheers and hollers coming from all sides. I glanced at Phebe and saw her eyes blazing with exhilaration at Lloyd's bold gesture. Helen was clapping her hands and bouncing on her feet in solidarity with her husband. I am ashamed to admit it was difficult for me to watch the document burn, our founding principles from the fathers of our nation, which were, at least ostensibly, based on tenets of liberty. I saw a few other faces that appeared affronted by the blasphemy of Lloyd's actions, but mostly, there was elation, glee, belligerence.

"There is more!" he declared, as he dropped the burning document into an iron cauldron on the ground beside him. "This," he said, holding aloft a new document, "is Commissioner Loring's disgraceful decision of last month, remanding Anthony Burns." He proclaimed again, "No! We in Massachusetts will tolerate it no longer!" And then he set that horrid document on fire as well. As he roared his resistance, the crowd roared along with him.

Finally, he held up a printed copy of the Fugitive Slave Law and added that to the flames.

"So perish all compromises with tyranny!" he shouted into the mayhem. "And let us say, 'Amen.'"

My eyes traveled then to Wendell, who stood near the side of the stage, awaiting his own turn to address the audience. As usual, my husband was surrounded by admirers, mostly other men who were clapping and cheering along with him. There were also two young women I'd not seen before, each more smartly dressed than the other. One would think I'd have grown accustomed to beautiful women attempting to enchant my husband, but still, I wondered how long it would be until my sweet Wendell noticed that one of those women had so much more to offer him than I. At least at the moment, he seemed significantly more focused on Lloyd up front than any of the adherents vying for his attention.

Now meandering his way across the stage was the middle-aged poet Henry Thoreau, a transcendentalist, as they called him. Mr. Thoreau had not been listed on the program as a speaker for the day, and I could not say whether his decision to speak had come at the request of the Society or if he, himself, had asked belatedly to participate. He was a fair looking man, with dark hair, deep-set eyes, and a thoughtful twist of his mouth above his trim beard. Even from a distance, I could see that his eyes were of a blue so light as to appear nearly translucent.

As he reached the podium, he stood motionless, staring out to the crowd, awaiting their attention and silence. Something about the man's calm was utterly arresting, and it was only a moment before all eyes were upon him, waiting to hear what he would say.

"Again it has happened," Thoreau began "that the Boston courthouse filled with armed men, holding prisoner and trying a man, to find out whether he was not really a slave. Does anyone think that justice or God awaited Mr. Loring's decision? For him to sit there deciding, when this question was already decided from eternity to eternity, and the unlettered slave himself and the multitude around had long since heard and assented to the decision, was simply to make himself ridiculous. We may be tempted to ask from whom he received his commission, and who he is that received it; what novel statutes he obeys, and what precedents are to him of authority. Such an arbiter's very existence is an impertinence. We should not have asked him to make up his mind, but to make up his pack.

"The whole military force of the State was at the service of a Mr. Suttle," Thoreau continued, his speech calm and even, though his words scathed, "a slaveholder from Virginia, to enable him to catch a man whom he called his property; but not a soldier was offered to save a citizen of Massachusetts from being kidnapped! Is this what all these soldiers, all this training, has been for these seventy-nine years past?"

I understood now that Mr. Thoreau was attacking the claims of politicians who asserted that slavery was mandated by a higher law. Such thinking could hardly be more ludicrous. He was pulling us all in, this gentle poet, with his calm demeanor and frightfully precise words.

"Massachusetts sat awaiting Mr. Loring's decision," he said, "as if it could in any way affect her own criminality. Her crime, the most conspicuous and fatal crime of all, was permitting him to be the umpire in such a case. It was really the trial of Massachusetts. Every moment that she hesitated to set this man free, every moment that she now hesitates to atone for her crime, she is convicted. The commissioner on her case is God; not Edward G. God, but simply God. The law will never make men free; it is men who have got to make the law free. The law is enslaved by its need to protect property above all else. I would remind my countrymen that they are to be men first, and Americans only at a late and convenient hour. The point is, no matter how valuable law may be to protect your property, even to keep soul and body together, it is of no value if it fails to keep you and humanity together.

"What should concern Massachusetts is not the Nebraska Bill, nor the Fugitive Slave Bill, but her own slaveholding and servility. Let the State dissolve her union with the slaveholder. She may wriggle and hesitate and ask leave to read the Constitution once more; but she can find no respectable law or precedent which sanctions the continuance of such a union for an instant. Let each inhabitant of the State dissolve his union with her, as long as she delays to do her duty."

As cries of approval erupted around me, I realized I, too, was jumping and applauding my encouragement at Mr. Thoreau's beautiful words. Though he read from notes, rather than memorizing his address in advance as Wendell would have, I was fairly certain his remarks had stolen the day. He put voice to the exact feelings so many of us were experiencing. The anti-slavery cause was no longer simply a political position. It had become, for so many of us, religion.

After the crowd calmed from the fervor induced by Thoreau's words, we were treated to a speech by Charles Redmond, a well-known abolitionist and self-proclaimed representative of the Negro community. He applauded Lloyd's burning of the Constitution and declared that any naysayers were simply "Negro haters." Following Mr. Redmond was the young Moncure Conway, a student at Harvard's Divinity School and a former resident of Virginia who had been personally acquainted with Mr. Charles Suttle. He told the crowd that he had found as many slaveholders in Massachusetts as he met in Virginia, simply by virtue of complacency. The members of the crowd made clear their agreement.

As riveted as I was by his words and as heartily as I hoped to discover how this Southerner had been converted to the Cause, I found myself tiring greatly. With all the people on their feet around me, I feared that simply lowering myself back onto the blanket would result in my being trampled. I tapped Helen and Phebe and pointed toward the back of the clearing to let them know where I intended to move.

They both nodded and turned their attention back to the stage, but I patted Helen a second time.

"You'll keep an eye trained toward her?" I asked into her ear.

Helen glanced toward Phebe and nodded emphatically in my direction. I knew, of course, it was silly for me to worry over Phebe, now that she had reached the mature age of seventeen. Even so, I couldn't seem to treat her like the adult that she was becoming.

I made my way toward the back of the Grove, where the crowd finally began to thin. My garments were sticking to my sweat-slicked skin, and I longed for even the slightest breeze. My legs ached and a pounding had begun to move from my head down into my neck. I was reluctant to admit to myself that my attendance today had been a mistake, but my limbs were offering clear indictment. At the back of the field, there were several carts with food and drink on sale and a few wooden benches. As I continued toward the benches, I felt myself stagger, my ability to remain upright waning fast. It wasn't so much farther now. If I could only reach a suitable place to sit.

And then, as if from nowhere, a young man was taking my arm. I looked up at his comely face, not bothering to hide my surprise.

"Ma'am." He smiled kindly. "If I might escort you to a seat?"

I lacked the energy to respond verbally and simply nodded as I placed probably too much of my weight against the stranger's arm. When we finally reached an open bench, I wasted no time lowering myself onto the warm wood. I was grateful that at least the chair was not made from iron, which would have been simply unbearable under current circumstances.

"George Washburn Smalley," the gentleman said, introducing himself. He appeared to be only slightly older than Phebe, with a head of thick brown hair, bright eyes, and a beard that was just full enough to give it character without rendering it unkempt. "Shall I fetch you a beverage?" he asked, looking toward the carts farther up the hill.

With the support of the bench beneath me, I was able now to find my voice. "Thank you, Mr. Smalley," I answered. "I will be fine." I was hardly unused to discomfort, wasn't I?

"Mother!" Phebe called to me, and I turned to see that she had followed me and was now hastening up the hill. She must have seen me stumble. "What can I do?" she huffed, as she reached me, her cheeks pink and her hairline damp with perspiration.

"Phebe," I said, steadying my voice, "this nice young man has already seen to me. You mustn't miss your father's speech. I'll need you to report back on every last detail. Mr. Smalley, do you think you might escort my daughter, Phebe, back toward the stage?"

Mr. Smalley was studying Phebe already with great fascination. "It would be my honor," he answered, a look of pure enchantment in his eyes. I realized then that Phebe was growing up whether I was ready or not.

I watched the two of them make their way back toward the speakers and fought the urge to close my eyes. It wouldn't do to be seen sleeping in public.

I WAITED FOR MY ENERGY TO REPLENISH itself so that I might maneuver back down to the crowd and listen to Wendell when he spoke. Unfortunately, such replenishment continued to elude me. After some time passed, I heard Wendell's voice booming forth from the stage. I could hear only the familiar cadence of his words, the rise, then lull, then rise again, as recognizable to me now as the folds of my own skin. I already knew what he'd be saying. I too could recite the words I had written for him from memory. He would be speaking about how we, as friends of freedom, sought to find a space, no matter how small, that truly could be called free, a place where a fugitive slave could find actual refuge, such that once he stepped a foot onto the dirt in such place, he would never, ever be sent back to bondage. Then Wendell would call for Commissioner Loring to be removed from his post, a campaign that would surely be well received by the audience.

At intervals, the crowd roared in reaction to various comments he made. I was pleased for him and ashamed that my own lack of physical fortitude kept me so far from the stage. Even so, I remained there on that bench until the entire meeting came to conclusion.

SOME TIME LATER, AS WE RODE by carriage back toward Essex Street, Wendell said again, "I'm sure that was the best speech I've heard from Thoreau."

I was too tired to respond thoughtfully and so I just listened as Wendell again reviewed the events of the day. I glanced over at Phebe, who had been staring distractedly into the distance for nearly the entire ride. Something in the whimsy of her expression told me she was thinking still of that Mr. Smalley. Perhaps it was the way her lips were upturned, ever so slightly, as though she was in possession of the tastiest secret.

"At last!" Wendell said as we reached home. He stepped down to the street first and then reached out a hand to help me. As I landed on the street beside him, there was sudden commotion. Heavy footfalls and shouts startled me as four officers of the law swiftly surrounded the two of us.

"Mr. Wendell Phillips?" one of them demanded.

"Yes?" Wendell looked in confusion from one officer to the next. Meanwhile, a third officer grabbed onto Wendell's hands, forcing them behind his back and locking them into metal cuffs.

"What is the meaning of this?" Wendell demanded.

"Mr. Wendell Phillips, you are under arrest under indictment by order of Attorney General Benjamin Hallett and Benjamin Curtis of the Supreme Court for obstructing the process of the United States and for the attack on the federal courthouse on the night of May 24." As he spoke, the officer began to push Wendell in the direction of a waiting cart.

"Wendell!" I yelled.

"Phebe," Wendell said, his voice calm as ever, "bring Mother inside. Then go fetch Theodore or Lloyd."

"Wait! They cannot take you!" Phebe shouted, jumping down to the street.

"Not to worry," Wendell told her. "I'm sure we will get this sorted straight away." And then he looked to the officer prodding him toward the cart. "No need to shove, gentlemen. I will comply."

He climbed into the back of their cart, lowering himself onto the bench, his back straight as could be even with his arms bound behind him, his bearing as regal as ever. As the driver set off and I watched Wendell retreat into the distance, he held himself steady and proud, as if a king of men, setting off on royal procession at last.

ANTHONY

Richmond, July 1854

It was easy to lose time in Lumpkin's jail, but Anthony tried anyway to tally up the days. After they stopped bringing him broth, another fourteen or fifteen days passed all in the same way. They put him back on the same mush he'd started with, but at least they continued bringing fresh water. They'd left his hands free so he could sit upright to eat proper, though his ankles were kept shackled like before. A guard would come each day to remove the irons and bring him out to the yard again. He had to stand out there day after day, listening to the people of Richmond shouting insults at him, calling for his hanging, flogging, castration. He kept searching for a certain glint of blonde hair beyond the fence, but always in vain.

Back when he was still getting broth, there was one day when his keepers made a mistake. When Anthony finished drinking the liquid that time, the guard watched the Negro boy carry out the bowl as usual. No one took any notice that the boy forgot the spoon, just left it sitting right there on the bench. Anthony's head was still pounding with the sickness, but he knew he had to act. As soon as they closed the door, he grabbed that spoon right up, wondering where he could hide the thing until such time he found a use for it. His eyes traveled round his small den, searching for where he might stow the thing. His quarters being so small, everything was out in the open. Just the bench and the chamber pot in there with him, and a small bit of crumbly floor.

His eyes skated toward the trapdoor that was used for entrance to his cell. He wondered if maybe he just left the spoon on the floor in the corner behind it, that might be sufficient to keep it hidden each time the door was opened. But the spoon might make a sound, the banging of metal against the door or the bricks of the wall. He called on God then, as he did often during those days, asking for His assistance. As Anthony moved his eyes skyward, thinking of Jesus in heaven, he noticed small holes between the bricks of the wall, some up by the ceiling just about big enough. He jumped up and tried the largest of the holes, and the spoon slid right in, vanishing inside. When he saw how well it disappeared, he reached deep in his pocket for the pen he still had hidden away, and he put that in another small hole. The coins he left in his pocket, thinking that if one hiding place was discovered, at least not everything would get taken.

As more time passed, he began to suspect that Master Charles planned for him to live the rest of his days in the prison. In the evenings, he would lay on his bench, listening to the sounds of slave voices coming from the communal cell beneath his own. The voices were muffled by the floor between the cells, and Anthony heard only enough to know discourse was happening. How long it had been since he'd said anything other than "Yessir."

One night when his despair was threatening to destroy him altogether, he climbed off the bench and put his ear to the floor, trying to listen in on what was happening below. As he lay there, making out a word here or there, he remembered suddenly about the spoon. He jumped to his feet and grabbed it down. He was rough in his excitement and knocked loose the brick beside it too. He placed the brick back proper, and then moved to the corner of the cell. He used that spoon and started digging into the rotted floor in that spot behind the trapdoor. The floor was so decayed it seemed more like dirt than wood, and it didn't take long before he began to make a hole. He dug with that spoon like it was a shovel from God, and he just kept at it. Soon, a pinprick of light began to show through. That pinprick was enough to set him on fire, and he dug all the harder. Not too much longer passed before the hole was as big as his eye.

He pushed his face against the floor and found he could see the folks below him! There was a Negro woman on one bench, dozing in candlelight. There were also two Negro men sitting beside each other on the floor, a pile of small sticks between them like they were playing some game. There was another person too, but Anthony was able to see only the feet and couldn't say if it was man or woman. He started digging again, keeping on until the hole was the size of a child's fist. He realized then that if there were still candles burning, maybe the guards hadn't cleared out for the night. So he waited, his heart galloping all the while.

Finally, the yellow glow of candlelight disappeared and all grew quiet below. There was only the smallest trace of light, which was likely coming from somewhere outside. He waited still for what he wanted to do.

The minutes dragged on until at last, he put his mouth right up that hole and whispered a sound.

"Psst," he said, and then quick switched to put his eye to the hole. Nobody moved. They must all have been asleep, so he placed his mouth back at the hole.

"Psst!" he tried again a little louder. "Psst!" And then he flipped his eye again back to the opening.

"Ho!" called out a man's voice below. Anthony watched the man look round the cell, trying to figure from where that voice was harking.

"Up top," Anthony called in a quiet voice.

Now another Negro man was standing beside the first, and they both looked up at where Anthony's eye was the only thing showing through.

The men looked at each other then back at Anthony.

"You're Burns," said one in a low voice as they both walked closer to stand just beneath the hole.

"Listen here," Anthony said, putting his mouth to the opening again and lowering his voice back to a whisper. "I need ink. Can you get it? And paper?"

They hesitated before answering.

"I got coins," Anthony said, "I can pay."

"And you'll tell us about the North?" one of the men replied.

IT WASN'T BUT FOUR NIGHTS LATER THAT one of his new friends called up to him.

"Burns!" It was a whisper and a shout all in one.

Before he even reached the cutout, there was paper pushing through, rolled up tight like a scroll. Anthony scurried to grab it and pull it through. Next, they pushed up a small bottle of the ink he had begged them to find. As he held that little bottle in his fist, his heart pumped with joy at what he would now be able to do. For the first time since arriving in the Trader's Jail, he was looking forward to morning.

He hardly slept at all that night, waiting for day to break so he could put pen to paper. As the first shards of light began to spill through his window, he realized the mistake he had made. He had failed to ask his new friends to find envelopes. But he would! He still had two of his four coins remaining in his pocket. He jumped from his bed and set himself to his task.

He began to write, taking his best guess at the date, as the pen wobbled in his shaky hand.

Richmond, July 23, 1854

Dear Mr. Dana,

I am well enough at this time, and I hope that this letter finds you and all my friends in Boston in acceptable health. I am able to tell you that the God of our heavenly father has been with me here where I am, and so I was able to secure these items necessary to send you a letter. I am here in jail, but I believe I may be for sale. I am bound in the Trader's Jail in Richmond. If you, all my friends, will please help me, to you all I will be a friend the rest of my days. Send some of your Boston friends to Alexandria and ask where Mr. Suttle keeps store. And then ask him if he has a single man to sell, and maybe you can even get me low. He would take even $800 for me now. I pray in the name of the Lord, please help me out of this suffering this one time please.

He read it over top to bottom, hoping up to heaven that Mr. Dana would be able to find some folks to do as he asked. Then he signed his name and folded up the paper small as it would get so he could pack the letter into the wall while he waited for an envelope.

By day, he took to staring out from the cell's small window, trying to figure out the next part of his plan. Mr. Lumpkin had his lodgings on this same piece of property as the prison, and Anthony found that if he stood at the window just so, he could see into a bedroom over at the man's house.

One day, Anthony was studying that bedroom, staring straight in and wondering how it was that Lumpkin lived, what it'd be like to be that white man managing all those Negroes in jail. Anthony had heard one of the prisoners below talk about Lumpkin's yellow wife, how no white woman would marry the man, on account of his disreputable job, so he had to settle for a yellow woman instead. But Anthony didn't see any yellow woman walking past that window, only a dark-skinned Negro slave, doing her business to tidy up and such. On that one day, as he was watching to see the Negro woman, she came over by a window and opened it wide to throw out some ash. Anthony thought better than to holler, but he pushed his hand out through the bars and waved it all around. The movement caught her eye, and he thought that now, maybe he had his plan for how to get that letter sent.

The woman looked over at him, like she was trying to figure out what he wanted. He stuck his face up close to the bars so she could see him good, and then he waved again. She nodded back at him, a quick but strong dip of her head, before she turned away. Then she was back about her tidying, picking up a basket, and moving to where he could no longer see her. He waited the rest of the day at that window, but the woman didn't appear again.

The next day he was back at the window all day. He kept waiting for a sight of the slave woman, but all he saw was empty space. His eyes started wandering toward the street beyond, folks passing by to go to the iron works or maybe the slave market, or any number of the factories down in Shockoe Bottom. He was watching one elderly Negro carrying a large box up the street when he spied movement across the way.

There was the slave woman in back of the house with a large blanket in her hands. She shook out the dust, and then started beating on it with her hand to get more dirt to fly. Anthony was reminded of the way his mama used to beat rugs with one of Mistress Suttle's old brooms when it was time to freshen them up. He didn't want to think on his mama just then though, not when she might be worrying for him, knowing he'd failed to stay free. It was one kind of thing to separate himself from her when the reward was freedom, but it was a whole other kind of ugly to think of never seeing her again when the reason was prison.

He watched the sturdy-looking slave woman as she aired out the blanket. Her hair was covered by a kerchief, long braids peeking out from the bottom. When she finished beating on the blanket, she looked over in his direction. He pushed his hand out from the window and waved it about in greeting. She didn't wave back, but she put a hand above her eyes to shield them from the sun and kept on still, just looking toward him. They stood there considering each other. Then she nodded again the same way as the day before and turned round to head back inside. He wasn't sure what had passed between them in that moment, but he got the sense it was a good thing. He had a feeling that something, some change, might be coming to him because of that woman. He couldn't say exactly why.

His suspicion was confirmed later that night when he lowered himself to the floor to visit with his friends in the cell below.

He called out with a "pssstt," and then heard some of them moving closer to the hole in the ceiling.

"What'd you say to Hattie?" one of the men called up.

"That you talking, Toro?" Anthony asked. "I don't know any Hattie," he added, but already he was thinking of the slave woman.

"She belong to Lumpkin," Toro said. "She come in with Mistress Lumpkin to tell us scripture when the master gives them say-so. She wanted to know all about you, asking us what you need."

"And?" Anthony asked, "you tell her?"

"Yeah," he said into the dark, "we told her about them envelopes."

"What she say?"

"She didn't."

Though he couldn't see Toro, Anthony imagined his friend shrugging his shoulders like that was that. Anthony didn't feel defeated though. Each time he found a new reason to hope, he grabbed onto it, holding fast and putting his energy there.

And wouldn't you know, it was only two nights later that Toro was pushing a few rolled envelopes up through the floor for him.

COLETTE

Richmond, July 1854

I was sitting at the writing desk in my chamber, finishing a letter to Fay. I'd promised I would keep her well apprised of the pregnancy, but at less than three months along, there wasn't yet much to report. I just kept on, drinking those awful tonics every morning. Maman's last letter recommended that I rest my body as much as I possibly could. So it was that I took to spending entire afternoons recessing in my chamber. I ran my stockinged foot over the curved leg of the desk beneath me and tried to determine if there was anything more I might tell Fay.

The only excitement we'd had recently was the visit to Shockoe Bottom, and I could hardly report to my sister on that. Adelia and I went down to the Bottom in hopes of catching sight of Anthony at the slave prison. After his arrival in Richmond, his whereabouts had been a mystery for so many days. Reports circulated that he was at the Trader's Jail, but when no one saw him in the yard with the other prisoners, people began conjecturing and painting all sorts of false pictures. We heard he'd been sold south, or he'd been sold to abolitionists up

North, or he was back in Alexandria with his master. There were even whispers that he had taken his own life. Day after day, there was news in the papers about "rabid abolitionists" up North and the debate about disunion, but as far as Anthony was concerned, the reports were scant.

Then finally, word got out that he was indeed imprisoned at Shockoe Bottom. A big fuss was made over the first day he would be put on view in the yard. When I saw the announcement in the paper, I told Adelia we had to attend. I wanted to show Anthony that despite everything, he still had friends in Richmond.

Except once we reached Shockoe Bottom, I became cowardly. As we approached the jail, onlookers were already assembled on the dusty road beside the prison yard. They were riled up with bitter energy, shouting and pushing at the fence. As we grew closer, I saw Anthony standing alone in the yard. Even from afar, I could see that he was so much thinner than when I'd last laid eyes on him. His body seemed bent inward, as though he'd been twisted into a state of disrepair. The crowd hollered horrible insults and threats at him.

"Rip his skin from his bones!" a man in the mob bellowed.

Another fellow right in front of me called out, "That piece of trash deserves a flogging and the pit!" The spectators surrounding him uttered various sounds of agreement and encouragement.

"Tear him apart, limb by limb!" yelled another man who was closer to the fence.

Adelia tugged on my sleeve and leaned toward my ear. "We best move along," she said. "This ain't no place for a lady."

But I couldn't tear myself away from where we stood at the rear of the group. I watched through the gaps between the bodies in front of us as a man threw rotten vegetables into the yard. A gourd struck Anthony in the side; a turnip collided with his head, but he just stood there, stock still, staring at the ground and listening to the insults. I had hoped, before we arrived, that I would have opportunity to say at least a brief how-do or even raise a hand in greeting, but clearly there would be no such chance, not if I wanted to return to Fifth Street unharmed. I now understood that the attention Anthony received from the newspapers had rendered him an enemy to all those who supported the institution of slavery.

WE DID NOT RETURN TO THE PRISON. My attempt to communicate with Anthony had been foolish. I could hardly walk myself up to the front of the crowd at the prison and inquire how he was doing, ask after his travels, and whether he enjoyed the brisk air in Boston. If our friendship had been infeasible before he left Virginia, now that he returned as the most infamous slave in all the South, the idea of any relation between us was nothing short of delusion. *But Adelia,* I wondered again, *perhaps there was some way she could see him.*

"Mistress," Adelia startled me from my reverie as she held two dresses side by side. "Which one?"

I barely looked at the options before answering, "The green is fine."

Elton's new friend, Foushee Ritchie, and his starlet wife, Anna Cora Mowatt, would be joining us for supper. If I were not so preoccupied about Anthony all the time, I might have been excited about spending an evening with the famous actress.

"Delly," I said tentatively, knowing I was going to aggravate her by broaching the topic yet again. "Can't we think of anything, anything at all, to help poor Anthony?"

Adelia sighed loudly then and laid both dresses flat on the bed before turning to address me. "How many times you going to ask me that, Mistress?"

I felt myself deflate again. "I just . . . how long can we just leave him there like that?"

"And what are we going to do, Mistress?" she asked. Something about the way she was looking at me made me feel like a child she was reprimanding. "Are you willing to risk your own skin? This life?" She motioned to the room around us.

"Adelia!" I snapped at her insolence.

She twisted her lips, as though she knew she had overstepped and was trying to hold the remainder of her words inside. Her voice held a particular inflection of harshness that I'd not heard from her since we were children, when she didn't yet know better. Until she resurrected those tones of bitterness just then, I'd forgotten the sound of her true sass altogether. I had allowed myself to believe that because Adelia and I were more familiar than was common between mistress and slave, that she was frank with me. I realized then that there must have been so many other moments when she kept her true thoughts inside.

"Delly," I lowered my voice. "What is it you're not saying? You can be direct with me. Please."

"I don't think so, Mistress," she said in a more subdued voice, and she returned her attention to the dresses in my wardrobe.

"Delly," I argued, "I am giving you permission. I want to know what you think I should do. Your *honest* answer."

She looked up from the shawl in her hand, meeting my eyes directly, and shook her head. "There ain't nothing you can do unless you want to destroy your own life. Now especially with the babe on the way, I'm thinking you don't want none of that. We all just do what we can, Mistress."

"What would you say, Delly, if I weren't your mistress, if I were your sister, and you could be truly blunt?" Suddenly, I was desperate to know what was inside Adelia's mind.

"But you ain't my sister, Mistress, and it's best I keep some thoughts to myself sometimes, just the way you do with Master Elton."

The idea that Adelia would censor herself in front of me the way I did with Elton was maddening. "Adelia, please. There will be no repercussions."

When she still didn't say more, I asked, "When have I ever punished you, Delly? Ever? What aren't you saying?"

"All right, Mistress." She crossed her arms over her chest and took a deep breath. "You think you're so different from the other folks down here because you speak kindly to the slaves, say please and thank you? Because you don't tolerate beatings? But you still *owning* us," she said. "You are still the problem."

"No, I . . ." I couldn't think how to answer.

"Who's cleaning up the floor after you retch every morning? I don't see you getting down on your hands and knees. You always handing me your things to hold, your dresses to press, your chamber pot to empty. Why do you think Anthony is where he is? People just like you."

"Adelia!" I scolded. "How dare you speak to me like that!" As soon as the words left my mouth, I realized that she was absolutely right.

She took a step back from me and looked to the floor, contrite. She was worried she had gone too far. I worried the same.

"I don't like what you said or how you said it," I told her, "but I asked for your thoughts. You needn't be afraid. Not of me."

I turned toward the writing desk and lifted my pen again, as if I were writing another letter, but I simply couldn't look her in the face. I *was* angry. I *did* want to punish her for speaking to me as she did. The worst part was that I realized the truth of her words.

Adelia remained in the room, moving gowns in the wardrobe from one spot to another, probably unsure what to do with herself.

I finally took pity on her and turned back in her direction. "If he saw me tending to my own pot," I said, motioning toward the side of the bed where we hid my chamber pot, "Elton would make me pay."

Her eyes were focused on the green dress that she was now removing from its hanger, but she nodded. "I know, Mistress," she said. "We all do only what we can."

AS WE WAITED IN THE DRAWING ROOM for our guests to arrive that evening, I was still ruminating on Adelia's words, her accusations. Elton sat across from me, flipping idly through another report about the quality of certain crops in the Virginia-Carolina tobacco belt.

When Tandey finally showed the Ritchies into the room, my unhappy thoughts were abruptly suspended by the appearance of Anna Cora Mowatt Ritchie. She was every bit as resplendent as people said. Her long dark hair held an exceptional shine and was curled to perfection, framing her face with short pieces in front and cascading halfway down her back. Her dress, too, was of the latest fashion, a violet color bright enough that the silk fabric of it seemed aglow. Her skirt was so wide, I imagined she must have been wearing as many as eight or nine petticoats beneath it. As I took in her small waist, the sloped shoulders of her gown, and its dazzling passementerie trim, I felt rather frumpy by comparison. Though I was nearly a decade her junior, my less inspired garments, as well as my growing middle, had me battling an unfamiliar sense of inferiority.

I worried that Elton, too, would notice how Mrs. Ritchie eclipsed me, and that I might suffer for it. But as we all greeted each other, Elton's smile was wide.

"My Foushee tells me we have a great deal in common," Mrs. Ritchie said as she took my hand, her Northern accent more eloquent than any I had heard before hers.

Elton interrupted before I had a chance to answer. "We'll have drinks on the patio before we dine. Come," he said, motioning toward the French doors that were already ajar at the rear of the drawing room.

We made our way to the brick patio where a wrought iron table and chairs awaited. Louisa and Cook had prepared an array of beverages and a few small plates of hors d'oeuvres for us. As we stepped outside, a door opened from the other end of the house, and Louisa appeared. She made her way to us and began pouring sweet tea into glasses.

"Please," I said to our guests, motioning toward the table, "try the *canapés*." The endless news articles I'd seen about their wedding had contained great detail about the food served at the event. I hoped Cook's peach and prosciutto *canapés* might rival the lobster and mushroom torte from the wedding. Elton had mentioned that particular dish to me no fewer than three times in the past week.

"Oh, how lovely," Mrs. Ritchie declared as she lifted a sample for herself. "Now," she said, placing her free hand on my arm, "tell me all about yourself." She guided me toward two chairs at the side of the patio, as though it were she who were hostess.

"Yes," I agreed, delighted by her manner in spite of the competitiveness that was eating at me. "But first you, the new-lywed, and newcomer to Richmond. So many adjustments, I'm sure. How are you settling in?"

The men, who had been listening in on our chat, turned toward each other at that, and began a conversation of their own.

"It's been a modification to my usual life, for certain," she said, sounding a bit wistful. "I've stopped touring, as you may have heard, which I was loath to do, but it was the only way. I do adore the lifestyle down here, the constant socializing and endless refinery suit me just fine. Though I must confess," she lowered her voice as she glanced toward Louisa, "I'm not accus-tomed to owning slaves, and I'm having some trouble learning to manage them. I can't seem to get comfortable with it."

I blinked at her words, hoping not to betray their effect on me. The topic was rather raw for me still, and I worried I would not be in a position to provide the advice she sought. I looked over at Foushee, wondering what it was about him that had motivated this dazzling woman to surrender not only her life's work but also to relocate to a place so foreign to her. He was gesticulating with his hands as he talked with Elton, and there was a vitality to his nature, which I thought was perhaps what had entranced the famous actress. Only after a moment did I take note of the content of his words.

"Secession," Foushee was saying, "is certainly the only sensible approach at this point. If they cease to enforce the Fugitive Law in the North, what will be next? How else will they hamper our rights?"

I sighed, more loudly than I should have, and then looked back at Mrs. Ritchie.

"I know," she said, shaking her head. "The constant discussion of politics can grow rather tiresome." She sipped the last drops of her tea and placed the empty glass upon the small table beside her.

Louisa was beside us almost instantly. "May I take your glass to refresh it, ma'am?" she asked Mrs. Ritchie.

"I'll take care of it," I said taking her glass, as well as my own, and walking across the patio to the pitcher of sweet tea. As I began to pour, I felt Elton watching me, but I didn't dare glance in his direction. My hand began to shake before I finished, and I realized that I was too much a coward even to fill the second glass on my own. It turned out that Adelia was decidedly correct about everything she'd said that afternoon, and even more so, about the parts she kept to herself. If I could not relieve Louisa from the duty of pouring drinks without shuddering in fear of my husband, how could I ever do anything truly helpful for Adelia, or Anthony, or any of the millions of others trapped in bondage?

ANN

Boston, August 1854

Wendell was released on bail only a few days after being arrested. His trial, along with those of the other "courthouse rioters," as they were being called, had been postponed because of a legislative decree that prosecutions under the state liquor law must be given priority over all other criminal justice cases.

Thus, we still managed to summer with my brother in Milton. Once summer concluded and we journeyed back to the city, I wished I could declare that the country retreat had been restorative to my well-being. At best, my health was no worse than it had been when summer began.

Not more than three hours after we returned from Milton, Richard Dana came knocking at our door. Wendell and I had just begun sorting through the mail and packages, which Cara had collected for us all summer long.

"Forgive me," Mr. Dana said, as he removed his hat and stepped into the entryway, "for just appearing like this."

"Nonsense." Wendell made a dismissive motion with his hand and ushered Mr. Dana into the sitting room.

As we took our seats on the room's opposing sofas, Mr. Dana pulled a tattered envelope from his pocket. I could see he still had a purplish mark on his forehead from the attack he suffered in June. Perhaps the scar would remain permanently.

"I met Lloyd Garrison earlier, and he mentioned you would be returning today," Mr. Dana said, looking from Wendell to me. "Your timing is fortuitous, as I received this just yesterday." He reached out to hand the envelope to Wendell. "It was delivered first to a distant cousin of mine and took a rather long time to make its way to my door."

I looked down at the envelope in Wendell's hand and saw that it was addressed only to "Lawyer Dana, Boston, Massachusetts." It was a wonder the letter had found its intended recipient at all.

As Wendell began unfolding the wrinkled paper, I started to divine the sender.

"Anthony Burns!" Wendell nearly shouted as he looked down at the paper in his hand.

"Move it closer," I said, sliding nearer to Wendell so that I might read along with him.

We were silent as we read the words asking for someone to journey to Virginia in pursuit of purchasing Anthony's freedom.

"Do you think there's truly a chance Mr. Suttle would sell?" I asked as I looked up from the page.

Mr. Dana shook his head. "It's too high profile," he said. "From what I understand, Southern newspapers have only just quieted down about the political implications of the case. If Mr. Suttle plays any part in returning Burns to freedom, he will be credited with a blow to slavery and the South as a whole. He will hardly want to bear responsibility for that."

I remembered that awful Saturday back in June when Pastor Grimes nearly convinced Mr. Suttle to sell Anthony for $1,200. The district attorney found every possible impediment to the sale, and eventually Mr. Suttle declared he was no longer willing to cooperate. I wondered if perhaps Mr. Suttle's position might have shifted in the many months since the trial.

"But surely, if he's brought Anthony all the way back to Virginia only to have the man locked in a prison, he must want to be rid of him now," I argued. "Who pays for Anthony to stay in the jail?" I wondered aloud. "And the notoriety can't be to Suttle's liking, besides."

"But what is the message?" Mr. Dana asked, "If we purchase the man, we line the pockets of a slaveholder with more ill-gotten funds."

"Right," Wendell nodded. "And we have achieved nothing for the Cause, except to reinforce the feasibility of buying and selling human property."

"But what of the man?" I demanded. "If we have the means to save him, how do we refrain?"

Wendell looked at me sadly, "And then what? Do we purchase all the other prisoners at the Trader's Jail along with him? All the other slaves in Richmond? In Virginia? Where does it end? If slaveholders can continue profiting off the sale of human property, how are we moving any closer toward the goal of eradicating these practices?"

"I think you should at least alert Pastor Grimes," I said.

"I wouldn't stand in the way of Mr. Dana," Wendell said, looking from our guest back to me, "if he wanted to share the news with the pastor, but I can't say I see the point."

Mr. Dana nodded. "It will only upset him," Mr. Dana said, "to hear what has befallen his friend. Especially when he is powerless to help."

AFTER MR. DANA LEFT, WENDELL AND I retreated to separate rooms, I suppose to nurse our respective frustrations. He went directly to his study, and I moved to the back parlor with Phebe to continue working through the large pile of mail.

Much correspondence had been forwarded to us in Milton, but so many parcels and letters had still made their way to Essex Street. I was certain it would take several days to respond to it all.

"Here is the one from Ticknor and Fields," Phebe said, knowing I was looking forward to its arrival.

"Aha," I said, taking the heavy package from her and hastily unwrapping the brown paper. Inside was a shiny leather volume, the word "Walden," printed on its spine. It was Henry Thoreau's new book, and I had so been looking forward to reading it. Yet now, thinking of Anthony Burns shuttered in a prison in Virginia, I found I could hardly summon any joy at all. I ran my fingers over the volume, subtitled, "Life in the Woods," and I remembered again Mr. Thoreau's words at Framingham on the Fourth of July.

Who but God, he had posited, could decide whether man should be slave or free? I found myself wanting to march straight up to Wendell and demand an answer of him. Who was he, and who was Richard Dana, to decide we should not purchase freedom for Anthony Burns? Though perhaps the real question I needed to ask myself was: Who was I?

ANTHONY

Richmond, August 1854

Toro pushed the tobacco and matches up through the hole in the floor. Anthony never had much interest in smoking, but Toro and Ansel convinced him, told him he had to find joy in this life where he could. All the hours spent by his lonesome in that cell, the isolation of it was starting to addle his brain. He'd sent no fewer than six letters during his time in the jail, and he couldn't say if one of them had reached its destination. He looked out from the window each day wondering if Mr. Dana had read his message, if one day soon, a person might approach Master Charles and come looking to purchase a man like himself. Day after day, he waited, but nothing. More likely, he figured, his Northern friends had forgotten him, just as he'd feared.

He'd gotten so desperate for company that he took to lying himself on the ground all the day long and watching the happenings of the cell below. When he could see their faces, he didn't feel quite so all alone. The solitude got to him so bad that he even sent a letter to Master Charles. Anthony told him all about how he was being treated in there, how he'd been left for weeks in his own filth and how he'd grown so ill. He asked if maybe it was time Master Charles forgave him and came back to get him from the prison. He thought if Master Charles had gotten that note, his old master would at least have come to check on Anthony's upkeep, or sent Master William to see what was what.

That afternoon, Anthony was lying there watching Ansel play a matchstick game with the woman they called Sable, when suddenly all the bodies he could see jumped to their feet.

Anthony rolled fast away from where he was watching, lest whoever was coming might look up and catch sight of his own eye staring through the ceiling.

Then he heard Mr. Lumpkin barking commands at the prisoners, telling them to line up and stand this way and that. Anthony often heard Lumpkin tormenting the captives below. One small mercy was the fact that the foul man never came up to where Anthony was locked away. But after a few minutes of Lumpkin grousing about below, Anthony heard footfalls on the steps outside his cell.

He hurried himself onto the wooden bench and sat stock still.

The door opened, and there stood thick-bodied Mr. Lumpkin with the guard behind him.

Lumpkin didn't say anything as he climbed inside, just let his eyes roam all across the cell, like he was searching for something. Anthony followed his gaze as it traveled across the floor. Thankfully, the hole he dug with the spoon was well covered by the trapdoor. He hoped Lumpkin wouldn't think to move the door and look behind it. But then the man was looking at the walls, and Anthony's breath caught, knowing what was coming.

He saw the moment Lumpkin's eyes caught on the pen. Anthony had been careless about pushing it all the way into the hole in the brick wall. Just the end was poking out, but it was enough to give him away.

"I was wondering why," Lumpkin said, as walked to the wall, and grabbed down the pen from where it sat between two bricks, "I received a visit from William Brent this morning."

Anthony didn't say a word, but just kept his eyes to the ground, sure he was going to be whipped. Or worse.

"Now, I don't know how you got a letter from up in this here cell all the way over to your friend Suttle in Alexandria," he said, as he walked toward the window and glanced outside. "But you sure put some people into a fit, talking about how poorly you's being treated. Like to make them think you're dying up in here." He looked back at Anthony, maybe waiting for a response, but Anthony didn't dare speak.

"Now normally, I'd need to beat you good for what you done." He ran his hands over the bricks as he talked, and Anthony prayed he'd done better hiding the spoon than the pen. "Now where'd you put that ink you used?" Lumpkin spat on the floor as he continued exploring the wall with his hands. "Seems Suttle is ready to have you sold. Realized you're nothing but trouble for him. I got half a mind to whip you good, now, but nobody at auction wants a Negro showing fresh blood on his back. Just make you seem like the bad investment you are."

He stopped talking as he caught sight of another hole between the bricks. He approached the wall, peered in, and then he let out a mean kind of laugh.

"Now what'd you figure on squirrelling away a spoon for?" He reached his two fingers into the hiding space to pull it out. "Not much of a weapon, is it?" He studied the spoon, and Anthony was grateful he'd wiped the dirt from it so it wouldn't bring to mind the digging on the floor.

"Although," Lumpkin said, pausing as he ran his finger along the edge of the scooping part, "maybe if I scrape long enough, I could cause some damage with this thing. Should we try?"

Anthony kept his eyes toward the floor. "No, sir."

"What do you think, guard?" There was a smile in his voice as he looked over at the gruff fellow who'd been bringing slop to Anthony's cell each morning.

"I think any Jimbo who wants to send letters complaining about us, he's got a lot more coming to him than a spoon," the guard said.

Lumpkin sighed loud, like he was suffering the most of all of them. "Why they had to decide on selling him now," he said, shaking his head. "But here's an idea," he said as he stepped closer.

Anthony felt his heart start to pound. He knew something bad was coming, and there wasn't anything he could do to stop it.

"That wrist of his," Lumpkin said, looking down at where Anthony's bone always stuck out, "everybody knows it's been defective for years. Nobody'd notice if it got worse. Let's put this here spoon to the test, yeah? See what it can actually do."

And then his hand shot out like a viper and he grabbed Anthony's arm, yanking it toward himself.

"No, sir," Anthony argued, trying to pull back, "please."

Lumpkin laughed out loud. "Oh, I wouldn't struggle if I was you, Burns. It'll just make a messier job of it. Guard, tie him down."

The two of them came at Anthony then. The guard had the irons and attached one to Anthony's good wrist, the other to the leg of the bench. Then they did his feet, and there wasn't nowhere he could go or nothing he could do. He flopped around like a fish fighting for breath as the two men took hold of his arm.

"Now, you're already famous for having bone exposed, ain't you?" Lumpkin barked.

"No, sir!" Anthony yelled. "Please!" he begged them, "Please, no sir! Don't!"

And then Lumpkin took the spoon and started digging right into the skin of the wrist, the same way Anthony had done his digging of the floor.

The pain was instant and searing, like nothing he'd ever felt.

"Please!" Anthony begged again, "I'm sorry, Master!" he shouted. But Lumpkin didn't slow. "Stop! Please!" Anthony couldn't free his wrist from the man's grip.

Mr. Lumpkin, he just laughed as Anthony hollered, and he drove the spoon deeper into the wound he was creating.

"Really have to push hard with this thing, don't you?" Lumpkin said, almost to himself.

Anthony yanked and pulled all he could, but for nothing. As Lumpkin pushed that metal in deeper, Anthony tried to take himself away, to move his mind as if he weren't even there. He tried to turn his thoughts over to Jesus, but he couldn't escape his own screams, nor the scraping sounds . . . the horrid noises the spoon was making against his skin and bone.

At some point, he passed out from the pain.

WHEN HE AWOKE, HE WAS ALONE AND the room was dark, but the ache was something straight from the devil. He wished he could pass right out again.

As the heat burned all the way up his arm, his mind was brought back to the day when the engine at the sawmill first spoiled his wrist. He remembered how he'd looked right into his own arm that day, how seeing his innards made him want to be sick just from the way everything oozed. He couldn't bear to turn his head now and see what damage they'd done him. He heard a noise, and only after the sound came out did he realize it was him, just whimpering and sobbing where he was.

Then came a low whistle from below, a signal from Toro to come and see him through the hole.

"I'm shackled," Anthony called. "Can't get over there."

There were sounds of shuffling and then he heard Toro's voice just beneath him.

"You all right?" Toro called up. "Sounded like they done you real bad."

"Real bad," Anthony answered in a whisper, knowing it was too quiet for anyone to hear.

AFTER THAT DAY WITH MR. LUMPKIN, Anthony took up with a fever from the wrist.

A new guard started coming every day, taking care of him like that last time he fell ill in the prison. The guard had hair the color of rust and thick muscles in his arms, but he wasn't mean like the others. He said his name was Mr. Tucker, and he came three times each day, bringing Anthony fresh soup and clean water. He tried each day to make Anthony eat because the auction was only one week away.

As the fever eased, memories kept coming back at Anthony from when Mr. Lumpkin was tearing his wrist apart. Anthony tried to push the visions away, but something Mr. Lumpkin said to the guard when he was doing the butchering kept repeating in his head.

"Don't know why we've got to keep him in one piece, anyhow," Lumpkin told the guard. "Nobody wants to buy a boy who's run. 'Specially not this one, when he's famous for it."

Anthony couldn't let himself think about what might happen if he didn't get sold. If he was still on the block when the auction ended, they'd bring him right back into the prison, and he'd be stuck in the same fires of hell he'd met up in there already. Except that they'd no longer have reason to keep from spoiling all the other parts of his body too.

ANN

Boston, September 1854

Wendell had been invited to deliver a lecture in New York, the one he called "The Lost Arts." He had given the talk hundreds of times already, though from what he told me, each time he presented it, the content varied greatly. Wendell's fees for his speeches had grown steeper over the years, but as usual, he responded to the invitation from New York offering to speak for free if they would only allow him to present on abolition instead. But no, they wanted the talk on the arts.

As usual, we packed a full container of his favorite tea and a large shawl that he could spread between the bedsheets at the boarding house if the bedding proved scratchier than he preferred.

"I expect," he told me as he placed a shirt into the valise that was open on the bed, "the audience will be somewhere around two thousand. I will miss you terribly though."

"Oh, go on," I said, waving away the endearment and lowering myself onto the chair beside me. Wendell and I had already debated at length whether he ought to accept this invitation from the New York Society of Culture to speak at their annual conference. It was hardly the first time he had been asked to travel to address a crowd. For years, he had been participating with the New Bedford Lyceum, delivering orations on topics ranging from foreign affairs, religion, and biography to finance and various types of social reform. The idea of leaving home this particular time unsettled him for reasons I could not ascertain.

"But you're sure you'll be sound without me?" It was as if he wanted me to beg him to stay.

"Enough, Wendell. It is but three days and then you will be home." I smiled to soften the statement. Much as I would have preferred Wendell's company at home, I refused to hold him back from the path he was meant to follow. I would not be responsible for limiting the achievements of a man with his potential. My own selfishness motivated me to force him from our nest. I would not have him resenting me for limiting his reach in life. Each time he was invited to speak at a distant location, I made certain he felt my hand against his back, pushing him out the door.

This time, I had additional reason to welcome his brief departure from town, though I could not admit as much to him.

There was a light knock at the open door of Wendell's room, and I looked to see Cara waiting.

"Mr. Phillips, you best be hurrying along now," she said. "It's coming on time to get to the station, ain't it?"

"Cara's correct," I said, pushing myself from the chair. A jolt of pain shot from my lower back down into my leg as I rose, but I did not allow myself to wince. If Wendell thought I needed him at home, he would cancel his speech without a second thought, and we could not have that, not today.

The three of us proceeded from the room. As we walked in tandem down the narrow staircase, I caught a strong scent of citrus in the air.

"Phebe," Wendell called toward the kitchen, "perhaps too much on the perfume."

"You can detect it from there?" Phebe called back. She emerged from the kitchen holding a scone in her hand. "I spilled the bergamot," she said sheepishly. "It's all over me now, but this is the dress I wanted to wear."

She had accepted a date for that afternoon to walk along the Charles River with George Smalley. How fortunate that she had run into him outside the market a couple of weeks earlier, after pining away for him for nearly two full months following the Fourth of July. Aunt Maria would be joining them as chaperone on their walk, and I would be free to pursue my own activities with no one the wiser.

Phebe's hair was freshly arranged with a part in the middle and loops piled above her ears. Like most of the women in our circle, Phebe generally preferred modest dresses in dark colors, but she had one frock of pale blue that I knew she favored best, and there she was, showing it off to its greatest advantage.

"Perhaps when you're walking outside, some of the scent will wear off," I offered. "Or a drop of my jasmine water might cut the aroma. It's atop my vanity in the pale green bottle."

Wendell stepped closer to her and took the scone from her hand, taking a large bite before handing it back to her.

"Father, am I not getting too old for you to pilfer my every pastry? In fact, are you not getting too old, as well?"

"Never!" he declared gamely, gathering her into himself and folding his arms around her. "Now give your father a good send off."

"You'll muss my hair," she complained, even as she fell into his embrace.

"Oh, dear me," he joked, "we wouldn't want to tousle any part of your appearance before precious Mr. Smalley sees you."

"Enough of this, you two," I said as I pushed past Wendell and opened the door. "Your train." I smiled brightly, trying to prove my readiness for his departure.

He kissed Phebe atop her head and then called toward the kitchen. "Take care of my girls, Cara!"

Phebe returned to the kitchen then, allowing Wendell and me a moment for a private goodbye.

"Promise me you will miss your Gra?" he asked.

I felt my cheeks warm at that, still affected by his nearness and his use of my special name for him. Here we were, an old married couple, and he could still make me blush like a school-girl. "Enough with your dallying. Go on now so you can start hurrying yourself back to me."

"Indeed," he answered, studying me fondly. And then he was off.

THREE HOURS LATER, I WAS WALKING myself toward the Twelfth Baptist Church, fighting against the pangs that assaulted my ankle each time my foot connected with the cobblestones. I tried to focus instead on the bright September sky and the trees lining the streets, their leaves just beginning to show a teasing hint of yellow.

As I considered the foliage, I did not notice the approach of our friend, the Negro abolitionist Lewis Hayden, walking opposite me along Warren Street.

"Good afternoon, Mrs. Phillips," he said kindly.

"Oh! Mr. Hayden." I gasped, stopping to greet him properly. "I am too lost in my own thoughts today. I'm just heading over to the church to visit Pastor Grimes."

"You won't be finding him over there," Mr. Hayden told me. "He'll have just finished his midday meal with Mrs. Grimes. Their home is just yonder, on Southac. You go on up there," he said, pointing. "He'll be glad to see you, I'm sure." He told me the house number and encouraged me on my way.

When I reached the correct residence, I raised the knocker somewhat tentatively. I hated to call on anyone unannounced, and I was hardly so familiar with Pastor Grimes to excuse the infraction. I thought of turning round for home, but then I pictured the face of Anthony Burns and the conditions in which I imagined him suffering at that very moment. I pounded the knocker against the door and waited.

When the door opened, I was greeted by the full-figured Mrs. Grimes. She had a baby on her hip, and another small child was hiding behind her skirt.

"I'm so sorry to arrive unannounced, Mrs. Grimes. I'm Ann Phillips."

"I know who you are," she said. Her tone was not unkind, but wary. She continued to stare at me, waiting for me to state my purpose. I had seen Mrs. Grimes at certain women's auxiliary events, but we had never before spoken with each other.

"I have a matter of some importance," I said. "I was hoping to speak with your husband."

"He's just finished eating, readying to head on back to church now," she told me. "Move aside, Julia," she said to the little girl, opening the door wider so I could pass.

I heard Pastor Grimes before I saw him, his deep voice strong and melodic.

"Octavia, who was at the door?" he asked as he emerged into the entryway. He was a tall man of a light brown complexion. Catching sight of me there, he pulled his waistcoat closed over the shirt beneath, affixing the center button into place.

"Mrs. Phillips, isn't it?" he asked, politely. "What can we do for you?"

"If we could please sit for just a moment before you go, I have news I thought you'd find important."

His eyes widened slightly, perhaps at my boldness, but he gestured for me to follow farther in all the same. "We'll just sit a spell," he said.

I followed them to the small sitting room, where I was directed to a chair that was ample and comfortable. A small collection of baby toys was spread haphazardly on the floor in the corner of the room, and all else seemed perfectly in place. Mr. Grimes sat opposite me, and Mrs. Grimes stood near his chair, watching. As I sank into the cushion beneath me, I was grateful to be off my feet for a moment.

As they regarded me, I remembered my intention to inform them that I'd engaged in this visit without my husband's knowledge. I had been planning to ask the pastor to keep the fact of our conversation to himself. But as I watched the way his wife stood behind him, as if she were an afterthought, I worried. Such a request for secrecy from me might burden the man's conscience and result in the opposite of the desired effect. If he disapproved of my insubordination, he might feel a pressing need to alert Wendell.

"Mr. Grimes," I started, deciding to go straight to business instead. "My husband and I were recently visited by Richard Henry Dana."

The pastor nodded.

"Mr. Dana received a letter from Anthony Burns."

"From Anthony!" Pastor Grimes's hands flew to the armrests of his chair, as though he was readying to push out from his seat, to give chase and rescue Burns from wherever he was being held.

"He's in a slave prison." I hated to deliver such bleak news, and I watched with dismay as varied emotions crossed the pastor's face. Meanwhile, his wife behind him was stoic, her features betraying nothing of what was inside her mind. Only her thumb on the back of her husband's chair began bouncing up and down, with a rapid ticking noise, as if she was racing through some thoughts herself.

Finally, the pastor's eyebrows drew together, as though he was ready to start puzzling out a plan.

"He knows where he's at? What city and such?" Pastor Grimes asked. "Octavia, please!" His reached up toward his shoulder, his hand landing firmly atop his wife's in order to halt the rhythmic tapping.

"He knows," I nodded, pleased I had at least that information to provide. "They're holding him in Richmond, and he thinks he might soon be sold. He suggested sending a man to inquire of his owner. Now, my husband and his compatriots believe purchasing Mr. Burns at this juncture will not serve the anti-slavery cause. I thought you might like to know the whereabouts of your friend regardless—in case you had other ideas about how you wanted to proceed."

That was the most I could offer the man without directly contradicting Wendell.

The pastor rose from his chair and walked to a small bookcase, where I could see a few volumes of religious texts, as well as several carved trinkets that looked to be the handiwork of their children. He removed a thick folio from the top shelf and turned back to me.

"We started taking up a collection back in June," he said, opening the book and removing some bills. "It's not enough yet to buy freedom for a man, but I could get back to work, start raising funds the same way I did for building the new church."

"I can hardly tell you how to proceed." I looked from the pastor to his wife. "If you choose to continue raising funds, I imagine it will take some time."

"You know we lost one third of our members when they passed the Fugitive Slave Law?" he asked me. Before I could answer, he continued. "So many refugees come up to our church, and now they're too frightened of what might befall them if they stay, so instead they hasten on to Canada."

I nodded, well aware of the horridness of that law. "You might consider, as the collection grows, whom you would send to Virginia as a representative to complete a purchase of Mr. Burns."

The pastor's lips turned down at my words. "What you're telling me is that none of you white folks will volunteer."

I looked down at my hands folded in my lap. I was ashamed I couldn't offer more.

"Mrs. Phillips," Pastor Grimes said evenly, "I appreciate you taking the time to tell me about the letter. I will have to think on what to do next. But truly, I thank you."

As I was clearly being dismissed, I pushed myself out from my seat, moving slowly to protect my fragile joints. Even so, a single pain shot across my back as I rose, causing me to blanch in spite of myself.

"You all right there, Mrs. Phillips?" Pastor Grimes asked.

"It's nothing. I will let you get back to the church," I said, trying not to grimace.

Mrs. Grimes walked me to the door, the child still on her hip, sucking on his own fist.

"Mrs. Phillips, wait one moment," she said, and she disappeared beyond the entryway to the kitchen. Just as I was beginning to wonder what was keeping her, I heard a cupboard door shut, and then she was back, handing me a small pot of cream.

"For the aches," she said. "It won't cure nothing, just covers the pain for a time. Might be it'll give you some relief." She held the little jar out for me to take.

"Oh!" I was so surprised by her kindness that I hesitated to say more. I accepted the jar and studied it a moment.

She seemed suddenly embarrassed by the gesture and stepped back. "You can't pass so many years helping fugitives without picking up some healing knowledge is all. It's made from spicy peppers and a bit of primrose oil. You looked as though you could use it." She shrugged sheepishly.

I peered at the jar and the amber-colored liniment inside, and I felt an unexpected swell of emotion. "I am enormously appreciative, Mrs. Grimes," I said.

"Make sure you give it a try. At least one try," she added with a marked insistence.

After we said our goodbyes and I began making my way back toward Essex Street, I hoped with all my heart that the pastor would find a way to help Mr. Burns. I remained appalled that neither Wendell nor I was doing more. Had I been the husband and Wendell the wife, I liked to think we would be proceeding differently. I wondered if the same could be said of the pastor and his wife as well. And then I had a surprising thought. I'd only walked a few blocks from the Grimes' house when I stopped in my tracks. Looking down at the jar of ointment in my hand, and wondering at my own ideas, I twisted the cover off. There, resting atop the clump of cream was a folded note from Mrs. Grimes.

ANTHONY

Richmond to Rocky Mount, October 1854

They didn't bring him to auction after all. Instead, he watched each week from the window as new Negroes were brought into the yard. Some of them got cleaned up and taken straight away to the auction block down the other end of the lot. Others, they pushed into the large cell beneath his own, sometimes crowding it up too much for him to talk to his friends in there at all.

The days kept rolling on, and Anthony reckoned they had him up in that tiny cell going on about four months. Weeks had gone by since the last time they took him out to the yard, and he was wondering if he'd ever again get to look straight up to see the sky. Then one day, he heard heavy footfalls outside his cell.

The door pushed open, and there stood Mr. Lumpkin. Anthony started shaking at the sight of him, wondering what cruelties might be coming.

"We got to get you cleaned up, boy. Going to a fair today."

Anthony couldn't guess why he would go to such a place, except if to be sold. He'd been lying in that tight space so long, he felt a sort of relief at the idea of going anywhere, but that feeling was getting all mixed up with the dread of what might follow, where he'd end up. Just like the compounds he used to mix for the apothecary, where two things came together to make a third, the feeling was something entirely new. They took off his irons and got him trimmed up nice, and then he followed them down to the yard.

It turned out they were only taking him across the lot to the auction house. Lumpkin's talk of a fair had been meant as mockery, he figured.

When they walked inside, the room was already crowded with white men of all sorts. Bodies pushing against each other, tobacco smoke, and the hum of loud conversation filled the place. Down the far end was a large platform where several Negroes were already waiting. Mr. Lumpkin pushed Anthony forward.

"Hurry on, now," he said. "Over there with the others."

Then Anthony saw the kindly guard, Mr. Tucker, waiting for him. The guard came and took Anthony by the arm, leading him deeper into the packed room. Mr. Tucker didn't say anything to him, and Anthony figured maybe in there, they weren't friends at all. So he just kept quiet and went where the guard bid.

Mr. Lumpkin followed a little ways behind them, chatting up the people in attendance as they passed through. When they reached near the platform, Anthony heard a voice call out toward him.

"Hey there, Tony." It was Master Charles, all turned out in a fine suit. "You fetch me a good price up there, you hear?" He didn't wait for an answer before he turned to Mr. Lumpkin. "Now you make sure you don't sell him to a Yankee, you understand?"

Anthony didn't hear Mr. Lumpkin's answer because Mr. Tucker was already pushing him on, directing him to stand in place between two other colored men.

A young woman was shoved up onto the stage then, and Anthony realized there was no official start to what was happening. They were just putting up merchandise and waiting for anyone to shout out how much they were willing to pay. Meanwhile, the white men in the room just kept on smoking, drinking, and chatting to their friends like they were at the pub.

Anthony watched the woman on the stage, waiting to see how it would go. She had her hair pulled back under a scarf, and she wore a starched, buttoned-up dress, making him think her last job had been house slave. As she stood on the platform with her eyes focused on her toes, a heavyset white man stepped up beside her and yanked the scarf from her head. She stumbled a bit from the jostling but kept her eyes turned down. He walked round her in a circle, considering her. Then he started squeezing different parts of her body, like she was a melon he was checking for ripeness. Her arms, her buttocks, her breasts. He stuck his hand inside her mouth, made her show her teeth. Then he told her to take off her dress.

Anthony thought for sure she'd tell him no, but she just started undoing the buttons, one after another. It fell to the floor, and she had nothing on underneath. Anthony dropped his own eyes then, not wanting to make her shame any worse. All those years of hiring himself out, a boss might have felt for muscles in his arms, but never more than that.

The man shouted out that he would buy her for $600, and he marked a paper that he handed to a fellow on the side of the stage. The woman hurried to put her dress back on, and then the heavy man was back beside her, pulling her by the arm.

Anthony watched as this process happened over and again. An older woman with sagging skin fetched a price of $350, a small man with wiry muscles sold for $750, a pretty, young girl with pale yellow skin went for $1,150. Each Negro was poked and fondled, but they all somehow kept their thoughts to themselves. All the while Anthony was watching, he wondered how he would be able to do the same.

When he was the last man remaining behind the platform, Lumpkin appeared again and pushed him toward the stage.

"Up you go," he said, and then he surprised Anthony by climbing onto the wooden platform right there beside him.

"Fellas!" Lumpkin called out to the room. "This here's Anthony Burns of Alexandria, Virginia. He's the best deal I got today. Young strong buck, good for working and for stud," he said, pausing to look Anthony over, and maybe encouraging his audience to do the same. "Normally he might sell for upwards of $1,500. But today, I'll give 'em to one of y'all for an even thousand."

Some man at the back of the room shouted up to the jailer, "Give us a break, Lumpkin. Nobody'd buy him for $1,500 even if he weren't a runner."

"Sure they would," Lumpkin called back. "Young enough to stud a farm full of his 'ninnies. Years of good work left in him." He looked out at the men settled around the room, waiting for the bidding to start.

"Take off your shirt, boy," he told Anthony, and then he turned back to the crowd. "Fine, we'll start off at $950. Do I hear $950?"

That was when the men started heckling the jailer.

"Nobody wants that runaway trash, Lumpkin!" called one fellow.

Another voice followed, "He'll just stir up trouble wherever he goes."

"Everybody'd be better off with that one dead," called another. "Filleted first!"

Soon everyone was hollering all at once, and Anthony worried those angry men might come take care of him themselves. Lumpkin held up his hand though, and to Anthony's surprise, the crowd quieted again.

"Now listen here," Lumpkin said. "This here's a gentlemen's sale."

Anthony didn't think Lumpkin had any part of gentleman to him, but nobody saw fit to argue the point.

"I'll lay out his credentials," Lumpkin said, "and if nobody wants him, so be it." He pulled a paper from the pocket of his trousers and began to read off what it said. "Young buck, approximately twenty-two years of age. Of solid body with only a scar to the wrist and the cheek. Well-trained in factory work, hauling, and housework. Well-fit but not trained for field work. Slave preacher."

When he finished, he folded the paper and waited. That crowd just stared back at him, and Anthony was starting to feel sure the prison was where he'd remain until his last days.

A man sitting right in front chewing on tobacco called up, "Lumpkin, nobody even wants the boy for free. Time to put him to pasture."

"How about you auction off his beating?" someone hollered out. "Show folks what happens to the ones who run." Men started cheering, and Anthony's heart thumped harder in his chest.

But then another voice called from back of the room, "Nine hundred dollars! Final offer."

They all turned round to look toward the bidder. Anthony wanted to crane his neck and look too, but he knew he had to keep still, to make it seem there was nothing at all in his mind.

Meanwhile, the crowd seemed to object to the offer, lots of rumbling and booing as Lumpkin clapped his hands twice, trying to quiet everyone.

"Anyone want to raise higher than $900?" he called. Spittle flew from his mouth with each word. "Do whatever you want with him once he's yourn?"

Nobody called back in response, and after a moment of more grumbling from the crowd, Lumpkin clapped once more.

"Sold to the gentleman in the grey vest for $900."

After that, people rose from their seats and began making their way back outside. Anthony got to thinking most of those men had only been there for the show of it, getting to see the famous runaway and where he'd end up. Folks were probably disappointed he got sold rather than flogged. While the crowd thinned out, he put his shirt back on, and then he kept to his spot, waiting for whosoever might come fetch him.

Finally, he caught a better glimpse of the man who'd purchased him, handing some bills to Lumpkin. Anthony didn't mind the look of him, with broad shoulders and sandy-colored hair curling near the collar. But he knew well enough not to judge a man on just how he appeared.

The fellow walked over to Anthony, and he spoke mean.

"Now listen here," he said, eyeing Anthony whole, taking the measure of him. "I won't have you preaching to my slaves. You want to do any preaching, you preach yourself at me, you hear?"

"Yes, Master," Anthony said.

The man seemed satisfied enough and led Anthony outside to a wagon. Unlike many of the other coaches, where drivers waited for their masters, this man's carriage sat empty. The lack of a driver had Anthony worried his new owner was a poor man, taking them to a shabby place. Before he stepped up, the man turned back to Anthony.

"You'll give me your word now then, that you won't be preaching to my slaves?" he asked.

Anthony knew he might regret what he was about to say, but he couldn't stop himself from being honest.

"I won't offer to preach for nobody," he said, "but I can't promise what I'll do if somebody ask me for it. A true preacher can't turn away a body in need of prayer. I'm sure Master knows that too."

The fellow looked back a moment in silence, so Anthony took the chance to say one piece more.

"I could promise you I won't run from you though, at least not without warning you first. So long as you good to me, I'll stay close."

The man stared back at Anthony, his eyes wide with surprise at the bold statement. But then he barked out a loud laugh.

"All right, Burns," he said, his voice warming up. "I guess you've made yourself clear, then." He smiled some and shook his head, like he was enjoying a good joke.

They climbed into the wagon, and then to Anthony's surprise, his new master started chatting with him like they were friends.

His name was David McDaniel, he told Anthony, and he lived in a place called Rocky Mount, North Carolina.

"Now Burns," Master McDaniel said as the wagon came to a stop outside a hotel in the center of town. "Plenty of men around these parts won't take kindly to me having bought you. Folks want to see you strung up. We'll go up to my rooms and wait until dark. Then we'll make our way."

They did just as he said, and nobody gave them any trouble as they traveled beyond the city limits into the dark night. Now Anthony didn't know why Master McDaniel wanted to risk his own name on buying a man with such a bad reputation, them having to sneak out of the city and such. Maybe he just couldn't pass up a good price. Anthony remembered what Master Charles once said a strong young slave was worth. Now that he was known for running, Anthony supposed his price had dropped and he'd become good labor at low cost. Whatever the reason, he was glad enough to see Richmond fade into the distance behind them. He didn't feel bad about the growing length between himself and the Devil's Half-Acre. No matter what came next, he'd never let himself be sent back there. He would make sure to die first.

ALL ALONG THEIR RIDE, ANTHONY TOOK note of how clean the air smelled. The scent of pine and oak, and even the fresh dirt alongside the road, was like manna from heaven after the months he'd spent inside that putrid cell.

His new master said not to fuss with surnames and just to call him "Master David." The man asked so many questions about what Anthony had done in other jobs, and then he grew quiet, making little marks in a journal now and then along the journey. The farther they traveled from the Trader's Jail, the more Anthony found himself wondering about what lay ahead.

Somewhere along the way, Master David had said he lived on a cotton farm. But when they finally reached their destination and rode up the driveway, Anthony was greeted by the largest home his wide eyes had ever beheld. It was as grand a cotton plantation as he'd ever seen. It turned out that Master David was also a merchant, and he ran three different businesses from his home. He was a planter, a horse-dealer, and a shopkeeper, all at once. Anthony used to think Master William lived in a great big mansion, but now he understood there were levels to being rich, and his new master's kind of rich was something else altogether.

Master David directed Anthony to pull the coach to an outbuilding around the side of the house. The structure was long and wide, with a roof painted dark green. From the outside, it looked like they could keep near forty horses inside if they had a mind to.

"Pull to the side just there," Master David said, directing them toward a wide door. "Go on inside and find Victor. Tell him you're the new coachman, and he'll show you what you need to know."

Well, that was the first Anthony heard that he'd be working as a driver. He understood now why Master David had asked so many questions about the driving he did back at Master William's, and he was grateful he had the right experience. Mostly, he was relieved he wasn't being put to field work.

He tied up the wagon to a post and then made his way into the stable. It took a moment to adjust to the dim light, but then his eyes settled on a young Negro who was adding feed to a stall at the back. Anthony made his way through the cool air toward the fellow.

"Ho!" Anthony called as he approached. "You Victor?"

The man turned, and Anthony saw a face that wasn't young at all, but showed as many as three or four times Anthony's own years. The fellow looked at Anthony questioningly, but his expression was not unkind.

"I'm Burns," Anthony said. "Massa says I'm to be the new driver. Said you'd show me what I need."

"How do, Burns," the man said, straightening up and wiping his palms against his pants. His dark skin had deep folds around his mouth, and he was missing two teeth up top, but he had a kind smile all the same. "Let's get them horses cooled down, and then I'll show you up," he said, pointing toward a ladder at the back of the barn. "Quarters for the stable boys."

Now Anthony knew there were some things he could feel sad about just then. First, that he had traveled even farther south than Richmond, and that nobody up North would know where he'd got to, if anyone thought to look. But he chose in that moment to feel glad about being free of that six-by-eight cell and to take solace in making a new friend. After all that time locked in, sleeping in a barn would be an improvement, so long as there was soft hay and room to stretch his legs.

As the two of them saw to the horses, Victor told Anthony all about caring for the livestock and also about life at what he called "Great Falls Farm."

"Been with Massa near two decades myself," Victor said as he removed the bridle from the horse and placed it to hang over a hook on the wall. "Came on with him when the whole area here was still called 'Great Falls at Tar River.' Now everybody calling it 'Rocky Mount.'" He shook his head a little, and Anthony could see he felt this area was home. It made Anthony hopeful that life at Great Falls Farm was gentler on folks than some of the other places he'd seen.

"There's another stable down yonder," he said, pointing toward the back of the barn. "In there's the mules and more horses. Ones for the coach always get stalls up front," he said. "Those be Massa's favorites, so they's the ones you tend most careful. Don't get too attached to nobody here, and you'll do fine. Massa always selling his slaves, just as soon as he gets a better price than what he paid. Just a few of us he keeps on for the long time."

"There a mistress?" Anthony asked.

Victor's lips twisted as he took a wet cloth from a bucket and started running it over the horse standing between them. "She either love you or hate you. There ain't no in the middle with her." The way he said it, Anthony reckoned Victor was on her wrong side.

It turned out that Victor liked to talk and talk, but Anthony didn't mind. He learned that Master David had more than a hundred and fifty slaves on the plantation and that he was respected as a businessman round town. Victor said the man was always buying and selling, whether it was land, slaves, horses, or cotton. "The slaves here is always for sale," Victor said again, "so you just keep that in your mind."

ONCE EVENING FELL, ANTHONY'S BELLY was more full than in all the time at Lumpkin's, and he slept solid that first night in the barn, like a sated bear finally come to nest.

So he was feeling fine with himself when the mistress came to see him the next morning. She looked younger than Master David, with a small body and a thin nose that had Anthony thinking of a sparrow.

He and Victor were just finishing portioning out the morning feed when she walked into the stable wearing a bright pink dress and holding a book in her hand.

"You're the new coachman?" she asked, looking Anthony over.

"Yes, Mistress," he said, moving his eyes fast from her face and fixing them on her toes.

"You'll be driving me to town this morning."

"Yes, Mistress." He saw a shadow come up behind her then and looked up to see Master David approaching.

But Master David held up a finger to his lips, like he didn't want his wife to know he was standing there.

"Take the horses from the first two stalls, and make haste," she told Anthony.

"Hazel," Master David said then, and her eyes opened wide. "I only just finished telling you I was planning to use those very horses this very morning, now did I not?"

Mistress didn't turn round to face him, but just raised her voice at Anthony. "Now hop to!" she said. "I haven't got all morning to wait."

Anthony looked from Master David back to Mistress Hazel, unsure how to proceed, but Master David said nothing. He just waited to see what Anthony would do.

Now Anthony knew he was going to get himself into trouble with one or the other, but he had to make a choice.

"I'm sorry Mistress," he said quietly, his eyes still on her shoes, "I can't be giving you Massa's horses today. But I know there's some fine horses just yonder." He pointed behind himself toward all the full stalls.

She didn't answer, but just turned to face Master David then. "Look at you," she said to him with venom in her voice. "Turning them against me, right from the start. Well done, David." She huffed off back in the direction of the house.

Master David walked to where Anthony was standing and the two of them stood quiet, watching the Mistress march up the path. "Burns," he said, clapping Anthony on the back, "you and I are going to get on just fine."

COLETTE

Richmond, December 1854

I was rising from the breakfast table when I felt the first pain stab me in the side. I yelped and doubled over at the sudden agony.

"Mistress!" Adelia was at my side near instantly. "You all right?"

The blow began to subside, and I straightened myself back to standing.

"The baby," I said, putting a hand to my taut middle. I had grown so large that even the widest hoops could hardly hide my size any longer, and I'd become accustomed to all sorts of kicks and aches. "I think I'm all right now," I said, "just a twinge."

But as soon as the words left my mouth, another pang came and pierced me again. I hardly had time to holler out my anguish again before I felt a rush of fluid burst forth from my body onto the floor below.

"It's coming!" Adelia declared. "Louisa! Help me with the mistress!" she shouted out toward the hallway.

The two of them led me up to my bedroom, as I was folded over myself in pain most of the way.

"It's too soon," I huffed as I hauled myself onto the bed,

my legs still slick with my own mess. "Delly, fetch the doctor. Hurry, please!"

Adelia and Louisa exchanged a look.

"Best let me go, Mistress," Louisa said. "Delly, she got know-how if the babe come quick."

"No!" I shouted as another pain took hold and I grabbed a fistful of the coverlet beneath me. "I am not having this baby yet!" I growled.

"Still and all," Adelia said, coming toward the bed and adjusting a pillow. "Best I be here in case. You go on now, Louisa."

Louisa spared me a quick glance, and when I didn't argue, she fled the room.

I laid my head back and shut my eyes, trying to calm my body. I couldn't lose this baby, not when the idea of a child was the only thing getting me through my time inside this house. I thought I'd soon find respite from the long days filled with frippery and needlepoint, having myself an infant to occupy my time.

Elton, too, I realized, would be so greatly disappointed if we lost the child. He would blame me, and he'd make me pay. He was taking those tablets of his with ever-increasing frequency, and he refused still to discuss their purpose or their origin. Even so, I imagined there was no amount of medicine that would calm him if I lost the heir he longed for so desperately.

"Delly, please," I begged. "Don't let the baby come."

"Hush, Mistress," she said, her voice kinder than I'd heard for so long. "You just lay back."

I did as she said, resting my head on the thick pillow and willing the pains to stop. Meanwhile, Adelia raced around the room making preparations. When I heard her fussing with something near my head, I opened my eyes to see her tying a white sheet to the bedpost.

"Why are you doing that?" I asked.

"It's for you, Mistress, to clutch when the pains come." She placed a hand against my forehead to feel for fever. Seeming satisfied, she propped me up to a sitting position. "Best we remove the gown," she said as she began unfastening hooks in back.

Relations between myself and Adelia had felt strained ever since the day we argued after seeing Anthony in Shockoe Bottom. She had been polite but distant, and I grasped better now where we stood with each other. Yet today, I could feel her concern for me, and I knew it to be genuine. As she finished with the hooks, I grabbed onto her wrist.

"Delly," I said, grimacing as my middle seemed to tighten in on itself. "Thank you."

She looked down at me and nodded quick. "Ain't no time for none of that now, Mistress," she said. "There's work to do."

Not long had passed before Louisa was rushing back into the room. I was covered in perspiration and the pains had not subsided.

"Doc Cherry on a hunting trip," she said through ragged breaths. "I could send Tandey to fetch the master?"

"No!" I shouted. "I am not having this baby today!"

"Mistress," Adelia said, "your water done broke. This baby coming with or without our say-so."

AND SHE WAS RIGHT. WITHIN A FEW agonizing hours, Adelia was holding the baby in her arms.

"She's here," Adelia said with awe in her voice.

"It's a girl?" I asked. "Is she, is she . . .?" I couldn't finish the sentence.

At the ringing of the baby's cry, Adelia and I smiled at each other with relief.

"She a small thing," Adelia said, holding up the baby's curled, wet body, "but she look like she just fine. Sound that way too."

Then suddenly there was a pounding of feet outside in the hallway. A moment later, Elton's face appeared in the doorway.

"Colette?" His features were etched with concern. Adelia hurried to adjust the sheet so my body was shielded from view.

"It's a girl," I smiled at him. I was so relieved that in that moment, I felt almost kindly toward Elton, thankful that he'd given me a child to love.

"A girl!" he said delightedly. "Can I see?" he asked, looking not to me but to Adelia for permission.

"Won't be but a few minutes, Massa, until we get her cleaned up."

"All right," he said, his face flushed with joy. "All right," he said again. "I'll be here. Just right here," he said as he closed the door.

I wondered if maybe this could be the beginning of a new start for Elton and me. Now we would be a family.

When Adelia finally admitted him into the room, it seemed that Elton felt the same way. The baby was wrapped neatly in my arms, swaddled up in a clean white cloth that Louisa had brought.

"What shall we call her?" I asked as Elton hurried over to my bedside and looked down into our daughter's scrunched little face.

"So tiny," he said in a hushed voice, staring down at her. Then he broke into a broad smile, just looking at her.

We stayed there like that a moment, only the three of us in the room, Elton and I just staring at her perfect little body. She couldn't have weighed even five pounds.

"Does her breathing sound shallow to you?" I asked, looking up at Elton.

He spared me but a glance before looking back to the baby. "Maybe just because she's so small," he said. "I'm sure her strength will build as she grows."

"How about we call her Dolly?" I asked.

"Too common," he said with a quick shake of his head. "We'll call her Celestina, after my mother."

I knew better than to argue. My mother-in-law had never been kind to me. Even though she'd passed on a couple of years earlier, I hardly wanted to think of her every time I looked at my lovely little girl. I would just have to find a way to make the name palatable. Maybe we'd call her Tina, which wasn't so objectionable.

I was so amazed by the new little being in my arms that hardly anything could have upset me then.

Adelia reappeared at the door holding a full tray. "Mistress going to need her strength," she said as she approached.

"Let me hold her a moment," Elton said, reaching out. He lifted the baby from me, and Adelia placed the tray in my lap.

She glanced over at little Tina, who appeared even smaller in Elton's wide arms. "She too blue," Adelia said.

Elton didn't look away from the baby's face. "No," he said, good-naturedly, "she's just adjusting to being out in the world. She's fine. Aren't you fine, Celestina?" He started rocking her gently.

"I thought her breathing seemed shallow," I told Adelia. "Do you think she's all right? Please, Elton, let Delly check her."

Elton emitted a little laugh. "Adelia's a doctor now? Celestina is quite all right. Aren't you, sweetheart?" he asked, leaning even closer to her face.

Adelia was still looking at the baby, her eyes filled with worry. "Please, Elton, what will it hurt?"

He sighed, as though I was asking a great deal of him, but then he handed the baby to Adelia all the same.

Adelia placed the baby gingerly on the bed beside me and unwrapped the little blanket. She put her hand to the baby's chest, and we all waited. After a moment, she looked up at me with alarm. "She not getting the air into her the way she should," Adelia said.

"What do we do?" I demanded. "How do we fix it?"

She pushed her lips together and shook her head. She

wrapped the blanket closed around Tina and lifted her again. "Nothing we can do for her except wait and hope that she gets stronger as the hours pass." She looked away from me as she said it, and I felt a sudden dread.

"No!" I shouted. "She has to be all right."

"She could be," Adelia said. "You both just hold her and give her all the love you can." She handed the baby back to Elton, whose face had fallen. It seemed he was trusting Adelia's opinion after all.

"We'll send Louisa back for a doctor," he said as he cradled the baby. "Cherry's not the only physician in Richmond. Tell her to find someone else. Just get someone here."

"Yes, Master." Adelia hurried from the room.

Elton looked down at me, and I noticed his cheeks were bright pink. He was more frightened than he was letting on.

"We will not lose this little girl," he said.

IT TURNED OUT THAT ELTON'S SURETY WAS nothing but an empty promise. Little Tina held on for only two days before her body gave up and she closed her eyes a final time.

I kept to my room for nearly three full weeks after that, refusing to rise from my bed. Finally on a rainy Saturday morning, Elton came to see me in my chamber.

"Enough with this, Colette," he said as he walked into the room, bypassing the bed to open the drapes at the windows beyond. "You've had your chance to mourn. Now you must get up and return to your duties."

My duties? I wanted to ask. I was failing well and truly at my duty to provide him with children. What else, really, was I needed for? I turned my head away from him, fixing my sight on a point beyond the open bedroom door.

My recalcitrance seemed only to enrage him. He marched over to the bed, but I kept my head turned away.

"You think this is easy for me, do you?" His voice was rising. "She was my little girl too. I can't have you moping like this. You need to get up and return to your life. We will try again."

There would be no new baby. It had taken so long for me to conceive the one time. What confidence could we have that it would ever happen again? And even if it did, would I carry another child only to watch it die mere days after arriving in the world? I could hardly bear it.

I squeezed my eyes shut and kept silent, willing Elton to leave.

"Don't you shut me out!" he shouted. He yanked the coverlet off me and tossed it to the floor.

The shock of the cool air against my body woke me from complacency.

"Get out!" I shouted. "I will not have you coming in here and making demands on me. Not anymore!"

His eyes widened in shock at the bold manner in which I had spoken, and then his expression turned to rage. "How dare you!" he said, and he raised his arm as if to strike me. But before I could even flinch, his eyes bulged and his red face suddenly grew near purple. He croaked out a pained sound and then fell to his knees.

"Elton!" I exclaimed.

He appeared stunned and unable to speak as he stared up at me helplessly. I worried he was having an attack on his heart.

"Your tablets!" I cried. "Where are your tablets?" I started patting down his coat, searching for the small bottle, finding nothing.

"Adelia!" I called toward the hallway. "Delly!"

As I removed my hands from Elton's body, he seemed to crumple entirely to the floor as his hand flew to his chest. His eyes were no longer focusing, and the noises coming from his throat made it sound as though he was being strangled from the inside.

As I stood over him, my panic began to subside, and I found myself growing oddly calm.

I took in his state of distress and had the realization that he looked rather similar to how I felt day after day, during all my years of being trapped with him. I took a step away from him then.

As I welcomed my resentment, I became bold and cruel.

"Does it hurt, Elton?" I asked as I looked down at him. "Poor thing," I mocked. "Are you feeling suffocated? Smothered? All these years with you, Elton. I know just how it feels. I called for Adelia, didn't I? But oh well." I shrugged. "It seems you are just on your own."

He coughed loudly then, and I started, worried that he was recovering; surely I would pay for my behavior. But then, just as suddenly, his eyes shut and he stilled completely.

I can hardly say how long I stood there staring down at him. Adelia finally appeared in the open doorway, and she was greeted by the strange sight.

"Mistress!" She rushed into the room. "What happened?"

I looked back at her and blinked a few times, as if I had just awoken from a slumber. "I think he's dead." My voice sounded far away, even to me. "He had an attack, and then he just plum collapsed."

Adelia hunched down over him and put her hand against his chest, feeling for breath, or maybe to check his heart. We were silent as she waited for signs of life. After a few moments, she shook her head and rose back to her full height.

"He's dead," she said. Then she looked me square in the face. "Mistress, you is free."

ANTHONY

Rocky Mount, December 1854

O ver time, Anthony came to think his new owner had a better head for business than Master Charles. Nearly every day, folks were coming to the house to buy or sell one thing or another, and Master David was always happy and smiling after they left. Didn't matter if it was horses, lumber, or slaves. The plantation seemed almost a side business—his main concern was always all that buying and selling.

Anthony knew there were places worse than Great Falls Farm, and so he aimed to avoid being one of the bodies sold off. He heeded what Vincent said about the master choosing favorites, and he decided to make himself someone the master couldn't lose. He also sought to make peace with Mistress Hazel.

He took to checking with her each night, asking if she wanted a ride anywhere the next day. Then he'd fetch up the horses, groom them real nice, and be ready and waiting with the carriage before each trip. Mistress seemed to like the special attention, and one afternoon, she even thanked Master David right there in front of Anthony.

She was stepping out of the carriage after a trip to church and Master David was walking from the barn to the house, when she called to get his attention.

"David, dear, a moment?" She spoke kindly, but when he turned round, his eyes said he didn't want to be bothered none.

"I can't argue with you right now, Hazel." He didn't slow his pace as he continued toward the house. "I've got men coming in a few minutes from Cooper's."

"I just wanted to thank you," she answered, her voice sweet.

He stopped and turned back again.

"The new driver is passable," she said. "I can resume my visiting."

Master David glanced at Anthony where he was adjusting a bridle, and then looked back to Hazel.

"Oh," he said. "Well, good, very good." And then he was back on his way.

LATER THAT AFTERNOON, AS DAY WAS turning to evening, Master David came to see Anthony in the stables. Anthony was mucking out one of the stalls when he heard the master call.

"Burns," he said, "what have you done to make the mistress so pleased?" He was dressed in only his shirtsleeves, which was a signal that he was finished doing business for the day.

"Well," Anthony said as he put the shovel blade down against the ground. "I just been making certain the coach is clean and ready whenever she need. Clean up the horses extra fresh before each ride. Drive her smooth to where she ask to go." He shrugged. "Only trying to do my job proper."

"Anthony," he said, "I'll tell you something. The mistress and I, we don't get on like we used to. She can be . . ." He paused, looking up to the rafters like he was searching for a word. "Particular," he finally said. "She didn't care for the last driver. Nor the one before him. Stopped leaving the property all together. I figured that was how it would stay and you'd be driving only for me." He walked toward the horse in the next stall and reached out to pat its nose.

Anthony just kept quiet, waiting for what else Master David might say.

"Things are better for us when she goes out and does her visiting. Lots of reasons why."

Anthony nodded, glad the master was pleased with him.

"Tell you what," Master David said, his eyes traveling toward the hayloft where Anthony and Vincent kept nights. "I've got an office down the south end of the house that's lying empty. It's small, but maybe more comfortable than the stable, if you'd like to set yourself up in there."

Well, with the nights getting colder as they were, Anthony was glad enough to find himself better shelter. "Thank you, sir."

"Well, then, come along." He motioned for Anthony to follow. "I'll show you now, and then you can come back out to finish for the night and get your things."

Anthony rested the shovel against the wall and did just as he was bid.

MASTER DAVID BROUGHT ANTHONY TO A room that was big enough for a writing desk and a large seat that he called a davenport. That's where Anthony was to sleep, and looking at the fat cushions on the thing, Anthony felt it would for sure be better than the barn.

Master David looked round the room one more time, making certain there weren't anything else he needed to pass on about the place. "I'll let the mistress know," he said, "so she doesn't jump out of her boots if she finds you here."

"Yes, sir," Anthony answered.

"And you might as well take your meals in the kitchen now, with Cook and Jenny and the others."

"Yessir," he nodded, thinking of the hotter, fresher food a body got inside the house.

"Right, then," Master David finally said, and then he walked out.

Once Anthony was alone in the office, he tried to feel cheerful about his good fortune. Yet now that he'd seen Boston, what once might have pitched his spirits toward the sky felt like only modest improvement. The longer he stayed down there with Master David, the more he saw his chance at freedom slipping away. How long would his Northern friends search for him? He ran his hand along the smooth wood of the writing desk in front of him as he remembered Coffin Pitts and how it felt walking himself to a paying job at the clothing shop each morning.

On impulse, he opened one of the drawers of the desk. Inside, there were some old books that looked like ledgers. He rose and closed the door of the office, and then he returned to the desk to open a ledger. Maybe moving to the office was more of an opportunity than he first realized. He thought maybe he could tear a sheet from the back of the book and use it to send another letter north. His blood pumped hard as he flipped pages looking for empty sheets, but page after page was so filled with numbers and figuring that there wasn't a single space free. He took up the next book and the one after that, flipping through faster and faster, but all he found was the same. When he'd gone through the last, he put them all back and closed the drawer with an aching heart. It was high time he stop hoping, hoping all the time. It only made the letdown hurt worse when nothing came of it.

He opened the next drawer feeling like there wasn't any purpose to his actions, and he was right. It was nothing but an empty drawer. There was a larger drawer at the bottom, and when he pulled that one out, his breath hitched. There was a pile of old correspondence, several letters with only a few words to a page. He could easily use the back of one to write a letter of his own, even maybe reuse the envelope. He got to thinking about how he might pass by the post the next time he took the mistress to town, maybe slip back there while she was busy visiting. He got to work that very night drafting another letter to Mr. Dana so that as soon as the mistress told him to drive her elsewhere, he'd be ready. He'd keep that letter always in his pocket, just waiting to be mailed.

THE VERY NEXT MORNING, ANTHONY THOUGHT his opportunity had come along, but it turned out he mistook why the day's journey would be important.

Mistress sent a boy name Carson to the stable to tell Anthony to ready the coach. He pushed his hand against his pants pocket, feeling for the letter hidden inside. The note he'd written told Mr. Dana all about how he was now in Rocky Mount, but that his master didn't want to sell him off. Anthony told Mr. Dana to write back, but to address the letter to Mr. James Black of Rocky Mount, else if he put Anthony's real name, the message would get taken before it ever reached him. Anthony thought his Northern friends might be able to persuade Master David to sell, if they did it proper.

His heart raced all that morning as he waited for the mistress to appear and tell him where to carry her. When she finally came out to the drive in her bright coral day dress and a matching shawl for keeping warm, Jenny from the kitchen hurried behind her holding a basket packed with food. Jenny came and handed Anthony the basket to load into the coach.

He leaned in close and asked her, "Mistress picnicking?" A picnic could mean his services would be required the entire time they were out of doors. If he ran off to the post, he would be missed.

Jenny shook her head and glanced at the mistress, who was climbing into the carriage. "For the drive," she said and then turned back to the house.

Mistress called down to Anthony from her seat. "Let's hurry now, Burns," she said. "We've got a journey ahead."

And just like that, he started feeling low again. He climbed to his seat with the knowledge that the outing wouldn't be taking them near the post after all. He drove along where Mistress told him, far out to the country. Finally, after nearly two hours, they pulled up in front a large white house that looked very similar to the McDaniels' plantation home.

Several young women hurried from the front porch to call out and embrace Mistress. Anthony gathered from their chirping that these were cousins she hadn't seen in a long while. As the ladies went inside, a stable hand walked to the coach.

"I'll show you where to tie up," he said, motioning Anthony to follow.

Anthony did as the stable boy instructed, and then he sat there on the driver's bench waiting out Mistress's visit. He kept thinking he should stop feeling sorry for himself. Wasn't he already better off than he'd been at Lumpkin's jail, now that he was sitting there in the fresh air knowing he'd have a soft place to sleep for himself that evening? It was unusually warm for December, and he reminded himself God would want him to appreciate the blessing of the mild day. It was hard not to be angry though. Each day, he felt he could only stand being a slave one day longer.

As he sat there chafing at what had befallen him, the doors opened at the balcony just above where he was sitting. Out came Mistress and three other women, all of them in brightly colored shawls. One of the women pointed toward the fields beyond the house as she talked to Mistress. They were far enough away that Anthony was unable to make out all their words, but he caught some. The woman was describing something new to be built on the property. He looked in the direction of the fields and wondered what these people could possibly need to add to their lands. He stared out that way so long that when he finally turned his eyes back toward the balcony, all but one of the ladies had gone. The woman remaining stared down at him. He looked away quick, but not before his pulse kicked up. She was looking at him real sharp. He was sure he'd never seen that woman before, but hand to God, she was looking at him like she knew exactly who he was.

ANN

Boston, January 1855

For two days, my legs had been causing me such trouble that I
could barely use them. Cara helped settle me on the divan in
the front parlor, covering me with a wool blanket and encouraging me to stay put for the whole day through. Beside me
just then sat Wendell, who had brought in the day's mail and
was sharing with me the contents of various correspondence. I
never saw a man receive as many letters as my husband, but he
relished them all, and he was always fastidious in responding
to every last note.

"Aha!" he said, as he picked up the next envelope in the
stack, as though he'd been waiting for that one in particular.
"Harriet Tubman writes," he said as he opened the envelope.
He began to read aloud.

Dear Mr. Phillips,

*Please accept my thanks for your kindness in
forwarding the books and pamphlets. I have not yet
read them. My head is very poor at present and I find it
difficult to attend to anything requiring much thought,*

but I have a presentiment that your position is the true one, at least in some respects.

But I am still most excessively annoyed in reading the account of Parker Pillsbury's late debut before the Anti-Slavery conference in London. I have always had an instinctive aversion to that man, founded on a deep impression of want of honor and purity in his character—this confirms it in a most striking manner.

"What has her in such a dither?" I interrupted. This was obviously a continuation of a conversation that had already begun between the two of them.

Wendell sighed and laid the letter on the small table beside his chair.

"She's lost patience with the more extreme members of the group," he said, "and she's frustrated with the American and Foreign Anti-Slavery Societies. Neither one espouses views precisely in line with hers. Yet, she has been falsely cited by all of them as aiding their workers."

"Go on, then," I told him.

He took up the pages again and pushed his spectacles higher on his nose.

I do not believe the course of the American Board has been what it should be, and had Mr. Pillsbury told the simple truth about them, I would have been well pleased. But these monstrous charges I read with indignation greater than I have felt since the recapture of Burns and of the same sort—

I couldn't help but interrupt again.

"She is so disturbed because Mr. Pillsbury too aggressively criticized the Anti-Slavery Society?"

"Indeed," he said, reaching back into the envelope and

removing a pamphlet. "It seems she's included an issue of *The Independent* containing the full account."

Before he could begin reading from the pamphlet, there came knocking at the front door. Wendell rose from his seat just as Cara appeared from the kitchen with a wooden spoon in her hand.

"Let me, Mr. Phillips," she said, shooing Wendell away with the spoon.

Cara opened the door to reveal Leonard Grimes and Richard Dana. At the sight of Pastor Grimes, my heart jumped to my throat.

"Good day!" exclaimed Mr. Dana with exuberance as he looked from Cara to Wendell. "We have news."

Cara pushed the door wide so they could pass. Wendell ushered the men into the parlor, and I saw that Mr. Dana's cheeks were flushed with excitement. In fact, both he and Mr. Grimes were practically quaking head to toe.

After abbreviated pleasantries, and before even taking their seats, Mr. Dana announced the purpose of their visit. "There has been a development with Anthony Burns!"

I gasped aloud, causing Wendell to glance over at me.

"Ann, this is perhaps too much commotion on a day when you're already suffering so." He looked about the room as if he would invite the men to deliver their account to him elsewhere.

"Absolutely not!" I was perhaps too forceful in my response, but I was desperate to know whether the efforts to which Octavia and I had gone had proved fruitful. Thankfully, Wendell was sufficiently distracted by our visitors to remain unmindful of my behavior.

"Well, come then," Wendell motioned the men to sit.

The last any of us had heard about Anthony had been weeks earlier, when Mr. Dana received an unexpected letter from a Reverend Stockwell of Amherst, Massachusetts, a man whom none of us had ever met. The Reverend Stockwell reported that one of his parishioners had been down South visiting family when she'd recognized Anthony Burns. It had been a relief to us all to learn that Mr. Burns was still alive, as we'd lost track of him following his departure from Lumpkin's jail. The parishioner had unfortunately also reported in her letter to Reverend Stockwell that the owner would never agree to sell because Anthony was the mistress's new favorite.

"But that woman," Wendell said, and my heart sped only faster as he continued, "the good Samaritan, did she not say Anthony's fate was sealed?"

Cara appeared then with the tea service. "I thought you might be liking some refreshment for your visiting." She set the tray before us and hurried off.

As hostess, I should have begun to pour the tea then, but I worried my hands would shake with nerves. It was better to let them all conclude I'd forgotten my manners. I had Octavia to think of too.

"It seems that the good Reverend Stockwell sent a letter south anyway," Mr. Dana declared with glee, "offering to purchase Mr. Burns from the owner."

I stole a glance at Pastor Grimes. Our eyes met briefly, and I detected not the slightest note of disapproval or indignation. It was only then that I was I able to release the breath I'd been holding.

"It seems the reverend directed the owner to send a response to us here in Boston," Mr. Dana continued. "I just received this letter from a David McDaniel of North Carolina, addressed to both Mr. Stockwell and myself." He pulled an envelope from his jacket.

Before Mr. Dana unfolded the letter, Pastor Grimes told us, "The owner has agreed to part with Burns for a price of $1,300. His letter directs Reverend Stockwell to meet him in Baltimore at the end of next month, at which time they will make the exchange."

I wanted to jump with excitement and throw my fists into the air at this success. But then I remembered that the battle was not yet won. I looked over at Wendell, fairly certain I knew what he would say. Still, I cringed as he said it.

"I'm sorry." Wendell shook his head. "I'm glad our friend is alive and out of that horrid prison, but we cannot purchase his freedom."

"Wendell," I implored, "we must."

I could see the indecision play across his face, and I knew I must seize this opportunity.

"Please, Wendell," I said, allowing my breath to grow a bit ragged. "Who knows how much longer it will be before my body expires entirely. Please let me see at least this one man reach freedom."

Wendell looked from me to our guests and then back to me again, struggling over the decision. "I cannot in good conscience fund this transaction, but I will make no effort to thwart you should you like to participate in raising the money."

Pastor Grimes cleared his throat. "Actually, Mr. Phillips, I've already been to see Charles Barry at Boston's City Bank. He drew for me two checks on the Union Bank of Maryland. One is for $676, an amount I already raised for a possibility just such as this." He glanced at me then, and I, ever so subtly, shook my head. Thankfully, Mr. Grimes seemed to understand, and he did not disclose anything about our prior discussion at his home.

"What of the other money?" Wendell asked.

"Mr. Barry advanced me the remaining $624 on his own."

I hardly knew Mr. Barry, but I was aware he served as the secretary for the Pine Street Anti-Slavery Society.

"Well, what is next, then?" Wendell asked, and I could see he was growing increasingly excited at the prospect of Burns's freedom, even though he might not have been a proponent of our methods.

Mr. Dana looked pleased as well. "Someone needs to inform Reverend Stockwell of the meeting," Mr. Dana said.

"I can do that," I said. "Just leave the address, and I'll draft the letter."

Mr. Dana nodded, and I hoped my relief at being permitted the task did not show on my face.

"And someone needs to bring the money," Mr. Dana said, turning back toward Wendell. "We thought perhaps since you were such a friend to Burns when he was here, you would go."

"Nonsense," Wendell responded gamely. "Pastor Grimes has been the truest friend to Mr. Burns, working to secure the funds as he has. I could hardly take his seat on the train." Wendell smiled graciously at the pastor.

Pastor Grimes shook his head. "That McDaniel—surely he will sell only to a white fellow."

"No matter," Wendell argued, "so long as the man knows that the minister, Reverend Stockwell, is coming, I'm confident that will be enough. You must go with the reverend and meet your friend again. And then you bring him home to freedom."

ANTHONY

January–February 1855

Victor had fallen ill some three days past. He was laid up in the sick cabin, and it was beginning to look like he mightn't ever return. Anthony was still working the barn in the meanwhile, shivering away in the winter cold, while he tried to do Victor's job along with his own. He was making certain all the horses had their water for the morning when he heard Master David calling.

Anthony found him waiting near the tack room, running his hands over a bridle that was hung-up on a hook.

"There you are," he said as Anthony approached. "I thought we might go for a walk."

Now, he knew better than to ask, but Anthony was worried why the master wanted to go strolling together in that biting cold. Instead, he just nodded and followed along.

They made their way toward the creek down the hill, stepping around fallen branches and root clusters as they walked. When they reached near the water's edge, Master David stopped. Then he squatted down to pick up a shiny stone from the sediment.

"There's something I need to ask you, Anthony," he said as he crouched, gazing out toward the icy water. "Now, I know you say you'll always be honest with me, so I hope that's the case now, as well."

"Sir?" Anthony asked, fretting at those words.

"Have you been sending letters north?"

He nearly lost his footing then. He felt a twinge in his wrist, remembering what happened the last time he'd been caught out.

"Lots of folks up North probably wondering where I am," he answered, pushing the words past the knot forming in his throat, not really answering what he'd been asked.

"Sure do," Master David said as he stood back to his full height. He pulled his arm out to the side, the smooth stone still in his hand, and with a flick of his wrist, he sent the stone skipping along the ripples of the creek. "Well, I might as well just tell you," he said, as he dusted off his hands. "I received a letter from a man named Reverend Stockwell asking whether he could purchase you for the purpose of setting you free. Would you like to be free, Anthony?"

Now Anthony knew he had a special place with Master David, that he was the recent favorite. But he wasn't certain if maybe Master David was trying to trap him somehow, angered about his letter writing. Anthony had never heard of any Reverend Stockwell before. When he hesitated to answer, Master David spoke again.

"He's offering quite a sum of money for you, much more than what I paid. Might make it worth my while."

A vine of excitement started creeping up from deep in Anthony's gut, but he didn't want to get himself fooled, neither. "This reverend, he's not a body I know," he told Master David. "You think I could see his letter?"

Well, Master David had the note there in his pocket, and he took it out and passed it over. Anthony studied the flowery script of the letter while Master David kept quiet. There was only the sound of birds above the rushing creek and the field workers chanting a work song in the distance. Sure enough, that letter said just what Master David had described. Anthony handed it back and tried to think what to ask. But Master David, he had more to say on the matter.

"Folks around here, you know they won't look kindly on me for letting you get your freedom. You can't mention a word to anyone, you hear? Not even the mistress."

"No, sir," Anthony answered, "I won't do no such thing." He put a hand to his chest, like a promise.

"It's a risk to me, as well, you understand," he said.

"Yes, sir." Anthony wondered if it was money or conscience pushing Master David toward considering the sale.

"Very good," he said, tucking the letter back in his pocket. "I will get everything arranged."

DAYS WENT BY AFTER THAT WHERE Master David didn't say anything else on the matter. He'd send Anthony to task on this or that, even sometimes ask after his comforts, but he never mentioned the talking they did down by the creek. There were days when Anthony wondered if he'd imagined it all, especially since he didn't ever know a Reverend Stockwell. All his guessing about how the reverend might be acting as agent for his Northern friends started to break apart as the days passed on. But then early one Monday morning, the master appeared as Anthony was carrying feed down from the storage shed and told him to return to his room in the office, to take whatever belongings he had.

"Hurry back," Master David directed, "and ready the coach. I'll get Curtis."

Curtis was the boy they got to replace Victor, after the sickness brought him to his maker. Anthony missed Victor and his talking, talking, talking, but Curtis was all right. And maybe his kind of quiet was better for their journey anyhow.

As Anthony looked round the small office and collected his other set of clothing, he was brought right back to that moment when he made his escape from Millspaugh, when he put on all the shirts and pants he owned and hurried to the docks. He remembered the hawk his father carved and wondered if it was still sitting safe at Coffin Pitts's house, waiting for him to return.

They drove with Curtis to the Rocky Mount station, just south of town. Master David had brought along a valise that Anthony carried as they made their way to the platform to await the train. So many other bodies milled about down there at the station, but Anthony just kept his face tilted to the ground, like Master David said, so he wouldn't be recognized. Anthony didn't think any of the white folk around there would remember about him anyway. More than three quarters of a year had passed since the trial in Boston. A few men greeted Master David as they passed, but nobody took interest in Anthony skulking along behind him. He figured he looked just like any other slave accompanying his master on a journey.

Master David paid the conductor for their tickets, and then Anthony followed him to their seats. His heart was banging so hard, like it was a child locked in a closet just wanting to get out. He couldn't wait for that train to start rolling so he could start moving closer to his freedom.

It was his first time riding the railroad. They settled onto the wooden benches of that Wilmington & Raleigh Railroad train car, with Anthony taking the spot just behind Master David. More folks kept coming onto the train, bringing with them the scents of tobacco and different foods they must have packed away with themselves. All the while Anthony worried something might go wrong. Mostly, he worried Master David might change his mind. But then finally, a whistle sounded. The train began to rattle and sway, making all sorts of racket, but the noise wasn't a bother to Anthony. No, it was the sound of celebration in his heart. By the grace of the good Lord and the mysterious Reverend Stockwell, after all he'd suffered in Lumpkin's jail and all the time that had passed, finally, he was back on his way.

They were riding east, toward Tarboro, so they could get themselves to Norfolk, where they would then be boarding a ship. Master David told him all this on the ride to the train station, when he asked one last time if Anthony was sure he wanted to leave. Master David said, Wasn't Anthony happy living at the plantation? Wasn't he treated good? Master David may have been the best master there was, but what man wanted any master other than himself?

The moving train brought up the wind, and Anthony wrapped his arms around himself for warmth. They hadn't been riding but ten minutes when someone called out to Master David.

"Hey-o, McDaniel!" came a greeting from a man a few benches beyond their own.

Master David tipped his hat in the direction of the caller, but then the man stood up. He was a medium sized fellow, dressed in a fine dark coat.

"Who's that darkie you're carrying with you?" The man pointed his stubbled chin toward Anthony. "That wouldn't be the Burns boy? On a train headed north?"

"Burns?" another rider asked, ears all along the train suddenly perking up, so many passengers turning to look their way.

"That'd make you a traitor, wouldn't it McDaniel?" someone else called. "Bringing the boy up North."

The first man turned to look at the others sitting around him. "Now we can't be abiding that. We best escort Mr. McDaniel clear off the train," he said, "and his Negro along with him!" Calls of agreement rang out from the other passengers.

Master David rose to his feet. "Gentlemen!" he hollered at them. "We're going only as far as Norfolk, where I've got business and needed a man to accompany me. If you'll please let off with your yelling."

The conductor had hurried over at the sound of the commotion and now shouted at the rowdy passengers. "What's
the meaning of this?" he called, and then his eyes settled on
Master David.

That man who recognized Anthony first came forward
to answer. "McDaniel here is trying to take that Burns boy
up North."

Anthony felt the conductor looking over at him then, but
he kept his face down, his eyes on his shoes.

"Burns?" the conductor said, and Anthony hoped the man
had never heard of him. "You mean the runaway?" He came
closer, probably to get a better look. Then he turned back to
Master David. "If I'd known you was bringing that boy onto
this here railcar, I never would've let you board." He sounded
real angry.

"So let's put him out! Stop the train!" another man called out.

The conductor looked round the train car a moment, as
though he was considering the best way to send Anthony home.
"Can't do it now," he said with frustration in his voice. "We
got schedules to keep."

Several of the men started shouting again at that, saying
Anthony shouldn't be permitted to travel anywhere.

Master David spoke again in that stern way he had. "This
matter doesn't concern y'all. Ronald Heathcote," he called to
one of the men who'd been heckling them. "I know you don't
want to jeopardize future feed contracts over this."

The man looked contrite and after a moment, he sat himself
back in his seat.

"Or you, Henry Wilkens. You want me to find another
supplier for rice down at the store?"

The man named Wilkens shook his head and then glanced
at the others around him before returning to his seat too, just
like the fellow before him.

"Do I have to call all y'all out by name, or can you just

button yourselves back up?" Master David fixed his hands on his hips as his eyes traveled round the railcar.

Nobody answered, but slowly, the other men began to retreat, and it wasn't too long before everyone was sitting docile again. Maybe it was because of being one of the richest men in town that Master David had some power, or maybe it was the way he just expected folks to give way. He huffed, to show his annoyance at the ruffian behavior, and then he too sat himself down. He didn't look over at Anthony.

The remainder of the long journey to Norfolk passed without incident. When the train began to slow, Master David leaned over. "When we stop," he near whispered, "we must make haste to be first off the train, you hear?"

Then he motioned for Anthony to move with him and stand close to the exit, so they could hop off quick when time came. Anthony was plenty stiff from the hours of sitting, and he figured Master David was too, but the man moved fast once he stood, and Anthony hurried along after him just the same.

When the train began to roll up alongside the platform at the depot, Master David signaled that the time had come, and they both jumped off before the train even came to a full stop.

They hurried into the station, passing through a thick crowd of travelers inside before coming out the other end, onto the bustling streets of Norfolk. Anthony wasn't sure exactly where they were heading, but then he saw the water coming into view, and he reckoned they were making for the steamer directly.

Master David said earlier that he had some business to conduct before they set sail from Norfolk, but it seemed he'd changed his plans. Anthony barely had a moment to look around at the new town, except to notice the crowded streets and the smell of tobacco and manure, just like back in Richmond. The afternoon sun was reflecting off the water, and he had to squint his eyes from the glare. When they reached the wharf, Master David near shoved him toward an open gangway.

They hustled themselves onto the waiting ship, slowing only for Master David to show a man their tickets, and then they hurried down to the cabins below deck. Master David found a sailor in the dark hallway and asked him to direct them forthwith to their compartment. Once they were alone in the cabin, Anthony looked round at the small space. There was a neat single bed, as well as a bureau, a writing desk, a tall floor clock, and two tidy-looking armchairs. He didn't want to think what this room was costing or whether Master David took account of the expense when he decided how much would be Anthony's price.

"I have business in town," Master David said, making clear his plans hadn't changed after all. "You should be safe on this vessel until I return."

"Yes, sir," Anthony answered, hoping Master David wouldn't meet any of those men from the train back on the street. They'd want to know where it was the famous slave had gotten to. Anthony didn't say any such thing to Master David. He just walked to the thick wooden door after he was alone and made certain the latch was secured good and tight.

He sat himself down on one of the armchairs and waited. He looked round the little cabin again, then down at his hands, studying his fingernails and picking at the edges where they were cracked and flaky from long days handling all the horse tack. As the minutes ticked by, he began to grow restless.

It'd be near two more hours before the vessel would set sail for the overnight trip up the Chesapeake to Baltimore. He thought about Master David saying it was safe there on the ship, and he rose from the chair to unlatch the heavy door. He peered out into the hallway, where other passengers were meandering to their quarters. Nobody spared him a second glance as they followed crew through the narrow hallways to their cabins.

He hoped time enough had passed now and the fellows from the train might have forgotten him, maybe getting on toward their evening plans instead. He decided he would go back up top after all and have one last look at Norfolk before he left the South forever. When he reached the open deck, he saw it was full-up now with passengers who arrived during the time he'd been in the cabin. Despite the January chill, groups of white folks were perched together on wooden deck chairs, men and women turned out in fine coats and hats, laughing, smoking, drinking, ready to set off on a grand adventure. He smiled as he climbed the last steps, feeling their excitement mix with his own.

He wandered toward the back of the vessel, where the deck grew narrower before it came to a point. The sun was creeping closer to the rooftops of all those city buildings, but he could see plenty of folks still bustling about finishing whatever business they had in town. He looked over toward the gangway then, wondering how much longer it'd be before Master David returned, and that's when he recognized one of the white men crossing the deck with three others close behind.

"Well, look who's here!" the man called as his eyes landed on Anthony. It was the same man who'd started the fussing on the train.

Anthony turned quickly to find the stairwell, but the deck was now so crowded that he couldn't see for sure where that opening was to get down below.

The men were nearly upon him, and it seemed there wasn't anything he could do but face them.

"Please, I don't want no trouble, sirs," he said, keeping his voice the way some white folk preferred, just plain and simple. He backed himself up as they approached until his body was pushed flush against the railing.

The man from the train laughed loudly as he stepped close to Anthony's face, and then he looked back at his friends. "He don't want no trouble," the man said to the others, and then he looked back at Anthony. "No trouble, eh?"

"No, sir." He turned his gaze to the floorboards, praying they would leave him be.

"Should have thought about that before you ran. Before you kicked up such a spectacle in Boston too. Ain't that right, boy?"

A crowd was forming around them with people asking what the excitement was about.

"That's Anthony Burns!" one of the men in the group shouted. "The runaway they nabbed up in Boston."

A big holler went up at that, folks growing crazed that he was here in their city, making his way north. More men seemed to be joining the group, ready to do Anthony harm.

The noise around them grew louder still, and he cursed himself for leaving that cabin.

One of the ship's crew approached and tried to calm the growing mob. "Gentlemen! Order! Order!" the uniformed man said.

Several others in the crowd started shouting back at the sailor.

"He's a fugitive!"

"A criminal!"

"Get him off the ship!"

Then Anthony caught sight of Master David pushing through the crowd, making his way until he was upon them. He pushed himself between Anthony and the others, facing the agitators straight on. He didn't say anything, but just raised his arm into the air, pointing a shiny pistol up toward the sky. Anthony hadn't known Master David brought a weapon with him. As people noticed the gun, the noise started to settle. It kept quieting until just about the whole crowd had turned their attention from Anthony over to Master David.

"Now!" he shouted the word like a command, "I have given my word that I will deliver this Negro to Baltimore. Is there a man here who would like to be responsible for causing me to break my word?"

There were some murmurs and rumbling from the crowd, but nobody answered directly. When the mob did not disperse,

Master David spoke again, "I am a man of my word, fellows, and I intend to keep that word, even if it costs me my life." He cocked his gun then, as if he was getting ready to shoot.

"Man alive, McDaniel," the ringleader answered back. "You're willing to stake so much on this Negro? Why?"

"Maybe you should ask yourself that same question, Heathcote," Master David said, as he changed the aim of the gun and pointed it directly at the man. "Just get on with yourselves. Off, off you go!" He waved the gun around, dismissing Heathcote with it, and the onlookers too.

"You win, McDaniel," the man called Heathcote said, "but if you're so strict with your *word*," he said the last part with a mocking tone, "why don't you give those of us here your word too?"

"How's that?" Master David asked.

"Your transaction doesn't go through in Baltimore as you expect, you come back to Norfolk and deliver that Negro to us?"

"You offering to buy him?" Master David asked.

"Sure am," the man said. "Then leastways, I knows he's staying put in the South."

"No," Master David said. "I don't think I'd sell to you. But I'll give you my word that if the deal falls through, I'll bring him back to North Carolina with me."

That seemed to satisfy the man enough and the mischief-makers looked like they were about ready to surrender. Anthony thought that fellow, Heathcote, was just trying to end the meeting without looking like he'd been defeated.

Master David was a formidable man even without a weapon, so Anthony wasn't surprised that he got the others to back down. He was more bewildered by how firmly his master had defended him. It made him almost sorry to be leaving the man—but not sorry enough to stay.

MASTER DAVID DIDN'T SAY MUCH ABOUT what happened up on deck. He just carried on like everything was regular. He told Anthony about the steamer that was carrying them and when they would arrive in Baltimore. The vessel was part of the Old Bay Line, he said, an outfit that had been running an overnight route between Norfolk and Baltimore for more than a decade. The only mention he made of the ruffians outside was to say Anthony should stay the night in the cabin for safety. Master David seemed to sleep peacefully through the night aboard the ship, but not Anthony. He spent the dark hours in the wooden chair in the corner, moving between panic and excitement, drowsiness and fear, as the vessel rocked beneath them. The chair was firm and tight, hardly meant for a comfortable sleep, but it was still better than his first sea journey toward freedom, when he suffered so many days inside that box.

After Master David rose and dressed, they made their way together onto the ship's deck to watch the sailors bring them into port. All the while, Anthony was scanning the people around them, wondering if there would be more trouble, worrying whether freedom would remain only a dream.

Finally, he heard the skipper call out, "All ashore who's going ashore!"

They didn't waste their time getting off that packet ship. He hurried along the dock behind Master David, the smell of fish and brine tickling his nose as he looked toward the city where his freedom was to be purchased.

As far as he could tell, Baltimore wasn't all that different from the cities he'd known in Virginia, except it had a monument near its center that stood taller than all the brick buildings around it. Even from afar, it was clear that the statue was built from white marble, and it made Anthony think of Master Charles and the stone quarry the Suttle family owned for all those years. Would his old master ever learn of him being sold to freedom? He hoped so. He wanted the old man to feel sorry for all the wrong he'd done in this life, but Anthony didn't expect it.

They made their way deeper into the city, passing shops and hotels until they reached an area called Monument Square. They passed close to another marble statue, smaller than the other, but still keeping the quarry on Anthony's mind. Then Master David pointed toward a large square building on the corner of North Calvert and Fayette.

The building looked to be about four stories high, with flags bearing the word "Baltimore" waving from the roof. Something about the structure's stout appearance and the bursting balconies brought to mind Boston's Tremont House.

As they stepped into the front corridor of the building, he had to stop himself from gasping aloud. He'd never been inside a hotel before, and he wondered if they were all just like this, with shiny floors and high ceilings, the hanging chandeliers above them even bigger than at Master David's home. He wondered who dusted all those crystal orbs hanging from the fixtures and how long it took a body to keep them so fresh.

There was a large desk ahead of them, and behind it was a man wearing a dark red uniform with brass buttons in two rows down the front. The fellow had a tidy hat to match.

"Good morning, sir." He smiled as Master David approached. "Welcome to the Barnum Hotel. How may I help you?"

Master David gave his name and said they were meeting a man from Boston.

"Ah," the clerk nodded. "Yes, your companion has already arrived. I understand you are to have a meeting."

"Has he been here long?" Master David asked, turning to glance at the grand stairwell.

The hotel man looked at the small clock on the desk. "About two hours, I'd say. He's just stepped out, but he left the key for you to wait in the room, if you'd like." He held up a brass key with a tassel hanging from it, the fringe in the same dark red as his costume.

Anthony followed Master David up to the room where they were to await Reverend Stockwell. He supposed the sale was to be done in privacy in order to protect their safety. The room they waited in gleamed the same as the large hall below, and he was careful not to touch anything. Master David sat himself down in a large chair that looked to be covered in velvet. He took the diary from his carrying case and started making marks in it, so Anthony moved to the window and turned to watch the people hurrying about on the street below. He wondered if he might recognize the Reverend Stockwell when the man arrived.

They didn't wait long before there was knocking. When Master David opened the door, Anthony couldn't believe the sight that greeted him.

Walking into the room was his very own true friend, Leonard Grimes!

Anthony nearly shouted in delight. "I knew it must be you! All the time, I was thinking it—it's my good friend Leonard finding a way to come for me!" He was so overcome that he forgot himself in front of Master David. He took Leonard's hand in his own and shook it up and down so hard that Leonard laughed.

Master David let out a chuckle then too, and Anthony remembered then to explain.

"This is the pastor," he said, "Mr. Grimes, who I told you of."

Master David looked for a moment beyond Leonard to the hallway. "Reverend Stockwell is not with you?" he asked Leonard.

"The good reverend has, unfortunately, not appeared." Leonard said. "As it happens, I am in possession of the funds required."

Anthony had forgotten how well Leonard spoke, and he was proud of his friend in front of Master David. Leonard was dressed in a fine suit too, his long coat fitting him neat and trim.

"Perhaps we'll just wait for the reverend," Master David said. "Has there been any word from him?"

"Sadly, there has not," Leonard answered, "but there is no need to inconvenience yourself and prolong your time away from home or business. I have everything required for the sale."

Master David was quiet a moment, thinking about the pastor's words. Anthony made not a peep as he waited to hear what Master David would say. Would he refuse to do business with anyone but the white man who had promised to make the purchase? A chill ran down Anthony's neck as he imagined stepping back onto a ship bound south.

Master David pulled his pocket watch from his breast then to check it. Staring down at the time he let out a sigh. "Come," he said to Leonard, "let us sit."

Pastor Grimes had somehow got right to the heart of it— Master David was always a man who valued his time. As the two men settled at the small circular table, Anthony stood to the side.

Leonard reached into his pocket and pulled out a paper that he handed to Master David. "Full remuneration for the price you posted."

Anthony's body was rumbling with excitement from top to bottom. Much as he prayed and prayed for the good Lord to bring him to this moment, he was struggling to believe that here it was; the Lord was truly delivering Anthony's greatest wish.

Master David took the check from Leonard and looked down at it with a troubled expression. The way he sucked his teeth brought Anthony's elation to a halt. Was he readying to back down from what he'd promised?

"Well, yes, that is the correct amount," Master David said, "but I'm afraid I'm going to need cash. You understand, I can hardly put all my faith in a check, especially in this circumstance." He held the paper out for Leonard to take back.

Leonard looked off toward the window, like he was trying to think. Anthony reckoned his friend had no such cash with him. But then Master David perked up.

"Not to worry, fellows," he said. "If the check is good, you should have no problem exchanging it for cash at the Bank of Baltimore. We can go directly."

They followed Master David back out of the hotel and down the street to the bank.

The aging bank clerk took the check from Leonard and studied it for a long moment. All the while, Anthony's heart thundered against his chest.

"I'm sorry," the white man said, handing the paper back to Leonard, "but I cannot cash this check. Bank rules. You must either be a citizen of Baltimore or find a citizen of Baltimore to attest to your identity."

Anthony didn't need to hear Leonard say that he didn't know a soul in the whole of Baltimore. It seemed that even after everything Anthony had been through to get here, all might be lost after all.

Master David was quiet a moment, and it seemed maybe that was the end of everything. But then his eyes changed, and Anthony remembered that Master David never liked when a person told him he couldn't do a thing.

"I have an idea," Master David said.

They followed behind him again back to the hotel, not knowing what he was figuring to do. When they reached the main entry, Master David strode straight toward that same uniformed man at the desk.

"If you would, please, sir," he said to the man, "direct me to the proprietor of the hotel?"

"That would be me," called a well-dressed white man who had been walking toward them already. "David Barnum," the man said, extending his hand to Master David. Then, to Anthony's surprise, the man reached out to shake hands with both Leonard and him too.

Master David explained the problem with the bank, and Mr. Barnum answered kindly, "Well, it seems you've come to the right place. I was just heading to the bank myself, and I'd be honored if my new friend, Mr. Grimes, would accompany me. I'd be delighted to attest to his identity."

It wasn't clear why the man was willing to help, but they all three seemed to sigh at once.

They returned then to the bank, and the check was cashed without issue, thanks to Mr. Barnum. Finally, they were able to return to the hotel room so that Leonard and Master David could finish with the purchasing part of the transaction.

Anthony stood back at his post to the side of the table. Master David accepted the cash from Leonard and then pulled a page from his carrying case. Anthony held his breath as he watched Master David sign his name to the paper and then hand it over to Leonard.

"Relax, Anthony," Master David said with a sort of sadness in his voice. "It's done." He rose and began collecting his belongings. Anthony watched as if he was in some sort of stupor.

Could it really be true? Had Leonard really just bought his freedom?

"Mr. McDaniel," Leonard said, and Anthony got worried for another holdup. "Now that you've received this premium price today, perhaps you'd be willing to make a gift to Anthony of $100? Simply to start him on his way?"

Master David let out a quick laugh at that. "This business of the sale has already cost me plenty. No, he will have to make it on his own from here." He turned toward Anthony and added, "I wish you only the best of luck, Anthony."

"Thank you, Master David," Anthony said.

"No. Not 'Master' anymore. Just 'Mr. McDaniel,' now." He nodded at them, put his hat to his head, and walked from the room.

AS SOON AS THE DOOR CLOSED BEHIND HIM, Leonard turned to Anthony.

"No time to celebrate," he said, still all business. "We've got to get you out of this state."

Though they were two free men, down in Baltimore they had barely any protections as citizens. Leonard was right that the sooner they could quit it, the better.

They made haste to the train station, but wouldn't you know it that when they made to step on the northbound train, they were stopped yet again.

"Sorry fellas," the ticket man called out to them from behind the window at his booth. "Can't let you board unless you find a white man to give permission. Too many runaways in these here parts."

A conductor stood in the entry to the train, listening and nodding along.

They returned fast as they could to the hotel, hoping that Mr. Barnum's capacity for kindness was even greater than they first saw. He greeted their request graciously, rising from his desk in the back office and telling them to follow along with him back to the station.

"It's the railroad company being frightened of liability, you see," Mr. Barnum explained along the way. "They don't want to find themselves in court over ferrying Negroes north. But it turns out to be an awful lot of hassle."

When they returned to the ticket man, Mr. Barnum marched straight to the window, never minding the others lined up waiting their turn. When nobody complained about his cutting up front, Anthony thought that Mr. Barnum must be an important fellow there in Baltimore.

The ticket man explained that Mr. Barnum had to post a $1,000 bond to protect the railroad company in case anyone should complain about the two Negroes being permitted to board. When Anthony heard the ticket man say that high price, he looked over to Leonard and wondered if they should forget about the train and start walking themselves north fast as they could.

But before he could open his mouth, Leonard held up a hand and motioned with his chin back toward Mr. Barnum. And sure enough, there was Mr. Barnum, hunched over the counter, a pen in his hand as he signed his name to a paper.

Anthony still could not say why Mr. Barnum was so good to them that day, but the next train was on its way, and he didn't dally to find out.

They boarded themselves onto that train into the third-class car, which some folks called the emigrant car. That part of the train was rougher than the rail he rode up from Rocky Mount the day before, but to him, it was a beautiful sight. There were only two ungainly benches lining the sides of the car, and they were almost full-up. He and Leonard found enough space where they could sit with their shoulders pushing firm against one another. Riders who came on after them would have to stand for their journey. As the whistle blew and the train started rumbling along, Anthony felt he could cry with joy.

"Here," Leonard said after the train had been jiggering along for about ten minutes. He handed Anthony a few papers and told him, "You'll be wanting to hold onto those. That's your proof of freedom."

Anthony clutched those papers tight and felt his heart grow near to bursting with fullness. It was like he was taking that testament of liberty into himself and finally, finally, making it part of who he was. At last, he could look with true joy on all that was going to be.

COLETTE

Outside of Richmond, November 1855

I was just finishing at the stables when I saw Rafael returning from his visit to the post. I met him in the drive before he reached the kitchen.

"Any letters?" I asked.

"Not today, Mistress," he answered, and I tried not to let my disappointment show. "Your papers though," he said, holding out the three Northern newspapers to which I'd begun subscribing earlier in the year.

"Ooh!" I reached out for them with delight. "Thank you!"

I hurried up to my childhood bedroom so that I could remove my riding clothes and scour the papers in private. As I reached the second floor, Maman was just coming from her room.

"Oh no, Coco," she said, taking in my disheveled appearance. "You must hurry and change. We have supper with the Franklins. *Dépêchez-vous!*"

"I know, lickety split." I smiled obediently. I had no intention of entertaining a courtship with taciturn Oliver Franklin, whom I'd known since I was a girl. In fact, I doubted I'd ever be interested in courting or marrying again. The only benefit to another match would be producing the children I longed for, but I doubted I could ever carry another child. The suspicion was both as to whether conception could occur and whether my battered heart could bear a repeat of the experience with baby Tina. No, I would lavish all my love on my sweet niece, Lettie, and any of her siblings that might follow.

After Elton died, it didn't take long for me to decide I would move back to my parents' home. They insisted that it was the only seemly course of action for a young widow like myself. I agreed, but only after they reluctantly accepted the condition that I would retain control of my own finances. My father helped me sell the Richmond home for a sum that would have greatly pleased Elton. The slaves, on the other hand, I insisted on handling myself.

It wasn't nearly as difficult as I'd expected to have their manumission papers drawn up and executed, not after I declared to the lawyer and to my parents that it was my husband's dying wish. I thought of my friend Anna Cora Ritchie and wondered if she would have been impressed by my performance. I told that elderly attorney again and again how devastated I was to be losing all those good workers, never mind the monetary loss, and he nodded along in agreement, even as he assembled the documents needed to grant my slaves their liberty.

I had hoped that Adelia would choose to stay with me for paid wages, but I was not surprised when she declined. No, she rode north on the train as an ostensible companion to Mrs. Ritchie when the woman went to New York to visit with family. Adelia told me she'd send a letter once she was settled somewhere new, but all these months later, I hadn't received so much as a scribble from her. I supposed I did not deserve any better.

I still read the Northern papers every afternoon, looking for news of her, or of Anthony. Though I couldn't confess as much to anyone other than Mrs. Ritchie, I enjoyed reading about the anti-slavery conventions and the Northern perspectives on what our own papers continued calling "rabid abolitionists." Now that I was widowed and I was free to return to teaching at the Female Institute, I declared that I was reading the papers to broaden my political knowledge so that I might better teach my students how not to behave. No one asked what I meant by that, and I knew better than to voice more specific opinions on the matter, even to my parents.

I closed the bedroom door before walking to the wardrobe, where I ran my hand over the gowns hanging inside.

Ruby, my mother's favorite house slave, knocked at the door. "Got to get you dressed now, Miss Colette," she said as she entered the room with an air of apology about her. She was a round woman with graying hair that poked out from her headscarf.

"I'll do the coral lace," I told her, choosing the gown that least flattered my complexion in hopes that Mr. Franklin would be unimpressed.

Ruby hesitated a moment, but she would not voice any objection the way Adelia surely would have. I removed the jacket from my habit and then turned so Ruby could begin unfastening the skirt. As she worked her ministrations behind me, my eyes strayed to the pile of papers I'd dropped on the bed moments before. I could see that the *New York Herald* was still reporting on the results of the recent elections, but I'd already had my fill of reading about the aggregate votes received. I leaned forward to push it aside so I could focus on the *Boston Evening Transcript*. The first headline pertained to General Walker and something about Nicaragua, a topic in which I hadn't the slightest interest. I scanned the remainder of the top sheet, seeing news about which ships had arrived and departed from the city. On and on it went about who had set off for foreign ports, who was arriving at home ports, etc. I finally pushed that paper aside in frustration too. My action uncovered a third newspaper in the pile, which I hadn't been expecting.

My shoulders deflated as I saw that the publication was only *The Front Royal Gazette*, a Virginian paper that my father enjoyed because of that city's proximity to the capital. As I turned away from it, not wanting to read whatever anti-Northern sentiments I might find there, a headline toward the bottom of the page caught my eye. Beneath the announcements of new rail lines was a bolded headline that read, "Anthony Burns Again."

"Hold one moment, Ruby," I said, taking the paper toward the light of the window to read.

The Famous Anthony Burns has been sent by his friends, the abolitionists, to Oberlin College, Ohio, to study for the ministry. He has applied for a letter of transfer in fellowship from the Church of Jesus Christ, at Union, Fauquier, Virginia, the house of worship at which he once claimed membership. The letter was promptly refused, and the proceedings of the church were published in the Port Royal Gazette with a letter from elder John Clark. That letter is reprinted below.

To all whom it may concern:

WHEREAS, Anthony Burns, a member of this church, has made application to us, by a letter to our pastor, for a letter of dismission, in fellowship, in order that he may unite with another church of the same faith and order; and whereas, it has been satisfactorily established before us, that the said Anthony Burns absconded from the service of his master, and refused to return voluntarily—thereby disobeying both the laws of God and man; although he subsequently obtained his freedom by purchase, yet we have now to consider him only as, a fugitive from labor (as he was before his arrest and restoration to his master), have therefore Resolved, Unanimously, that he be excommunicated from the communion and fellowship of this church.

Done by order of the church, in regular church meeting, this twentieth day of October, 1855.

WM. W. WEST, Clerk

I was astounded. To have found news of Anthony attesting to his continued survival filled my heart with joy. But that awful letter! *Such gall*, I fumed. *The Gazette* had thought to publish it, flaunting the excommunication from his Southern church as a last bit of punishment for Anthony. I huffed at their audacity even as I reminded myself that Anthony had accomplished his goal regardless of anyone's hatefulness—he was living free. I was meanwhile delighted to learn that he was studying the gospel at Oberlin, preparing to join the ministry. I thought that I might like to send a donation to help finance the remainder of his studies. But I was just as quickly distracted by another idea.

If I knew Anthony like I thought I did, he would never allow this letter from the church to go unanswered. I grabbed for my two Northern papers and flipped frantically through their pages, but there was nothing about Anthony whatsoever. I tossed everything back to the bed with a sigh, remembering now that Ruby was in the room, waiting for me.

"I'm sorry, Ruby," I said, walking back toward where she was still standing quietly behind the bed. "Let's finish this."

IT WAS NEARLY THREE WEEKS LATER THAT I opened the *New York Herald* and found the letter I had felt sure Anthony would pen in response to that abominable missive from his former pastor.

I did not even wait until I'd returned to the house but stood there in the middle of the gravel drive that afternoon, reading the letter in its entirety. The eloquence of the sentences I found showed that Anthony had clearly progressed in his studies since our last meeting. Even so, I recognized the quick wittedness and the force of his convictions as being decidedly his own.

In answer to my request by mail, dated July 13, 1855, for a letter of dismission in fellowship and of recommendation to another church, I have received a copy of The Front Royal Gazette, dated Nov. 8, 1855, in which I find a communication addressed to myself and signed by John Clark, as pastor of your body, covering your official action upon my request.

You have excommunicated me, on the charge of "disobeying both the laws of God and men . . . , in absconding from the service of my master, and refusing to return voluntarily." You charge me that, in escaping, I disobeyed God's law. No, indeed! That law which God wrote on the table of my heart, inspiring the love of freedom, and impelling me to seek it at every hazard, I obeyed; and, by the good hand of my God upon me, I walked out of the house of bondage.

I disobeyed no law of God revealed in the Bible. I read in Paul (1 Cor. 7: 21), "But, if thou mayest be made free, use it rather." I read in Moses (Deut. 23: 15, 16), "Thou shalt not deliver unto his master the servant which is escaped from his master unto thee. He shall dwell with thee, even among you in that place which he shall choose in one of thy gates, where it liketh him best; thou shalt not oppress him." This implies my right to flee if I feel myself oppressed, and debars any man from delivering me again to my professed master.

I said I was stolen. God's Word declares, "He that stealeth a man and selleth him, or if he be found in his hand, he shall surely be put to death" (Ex. 21: 16). Why did you not execute God's law on the man who stole me from my mother's arms? How is it that you trample down God's law against the oppressor, and wrest it to condemn me, the innocent and oppressed?

You charge me with disobeying the laws of men. I utterly deny that those things which outrage all just people are even laws. To be real laws, they must be founded in equity.

You have used your liberty of speech freely in exhorting and rebuking me. You are aware that I, too, am now where I may think for myself and can use great freedom of speech, too, if I please.

You have thrust me out of your church fellowship. So be it. You can do no more. You cannot exclude me from heaven; you cannot hinder my daily fellowship with God.

ANTHONY BURNS

Mon dieu! I wanted to hoot and cheer for my old friend. Such courage and strength of character he continued to display.

I had the fleeting thought that maybe I should take myself north to see him. But no, I knew that even in the North, there could never be anything between us. Better I should leave him to find happiness than interrupt the great progress he was achieving for himself and, I hoped, for our fractured country. I closed my eyes and pointed my face up toward the winter sun, holding the newspaper against my chest, as if I could take his words into myself, hoping I, too, could continue to change, hoping one day I would be brave like him.

ANN

Boston, April 1886

I can feel death coming for me. The sensation is different from
the suffering I experienced in my youth. The extreme fatigue
is similar, yes, but the heaviness in every limb and digit, the
tightness in my chest, the fog in my mind, they have a morbid,
ghastly quality that tells me all I need to know.

I always expected Wendell would long outlive me, but
somehow, I've managed to hang on these last three years without him. To everyone's surprise, it has been I, sickly Ann, who
has outlasted most of my dearest friends, as well. But now it
is time for me to join them. I have grieved the loss of so many
over the years—Helen and Lloyd Garrison, Pastor Grimes and
my dear Octavia, Theodore Parker, Richard Dana, Aunt Maria
and Uncle Henry too. And of course, there was Anthony Burns,
whom we lost all those years ago.

My mind drifts now to the memories of Anthony's return to
Boston back in March of 1855. How we danced with joy when
Pastor Grimes brought him to our door. There was a reception
held for him that same night at Tremont Temple. There must
have been over a thousand people who came to celebrate his

freedom along with us. With so much merriment, no one had thought it odd the way that Octavia and I clung to each other there, grasping hands and basking in our shared relief.

And still, as the years unfolded afterward, neither of our husbands, and in fact, none in their circles, ever thought to ask why Reverend Stockwell had decided to send a second letter to that Mr. McDaniel of North Carolina. Nor did they inquire why, after adamantly promising his participation, the man then failed to arrive in Baltimore for the sale.

We thought Anthony's arrival signaled a new day. And perhaps it did. He was the last runaway ever returned to the South from Massachusetts. Only a few years afterwards, the Civil War began. I'm hardly the only person who believes Anthony's case was the final catalyst in pushing people to lift their weapons and finally demand freedom for all. I wish still that Anthony had lived long enough to see the Emancipation Proclamation become law.

Soon after Anthony arrived to freedom, he enrolled at Oberlin College and managed to complete a deep course of study. I heard that his studies were funded through a generous donation from an anonymous female donor. No one ever learned her reasons for providing such significant financial support.

It turned out that Anthony was a gifted preacher. So adept was he that he was invited by P.T. Barnum to conduct a speaking circuit on the horrors of slavery and to enlighten crowds. Anthony, bless his spirit, was not interested in simply advancing the business enterprise of another and took to performing such speeches on his own, under his own auspices. He traveled throughout the Northern states and Canada, developing quite a following.

Perhaps it was those trips that inspired him to settle finally in Canada. More likely, it was the welcoming community of Negroes that he encountered in St. Catharines. He took a post at a church there and lived quite happily. Regrettably, it was only a short time later that consumption took him from his flock. He never fully recovered from the time he spent in that horrible prison in Virginia, and his health had been precarious ever since. We lost him before he reached the age of thirty.

And still, for reasons I cannot fathom, my own heart has continued to beat all these years. Here I am now, at seventy-two, finally heading toward my maker.

I can sense Phebe here, near my bedside. Periodically she holds a cool cloth to my head. I imagine her husband, George, is down in the kitchen.

I hope that when I cross to the other side, Wendell will be there waiting for me. We can talk of all the speeches he performed throughout the country that I never was able to hear. After watching Wendell fight for Anthony's freedom, seeing the way he dazzled rooms full of people time and time again, convincing crowds of our shared opinions, I pushed him on ahead. I persuaded to him to accept new engagements, despite the fact that such commitments might result in his extended absence from our home. No longer did his trips last only two or three days, but many required him to be absent from home for weeks or even months. With great effort, I convinced him that he did not belong always hurrying back to Boston, getting trapped all over again, as he tended to my needs. There was important work to be done, and my own ailments could no longer prevent him from spreading the abolitionist message to places far beyond his earlier reach. I saw no reason to mention how I might keep busy in his absence.

His decades-long lecturing career included speeches not only about abolition, but also about so many other topics he held dear, from the classics and art to philosophy. When a city invited him to speak on one of those other topics and proposed to pay him a hefty sum, he retained his practice of offering to appear for free if he would be permitted to speak about the rights of the oppressed instead, whether Negroes, women, or immigrants.

We sent so many letters back and forth during those years. Perhaps as we grew older, we never loved each other more.

History is a finicky friend, choosing favorites as she sees fit. I hope the records will at least remember my dear Wendell, how he championed the causes of the enslaved, the downtrodden, the persecuted, at every opportunity. I hope they will recount how he gave nearly everything he had to the Cause: his money and time, even his soul. As for those of us who will more likely be forgotten, I feel comforted that we were never motivated by hope of acclaim.

The weight upon my chest grows only heavier. I close my eyes and open my heart, ready now to find what lies beyond.

The End

AUTHOR'S NOTE

During the era preceding the Civil War, many citizens of Boston and the surrounding areas worked tirelessly to help end American slavery. In their fight for the Cause, they sacrificed much, including personal relationships, social status, and their own safety. Their efforts in spreading the abolitionist message and in denouncing laws like the Fugitive Slave Act played an integral role in precipitating the Civil War and eventually eradicating "the peculiar institution." Although Wendell Phillips and his associates garnered certain recognition for their efforts, many women who were equally committed were prevented by societal norms from receiving the same level of historical acknowledgment. Through this novel, I hope to shine a light on these helpers.

For those interested in learning more about the relationship between Ann and Wendell Phillips, there is a wealth of material showing that their marriage, while imperfect, was the embodiment of an intense, decades-long love affair. Their passion for each other can be traced through the many letters they exchanged while Wendell was touring the country speaking about causes of import to him. Ann never received a conclusive diagnosis regarding her health problems, but many now believe the condition from which she suffered was rheumatoid arthritis.

For further reading about Wendell and Ann, I recommend the following texts:

- Bartlett, Irving H. *Wendell & Ann Phillips: The Community of Reform, 1840–1880*. New York: W.W. Norton & Co., 1979.
- Korngold, Ralph. *Two Friends of Man: The Story of William Lloyd Garrison and Wendell Phillips and Their Relationship with Abraham Lincoln*. Boston: Little, Brown and Company, 1950.
- Sherwin, Oscar. *Prophet of Liberty: The Life and Times of Wendell Phillips*. New York: Bookman Associates, 1958.

There is regrettably less information available about Octavia Grimes, but records show that after the Civil War began, she founded the Colored Ladies Contraband Relief Association at the 12th Street Baptist Church, continuing to assist refugees well into her advanced years. As a starting point for more information on Octavia and her husband, see *The Liberator Files*: *Women Raise Money for Leonard Grimes' Twelfth Baptist Church*, May 2012 (https://www.theliberatorfiles.com/ladies-raise-money-for-leonard-grimes-twelfth-baptist-church/ and *NewAfrikan77: NewAfrikan Leonard Grimes & the Loudon County VA Underground Railroad DMV*, August 2016. https://newafrikan77.wordpress.com/2016/08/02/new-afrikan-leonard-grimes-the-loudon-county-va-underground-railroad-dmv-2-years-in-richmond-penitentiary/).

For reading about Contraband Relief Associations and how the African-American community mobilized to assist former slaves through these organizations, see Judith E. Harper, *Women During the Civil War: An Encyclopedia*, New York: Routledge, 2003.

It bears mentioning that the speeches performed throughout the story are taken almost entirely from historical record.

Alterations have been made to condense what were once lengthier addresses or to modernize language for the sake of the story's flow. I have attempted to remain as close as possible to the original language in these deliveries, including: Richard Henry Dana's courtroom arguments, each of Wendell's public speeches, all addresses performed at the Framingham Fourth of July gathering, including Henry David Thoreau's, and many of the speeches at the rallies and on the streets throughout the story. The same is true of all newspaper articles reprinted herein. Certain articles are the combination of multiple reports that I have condensed and combined, but much of the news recounted in the story contains direct quotes from the actual news reports of the day. For a sampling of the speeches and news articles in full, readers can refer to the following sources:

- Dana, Richard Henry Jr. *Richard Henry Dana Jr. Speeches in Stirring Times and Letters to a Son*, Boston and New York: Houghton Mifflin Company, 1910.
- Library of Congress digital newspaper archive; see in particular:

    Alexandria Gazette, May 30, 1854; The Daily Comet, Nov. 30, 1855; *The Richmond Dispatch*, June 13, 1855.

    Massachusetts Historical Archives, *William Lloyd Garrison's Fourth of July Speech*, https://www.masshist.org/database/431.

    Thoreau, Henry David. *Slavery in Massachusetts*, 1854, reprinted by the University of Pennsylvania African Studies Center, https://www.africa.upenn.edu/Articles_Gen/Slavery_Massachusetts.html.

The timeline of Anthony Burns's life has been pieced together from several helpful texts, which allowed me to ensure accuracy as to many locations and dates throughout the story. Anthony was reported to be a smart, kind, religious, and industrious man, and I have tried to portray those admirable traits throughout the novel. To learn about Anthony's life, I relied most heavily on the following texts:

- Barker, Gordon S. *The Imperfect Revolution: Anthony Burns and the Landscape of Race in Antebellum America*, Kent: Kent State University Press, 2010.
- Stevens, Charles Emery. *Anthony Burns, A History*, Boston: John P. Jewett & Company, 1856.
- Von Frank, Albert J. *The Trials of Anthony Burns, Freedom and Slavery in Emerson's Boston*, Cambridge: Harvard University Press, 1998.

Colette Randolph is a fictional character. Sadly, the plight of women like her, who were relegated to the position of baby-making machines and deprived of the opportunity to participate in other productive endeavors, was all too real in antebellum America. In addition to making an important statement about antiquated gender roles, Colette's character was also inspired by the actual anonymous female donor who funded Anthony's education at Oberlin. Similarly, historians believe that Anthony had a secret love interest in Richmond. There is no indication as to the woman's race.

Although Colette is fictional, many of the people she meets during the novel are borrowed from history. For example, James Cowardin was the true owner of the *Richmond Daily Dispatch* and Joseph Anderson was at the helm of the famous Tredegar Iron Works during the time period in which the story takes place. Similarly, William Foushee Ritchie was the editor of the *Richmond Enquirer* and the second husband of the famous actress, Anna Cora Mowatt. Although I found no specific evidence showing Ms. Mowatt to be the abolitionist sympathizer I have made her out to be, she was a Northerner who was ahead of her time in many ways, and I discovered no reason to conclude she was *not* an abolitionist sympathizer either.

Finally, many of the atrocities described within the story are drawn from history. For example, Lumpkin's jail and the cruel punishments meted out by slave owners are representative of actual historical conditions and events. Our country continues to confront the painful realities of a past blighted by slavery. The abolitionists described in this story dedicated themselves to fighting against such inhumanity. As diverse voices continue to join the chorus of storytelling about our collective history, my hope is that we move forward toward a future that is more fair and just for all.

ACKNOWLEDGMENTS

When pandemic lockdowns began in 2020, I was not unique in being overwhelmed. I had just completed my third novel and it was time to start the fourth, but I couldn't corral my thinking sufficiently to create anything worthwhile. So instead of writing, I began to research a story I had been made aware of years earlier. Learning about Ann Phillips, Octavia Grimes, and Anthony Burns, I escaped for a time. I felt myself living temporarily in their world, not mine. While I was powerless in the face of the modern pandemic, I found another way to channel my efforts into something constructive, which was to lay bare a story that has been buried too long. Though I will never be able to thank them personally, I owe an enormous debt of gratitude to Ann, Octavia, and Anthony for sharing their story with me and allowing me to retell it as best I could.

I am grateful for the many others who helped me turn the piles and pounds of research I collected from a nascent idea into the book it is today. First, to the wonderful team at SparkPress and She Writes Press, Brooke Warner, Crystal Patriarche, Lauren Wise, Samantha Strom, Shannon Green, and Krissa Lagos, who have put up with my continued refusal to commit to just one fictional genre and have helped turned my books into successful finished products across historical, contemporary, dramatic, and romantic categories. Publicity aces Crystal Patriarche, Taylor Brightwell, Hanna Lindsley, and Rylee Warner continue to energize me with their creativity, drive, and excitement. My editor, Nicola Kraus, whose insights always feel as wise as they are vital—thank you for being such a pleasure to know and for every last strike-through. To Kathy Schneider at the Jane Rotrosen Agency for her incredible instincts and enthusiastic support of my work, I feel so lucky to have connected and look forward to our future projects with eager anticipation.

This book could not have been written without the many historical sources on which I relied in my research. Though much history has been lost, I am grateful to all the historians who have written on the subject of female abolitionists and the trial of Anthony Burns. To see which texts I relied on most heavily, please refer to the Author's Note in this book.

Like so much in life, getting a book out into the world really does "take a village." I've been blessed to be surrounded by author friends who are collaborative, supportive, and astoundingly intelligent. In the heart of the pandemic, I somehow managed to find my best writing partners, who just so happen to be bestselling and award-winning authors. To Samantha Woodruff and Brooke Foster, thank you for everything, but especially for beta reading, for your thoughtful feedback, and for continuing to inspire me when I might otherwise have given up.

To the many other kind and generous writers with whom I've been lucky to build friendships since beginning this career, I must say that I'm growing rather attached. Thank you to: Corie Adjmi, Lisa Barr, Jenna Blum, Amy Blumenfeld, Karen Dukess, Elyssa Friedland, Heather Frimmer, Reyna Marder Gentin, Jane Green, Alison Hammer, Nicola Harrison, Susan Kleinman, Sally Koslow, Rachel Levy Lesser, Lynda Loigman, Anna-bel Monaghan, Zibby Owens, Camille Pagan, Amy Poepell,

Ines Rodriguez, Marilyn Simon Rothstein, Susie Schnall, Dan Schorr, Rochelle Weinstein, and Kitty Zeldis.

To the book bloggers, bookstagrammers, and bookfluencers, you are the lifeblood of this profession, and it is thanks in no small part to your efforts that reading remains as popular as it is today. Thank you for all that you do (and for letting me know, time and again, what I need to read next): Holly Berfield, Barbara Bos, Alissa Butterfass, Robin Hall Kominoff, Suzy Weinstein Leopold, Andrea Peskind Katz, Brad King, Lauren Blank Margolin, Zibby Owens (again), Sue Peterson, Jamie Rosenblitt, and Renee Weiss Weingarten.

To my friends from outside the bookish world who have gone above and beyond the call of friendly duty with each of my books, posting multiple reviews, showing up at my events, buying copies for every member of the extended family, and shouting about my books to anyone who will listen, your love and support mean so very much to me. Thank you to Jenny Brown, Jocelyn Burton, Lissy Carr, Bree Schonbrun Dumain, Amy Federman, Reena Glick, Ali Isaacs, Jessica Levinson, Jenna Myers, Nancy and Ari Mayerfield, Daria Mikhailov, Robyn Pecarsky, Michal Plancey, Aliya Sahai, Julie Schanzer, Renana Shvil, Aviva Seiden, Michele Sloane, Abby Schiffman, Amy Tunick, Stacey Wechsler, and Mimi Sager Yoskowitz,

Finally, I offer profound thanks to my incredible family. To my nieces and nephews who are nearing ages where they might soon read one or another of my books: I hope I do you proud. To Sheila, Bob, Allison, Ben, Samantha, and Mike, thank you for your enduring interest and excitement about my work. To my father, who can pick apart a sentence like no one else, our emails about word placement bring me continued delight. To Seymour, who I love dearly and who's not afraid to tell every passing stranger to read my books. To Kelly and Harry, whose unwavering confidence in me has given me more strength than they can possibly realize. To my mother, I strive at every moment of my life to make you proud because I admire and love you so much. To my children, my *raison d' etre* (go ahead and look that up). There are not enough words to describe the joy and wonder you bring to my life. And to Jason, the best choice I ever made, I love you with my every breath.

ABOUT THE AUTHOR

JACQUELINE FRIEDLAND is the *USA Today* best-selling and multi-award-winning author of *He Gets That From Me, That's Not a Thing*, and *Trouble the Water*. A graduate of the University of Pennsylvania and NYU Law School, she practiced briefly as a commercial litigator in Manhattan and taught Legal Writing and Lawyering Skills at the Benjamin Cardozo School of Law. She returned to school after not too long in the legal world, earning her Masters of Fine Arts in Creative Writing from Sarah Lawrence College. Jacqueline regularly reviews fiction for trade publications and appears as a guest lecturer. When not writing, she loves to exercise, watch movies with her family, listen to music, make lists, and dream about exotic vacations. She lives in Westchester, New York, with her husband, four children, and two very lovable dogs.

Author photo © Rebecca Weiss Photography

SELECTED TITLES FROM SPARKPRESS

SparkPress is an independent boutique publisher delivering high-quality, entertaining, and engaging content that enhances readers' lives, with a special focus on female-driven work. www.gosparkpress.com

He Gets That from Me: A Novel, Jacqueline Friedland, $16.95, 978-1-68463-097-4. A young woman serves as a surrogate mother for a gay couple in hopes of changing her own life for the better—only to discover ten years later that she accidentally gave away her own biological child.

That's Not a Thing: A Novel, Jacqueline Friedland. $16.95, 978-1-68463-030-1. When a recently engaged Manhattanite learns that her first great love has been diagnosed with ALS, she is faced with the impossible decision of whether a few final months with her ex might be worth risking her entire future. A fast-paced emotional journey that explores whether it's possible to be equally in love with two men at once.

Trouble the Water: A Novel, Jacqueline Friedland. $16.95, 978-1-943006-54-0. When a young woman travels from a British factory town to South Carolina in the 1840s, she becomes involved with a vigilante abolitionist and the Underground Railroad while trying to navigate the complexities of Charleston high society and falling in love.

A Dangerous Woman from Nowhere: A Novel, Kris Radish. $16.95, 978-1-943006-26-7. When her husband is kidnapped by ruthless gold miners, frontier woman Briar Logan is forced to accept the help of an emotionally damaged young man and a famous female horse trainer. On her quest to save her husband, she discovers that adventures of the heart are almost as dangerous as tracking down lawless killers.

Girl with a Gun: An Annie Oakley Mystery, Kari Bovée, $16.95, 978-1-943006-60-1.When a series of crimes take place soon after fifteen-year-old Annie Oakley joins Buffalo Bill's Wild West Show, including the mysterious death of her Native American assistant, Annie fears someone is out to get her. With the help of a sassy, blue-blooded reporter, Annie sets out to solve the crimes that threaten her good name.

Sarah's War, Eugenia Lovett West. $16.95, 978-1-943006-92-2. Sarah, a parson's young daughter and dedicated patriot, is sent to live with a rich Loyalist aunt in Philadelphia, where she is plunged into a world of intrigue and spies, her beauty attracts men, and she learns that love comes in many shapes and sizes.